COLLIDE

THE COLOR ALCHEMIST BOOK FOUR

NINA WALKER

PENDER COUNTY PUBLIC LIBRARY
BURGAW, NORTH CAROLINA

ADDISON & GRAY PRESS
WWW.NINAWALKERBOOKS.COM

Copyright © 2018 by Nina Walker. All rights reserved.

Characters, names and related indicia are trademarked and copyrighted by Nina Walker.

No part of this publication may be reproduced, distributed, or transmitted in any form or by any means, including but not limited to photocopying, recording, or other electronic or mechanical methods, without the prior written permission of the publisher, except in the case of brief quotations embodied in reviews or other noncommercial uses permitted by copyright law .

Published by Addison & Gray Press, LLC.

The characters and events portrayed in this book are fictitious. Any similarity to real persons, living or dead, is coincidental and not intended by the author.

Ebook ISBN: 978-0-9992876-6-8
Paperback ISBN: 978-0-9992876-7-5

*This book is for the dreamers and doers.
May you be both.*

ONE
SASHA

"You need to give this up before you get us all killed," Mastin huffed, his voice a low timbre that rolled over the dark landscape.

Traitor.

I spun on my heels and shoved him. Hard. He didn't budge. The man barely even blinked. Me and my "nice side" shouldn't have been on such good terms at that moment. He was lucky I was currently choosing to refrain from using my magic on him. One touch of yellow was all I needed to knock him out—we both knew it. Our eyes met, his narrowed into slits, and I glared.

"Nobody said you had to tag along," I snapped, stepping back. Tristan moved in between us, head cocked and arms folded, his stance diplomatic, ready to mediate.

"Keep your voice down," Mastin hissed. "Or have you already forgotten where you've so wittingly led us?" He motioned to the barren field that spread wide around the three of us. We were in the middle of no man's land, shrouded in darkness.

I forced the annoyance down, trying to replace it with humility. This was New Colony, and I knew better than to test my luck here.

"You're right," I said, the two words nearly killing me. Still, my eyes rolled. They couldn't be controlled.

Fingers pressing the blue stone on my necklace, I drew on its power until I was sure we were silenced. We could hear each other, no problem, but my form of blue magic worked as a noise-cancelling force field, preventing our conversation from straying too far. And for someone like me in a place like New Colony? That could mean the difference between life and death.

A shiver ran up my spine, both from the winter night and the weight of our situation. As if sensing my discomfort, Tristan placed a steady hand on my shoulder. The pressure of his touch calmed and grounded me. I breathed in deep, forcing the nerves to retreat.

"Arguing isn't going to get us anywhere." Tristan's voice of reason made me want to scream. He must have sensed it because he gently shifted my body toward him. He held steady hands on my shoulders and leaned down to meet my gaze. "Your sister is gone and obviously doesn't want to be found. We're in enemy territory. If we stay here, we'll end up getting killed."

"Or worse," Mastin added.

A flash of my time in the palace prison jolted my memories. My muscles tensed. I could practically feel the pain of the beatings I'd endured. *Just breathe.* I forced my lungs to fill with air and then slowly relax, clearing the emotions. Tristan was right. Mastin was right. Of course, they were only speaking the truth. And yet, the idea of giving up on Jessa made tears prick at the back my eyes.

I turned away. "Let's go back and talk to that farmer.

Maybe he has an idea of where she could have gone." When they didn't answer, I glowered back at them. "Well, are you in or not?"

Mastin shook his head as Tristan nodded.

"We don't have time," Mastin ground out, his bright eyes flashing.

"We could hurry," Tristan added.

A robotic ping sounded. I jerked back, heart accelerating. Mastin pinched his lips and pulled out his slatebook from his back pocket. It was a smaller device than most, but industrial and boxy. Military issue.

I eyed him wearily as he put it to his ear to take the call.

"We're almost done here." He paused for a long second, his pursed lips falling into a deep frown as he listened to the hurried voice on the other end, loud enough for me to make out the tone but not the actual words.

"What is it?" I asked.

In the shadows cast by the faint glow of the moon, it was tricky to make out his full expression, but he obviously wasn't happy. He lowered his head, essentially ignored me, and finished the call with a quick, "Yes."

"Well?" I questioned again.

"It's our pilot. He's not willing to wait much longer. If we're going to make it back to base, we have to leave now."

Another reason why they should've let me pilot the thing.

"Pull rank. Call him back and tell him to wait!"

"It's not that easy. I'm not going to ask him to risk his life any more for us. Let's go."

I growled but nodded. The three of us sprinted toward the chopper, kicking up clumps of hard earth in our wake. The dusty scent filled my nostrils and my eyes watered. The urge to cough gripped my throat. Inwardly, the battle between guilt and practicality raged. Jessa had been *right there*. How could I have let her get away? Just as I was about to get her out of this God-forsaken place and reunite her with our family, she had to run off like a total lovesick fool. Now what was I supposed to do, leave her here? Why would she choose this?

Love. That word again. There was no questioning that love was why she'd gone back. It had pushed her to find out for herself if Prince Lucas was actually dead. Even if that meant risking her life, it was worth it to her to find out the truth.

The emptiness spread around us in a kaleidoscope of gray and black. I studied the horizon, searching for a flash of her. In every sway of shadow, I questioned. Was it Jessa? It hadn't been long since I'd lost her to the darkness, maybe twenty minutes, so there was no way she could have gone *too* far, even with the magic. But as I scanned the scene, I knew in my gut that she was long gone. She had vanished, and so had my hope of finding her tonight.

Our speed increased as we neared the location where the helicopter had dropped us off. It waited, part of the darkness, our saving grace, our way out. Guilt ripped through me. A hand found mine and he tugged just enough to get my attention. Tristan. I met his eyes, trying to read his torn expression. He nodded once. He understood. Despite the undesirable circumstances, my lips quirked up in a smile.

"Are you sure about this?" he questioned, his voice barely a whisper above the intake of our hurried breaths. Our legs continued to pump us forward as we moved behind Mastin. He was in soldier-mode and paid us little attention, so zeroed in on his target he didn't catch what I was planning. I didn't mind. Mastin was good for a lot of things, but not for this. He wouldn't understand.

"I have to try. Don't I?" I panted.

"It's what I did for you." His full lips spread into a smile so wide, I could see his teeth shining in the dark.

Once again, I nodded, my heart swelling as I remembered how he had crossed the Shadowlands to help me. I squeezed his hand and then dropped it. I switched directions, taking off for the white farmhouse on the edge of the horizon. My boots thudded against the ground, the cold air rushed against my cheeks.

A few seconds later Mastin broke his protocol and shouted, "You have got to be kidding me!" His voice carried over the landscape and I cringed, but also, I had to suppress a laugh.

I felt for the energy of yellow and allowed it to pulse through me, the magic connecting like an internal power source. In a burst of alchemy, my legs swept me forward, and I left the two men far behind.

Mastin could head back to basecamp. That was his right. Tristan, too, though I doubted he'd leave me here. But I just couldn't give up on Jessa so easily. I'd spent my whole life running from family and I wasn't going to do that again. If needed, I'd hide out in New Colony, give it a couple of days. Most likely, my sister didn't have a plan. She was powerful, but not cut out for this kind of thing. If that farmer had a clue as to where Jessa was hiding before stowing her away in his cellar, then I would retrace her steps until I found her.

As I shot up the porch steps, the hum of helicopter blades caught my attention. It flew overhead, disappearing into the inky blackness. I didn't let myself turn to see if Mastin and Tristan were still on land. But at the back of my mind I wondered. Were they hiding out somewhere, watching, ready to jump in at any minute if things went south?

Of course they were.

And I owed it to them to focus, to make sure this didn't turn into another disaster. The house was silent and dark. I calmed my breathing, swallowing any panting leftover from the run. I stepped forward, clenched my fist and raised it to the oak door. The moment I was about to knock, a massive figure appeared from around the side of a wraparound porch. I jumped, adrenaline slicing through my chest. A man held up his hands in surrender as he inched closer to me.

"Hold on there," he said in a deep baritone.

Recognition calmed me; it was the farmer. He towered over me in both height and width. He wasn't overweight, just carrying a ton of thick muscle on his already large frame. His unruly beard framed his dark face, eyes shining like two small lights in the shadows.

"This is your fault," I snapped, folding my arms. "She was about to come with us when you had to run out and tell her about Lucas. Why did you do that?"

He sighed and cleared his throat. "Yeah … not my brightest idea. I see that now," he said. "But I've met the prince. He's a good man. I thought … I don't know, what I thought. That I was honoring his memory by telling her. That's his wife, you know? He really cared about her, made me promise to help her if she ever showed up here."

I squinted, making out the most earnest of expressions on his face. A tiny part of me understood his reasoning, even if it was the definition of stupid. Lucas had shown him kindness, and from the looks of this guy's barren farm and weathered features, he'd needed it.

"Fine. It's done. But now I need help finding her. Do you know where she was before she came to you?"

An upstairs light flicked on, the interruption illuminating the yard. The man's eyes widened, and he shot toward the door, fumbling with the handle.

"Wait. Where are you going?"

"My wife doesn't know about all this."

"Just answer my question."

"I don't know anything. Okay? Please, you need to get out of here. Treason is not something I'm going to subject my wife and children to."

"You're a little late for that." I laughed, shocked that he would help Jessa if *this* was how he was responding to me.

As he pushed open the door, a woman in a blue bathrobe stood in the doorway, one hand rubbing the sleep from weary eyes. Part of me wanted to shake her! *Really, lady? You slept through everything else tonight.* Behind me, leaves rustled and boots crunched against the frozen grass.

"Taysom Green," the woman chastised. "What on earth is going on? Who are these people?"

I spun around to find a smiling Tristan walking up the steps, his hand raised in greeting.

"So sorry for the inconvenience, Miss," he said, his voice as rich and smooth as butter. "We're Guardians of Color on assignment to check on your farm. Is there anything that my associate can help you with? She's a master healer." He winked at me.

"Uhhh," I faltered, but I quickly recovered and turned back to the woman with an equally pleasant smile. If anyone could play this game of make believe, it was me. After all, I'd had years of experience.

"Yes, we're so sorry for waking you," I said pleasantly. "We check on things at night when the citizens are asleep. We're not supposed to draw too much attention to ourselves. It's part of our protocol. But it turns out that your husband is a light sleeper."

Her eyes flicked back and forth between the three of us, as if she knew we were lying through our teeth. I continued to smile, until finally, her tense face relaxed, eyebrows softening, lips parting, and intense eyes losing a bit of their focus. She gave us a quick nod.

"I'm afraid everything's dead this season. Ground's already been tilled. We're planting again in a few months. Will you be back to help us then?"

I nodded eagerly, the shame of my outright lie ripping through me. There was nothing I could do for these people's dying farmland. And besides, we had a war to win. Once that was sorted, then I could help as many farmers as possible.

"Well, it's late, best be off with you," Taysom said, sliding into his home, his frame blocking his wife from our view. He shut the door in my face with a thud.

I clenched my teeth and fists, burning to bust that door wide open. But instead I closed my eyes and sighed. Inviting hothead Sasha to the party wasn't a smart idea, given our situation.

"Now what?" Tristan asked, putting a warm hand on my back. It only accentuated the cold night.

I took a deep breath, watching it hang in the air, as I considered our options. "I'm not convinced that man doesn't know anything." I leaned into Tristan and laid my head on his shoulder, pulling him into a hug. "Thank you for staying with me," I whispered. At least I wasn't alone in all of this.

I felt him nod and breathe me in. I did the same. He reached out and coaxed my tight fist to relax, threading long fingers through mine.

"Come on," he said into my hair. "We don't know the area. Let's hide out in that cellar while we figure out what to do next."

"You think we can trust him?"

"I do. He's spooked, so we'll have to move on soon."

I still wanted to stomp on the porch, to bang on the door, to demand answers. But Tristan was right. I let the frustration go, forcing it away with each step as I followed the man who would follow me anywhere, who was undoubtedly my best friend. We rounded the house hand in hand. Exhaustion ebbed at the corners of my vision. My body heavy, I reflected on my appalling lack of sleep lately.

I blinked as my eyes adjusted. Someone was waiting for us.

Mastin.

He leaned against the house with his arms crossed over his chest, a tightly wound expression held on his face. I knew deep in my core that he was livid with me, but I also knew just how grateful I was to see him still standing here.

"I can't believe you stayed," I choked on the emotion, smiling and scrunching my nose.

He didn't look at me, didn't acknowledge me in any way. He only pushed off the side of the house, threw open the cellar door with an angry clang, and stormed into the blackness below. His boots sent a mist of stifling dust wafting back out after him, as if to taunt me for what I had done to land us here for the night. I didn't blame him for being angry; this had never been in the plan. But my entire life hadn't gone according to plan and you didn't see me slamming doors. Typical Mastin. I refused to feel guilty.

I turned to Tristan, ready to make my argument, but he only chuckled.

Tristan took first watch. When he woke me a few hours later, I expected to trade positions straight away, so he could get some much-needed rest.

"I want to show you something first," he said, his voice a low whisper that tickled my cheek.

The sleep had come quick and heavy, despite the cold, hard floor. Mastin was still out cold, his back pressed against the side of the small room. The walls were dusty stone, the floor damp earth. There were a few blankets and crates pushed alongside one wall.

"Okay, I hope it's something good," I whispered, standing in a crouch because of the low ceiling and following him back up the short set of stairs.

Outside the sun met us in a brilliant pink light that illuminated the landscape. There wasn't another structure for miles, just dark earth kissing a new sky. Warmth caressed my face, and I sighed with a soft smile. I relished the peace—soon this feeling would be gone.

"So beautiful," I said, leaning against the house.

"Yes." Tristan nodded, watching me. His gaze had turned intense, a side of him he rarely showed me. His eyes were two questioning depths, staring back at me. A twinge of anticipation ran down my spine. I couldn't stop thinking about what he'd said that night on the beach. *Wait for me.*

Didn't he know I'd always been waiting for him?

"I wanted to talk to you about something," he whispered, his voice catching ever so slightly, but enough for me to know he was nervous.

It made me nervous, too.

What is there to be nervous about? This is Tristan. He was my best friend and the person I trusted most in the world. I'd known the guy for years, had seen him grow from a boy to a man. And truth be told, I'd spent several of my teenage years pining over him, a secret that I was pretty sure he'd known about. But we were almost six years apart in age and I'd always been too young for him before. Of course he'd never acted on anything. Tristan always did the *right* thing.

But things were different now.

"You can tell me," I said, shifting to get a better look. His dark eyes burned behind a fallen lock of midnight hair. The corners of his liquid eyes crinkled as he studied me for a long moment and then he shifted closer. When those same eyes flicked to gaze at my lips, anticipation burned inside. Was he going to kiss me? Did I want him to kiss me?

The truth rooted me to the spot. *Yes, I wanted him to.*

"I shouldn't have asked you not to date Mastin," he said, suddenly creating distance between us. He stepped back. The passion in his expression vanished, replaced by the familiar understanding and friendly gaze he always wore around me.

"Wait…what?" I sputtered, confusion and shame coursing through me like boiling-hot water.

"I know there's something there between you two. It wasn't right of me to ask you not to pursue that." He cleared his throat. "You're my best friend, but I don't own you like that, you know? It wasn't right."

So what was he saying? That he didn't have interest in me? That he thought Mastin was a better fit?

Or maybe he knows about your stupid crush on him and he's rejecting you.

A razor-sharp pain tore at me. All the insecurities of being a young girl fantasying over an older but romantically uninterested guy, surfaced in an instant. The embarrassment that rocked me sent burning hot tears to the back of my eyes, which only made everything worse.

Please don't cry. Please don't cry. Please…

"Thanks for your permission," I snapped. "I'll take it under advisement."

I kept my head down, sure my cheeks were bright red. This was so embarrassing! I stumbled back to the cellar door and down the stairs, steadying my breath as much as possible.

"Wait," he called after me, his voice torn in frustration.

But he didn't follow.

I plopped down in the corner of the cold room, glaring

at the boxes of root vegetables in across from me, the rudimentary brewery next to those, and Mastin's hunched over form in the other corner.

He wasn't asleep anymore. He watched me like I was up to something. Had he heard any part of my conversation with Tristan? The thought of it sent another wave of shame crashing over me.

"Everything okay?" he finally asked, his voice laced with a protectiveness that I hadn't heard from him before.

"He talks," I muttered, referring to the frustrating silent treatment he'd given me before we'd gone to sleep. I knew I was being a brat, but I couldn't seem to stop myself.

"When I need to talk, I talk," he replied, his voice softer this time.

I closed my eyes and rested my head back against the cool stone for a moment. "Yes, everything is fine. We're trapped in New Colony, but other than that, things are great." I made sure my tone dripped with sarcasm.

"You don't have to be such a brat."

I laughed because he had called me out on what I'd just been thinking moments earlier, though I wasn't amused. *I need to get a hold of myself. No more arguing with my guys.*

"I'm sorry," I finally relented, blowing out my breath and meeting his inspecting gaze. "I know this is my fault and complaining won't help the situation."

He studied me through the filtered light, flecks of dust floating between us. We hadn't turned on the lone light bulb, instead opting to keep the cellar door open. At least for now. Once the family woke up and found us, all bets were off.

"I'm going to get an extraction team out here as soon as possible," Mastin said. "Our base outside of Nashville isn't far at all, but I'm afraid it might be a few days with everything going on. I don't know yet, but I don't like sitting here. Richard's men are hunting Jessa and all we've managed to do is take her place."

"And women." I crossed my arms over my knees.

He raised a questioning eyebrow.

"You said Richard's men. But it's men and women. His number one officer, Faulk, is a woman."

He nodded. "Well, either way, I don't know if we can trust this guy," he said, pointing to the house above, "or his wife."

"Who else is there to trust in this kingdom?" I sighed.

But as I asked the question, an idea came to me. How hadn't I thought of it earlier? I'd been so distracted that I'd overlooked something important. I lifted my hip to the side and reached two fingers into my front pocket, digging for a moment. The thin slip of paper slid out like an answer to a prayer. I held it up to the light, a smile pulling at my lips. I pictured the day Branson had given it to me, remembered the shock of the moment when I'd learned he was Resistance. An email address had been written there, meant to give West America an inside source in New Colony's warfront. I was supposed to hand if off to General Scott, but had instead held onto it. I had worried that it was a trap. Or that if it wasn't, Nathan Scott wouldn't treat Branson right because of deep rooted prejudice. Tristan was the only other soul who knew about the email address. He hadn't liked that I'd kept the paper, but hadn't tattled on me to anyone, either.

"What's that?" Mastin's eyes narrowed, catching sight of my secret.

I stilled. Mastin and his "live by the rules set, adhere to your higher ranks" attitude was going to be pretty pissed when I revealed this secret. But hey, I wasn't known for following the rules myself. What did he really expect from me?

"Sasha, what is it?" A twinge of panic rose in his voice and

I smirked.

I avoided his question by asking one of my own. "How much charge is left on that slatebook of yours?"

His lips thinned, but he pulled it from his pocket and tapped at the screen. "A few days."

"Good." I flashed the slip of paper once more. "Because this just might be our ticket out of here."

TWO

JESSA

I crouched behind a dumpster, waiting for the already thin crowd of theatre-goers to disappear into the night. They streamed from the building, chattering voices floating on the cool air. Nobody looked my way. The stench of food waste and musky city streets wafted around me, encouraging me to move on, to take the risk now if only to get away from the stench. I didn't. Pressing my hand harder against my nose, I waited for my chance. It needed to be perfect.

The second it had been dark enough, I'd slowly traversed through downtown Marthasville. Careful to keep my head down, I'd dodged pedestrians and hidden in the darkest shadows I could find. If anyone got a good look at my face, I'd be in big trouble. Since the engagement, I'd become one of the most recognizable people in the kingdom. At least I was dressed better and more put-together than yesterday, since I'd stolen clean clothes this morning on my trek into the city. I had to steal the clothes right off a clothesline from one of the farms outside the city. No coat, but there wasn't snow here in the winters like up north. The dark green shirt was a little big for my frame, but it was long-sleeved and helped keep the shivers away.

The downtown area was compact, so it wasn't too hard to find the theatre. The people here weren't quite as well-to-do as the ones in the capital, but they still dressed in fine clothing and chattered like they didn't have a care in the world. Nobody noticed me in my hiding spot. The marquee across the street shined bright, the sight sending both hope and dread careening through me. I read the blocky words again: New Colony Royal Ballet. Tears pricked at my eyes. If only I'd been here a week ago, even a few days, I could have seen Dad. Held him, hugged him. But by the time I'd made it to Taysom Green's place after weeks of hiding with sympathizers and travelling in the dead of night, it was too late. Reaching out in the farm's cellar to Dad via our telepathic connection, I'd discovered he was just crossing the border. I squeezed my eyes shut and let one tear trickled down my cheek. I hoped Dad had made it into safe hands. I couldn't think about the alternative.

I slapped my cheeks, determined to be strong, to think back on my journey. Why couldn't I see just how brave I really was? None of it had been easy, but I had done it, I had made it through. And I would make it through tonight, too.

The possibility of failure needed to fall to the back of my mind for now. I needed to focus on the building in front of me, on the task at hand. This was my only chance at getting back to Lucas. I clenched stiff fingers against the inside of my sleeves and wrapped my arms around myself for warmth. Soon, I would be inside and wouldn't be cold. Soon, things would be better. I thanked my lucky stars that the ballet was still in town and I could find a way to get help.

It made sense the ballet was still here, even though I'd been plagued with worry they wouldn't. When the company traveled, they would stay a week or two in one place before moving on to the next. Most citizens couldn't afford a ticket, of course, but those with the best jobs and highest wages prided themselves on going. There was always an audience for ballet. Dressed in their finest suits and gowns, people would make a public spectacle out of the event. It seemed that was the case even in war time. Ballet was an old aristocratic tradition, even from way before New Colony, one of the few things that had stuck in the new kingdom.

The once-busy crowd had disappeared, voices fading as they went their different ways, some on foot, others in vehicles. The once-bustling area had emptied. The night had grown silent. This was my chance. I stilled, ready to make a run for it. I needed to make it across the street and around the back of the theatre. And I needed to be quick, in case someone was out here that still recognized me. That part of the plan was doable. But then I'd have to break into the back door of the theatre and find Madame Silver, *also* without anyone recognizing me. Considering I'd trained with these dancers, knew most of them by name, that part of my plan was *not* so doable.

Didn't matter, I had to try.

Head down, I darted across the pavement, eyes focused on the ground, lights and shadows dancing in the corner of my vision. I walked as fast as I could without running. Since I didn't want to draw attention to myself, I didn't connect with the stones around my neck or use yellow magic to quicken my strides. For all I knew, there was someone watching from a window, or lurking around a corner. My heartbeat pounded in my chest. Biting air whooshed against my cheeks, my clenched jaw aching, my ears burning. Seconds later, I made it to another darkened alleyway and pressed myself against the wall. Eyeing the street, I made sure I wasn't being followed. Nothing stirred. Nobody was there. It seemed that the street was still mercifully empty.

I crept around the side of the building, running my fingers along the smooth whitewashed stone as I searched, eager for a service or crew entrance that I could slip into undetected. It didn't take long to find a nondescript black, steel door with rust around the edges. Perfect! Using yellow, I pushed the magic from my stone into my body, channeling it instantly, and broke the lock with a snap. It creaked open with the faint grinding of metal against metal. I cringed, scrunching up my face. If only I had access to silencing magic. But I couldn't think about that, I needed to move. I stepped inside.

The familiar scent of being backstage surrounded me as I slipped into the darkest shadow. It was the mix of dust, heated plastic, floor polish, sweat, and paint that calmed me and also called to me. For the first time all day, I smiled. This was home. Longing enveloped me, but so did the comfort of what I loved. This was where I should have been all along. If only things hadn't fallen apart all those months ago.

"Good show tonight." The familiar stagehand's voice carried through the space. *Toby.*

I'd worked with him just over six months ago, but now those memories felt like they'd been years ago. Another Jessa. Another life.

"Another great performance," he called again, down a set of stairs. That meant the dressing rooms were down below—a common set up. I slipped further into the shadows, pressing myself against the wall and praying with every fiber of my being that Toby wasn't about to find me. He was the ballet's light guy, a ruddy character with a thick mustache and a round belly. I liked him; he always had a smile on this face. But that didn't mean I could trust him now. Heavy footsteps clopped across the stage and his familiar round outline protruded into my sightline, followed by the rest of him. He ran a finger and thumb down his peppery mustache as he hummed to himself.

Same old Toby.

Madame Silver had said others in the ballet company's management agreed to help me and Dad, but I didn't know if that included Toby. Nor did I know if things had changed since Lucas's reported death. No, it was Madame Silver who I needed to find first. I couldn't expose my presence to anyone but her. Everyone else was too much of a risk.

Toby strode across the stage again, a satisfied grin flashing from under his bushy mustache. The urge to run and enfold him in a hug overcame me. Instead, I held my breath and clenched my hands into fists. The velvety maroon curtain was down, its bottom barely brushing the floor, and most of the area back here was shadowed in inky darkness. I hoped it would stay that way. But Toby walked up to a light on the far side of stage right and started flipping a row of switches.

No! I stumbled along the wall, darting for the closest hiding place. The plywood scenery piece was my only shot. It hid me, but only barely. It wasn't very large, the shape of a shrub, and there was nowhere for me to go from here. I crouched and watched Toby carry a ladder to center stage and begin setting it up. Either he was adjusting some lights for tomorrow's performance, or he was collecting a few things before the company moved on to their next location. I wished it was the second option—that meant I could hitch a ride back north. Maybe.

I'd be one step closer to finding out if Lucas was really dead.

Grief threatened to overtake me. It would claw at my every thought if I let it, so I pushed it aside for the matter that was right in front of me, for what I could try to control.

Where was Madame Silver? I had to find her. It was possible she'd already left, but knowing her, that wasn't likely. Always the professional, she liked to see to it that all the dancers were out of the building before leaving herself. Were things different on tour? Perhaps this wasn't like dancing back in the Capital. I didn't know, and I hated that. I rolled my eyes and bit my lip, coming to grips with my desperate reality. Just as I was debating the best way to go about finding her, realization hit me. How had I been so stupid as to overlook it before? The solution was obvious.

It lay in the purple and gray stone warming my neck.

Madame Silver, I called out through our telepathic connection. *Can you hear me?*

I slunk even further behind the scenery piece and waited, grateful I had this magic tying me to her. *It's me, Jessa. I'm here and I need your help.*

Still nothing.

My head dropped into my cold palms. Overwhelming fear poured down my entire body, sinking me deeper into the floor. What if I was stuck here in Marthasville? What if coming back for Lucas had been a terrible mistake? Maybe I should have gone with my sister. I could be reunited with my family right now. But then, wasn't Lucas my family, too?

Jessa? Is that you? Our connection flared to life, like a lighted match dropping into a stream of gasoline. I gasped and slapped a hand over my mouth as the relief roared through me.

Yes, I'm here in the theatre. I'm backstage. My words would be flowing through her mind just as hers were in mine.

What are you doing here? We've been worried sick about you. Your father is gone now; I hope he's safe. We thought you'd be with him after your disappearance. Her words rushed at me, the flood of worry overflowing in her tone. *At least you're alive*, she added.

I smiled wider, once again filled with awe at this magic. Lucas's white invisibility would've been really handy at a time like this, but purple's telepathy was just as good. I rubbed the necklace around my neck, grateful for all it provided. But also, a little worried about where I'd find more purple once this stone was used up. It was almost gone as it was. There wasn't time to be concerned, I'd deal with it as soon as I had the chance.

Where can I meet you? I begged. *I need your help.*

Use the stage right stairs and head down to the lower level. I'll be in the first room on your left. Be quick. I don't know how long this hall will be clear.

Toby is up here right now.

She paused, as if talking to someone else for a moment. Unease rolled in my belly, but I reasoned that Madame Silver had always done right by me. She had saved my father's life, after all. And I hated that she was all I had. I was asking for her help, help that put her and many others in danger.

Madame Silver?

I just sent someone up to fetch him. The moment they head down the stage right stairs, you need to bolt for the left stairs and beat them down here, then hide in the room on your first left. I'll meet you there.

My whole body tensed. If I ran into anybody here, red alchemy would be my only saving grace. I didn't want to risk that. I *couldn't* risk that. Not on these people. They'd once been my second family.

"Hey Bossman, we need another pair of hands downstairs for a bit. Can you take a break from this?" A young man ambled up the stairs, dressed head to toe in black. I flashbacked to the Guardian uniform and shuddered. But no, this was just typical stagehand dress, nothing about this was formal, nothing about it spoke to the authority that had ruled my life these last months.

The kid had shiny blond hair and a youthful sureness to his stride. He must have been assigned to an apprenticeship under Toby. I didn't recognize him; he must've been new. Possibly as new as this tour.

"All right, Kenny," Toby replied. "But help me out here first, will ya? I've almost got this unscrewed. I'll pass it down."

Toby carefully lifted a large stage light from where he balanced near the top of the ladder, moving it into Kenny's upstretched arms. My heart raced when Toby leaned a tad too far for my comfort, but Kenny secured the light in his hands and strode back. Toby righted himself with the ease of a master.

"There you go," Toby said cheerfully, stepping down the rungs of the ladder.

I moved into a runners pose, calling on the yellow to flow through me. The second these two were out of view, I'd make a run for it. With the magic, I had no doubt I'd beat them downstairs.

"Whoa," Toby's voice ground out just as Kenny snapped, "Careful!"

But it was too late.

Toby slipped. It was his job not to slip, not to have an accident. And yet…

He crashed to the ground, the ladder rocking and toppling in the other direction with an ear-splitting shatter.

"No!" Kenny yelled. Another, smaller crash echoed through the area. The light was in pieces on the floor, an arc of glass around it, and Kenny was already on his knees in front of Toby.

I stared, horrified. Toby's body was bent at an awkward angle. An unnatural spread of limbs. He screamed out in pain, the sound so wild and guttural, that I jumped up.

I ran, all thoughts fading away. I slid next to Kenny, falling to my knees and running my eyes up and down Toby. I reached out, green magic flowing from my fingers in strings of effervescent light. The one measly stone on my necklace might not be enough for an accident this bad. I suspected his back was broken.

"Hurry," I said to the kid. "Can you find me a plant?"

"Don't touch him," he challenged, eyes drawn in confusion. "I need to get a medic. His back could be broken."

"I said get me a plant! I don't think I have enough with just a stone."

I widened my eyes at him, and his eyebrows drew in. Confusion and then recognition and then something like horrified-awe spread over his face. He nodded and sprinted off.

Toby's eyes were squeezed shut in two deep lines sunken into his reddened face as he howled in pain. I pushed the magic into him, feeling it work through his broken pieces. It would find the source and begin healing immediately, but I needed to act fast to mend bones properly. At least he hadn't snapped his neck because then he'd be dead right now. There were some things even magic couldn't bring people back from.

"Jessa!" Madame Silver ran onto the stage, her dark hair streaming behind her, her eyes round and frantic. "What are you doing?"

Her face drained of color as she took in the gruesome scene. Then she too fell to her knees beside me, her black skirt tucking against her thighs. "Is it working?" she asked, voice turning eerily calm. "How much longer? We have to get you out of here before anyone else sees you."

"Too late. Kenny already did. He went to find me a plant.

I need more green."

Toby was whimpering now; I felt terrible that I hadn't been able to completely numb his pain. I whipped my head from side to side, I searched, needing to get my hands on some more green. Where was that kid?

As if on cue, Kenny stumbled back onto the stage, footsteps hollow in the vastness of the theatre. "This was all I could find," he said, dropping a bouquet of fresh-cut yellow roses into my lap. I eyed the stems and leaves, and inhaled the scent of performances gone-by.

"Thank you." I pressed one hand into them, avoiding the thorns as much as possible, and held the other hand against Toby's arm. His flesh was warm and sweaty under my palm. At least he wasn't cold. "This should be enough."

I concentrated and sent the green magic flowing into Toby. After a long minute, his eyes fluttered open. His body relaxed. He shifted his head to one side, moved a hand to rub his head, and then slowly, he sat up. Bewilderment filled his entire expression as he blinked at me. I threw a worried glance at Madame Silver. "Jessa," he breathed. "I thought that was you. What are you doing here?"

Before I could answer, he added, "You saved my life."

"Your guy Kenny found the green," I supplied lamely, my cheeks heating. Kenny sat across from us now, equally shocked by everything he'd just witnessed. He stared at me like he either wanted to get my autograph, or run away. Either way, it was not a good sign. My heart sank.

"Please don't speak of this," I begged of the men, looking from Toby to Kenny. My voice trembled. "Please don't turn me in."

"We'd never." Toby smiled, eyebrows drawn in concern. He took my hand and patted it reassuringly, like a father would to his daughter. He helped me up and my heart rose with it, hope, foolish hope, filling me.

I stood wearily, shaking out my legs and getting ready to make a run for it, despite the pulse of a headache forming between my eyes. Maybe this had been a huge mistake. But as I turned around, fear slammed me, rooting me to the spot.

Streaming from the staircase was a crowd of familiar faces. The entire crew of dancers and staff must have had heard the commotion upstairs, and now, they were all gaping in my direction. Equal parts fascination and fear lined their features as they stared at me, the girl they all knew, the one who had been lost to magic. The one who was a wanted woman, a bounty on her head. My eyes burned. Dread washed through me. I stumbled backward.

Were they more shocked at seeing color alchemy in action? Or was it my presence that alarmed them? I was the runaway queen. And yet here I was, randomly showing up on their stage, once again disrupting their lives.

"Please," I croaked, my voice not sounding like my own. "Please don't turn me in." I stepped back, panic building.

But then, one by one, they did the strangest thing. The thing that I would have never expected: they lowered their heads and bowed.

"Your Royal Highness," someone called from the back, "you're alive!"

My heart exploded in a flurry of shock. Yes, I was very much alive. But with this many people privy to my whereabouts, there was a real possibility that I'd be dead by morning.

★

The train rumbled beneath me, a steady vibration that should have rocked me to sleep. But sleep wouldn't come. Not for me, not at a time like this. My guard was up, and I wasn't planning on taking it down. I couldn't.

I rested on the hard bed of the sleeper train, my back pressed against the cool wall, going over everything again and again. After explaining myself, the entire company had sworn to protect me. That was the part I hadn't seen coming. And still, I questioned if I was safe. I knew I wasn't, but I was also out of options.

When the crew had finished cleaning up and we'd loaded the train, I'd taken the offer to stow along. I desperately needed to get north, needed to find out the truth about Lucas. The train was the only way I knew how to make that happen. My connections with the Resistance were lost since being dropped off at Taysom's farm.

I could do this. I could make this work.

A light tapping pulled me from the bed. I stood and brushed past the paneled wall, opening the pocket door. Madame Silver waited on the other side, her downcast gaze sending a fresh panic through me.

"We need to talk," she said.

I ushered her inside and closed us into the tight space. "I'm not safe, am I?"

"I don't know." Her makeup now washed clean and hair brushed loosely around her shoulders, she looked older and younger at the same time. She sat down on the bed and patted the spot next to her for me to join. "Probably not for long. You can trust these people, but there's just so many of them, and that's what worries me."

"Me too," I agreed. "A few could have been locked down, but that was what, like forty people? Fifty? It's dangerous and not just for me. I keep thinking that every minute I stay with the company is another minute I put everyone at risk, including you. Especially you, given our history." My voice cracked on the last part as guilt swelled.

She sighed. "We've agreed to help you. That's already done. What you do next is up to you."

But what could I do?

"I've come to show you something," she said, slipping her slatebook from her silky pajama bottom pocket. "There was another broadcast earlier tonight. I think you need to see it"

I stilled, something deep within me knowing that the broadcast was about me. I took a deep breath and forced the tears burning in my eyes away. She fiddled with the device and then passed it to me gently. The screen lit up, basking the room in a blue glow, and King Richard filled the screen.

I recoiled, struck by his appearance. He was more worn down than ever, with dark circles under his eyes and a grim line to his lips. Even his hair looked to have grayed another shade since I last saw him a few weeks ago. None of that stopped me from hating him.

"Dear citizens, as you already know, my son has been murdered." His voice was as strong as ever as it boomed out of the slatebook speaker. "We believe a West American assassin is responsible. We've gone over everything from that night, and the startling truth is, one of the most trusted members of the palace was the assailant. We have him detained and a public execution is scheduled for tomorrow."

Richard hadn't named me as Lucas's killer? The stark realization allowed me to release the breath I'd been holding tight in my gut. The camera flashed from Richard to a man's photo. I squinted in disbelief.

"That's not Lucas's killer," I gasped. "That man has been in prison for weeks."

It was the same man I'd interrogated with Lucas, the one whose wife had been related to the gunman from Queen Natasha's funeral. I highly doubted he was a West American assassin, not when I'd used magic to question him. He was just someone caught in the crosshairs, someone who'd known too much.

"They're using him as a scapegoat." The truth hit me hard, like whiplash, throwing off everything else Richard had told the press. My eyes widened. Hope burst into flame within me. Did this mean Lucas wasn't dead? Or did it confirm the opposite? It was confusing, but I was leaning toward the former. Madame Silver sat still as a statue next to me and didn't offer a word.

"Because of the horrible murders that occurred during my wife's funeral," Richard continued. "I have decided Lucas will be buried in private. Thank you for understanding. I am burdened with more grief and anger than ever. I will stop at nothing to defeat our enemy and avenge not only my wife and my son, but also my daughter-in-law."

"What?" I sputtered. "Avenge *me*?"

"Just watch." Madame Silver squeezed my shoulder before resting her arm around me.

"We believe that our newest princess was kidnapped from her wedding bed. It happened the very night her husband was murdered, possibly before her eyes. Now that we've had more details come to light and a chance to interrogate Lucas's killer, we know the assassin wasn't acting alone. Princess Jessa Heart has been kidnapped. It is very possible she is still in New Colony. Please, if you find her, or know of any information leading to her discovery, call this number immediately and report it to the proper authorities."

A number flashed across the screen as dread prickled up and down my entire body. This wasn't good news for me.

"It is my belief the princess is being held against her will and is in grave danger. Help me in returning her to her rightful place, if not for me, do it for the prince you loved dearly. My son never would have wanted his beloved wife to be in such danger. Please, bring our princess home. A reward will be offered to anyone who can help us in this most important endeavor."

My image filled the screen along with a startlingly high reward price that flashed across the top. In the photo, I was standing next to Lucas at our wedding reception, smiling from ear-to-ear, happiness radiating from my eyes.

Madame Silver gently pried the slatebook from my shaking hands, but my eyes followed the image of Lucas's handsome face until she shut it off.

"Have they watched it?" I didn't have to say whom I was talking about; I was surrounded by people who knew exactly where I was.

"They watched it in the dressing room, before they found you," she said. "That's the good news—they already had this information before they agreed to help. The bad news is I don't know how long it will take for someone to second guess themselves and call that number. Not to mention, that reward…"

I nodded. "Okay," I breathed. I needed to run. "At our next stop, I'll sneak away. I won't say a word to anyone about where I'm going." Not that I knew where that would be.

"I'm going to prepare a pack for you," she said, concern etched in her words. Her faint wrinkles deepened around her eyes as her shoulders sagged under the weight of her words. "Food and clothing, whatever I can find that might help. I'll do that now."

We stood, and she hugged me tightly, my tall frame towering above her. I could practically feel the guilt she had over this.

"It's not your fault," I whispered. "I'll be fine. I promise. I've made it this far, haven't I?"

"You need to get out of New Colony." She stepped back and looked me up and down, her mouth falling into a sad frown. "You can't stay here."

I nodded.

She had no idea just how right she was. This was the worst possible place for me to be, but still, I had to know the truth. I still didn't believe Lucas was dead, and that broadcast had only solidified the burning questions in my mind. Why would the King accuse a false killer? Why hide the body like that?

Something wasn't adding up.

"I know. You're right." I smiled weakly. "But I can't put you in any more danger. Thank you so much for all you've done for me. I'll never forget your generosity."

She nodded, hugged me once more, and then slipped out the door.

I fell back onto the bed, overcome with the weight of the situation. How had things gotten so off track? Lucas should have come with me when I ran. Or I never should have tried to manipulate Richard's blood in the first place. Oh, there were so many things I could have done that would have avoided all of this.

All the regrets, they pressed down, threatening to suffocate me.

No matter. Don't focus on the past. I repeated the words in my head, trying once again to find the sleep that eluded me.

Don't sleep. You saw that broadcast. You're a wanted woman. There's a huge bounty on your head. You can't afford to sleep with so many people near.

So, I sat back up and I waited. Waited for sunlight. Waited for my chance to flee. Waited for the moment that I'd be on my own again, running for my life.

THREE
SASHA

"Check it again." I nodded at Mastin. My eyes flashed toward his pocket where he kept his slatebook. He shook his head slightly but still did as I said. Despite the warm sun, I shivered. Why was I suddenly so nervous? I should've been used to this kind of thing, this life and death thing. But no matter how many times I was faced with it, the possibility of dying always sent a cold shiver down my spine, always caused a shaking nerve, always made my breath quicken.

His mouth fell into a frown as he swiped the screen. "No news."

"I don't like this," Tristan added.

The three of us were bored, struggling as we waited in yet another cropping of overgrown bushes and trees. The afternoon sun had cut into me, pushing a sort of heavy lethargy deep into my bones. The constant rise and fall of temperatures weighed on me, but I didn't want the others to catch on to my weariness. I needed to stay strong, not only for them, but for myself.

"You hungry?" Tristan changed the subject, shifting the backpack that rested between the three of us. He rummaged inside and pulled out a canteen and a couple of long leafy carrots. "Lucky for us that farmer was willing to give us some of their winter provisions, eh?"

Mastin scoffed, rubbing the heel of his boot into the dirt. "Only to get us off his property as quickly as possible."

"It's better than nothing." Tristan smiled and tore into his sad lunch.

I shrugged and grabbed the extra carrot from Tristan, biting into it with a crunch. I rolled the thick pieces around in my mouth, trying not to think about the odd taste. I'd always hated carrots.

"Truth be told, I don't really fault Taysom for wanting us to go," Tristan said.

He was right to think so. We were a liability, a threat to the man's family. The kind farmer may have made an agreement with Lucas, but that was about Jessa's safety, not ours. He'd certainly never bargained for the three of us to come knocking on his door in the middle of a war.

"Neither do I, but that doesn't change the fact that we're stuck out here," Mastin said. I sighed and focused on my measly carrot.

We'd been traveling northeast for the better part of two days, keeping out of sight during the sunlit hours and moving through the long dark nights as quickly as possible. The area was a mix of farmland and forests, with a few rolling hills for good measure. But mostly, the land was desolate and underpopulated. That played into our favor. Now we were only a couple miles from our destination, and the closer we got, the more tense I became, my thoughts turning toward all the worst-case scenarios I could conjure in my mind.

Just breathe. Everything is going to be okay.

"What if this is a trap?" I said aloud, contradicting the lame mantra I'd been tossing around in my head.

The men turned on me at the same time, both with a mix of annoyance and frustration on their faces. Saying what everyone else was thinking didn't serve the situation, I knew that, but that didn't stop me. I held up my hands, carrot dangling. "I know, I know, this is what you've both been saying. I'm just ... okay. Maybe you're right; maybe we should turn back."

Not my strong suit, admitting I *might* be wrong. But, whatever, too late for that now.

"You're unbelievable." Mastin shot me a knowing look.

Tristan nodded slowly, his eyes drawn in as they studied me like I was some kind of unsolvable puzzle.

Inwardly, some small part of me ... okay, maybe a large part of me, stirred. These two ganging up on me was not cool, even *if* I was wrong. Weren't they supposed to hate each other or something? But no, the last couple of days they'd gotten along splendidly while I'd suffered with a chip on my shoulder.

"Let's go over everything again," Tristan said, leaning back on his elbows and looking up into the blue expanse of sky. I studied his profile, taking in his thick lashes and smooth tan skin. Why did he have to be so pretty? Why did they *both* have to be so pretty? It was annoying.

"You say Branson can be trusted? He was friendly with you back at the palace, but you never officially knew him to be part of the Resistance. Jasmine was careful to keep all her secrets to herself in the interest of protecting her people, so that part checks out."

"That's all true." I nodded.

Tristan continued, "And I had heard of his name at basecamp. That makes me think he's Resistance. And if he's really Resistance, then we shouldn't be surprised he gave you that email address. He probably knew he could trust you with it."

Mastin scoffed. "The address you were supposed to turn in to my father." He rolled his eyes.

"We can *still* give it to him. I'm sure *you* will," I countered. "I just, I don't know, I wanted to be sure ... "

I didn't add the rest of my thought, that I wanted to be sure West America wasn't going to continue to treat Alchemists like violent criminals. It was true I wanted New Colony to be defeated, or at least, I wanted to dethrone King Richard. Did that mean I *also* wanted West America to take over the kingdom?

Not if it meant the end of magic. And the verdict was still out on that.

"And now all we have to show for that email exchange are a set of coordinates and a time," Mastin replied. "It's vague. It could be a trap."

Yes, it very well could be. And that was exactly why I was beginning to feel sick to my stomach.

"Which is why we're going over everything again," Tristan said calmly. "One final time before we go through with it."

I bit my lip and brushed a wayward strand of hair out of my face. Yesterday morning we'd used Mastin's slatebook to send an email to the address Branson had supplied. All we'd said was that there were two soldiers and one Alchemist on this side of the border, who wanted to help in exchange for safe passage back to West America. I'd expected Branson to give us directions, a mission, something. When we'd replied with questions, reasonable questions, we never got an answer. And now we were almost to those coordinates, the time was almost upon us, and we still hadn't gotten a response.

What were we supposed to do?

"Coordinates and a time isn't a lot to go off of," Tristan continued. "But I do think Branson can be trusted, even if it is risky."

"We should've just crossed the border on foot," Mastin pressed, his closely cropped blond hair shining in the sunlight. He narrowed his green eyes as he rubbed at the dirt on his black boot. "Our Nashville base isn't even that far."

That had been his opinion from the start. It had quickly become clear that Mastin wasn't willing to risk any more of his men to come extract us, and neither was his father. When Mastin had contacted his father about what had happened to us, we'd been horrified to learn the newest update.

The helicopter that left us had been shot down at the border.

The pilot, dead.

This was the second time American soldiers had died trying to get me out of New Colony. It would be the last. Guilt had gripped me at the news; I'd fallen to the floor, dry heaving and sick to my stomach. Mastin had punched the wall and broken his hand in two places, something I'd fixed up for him later with green alchemy. And Tristan had gone silent for hours. All very reasonable reactions.

I glanced over at Mastin, not wanting to let the guilt rip me open once more. He rubbed his bruised knuckles, the frown still deep on his face. The bruises were still there since he hadn't let me entirely heal the broken bones he'd caused after punching the wall; those actions all watched over silently by Tristan.

General Nathan Scott's livid yells still echoed in my mind, so loud he may as well have been here and not on the other end of a phone call with Mastin. What was worse, I had agreed with him. Mastin should never have come with me and we'd been in NC too long. The whole call I waited for Mastin to blame me, say it was all my fault. He hadn't though. He only listened, never implicating anyone else for the damage done. Talk about laying some more guilt on my shoulders.

But worrying about that now wouldn't change a thing. Open countryside, farmland, marshes, all stretched for miles around us. No matter which way we traveled, danger awaited.

We were stranded.

"We can't just walk across the border of two warring nations without expecting to get shot," Tristan said. "We couldn't stay hidden at the farmer's place either. We weren't welcome there. So as risky as it is—"

"Branson is our best chance at getting out of here," I finished.

Mastin closed his eyes, face grim, but nodded. "Give me one of those damn carrots." Tristan tossed him one, and Mastin bit into it like it had personally offended him. "I'm going to case the area. I'll be back in ten." He jumped to his feet and stomped away, back straight, dark camo clothes blending perfectly into the scenery and disappearing before anyone could protest.

Tristan and I fell into silence.

We'd never talked again about our earlier argument. I forced my eyes to look anywhere but at him as it festered between us like an undressed wound. Shame pressed down on me every time I thought of his words, of how quickly he'd pushed me on Mastin. And now we had only a few more hours until we had to be at our destination, facing whatever surprises waited. If there were things we needed to say, now was the time.

I glanced at him, only to find him staring. His black,

unreadable eyes quickly flicked away. He reached for the canteen and took a long swallow. A tangle of confused emotions rose in me.

"I'm sorry," I blurted.

"About what?"

"Everything. This." I motioned to the cropping we were hanging out in, the backpack between us. "This situation. And ... everything."

His jaw tensed, and he licked the water from his lips. I took a deep breath. "I'm sorry, too. I don't think you understood what I meant by what I said."

My cheeks ignited in a warm blush, and I couldn't help but look away. "No, it's okay. I got what you meant. We're better off as friends."

His hand found mine and squeezed, his thumb sliding up my wrist.

An echoing boom exploded from behind us. We both jumped, panic bursting through my veins like dynamite. I pushed that away and replaced it with action.

"What was that?" Not waiting for an answer, I sprinted through the brush to get a better look, Tristan right behind me, his breath heavy on the back of my head. Branches and twigs scratched at me, but I barely noticed, intent on finding the source to the sound that now careened through the once-silent afternoon.

Mastin crouched behind a large oak, motioning for us to join him. Up ahead, on the edge of the horizon, a fire raged.

"What is it?" I asked, though the question seemed ridiculous the second it left my mouth. I already knew. I could see what looked like an outpost caught on the offensive. A row of buildings burned, and people ran to and fro, some getting into position, others trying to stifle the flames. Black smoke billowed upward, staining the crystal blue sky.

"That must be the frontline," Tristan said, voice eerily calm against the backdrop of chaos.

Mastin nodded, a slight smile pulling on the hard lines of his usually stoic mouth. "They are under attack."

✯

My chest burned. My legs ached. My throat tightened with nagging thirst. But that didn't matter. I hardly noticed any pain as I focused my attention straight ahead on our target. We ran together, at an all-out sprint, toward the mayhem. On the horizon, it appeared that several bombs had been dropped and at least one of New America's fighter jets had been shot down in the attack. The wreckage was spilled across an open field as it burned. Rows of uniform brick and metal buildings were engulfed in angry-red flames that reached into the sky recklessly.

The New Colony soldiers didn't notice the three of us as we approached, we were coming from the wrong direction. Several of them held massive hoses as they sprayed the flames, to little success. Others loaded their injured comrades on stretchers, running around a corner and disappearing toward more of the buildings that hadn't been hit. But the majority of the soldiers seemed to be running toward the airfield. Among the gunshots, the screams and shouts, the crackling of fire, was the sound of them calling out to each other, getting into position.

As we neared the area, it was evident that we couldn't just stay out in the open. We needed to take cover. Mastin led us to refuge behind a large dumpster. The three of us caught our breath and my brain ran through all the possibilities on our next move.

"Now what?" Tristan asked, looking up to the two of us

from where he had his hands resting on his knees. Sweat lined his forehead and adrenaline sparked in his eyes. Tristan was the kind of person who could easily take charge when needed, but also knew when to back down and let someone else be the leader. That came in handy in times like these.

"Let's go to the meeting spot," I offered. "Maybe Branson will still be there."

Mastin pursed his lips but he nodded anyway.

"Hold on," I said, reaching toward the men. "Stay close and I can help us." I felt the magic from my stone necklace begin to work its way into my body, like heat being poured through me. I sent out the blue as a protective noise bubble.

Gunfire, short pops followed by a series of successive clatters, punctured the afternoon just ahead of us. My heart rose up into my throat and I knew that I could do more for these men under my protection. It was my fault they were here; I needed to see they made it out of this alive. I glanced down to the necklace, taking in the sight of the stones. The colors were fading. After today, I'd need to refresh most of these, including the amber stone that glinted like solid honey in the sunlight. I prayed there'd be enough to get us through tonight.

"Okay, we weren't ever really supposed to do this," I said. "I don't even know if I can, not everyone is able to, but I should try ... "

More gunshots, this time closer.

"Sasha, we've got to get out of here." Tristan tugged on my hand, but I held him back.

"What are you talking about?" Mastin questioned. "Let's go. Now!"

I turned and looked at the men, trying to get them to understand with a single expression. "If this works …" I said. "Don't be mad at me, okay?"

Mastin was distracted, already in battle mode. His hand rested on his gun, his body was crouched into position, and his eyes were narrowed in singular focus. But Tristan had turned toward me, his eyes flashing in a slight accusation. He knew me too well for his own good.

"Why would I be mad?" The question came out of his mouth slow and testy. "What aren't you telling me?"

There was no use in hiding it. "Okay," I sputtered. "I might be able to give you some of this yellow magic. I'm not sure it will work, but if it does, we'll have a much better chance at making it to these coordinates without being shot dead."

Mastin swung his head around. "I don't want it," he growled.

I wasn't about to give him a choice. There wasn't time to hash out an argument with the man.

The yellow already spun in tendrils of magic around us, already making its way toward the intended targets. In a flash, the tendrils caressed the men's exposed arms and sank into their bodies like water through paper.

This is okay. This is going to work just fine.

Alchemists used magic on others for green alchemy. The King used it for his own persuasion, something I'd seen Reed do on more than one occasion. But some of the more volatile magics were kept to ourselves. We were trained to handle them, true, but more than that, we'd been *born* for the task.

"Just trust me. I don't have a lot of this color left on me, so we need to get moving now. Mastin, do you want to take point?"

He stared at me like I'd completely lost my mind. I shrugged. I hated giving him the lead, but it would keep his mind occupied from the magic.

Another round of shots echoed, once again, closer.

"We don't have time," I reminded them and raised my

eyebrows.

We took off together, first rounding the dumpster, sprinting for the closest building, and running along the back. As we moved, our speed at least five times a normal human's, I kept my head down. I couldn't bring myself to look at Mastin, or Tristan, for that matter. Tristan hadn't put up a fight at the magic, but that didn't mean I wouldn't pay for this later.

I'd kept this ability to myself for years. Would he judge me for it now? Would he think I'd been selfish? Would he understand that I'd been protecting him?

Mastin stopped abruptly, falling flat on his face in the process. Tristan jumped over him, only to skid and land on his butt with a heavy thud. They both groaned as they stood. I quickly checked to make sure the blue magic was still surrounding us. It was an inner knowing within me that called to the blue, since the magic was different than all the others. They were all unique in their own ways, each feeling slightly different from the last. But the blue? It was beginning to fade. And I didn't have much color left in the stone.

"Are you two okay?" I asked. "Anything feel broken?"

"I'm fine." Mastin jumped up, brushing himself off. There was a tear in his uniform, a small trickle of blood bubbled up on his exposed knee. I frowned and reached toward it.

"I said I'm fine," he snapped, moving out of my reach. I tried not to be offended that he wouldn't let me help him, but I had to grit my teeth to do it.

Tristan was also standing now, a teasing smile lifting his face. "You could have warned us."

"I did," I replied sharply.

He lifted an eyebrow.

"Kind of."

He laughed, two perfect rows of teeth shining. I rolled

my eyes, took a deep breath, and noticed the smoke was beginning to fade. The sounds of shouting had also faded out. The battle had progressed further ahead.

Mastin shook his head, clearly unimpressed by the two of us. "The meeting point from the coordinates is just around this corner and two hundred feet ahead."

"I'll go first," I said. "You two watch for me here and jump in if I need you. Branson knows me. This is best."

Before they could argue, I took off. It was a narrow alleyway, and deserted. *For now*.

Didn't mean we were safe.

Please be there, Branson. We need you. My gut twisted. He was probably too busy to make the meeting, that was assuming he'd made it out of the battle alive.

The two buildings were about to come to an end, a tank sat right in the center, pointed outward. The relative safety of the alley was all I had left. An open road up ahead filled with smoke, a few soldiers dashing past, shouts and gunshots continuing to pierce further ahead. Not about to step out into the open, I stopped and crouched low next to the army tank. It was parked at the opening, probably ready to join the battle if needed. Where was Branson?

"Over here," a deep male voice called softly from behind, as if he'd heard my thought. I turned, tensing when I didn't spot anyone. But a moment later, Branson stepped into view from the other side of the tank. Blood mixed with dirt and sweat ran down his temple, and his mouth was set in a grim line. I stilled and clenched my fists, ready to fight if this turned out to be a trap.

He held up his hands. "I was hoping you wouldn't show. You should go," he said, voice low and tired. "This is a bad time."

"I kind of figured that part out." I glared. "You should have emailed us back."

He folded his arms over his chest, glancing around. I could sense his worry in the tense set of his shoulders and the way his eyes kept glancing about, never quite landing in one place for more than a few seconds.

"It's okay." I motioned to my necklace. "I have shielding blue around us right now. No one can hear."

Hopefully that wouldn't turn out to be a mistake, considering Tristan and Mastin were now out of earshot too.

Branson's eyes finally landed on me, impressed, and he nodded. "Then I'll make this quick. I was going to have you take a couple of people with you to the other side. Faulk is closing in on them, and I wanted them gone before she figured out that they're Resistance."

"Who?"

"Doesn't matter." He shook his head. "They're caught up in the fight."

"Who?" I shifted closer and pressed the question again.

"They're safer if you don't know," he snapped. "You'll have to come back another time. Go hide and I'll email when I can. Things are getting tense around here. Be patient. It might take some time."

Disappointment washed through me in tiny pinpricks down my spine, but what else could I do? What else could *he* do? From the looks of things, no one had expected this attack today. Maybe if Mastin had communicated with his father better, we could have avoided this. *No use fretting about it now.* Branson stepped back as I turned to go.

"Look who I found," a sinister voice called out from the other end of the alley. I whipped around and gasped with recognition. Reed. He stood behind Tristan and Mastin. Both of their hands were behind their heads as the group shuffled forward. Tristan's expression remained steady, but

Mastin snarled, his teeth bared in disgust. My eyes darted to Reed, a smug smile and raised eyebrows drawing out all my anger. Reed caught my expression and pressed back with a cackle. Like pouring salt into the wound, he held their guns in both of his meaty hands and used his magic to break them in half. A flash of yellow sparked as the broken pieces clattered to the pavement. He laughed, gleeful and sadistic.

Behind him, two more alchemists were walking with a confident swagger in their step, fists up as if ready for a fight. Their black war uniforms gleamed with stones, the visors on their helmets pulled down so I couldn't recognize them, like I could Reed. They moved like a pack of lions, confident and out for blood. We were outnumbered, and worse, I was the only alchemist on our side of the fight.

Branson's hand reached around me, scrunching my shirt and ramming me back against the tank. I caught his low spoken words. "Still using blue?" His quick and violent movement caught me so off guard.

"Don't touch her!" Mastin yelled.

"Yes, I'm still using blue," I mumbled, between gritted teeth. "They can't hear us."

"This tank is unlocked. It's ready for you to go. I was going to have you take my friends in there, but it looks like the three of you will be going at it alone." I stilled as he wrenched my arms behind my back. "Now drop the blue before he catches on," he whispered again, sending another shove into my gut.

When I did, I think we both felt the magic fade away, because the moment it was gone, Branson immediately called out to Reed. "I got her!"

A few seconds later the lot of them closed in, boots clomping on the ground and angry curses and shoves between them. Branson shoved me in front of him, his beefy hands holding me in place. Reed's visor was pulled up. He strode over and sneered in my face. I could smell the sweat on him, the blood from battle, and the eagerness to prove himself.

I glanced at my boys and shook my head slightly, hoping they'd catch what I wanted. *Play along, follow my lead, I have a plan.*

"What were you thinking coming here?" Reed scoffed. "You really are the stupidest person I have ever met. You know that? We're going to torture you and your friends, Traitor. And then do you know what we're going to do?"

I glared, refusing to answer him. He leaned in so close, our noses were nearly touching. I fought the urge to spit in his face.

"I said, do you know what we're going to do?" he yelled, spittle flying.

"You spit when you talk," I replied with a growl. "And your breath is seriously rancid. Might want to rein that in, buddy."

He moved faster than I could react, his magic igniting him, as he backhanded me across the face. I jerked back into Branson's hard chest. Pain burned across my face, and I spat blood into the dirt. Anger rose in me tenfold, hot and ready to burst.

"Touch her again and you're dead!" Tristan tore out of his captor's grip as he went for Reed, but one of the alchemists tackled him to the ground before he'd made it a few steps.

"As I was saying before I was so rudely interrupted…" Reed moved back into my personal space. "After we torture and interrogate you, we will kill your friends. I'll do it myself. You can watch. And then? We'll execute you. I think the King will make that one public."

How had this guy gone from the friendly kid at the palace to this sadistic monster?

Dread gripped me and I lost my breath. My eyes flicked to Tristan and Mastin. Tristan was still sprawled out on the ground, an alchemist sat on his back, pushing his face into the ground. Regardless, he looked up at me with utter determination in his eyes. Mastin was no different, the fire rolled off him in waves. Reed inched back, turning to the other alchemists as he began barking orders.

Branson's grip on my arms went slack.

"Go for the tank!" I yelled.

Immediately, they went into attack mode. The superhuman strength and speed of yellow was still in their systems, something Reed and his little friends hadn't been expecting. Shock rang on the alchemists' faces as they shrieked and pounced. But Tristan and Mastin were both trained fighters, and with this newfound strength pulsing through them, they were quick to knock their captors down and sprint for the tank.

I pushed Branson off me with ease and ripped open the door to the tank. Adrenaline ignited the yellow alchemy and for a moment I thought I'd torn the door right off. I jumped inside, seconds later Tristan and Mastin's bodies rolled in after me.

"I got this." Mastin pulled the door shut and locked it. "Make sure all the other escapes are locked. Go, now!"

I dove for the door on the other end of the cab and Tristan leaned up to check the one on the roof. We were secured inside in seconds, Mastin already taking point behind the wheel. It roared to life with a loud rumble that vibrated up my bones. A panel of lights ignited on the dash, reminding me of a helicopter. Reed and his cronies were trying to get inside, banging on the windows and doors, but even with magic, the monstrosity was airtight and couldn't be infiltrated.

"You know how to drive this thing?" I asked Mastin, finally catching my breath.

He nodded, face grim. "Never had to use it in battle, though."

We jerked forward. A faint burning rubber smell made me cough.

"These things aren't always the fastest, but they're sturdy. If we can get out of here before someone catches on that we're in it, we might be able to get over the frontline and back into America."

"Won't your people just blow us up?" Tristan questioned.

"Good point. Here, call my father and let him know we're coming." He pulled out the slatebook and tossed it to me. I fumbled with the device for a moment before finding Nathan Scott's contact. Pressing send, it only took one ring before the General's face filled the screen.

"I'm a little busy at the moment, son!" he shouted. "We're trying to win a war here!" Then he looked down at the screen and saw me, his lips pinching, reminding me that he and Mastin shared the same blood. His face was ashen, eyes weary.

"Sasha." His voice clipped.

I quickly explained the situation, and he nodded.

"Fine," he said. "I'll relay the message. Ping me your exact location every few minutes until you get here."

Mastin took the lead, navigating the land with expert precision. There was a steering wheel, like any land vehicle, but all the buttons he pushed left my head reeling. I watched, fascinated, as he saved our lives. It was surprisingly easy for us to get out of the New Colony basecamp. Every inch we put between us and them, allowed me to relax a millimeter more.

"With the battle waging, what's one more tank, huh?"

Tristan said.

I turned to smile at my friend, only to notice that his skin had taken on a pallid tone. A slight sheen of sweat had covered his face and his eyes were clouded and beginning to droop shut.

"Are you okay?" My eyes searched his body.

He pulled up his shirt with a stifled groan. A trickle of blood oozed from a round cut in his abdomen. I leaned in closer.

"You've been shot!"

He smiled. "Actually, I was stabbed, and I might need you to fix that up for me." Then he had the audacity to wink before the rest of the color drained from his face and he slumped over in his seat.

FOUR
JESSA

I needed to get north. The sooner I could connect to Lucas, the better. I was running out of time. Correction, I was already out of time because he might be dead. But that wasn't going to stop me from at least trying to help. Everything in the world might be conspiring to slow me down and keep us apart, but one way or another, I would discover the truth. I would find Lucas.

I leaned back against the wall and sighed, ignoring the rumble of my stomach. It matched the rumble of the thin wall behind me. I was still here, still riding the train north. Part of me hated myself for doing it; I was putting others at risk. I'd spent the better part of the day justifying my actions. Nobody knew I was here. Nobody would be implicated if I was caught. And even though Madame Silver had prepared me a pack, I was planning to save most of it for when I really needed it again. At the moment, I was safe…

Relatively speaking.

Earlier this morning, when the train had made a stop, I'd left. I'd asked Madame Silver to relay the message to the others, something I was sure she would do. She wanted me away from her company just as I did. What she didn't know, and what nobody knew, was that I'd immediately circled back and stowed away in one of the prop cars. I was currently hiding behind a row of hanging costume bags. The space was stuffy, squished, hot, and miserable. But what other option did I have? If I'd actually run off into that unknown town, in broad daylight, someone would have recognized me. And even if I'd been lucky enough to make it out of there, then what? Walk all the way to The Capitol?

No. This was the only way. I would hide here as long as possible. I would be grateful that every minute I was traveling closer to my love.

My love.

When had things gotten so complicated? First, I'd hated Lucas. Then I'd fallen in love with him. Then I'd hated him again, and now I was back to loving him, this time more deeply than ever. After our wedding, I'd seen him for who he really was, for the selfless person, not just the prince doing his father's bidding. He'd saved me. Not only me, but my father and my older sister. When that farmer had said Lucas was dead, it was like I'd been buried right along with him. I knew it then, knew I'd forgiven Lucas, that I loved him, and that I wasn't ready to leave him behind.

My heart had been softened and now it was too late.

Don't say that...

I closed my eyes, squeezing them against the turmoil. My fingers traveled to the necklace that rested around my neck, relaxing against the comfort the stones provided. I stopped on one and looked down with a frown. I was almost out of purple. I'd been using what little I had far too often lately. The Resistance had been able to help me replenish some of my crystals, but amethyst wasn't easy to come by. It didn't just pop up in people's gardens.

My precious stone had turned completely gray all but for one small speck of purple.

That meant one more chance to use telepathy. Over the last couple of days, I'd questioned whether I should connect with Dad again. But Lucas needed me; I had to save the color for him.

Fatigue simmered just under my eyelids, and I stifled a yawn. Tiredness overwhelmed me, the hard floor was beginning to make my lower back ache, and there was barely enough room to spread my cramping legs out. But who was I to complain? Instead of focusing on my physical discomfort, I needed to focus on using my magic to help Lucas.

I glanced up at the clear bags hanging on the rail beside me. Maybe I could use one as a pillow, or drape it over my body to stay hidden as I slept. The closest bag contained a forest green dress, sequins glistening in the shards of light slicing up through the gaps in the floorboard. A stunning color. If only I could…

Wait! That was it. Adrenaline coursed through my limbs and I shimmied up the wall. I rummaged through the bags, searching through the rainbow of fabrics. There, a purple silk leotard.

Most of my colors had to be pulled from natural elements, but purple was one I was especially talented in when it came to alchemy. The synthetic material would work beautifully. Ignoring a little stab of guilt for ruining something so fine, I ripped a large chunk from the costume. I winced at the sound of tearing fabric, then quickly zipped up the bag and slid back to my hiding spot.

I ran a thumb over the smooth fabric. There was enough color here between my fingers for several more telepathic conversations. Telepathy was finicky magic. I had to be close to my target, but the stronger I got, the further and further away I could be to do it. I also had to make a physical connection with the person first. Okay, not always; there had been that time during the initiation trails where I'd been able to hear a young girl. But our connection had been terrible. I'd tested it with Madame Silver and figured out it was best to touch someone first. They didn't even have to know about it right away. Once the connection was there, it could be called upon again and again.

I stilled my mind, relaxed my body, and focused on my task. I thought of Lucas, thought of everything we'd been through together. And that centered me. I touched my lip as I remembered our first kiss, pictured the way he'd looked at me. I heard the low timbre of his voice when he'd told me he'd loved me, and the way his gray eyes had flashed silver when I'd said it back. I could see it all so clearly, could practically feel him, smell his spicy scent and touch his warm skin, as if he were in the little room sitting right in front of me.

Lucas, I called out. *Can you hear me? It's me. It's Jessa.*

I waited, sure that there was something on the other end, like a slight crackle when the slatebooks connected to each other, and I just needed to listen harder.

Lucas, I tried again. *Are you okay? Please, Lucas, if you can just give me a sign. Just say anything so I know you're all right.*

Still, nothing.

Frustration clawed at me. The purple magic pulsed through my body, ready to make a connection, like it too was beginning to panic. It buzzed around, filling me with anxiety.

Lucas, please!

This time, I already knew there wouldn't be a response to my pleading words. But even so, something was there, lingering, some faint energy on the other end. Surely, it wasn't all in my mind. I shoved the thick wad of fabric into the pocket of my jeans and dropped my face into sweaty palms, nearly ready to give up. Maybe all of it was in my mind, just wishful thinking, just a heart trying not to be broken. Silly. Hopeless.

Definitely foolish.

I stayed like that for hours, trying again and again to make a connection.

Failing.

Failing so miserably I barely noticed when my cheeks became wet and sore. I didn't know when I'd begun to cry, silent anguish dripping down my face. It lasted for longer than I'd care to admit. And when the tears could no longer flow, when there was simply nothing left inside to pour out, my mind drifted away.

It was the angry kind of sleep that found me. Not restful or a way to forget the world; there was no peace in it. Rather, it consumed me with heady nightmares, the kind laced with sinking horrors and twisted fears. Worst of all, it held me under and pinned me down with no way to wake myself, no way to escape.

★

The train had stopped, the low rumble gone.

"There she is," a sharp voice split through the fog.

My eyes popped open. Before I could react, hands grabbed me. I reached for my stones, but more hands beat me to it and ripped them away. Lights flickered on, illuminating the small area and momentarily blinding me. Yanked from my spot on the floor, my body, heavy from sleep, knocked over the long row of black garment bags.

I blinked, my heart racing, as the white Royal Officer

uniforms took over my vision, their badges glistening silver, their ominous weapons inches from my face.

Unmistakable black boots stepped forward. I looked up to find Faulk glowering in my face, her tall, wiry frame stiff, her smile triumphant, her eyes narrowed in pure hatred. She tossed a handful of gray clothes at me and pointed her gun. "Change. Now."

I debated going for the color since it was all around me. But most of it was synthetic and wouldn't grant me any favors.

"Now!" she yelled again, voice sharp as a knife.

I turned and stripped as fast as possible, shame and anger in every movement. Without color, I would be hopeless. But I had no way out of this situation, no other choice, but to comply with Faulk. Dressed in only a white bra and panties, I took a risk and slipped the ripped piece of purple fabric inside the cup of my bra. Then I threw on the gray top and shimmied into the thin pants.

Purple wouldn't get me out of this mess, but it was better than nothing.

"Jessa Heart, you are under arrest." Faulk grabbed me and pushed me against the doorframe, locking handcuffs around my wrists.

"For what?" I growled, automatically tugging against the grip of metal. She tightened the cuffs even more, the pain biting into my wrists.

"I think you already know," she snapped, voice right in my ear.

Oh, I did. For attempting to manipulate the King by going for what I thought was his red blood? Yeah, that had been a huge error on my part and arrest-worthy. But I'd never hurt Lucas, and I prayed I wasn't about to be blamed for whatever had happened to him.

"Is Lucas really dead?" The urge to have answers made me sound desperate, but I didn't care. I craned my neck to get a better look at her, to see if her reaction gave anything away, but she only shoved my face back into the doorframe. "Please, just tell me the truth. Is he okay?"

"If you know what's good for you, you'll shut up. If you don't, I'll shut you up." Her voice grew louder. "You're in a lot of trouble. I wouldn't be surprised if King Richard orders your execution the moment he sees you."

My gut twisted. I wouldn't be surprised either, especially if Lucas really was dead and the King had no leads. I was an easy target. He'd probably kill me himself.

She pulled me from the room, deliberately shoving me into the doorframe before pushing me into the small hallway. On either end of the passenger train, faces stared back, and I ran my eyes over wrinkled foreheads, hands over mouths, and huddles of my old friends.

"Why are you arresting her?" Kenny said, breaking from the crowd and moving in close. His eyebrows arched in concern, but guilt lit his expression. "I thought you said she was in trouble. You were supposed to help her!"

Faulk eyed him with disdain. "You got what you wanted, boy. You got your reward. Don't ask questions. We know what we're doing."

A dark cloud enveloped me, and I sighed heavily. Kenny. Kenny had turned me in. He'd seemed so trustworthy, helped me when I'd saved Toby. When would I learn that I could trust no one? Madame Silver stood behind him, her eyes wide with anguish. I couldn't blame her, she'd known this would happen. She'd been smart enough to get me out, but I'd been the one to go back on my word.

"You're sure nobody else knew she was in there?" Faulk asked Kenny.

"I'm sure," he sputtered.

"You know we have ways to detect if you're lying."

Dread crashed through me. If he told the truth, it would implicate the entire company. They would be punished. Severely. But, in retrospect, I had gone into that storage car alone. Kenny wasn't lying, he just wasn't telling the entire truth.

"I'm sure," he went on. "I went in there to get something and found her, so I called the hotline right away."

Faulk nodded. "My colleagues will be conducting interviews."

A wave of dizziness fell over me.

"And if everything checks out, you will be rewarded, as promised."

Kenny's mouth twisted but his eyes widened, and the dizziness running through my mind doubled. Of course, I couldn't trust these people not to turn me in. Money was money. Who was I to them when a fortune was on the line?

Faulk yanked me down the thin hall to the exit, down the steps, and out toward a waiting car. I'd spent enough time in black, shiny cars over the last six months, and just the sight of it made tears spring to my eyes. My stomach turned and before I could stop myself, I bent at the waist and lost what little I had in my stomach. It spread across the pavement and splattered Faulk's shoes. "Sorry," I muttered, not that I really cared. A small laugh escaped me.

"Oh, you've got to be kidding," she growled, spinning me around so quick the dizziness came back with a vengeance. She backhanded me across the face, hard enough for my breath to catch and my vision to blur.

Everything fell to darkness.

★

I caught the faint sandalwood scent of Lucas; it crashed me from the tip of weightlessness back into reality. My heart, so closed until now, fluttered open—my eyes, too. My surroundings took form, from hazy to solid—I was in his surroundings, too. I shot up, a mix of fear and longing clenching me so tight I could hardly breathe.

I was lying in the center of a large bed, in the bedroom we'd been meant to share together. The fireplace, the furniture, the long, sheer curtains—everything appeared as we'd left it, as if waiting for my return. Part of me wished I'd never left it that night. If I'd stayed here with Lucas, we might not be in this mess. Maybe I could have protected him from whatever happened, and maybe he could have done the same for me. Maybe he would still be in here with me now, instead of the wispy traces of his scent, a pale comparison to the real thing.

I buried my head into his pillow, tears filling my eyes. I'd gone and ruined everything and now that I was back, I was more of a prisoner than ever. And I didn't have Lucas. I didn't have anyone. But at least I was here. At least now I had a chance to find him. Somehow. Someway.

Maybe this was not only the better way, but also the only way. Maybe this was what needed to happen all along. It was the only hope I had, and it still didn't change the fact that I was once again in my gilded prison.

I sat up and peered around, noticing there was something a little off about the room. There was no usable color. I wasn't surprised. The furniture was dark oak, the linens were all white, and the floors the same polished alabaster marble found in most of the palace. Even the rug and wall hangings had been removed, and after checking the dresser drawers and the closet, I only found black, gray, or white, but nothing usable.

Deep in my gut, I knew that the doors would be locked,

the windows, too. Still, ever the naïve optimist, I rolled from the bed and checked them anyway. The silver door handle didn't budge, and the window was firmly shut in place. I ran a finger along the line of fresh nails buried along the painted windowsill and sighed.

At least I wasn't expected to wear prison clothes. That had to mean something. I went back to the closet to study the casual outfits and formal gowns, finding a group of pressed Guardian uniforms hanging in the back. Breath catching in my throat, I ran my fingers along the material of my old uniform and felt my heart kick in protest. I had been so close to getting away from this outfit and everything it meant. The idea of wearing them hardly seemed appropriate, but I could take a hint when I saw one.

Besides, I needed to get cleaned up while I still had the chance.

I hurried to the shower and got myself ready as quickly as I could, partly from the anticipation of what the day would hold for someone under arrest, but partly from curiosity as to why I was locked up in here instead of downstairs with all the other criminals. If I had to guess, I'd say I was going to find out what was going on sooner rather than later. Surely I wasn't just going to be accepted back into the fold as a Guardian? But according to the latest broadcast, I was still the princess. But that didn't make sense either, given the circumstances of my disappearance.

Dressing in the bathroom, I found the strip of purple fabric I'd stolen and returned it to the spot inside of my bra, tucking it against my skin. I felt a little silly hiding something there, because what would happen if they made me strip? I couldn't worry about that. It was all the color I had left, and it was coming with me, just in case. Freshened up and waiting for whatever came next, I sat back on the bed, foot tapping restlessly on the floor. Breakfast, perhaps? My stomach pinched at the thought.

I closed my eyes and relaxed, thinking of Lucas, wondering if he was near, hoping he was okay. I was no stranger to pain and sadness lately, but even imagining him no longer being alive tore a giant hole inside me. I was nervous to try the purple magic again for that very reason. What if it didn't work? What if it failed so miserably I had no choice but to accept Lucas's death? I touched my side, close to the purple fabric. If it didn't work, if he didn't respond now that I was back in our home, I swore my heart would crumble.

I swallowed and took several deep breaths, my chest rising and falling with effort. Whatever the case, whatever happened, I had to be strong. There wasn't any more time to question things. I was back in the palace, and if Lucas was hiding somewhere, he was probably close. I could do this.

Mind made up, the purple came to me instantly, quickening my pulse. With steady thoughts, I reached out for him. At first, there was nothing, but then a small flicker of familiar energy rose on the other end.

Lucas! I called out. *Lucas, are you okay? Is that you? Can you hear me?*

The door flew open. I blinked several times, instantly losing the telepathic magic. With the color safely tucked away, nobody would know what had just happened. I cleared the magic from my body and turned to face my intruder.

King Richard.

"You," he spat, striding into the room with clenched fists. A few guards shuffled in after him, and the door slammed with a thud.

I held up my hands in surrender, mouth falling open, unable to utter a word. He loomed over me, looking taller than I remembered. Bigger. And angrier than I'd ever seen him, the clarity in his steel eyes was startling. His hair was slicked back and his suit was pressed to perfection, the polished exterior did little to hide the animal within.

"You have a lot of explaining to do," he growled low, a thick vein in his forehead bulging, his sunken cheeks making his facial bones extra severe. "Unfortunately, Reed is still on the frontline. He's been rather useful to me there, but I'm starting to regret that decision." He eyed me with contempt as his presence overtook the room. "I'm going to give you one chance to tell me the truth, and if you don't, I swear on my wife's grave, I will drag you by that pretty hair of yours all the way to the frontline to beg at Reed's feet."

My stomach flipped. Reed was the most powerful blue alchemist in the kingdom and I had too much to hide. I should have been more careful than to end up here! With all the suspicion cast in my direction, and Reed to interrogate me about everything, I'd have to fight harder than ever to overcome him. But I'd done it before. I could do it again. Still, I needed that to be the last resort.

"Okay," I squeaked. I cleared my throat, grasping for confidence. "Okay, I'll tell you." How was I going to pull this off?

I gripped the edge of the bed sheet, wishing I could manipulate white and get out of here. I tried to clear my mind, noticing instead that my whole body had grown cold.

He leaned in front of me, eyes narrowed into angry slits. "Are you with the Resistance?"

There was no point in lying. I'd already tried and failed to manipulate the man's blood. He hated me, would never trust me again.

"Yes."

Slam! He slapped me across the face. It was so unexpected, so shocking, I didn't brace myself. I fell back onto the bed and cowered. He didn't seem to care either way. His face was beet red as he towered over me.

"How long?" he demanded.

"Since not long after I got here. Sasha and Jasmine recruited me."

"Who else?"

"What?" I sputtered, the terror multiplying.

"You know what!" he yelled, voice booming through the room.

How was I going to keep others out of this one? Lucas had been part of the Resistance for a time, and I couldn't possibly tell his father. Madame Silver had helped me, and she could be so easily implicated. That sweet old woman, Ruth, the farmer Taysom Greene and his family, and so many others ... even the couple at the palace. I couldn't turn these people in. They had helped me. Any suspicion on them would ultimately mean their deaths. I'd seen for myself how Richard had twisted things to punish anyone he wanted. There were no consequences for a king.

"Who else is Resistance?" he demanded again.

"I don't know," I lied. If it came to the point that Reed got the truth from me using his persuasive magic, then so be it. Right now, I was all about lying through my teeth for as long as I could manage.

"I don't believe you," he said slowly, once again clenching his fists.

"No, it was only those two. When Jasmine died, the Resistance died too," I pleaded.

Died... I gritted my death. Murder was the appropriate word for what had happened to Jasmine. I longed to say it, but given my vulnerable position, I needed to appear as cooperative as possible, but without revealing too much. I needed to appear chastised, apologetic.

"If that's true, then who has been trying to assassinate my family?" He began to pace the room, arms flying about as he spoke. His guards stood back, expressions placid. But they followed him with their careful eyes, as if they knew to watch out, as if they understood the viper was about to strike.

"I don't know, honestly, I don't," I said.

"Again, Jessa, I don't believe you. You're a liar."

He should know…

"Is Lucas really dead?" I asked, changing the subject to what I really longed to be discussing. Richard didn't take the bait.

"Where did you go? The night you attacked me, tried to ruin me, where did you disappear to?"

There was no way around this one. But I could bend the truth. If I stuck close enough to what happened, then maybe he would believe the lies I was weaving.

"Your son, he got me out."

He spun toward me, face growing pale, jaw slacking in shock.

"Lucas said you'd never forgive me," I continued, holding up my hands in surrender. "He thought you were going to have me executed for treason after what I did. He snuck me out of the palace. I've been traveling by myself ever since."

"My son snuck you out?" His eyes narrowed, realization dawning in them. "So you don't know what happened to him."

I shook my head. "I don't."

"Isn't it interesting that when we found you, you were stowed away on a train heading North. If you were really so eager to get away from me, then it seems your story doesn't add up."

I scooted back and crawled to the top of the bed, pressing my back against the headboard.

"I came back to see if Lucas was really dead," I croaked.

He silently strode to the window, peering out with his hands clasped behind his back. Outside, winter was nearing its end, but the earth was still in hibernation. I wondered if it reflected the rage simmering under King Richard's exterior.

He glared back at me and stalked forward, finger pointed. "Tell me the full truth. Who else helped you?"

I bit my lip as I shook my head. "No one."

Silence and thick hatred spread between us.

"So be it," he finally said, voice calmer than ever. "First thing tomorrow, you and I are going on a little trip."

I gulped. I didn't need to ask what that meant.

Once Reed got ahold of me, there was no telling what secrets would be revealed. I'd hidden so many in the dark for so long, the idea of them being exposed left me reeling.

He studied me for a minute more, then turned for the door.

"What about my husband?" I called after him. Saying the word husband felt like admitting just how much I loved Lucas.

But Lucas's father, his own flesh and blood, didn't bother to reply or even glance back. He slammed the door with finality, rattling the doorframe, leaving me to my imagination.

★

Lucas! I called out, homing in on our telepathic connection. *Lucas, are you there? Is that you?* I felt it, felt someone hovering on the other side of my thoughts. Tears pricked at my eyes. Hope flooded my heart. Hope and excitement.

Lucas, I continued, *it's me, Jessa.*

Jessa?

His voice hit me like a gasp for air. I couldn't breathe. My trembling hand slapped against my mouth, holding back the choking sobs. It was him. It was muffled, far off, but it was him. Hearing him was like coming up for air when I didn't even know I was drowning.

Oh, thank God. Are you okay?

There was a long pause.

This is Jessa? he asked, this time sounding somewhat confused.

And that confused me. I blinked, unease settling in.

Yes, of course, where are you? Are you okay?

Another long pause was followed by a sharp reply. *Go away. Get out of my head.*

I sputtered. *What? What do you mean?*

Do I have to spell it out for you? I said, get out of my head! The connection slammed at me, as if he was forcing me out. But why? Why wouldn't he want to talk to me? It made no sense. We hadn't left on the best of terms, but we were closer than we'd been in weeks. He suddenly didn't want anything to do with me? No. This wasn't how this was supposed to go. It didn't make sense.

I won't leave you alone until you tell me you're all right! I challenged. *You have no idea what I just went through, and what I am going to go through. Everyone thinks you're dead, Lucas. I thought you were dead. Do you have any idea what that did to me? I came back to find out the truth!*

Finally, his voice replied. This time not angry, not calm, not confused, but also, not anything. He was completely devoid of any emotion at all. *I'm sorry you had to suffer because of me, but you need to get out of my head right now.*

What? Why? What's going on, Lucas?

I don't know you, okay! he shot back. *This head injury*

has been tough enough as it is, and now I don't need to start hearing voices. So, I would kindly ask you to leave me alone.

I momentarily froze. Then I jolted from the bed. What was he talking about? He didn't know me? What was that supposed to mean?

Lucas, you're scaring me.

The feeling is mutual, Jessa. Whoever you are. Now get out! He slammed once again on the connection, this time severing it completely.

I fell back onto the bed. Bile rose into the back of my throat. I rolled to my side, drew my knees in, and clenched my stomach.

Lucas didn't remember me.

The realization of it crashed down, taking all my hopes for our future and turning them to dust. The room spun, and I closed my eyes. My body sank down into the bed, weightless and empty. The man I loved didn't even know who I was. All of this, all I went through, was for nothing. How could that be?

Except all wasn't lost because Lucas wasn't dead. I thanked whatever God was in heaven for that.

Lucas wasn't dead. But he had a head injury.

Lucas wasn't dead. But he also didn't remember me.

Not even a little bit.

And if he'd forgotten me, what else had Prince Lucas forgotten?

FIVE
LUCAS

"This is getting ridiculous." I tugged at the IV in my arm. The nurse, Cathy, raised an eyebrow but injected something into my vein anyway. It burned all the way up my arm. "Come on, Cathy, you could have warned me." I gritted my teeth but winked at her anyway.

"I thought I did," she mused, checking my vitals.

"I need to get out of here. I need to talk to my parents. Where are they?"

Three days. Three days of lying here in this bed. I was a prince and I felt fine, yet I was being treated like a child. And now my patience was wearing thin. Upon waking, I'd recognized the room as one not belonging to the palace or even a hospital, but to the orphanage Mom and I had organized a few years back. Once upon a time it was one of our royal estates, but now it belonged to orphaned children, which was better use in my opinion.

But none of that answered the question: what in the world was I doing here?

Doctor Lawson strolled in, white lab coat flowing behind him, a warm smile on his face. His calculating eyes looked me up and down from behind shiny glasses perched on the tip of his nose. "How's my favorite patient doing today?"

I rolled my eyes. "I'm your only patient."

It was true. It didn't take a genius to gather that something had happened to me and this was where my parents had decided to whisk me away. What it apparently did take a genius to gather was the reason why? Why hide me like this? I had spent the last two days conjuring up every possible explanation for what could be going on back home and I was about ready to burst.

"But why am I here?" I asked the doctor, noticing how he looked away.

It was one of many questions I'd been asking lately. I never got any answers. "Where are my parents?" I continued, lowering my voice and trying to sound reasonable. "Look, I just need to talk to someone who knows what's going on. The way I see it, I should've been placed in a real hospital, right? My parents have hidden me away and I want to know why."

Lawson and Cathy shared a pained look.

The alchemist strolled into the room at that moment, a small smile on her round face. She was cute, with curly blonde hair and thick black glasses. Cute, in a nerdy kind of way. I usually went for the more polished type, but I could bend my rules for this one.

"In a real hospital, you wouldn't have me," she said. "So count yourself lucky your father sent you up here to heal."

I rolled my eyes again.

"Thanks for listening in," I smirked at her, even though, that part was true. Her name was Callie, and she'd apparently been a huge part in my healing since alchemy wasn't something we did in hospitals. But that still didn't explain why I was here. She could have just helped me at the palace. Or broken protocol and healed me at the hospital anyway.

She shrugged, but I caught the pity in her eyes and as much as it killed me, decided to go with it.

"I need answers," I pressed, nodding toward her as if she were my only shot. "I'm not just going to sit around this place in the middle of nowhere while my parents are missing, maybe even hurt." My voice trailed off and I cleared my throat. As much as I was trying to reach them through the heartstrings, it didn't mean I wasn't telling the truth. I was worried.

The doctor fumbled with some paperwork, looking through his pages and pages of notes. I strained my eyes to get a peek, but his handwriting was atrocious. I fell back against the pillows and sighed heavily. Apparently, Doctor Lawson had decided to ignore me. Great.

"Let's go through these questions again, shall we?" he asked, voice clinical and never once looking up at me.

Oh, here we go again.

We'd gone through these questions every day since I'd woken, and my answers weren't just suddenly going to change. This was getting weirder and weirder. I sucked in a breath of the stale air and counted backwards from three, trying to relax into this. Maybe if I answered his questions, he'd finally answer a few of mine.

"What's your name?" he asked.

"Lucas Heart."

"What's the last thing you remember before waking up?"

I sighed. "I remember eating dinner with my parents and going to bed. That's it, nothing exciting."

"You don't remember any kind of accident or maybe an attack?"

Nurse Cathy, busy checking the heart rate monitor, stilled.

Doctor Lawson was no longer studying his notes, but studying me. I eyed him scrupulously. This was a new question and the whole room buzzed with that fact. "I've told you, I have no idea how this happened to me. What do you mean an attack?"

"And how old are you?" He returned back to his list.

I sunk back into the bed, frustrated. "I just turned eighteen." But that didn't stop me from watching him intently, and when his nose quirked, I narrowed my eyes. "What?" I questioned. "Why did you make that face?"

"I didn't make a face."

I spun on the nurse. "You saw it, right? Did he make a face?"

She shrugged and turned away.

"See! You totally did. What is going on, Doc?"

"I am not permitted to say anything until your father gets here."

"And where is my father?" I growled, finally losing my cool. "I woke up here, of all places. I've been sitting around for days with a constant pain in my head. And you keep telling me he's coming but I don't see anyone pulling up that drive, do you?" I motioned to the driveway outside the window, and the white-washed landscape beyond that. We were utterly alone out here.

"And anyway," I continued, "he can just call, can't he? I want my slatebook." I reached my hand out. "Or I can take yours. I'm sure *you* have one; it will have to do."

He bristled. "I'm sorry but I can't do that."

"Trust me," the alchemist girl, Callie, stepped forward. "You don't want to see the newsfeeds right now."

"And why not?" I snapped. Her eyes widened, clearly caught in the crossfire.

I threw my head back against the soft pillow, sighing loudly. "Sorry." I rubbed my eyes, a dull ache forming behind them. "I feel like I'm going crazy. I just want to know why I can't leave this room, why no one will tell me why I'm here."

The doctor shook his head, returning to his paperwork. "We have our orders."

"Can you at least tell me who Jessa is?"

His head popped up, eyes turning into round orbs as he strode forward, shining a light in my pupil.

I waved him off, only to find Callie's smiling face and nurse Cathy sighing a huge breath of relief.

"You remember Jessa?" doctor Lawson asked, a twinge of excitement in his tone.

"I hate to break it to you, but no. That's why I'm asking you guys who she is." I gulped, rubbing my temples. Were these people even listening to me? "She's been in my head or something ... I don't know."

"What do you mean she's been in your head?" the doctor asked, his expression still hopeful. His eyes searched my face, no longer interested in the pages of notes he'd been using for cover earlier.

But as much as I wanted to make progress, I wasn't about to tell the man I'd been hearing voices. I shrugged. "I don't know how to explain it, just that I know that name is important somehow. So, who is she?"

My eyes hopped between the three of them as they shared glances. A tension had gathered in the room; I'd hit a nerve.

"I'm calling your father," the doctor finally replied, breaking the tension and heading for the door. "This is a huge development. He needs to advise me on our next step."

Annoyance pulled at me like a string, tugging on my father and his unknown destination, ever the puppet master.

"Tell my *father* to come visit his *son*!" I called after the doctor. The man didn't pause as he left the room, didn't even seem to hear me. I turned to the nurse. She stood by the window, her arms crossed and her head cocked, studying me with pitying eyes.

"What?" I challenged.

She shrugged, shaking her head. She knew she couldn't say anything. We all knew it. But that didn't make it right

"How are you feeling today?" Callie held up her hands, a green stone centered in her palm. "Need another boost?"

I grimaced. "You know what I really need."

Answers.

Callie bit her lip, consideration flashing in her eyes. "You really don't remember her?" When I shook my head she frowned, her honey eyes filling with deep concern, like she was somehow invested in all of this, too. "Poor Jessa," she whispered.

What was that supposed to mean? Poor Jessa? What about poor Lucas? I let out a frustrated laugh and a sharp pain reverberated from the back of my head. I winced, rubbing the spot as it returned to a dull ache.

"You need to calm down." The nurse motioned to the heart rate monitor, which had begun to speed up. "You're aggravating the wound."

"What do you expect, given my situation? Am I just supposed to sleep and pretend I don't have a whole lot of questions?"

"The pain medicine will kick in any moment," she talked over me. "And yes, I would like for you to get some rest and put the worry out of your mind for now. It's important for your recovery."

She spun on her heel and hustled from the room.

"You sure you don't want some green alchemy before I go?" Callie asked.

I didn't answer. I just looked up to meet her stare. She had that same twisted expression from before, the one that told me she knew much more than she was letting on. I raised a hopeful eyebrow, wishing more than anything that I knew what she was thinking. Her eyes flashed once again. She felt sorry for me.

This was my chance.

"Please…"

"I can't say anything," she whispered. "It's my orders. If I break them I will get in so much trouble. So much. You don't even know."

"I swear I won't tell a soul. I just want to know what happened to me."

"I don't know how it happened, only that you hit your head really hard. Lucas, you have some sort of amnesia. The doctor thinks it's temporary, but it might be permanent."

I shook my head. Amnesia? But I remembered who I was. That didn't make sense.

"Are you messing with me?" I laughed, disbelieving.

"You've forgotten practically a year of your life," she finally relented.

My body sank into the bed like it was made out of quicksand. I didn't fight it, didn't even know how to move. A year of my life? How was that possible?

When I didn't reply, she continued on, wringing her hands, regretful eyes trained on me. "It's supposed to be temporary. I don't know. I haven't been able to reverse it with magic." Her eyes filled with tears. "What if it's not temporary? What will Jessa do?"

I squinted, breathing in the scent of antiseptic. "Who is Jessa?"

She twisted her lip between her teeth, studying me, searching for words.

"Who is she?" I pressed.

"I'm not supposed to say." Her voice came out, barely a squeak.

"Isn't it a little late for that? Besides, I'm your prince. Consider it an order."

That was total crap, and my father pulled rank, but she needed an excuse to tell me the truth. From the torn expression on her face, she wanted me to know.

"Just tell me."

She let out a slow breath. "Lucas, you're married. Jessa is your wife."

I laughed. Now, *that* was ridiculous. Was I honestly supposed to believe I was married? Even if I had forgotten a year, I certainly wouldn't have agreed to a marriage.

"It's true," she whispered. "You're madly in love with her. I've never seen anything like it, the way you look at her."

Confusion traveled through me, starting in my center and spreading to every inch of my body, of my memory, and of my life. "How is that possible? If I love her so much, then why can't I remember her?"

Her eyebrows drew in, and she glared. "Because you hit your head and forgot!" She strode to the door, locking it, then whipped out a slatebook from her back pocket. After few swipes, she turned the screen on me. "See!"

A picture shone back, leaving me grasping at the truth. It was a photo of me. Wearing a tuxedo, I had a massive grin plastered on my face as I looked adoringly at the woman next to me. My arm was wrapped around her, and she was dressed in a white gown so beautiful, it was obvious she had to be a bride. My bride. Her dark hair was curled loosely down and around her shoulders, and she leaned into me, beaming at the camera, bright blue eyes shining like a clear sky. It was most definitely a wedding photograph, but one I had absolutely no recollection of, nor of the woman.

I studied my expression, looking for a crack in the exterior, something to indicate this wasn't real, but all I could see was a man very much in love.

Heat poured over me. I finally let out a breath. Questions danced through my mind. What in the world was going on?

"That's my wife?" I asked. "Seriously?"

"Yes," Callie said, slipping the slatebook back into her pocket.

"I love her?"

"Yes."

"I'm assuming she loves me, too?"

"I always thought so."

I squinted. "What's that supposed to mean?"

She moved to the door faster than humanly possible, yellow alchemy at play. "I've said too much."

Before I could question her further, her small body, dressed head to toe in alchemist black, slid through the door. I debated going after her, demanding more answers and especially demanding she hand over that slatebook. But the IV was busy pumping fluids into my body and as much as I hated it, I couldn't rip it out. I needed it. I didn't really want to roll the thing around with me. My head pounded harder than ever and a sleepy fog was rolling into my mind, clouding all my thoughts.

I knew what came next. Every single time I thought I felt better, thought I could leave this stupid mansion and go back to the palace, more pain would crash over me. Next thing, I'd be laid out in bed within the hour and fighting the pain, drifting into the drug-laced sleep.

I needed to heal, to remember.

If I'd forgotten my wife, what else might I have forgotten?

I needed answers. But something tugged at me, a nagging

fear that had wormed its way into my mind. What if I found out the truth, and I didn't like it? What if it was worse than being left in the dark?

I groaned and dropped my head into my hands. My parents had better get here and explain what happened to me before I officially lost it.

★

For the first time since waking up in the estate, I was allowed out of my room. I enjoyed dinner with the children, chatting idly over a hot stew, I realized it was the first moment of peace I'd had since waking into this nightmare. Apparently, the kids had been instructed not to talk about my injury or my past, because the subject stayed out of the conversation.

That was until my favorite little boy, Joey, looped skinny arms around my neck and whispered into my ear. "I really hope Jessa is okay. We miss her."

Then he scampered off, leaving me, once again, feeling like everyone was in on the secret but me.

"Are you finished with that?" a staff member asked over my shoulder, motioning to my empty bowl. I licked my lips, the warm broth settling comfortably in my stomach, and nodded.

She reached to take it, and when I stopped her, her busied expression flushed. "It's okay," I said. "I can help clean up."

"Oh, we couldn't ask that," she replied, brushing a long strand of gray hair out of her face.

I stared into her weary blue eyes for a moment and smiled. "Really, it's okay. I've been bedridden for days and need to move my legs anyway. You'd be doing me a favor."

"Are you sure?" Her mouth set as she frowned, brushing sturdy hands on her apron. This woman, no matter her age, was used to doing her job well and keeping out of trouble.

"You see that doctor over there?" I pointed to the man seated with the nurse on the other end of the table. They were also finishing their meals, leaning close and whispering—probably about me.

She nodded.

"He's going to make me go back to bed at the first opportunity. This is my first time out of that stuffy room and I want to make it last as long as I can." I stood from my chair, picking up the mess and stacking it with the other bowls around me. "Please, let me help."

She chuckled low and shrugged. "You did this last time you were here, you know? Always such a chivalrous boy."

I paused. "Last time?" I wracked my brain, trying to remember the exact moment she was talking about. It had been a while since I'd shared a meal with the orphans. But then Joey had made it sound like he knew Jessa personally…

She clammed up. "Oh shoot, I messed that one up."

I eyed her with interest as her round face turned as red as a tomato. "Wait, last time? Was I here recently?"

She eyed the doctor for a moment and muttered under her breath. "You were here with your lovely fiancé not less than a month ago."

I stilled. "You've met Jessa? Tell me, what's she like?"

She smiled softly. "Kind."

I took in the room, trying to imagine us here, trying to make the connection. The furnishings were solid oak, made to handle years of use. The walls had landscape paintings on each, except for the far wall where children's artwork was featured, rows upon rows of imagination brought to life. But the aroma of hearty broth, the laughter and chatter, and the clinking sound of spoon-scraped bowls being stacked atop each other, didn't spark memories of Jessa. She was like a ghost that everyone else had seen, but I only knew the story.

"Oh, you two were so adorable. I really hope they find her soon," she whispered, eyes hopeful but mouth carefully relaxed.

I gulped, letting out a defeated sigh. "I'm sorry, but I don't remember her."

"Dearest me, I've said too much." She scampered off to take care of cleaning up the younger children.

A sense of disorientation whipped through me, unsettling any comfort I had previously felt. Apparently, my wife was missing?

As I moved about the room, helping with the clean-up, my mind tried fruitlessly to remember Jessa. Who was she, really? And how had she gotten into my head like that? The way she had just spoken in my mind, was I going crazy? Or was it the kind of rare and powerful alchemy, the kind I knew was possible, but that I had never experienced? An offshoot of purple, telepathic magic was something some people would kill to have, and others would do anything to keep hidden. If that was what Jessa was doing, if that was how she got in my mind, then which kind of alchemist was she? The kind who boasted her ability, or the kind who hid it among her deepest secrets?

As I considered the questions, I found my body growing tired. Irritated, I returned to my bedroom and plopped down on the comforter, resigned to end one of the most confusing days of my life. Maybe the doctor was right. Maybe if I got some rest, all of this would heal faster, the memories would return, and with it, the answers.

One knock boomed off the door before it swung open and my father strolled into the room. I sat upright, relief washing through me the moment our eyes met.

"Son!" he exclaimed, rushing forward and wrapping his

arms around me in a tight grip. His familiar smell of soap and spice calmed me further. "I'm so glad to hear you've had some of your memories return. I came as soon as the doctor called."

I hugged him back, though the question bothered me. "Why didn't you come when I first woke up?"

He stepped back. "I'm sorry. Things are ... complicated."

I raised a brow. "I've been awake for days, living in this bizarre stupor and nobody will tell me anything. I can't take it. What happened to me?"

His face stilled, and I stood to meet his expression. A long moment stretched between us.

He finally relaxed, jaw releasing, shoulders drooping, and energy falling. "Why don't you tell me everything you think happened and I can fill in the gaps?"

I ran a hand through my hair, stopping at the back of my head where the headache persisted. If only it were that easy. His steel eyes zeroed in on me, more intense than I ever remembered, and something deep within me faltered. "I don't know; that's the problem. I don't remember anything from the last year of my life."

He squinted. "Are you sure? They said you asked about Jessa."

I shook my head. I didn't want to get into it. If he knew I'd been hearing voices, it was likely I'd be stuck out here in no-man's land even longer. Which brought me to my next question. "Why am I here? Why aren't I in the palace or at least in the capital city? This isn't exactly the height of civilization."

He sighed and found the chair by the window. I sat on the edge of the bed and watched him carefully, waiting for the truth. He ran his hands through his hair, and I noticed how he'd aged considerably. His hair had become grayer, his wrinkles deeper, his eyes more sunken in, and he'd lost weight. Was he okay?

"A lot has happened, Son. I don't even know where to start."

"I guess, start with Mom. Where is she?" Even as I asked the question, a bubble of fear welled up inside me.

His eyes shot to mine, anguish filling his features instantly. "Your mother is dead. She was murdered. It happened five months ago."

I blinked, my body made of ice. "What?" I sputtered in disbelief.

He nodded solemnly. "It's a long story, but we believe she was murdered by West America. And by the way, we are currently at war with them."

I shook my head. War? We weren't a kingdom of war. New Colony had spent the better part of a century avoiding it at all costs.

"West America also tried to take you out," my father continued. "That's why you're here. We're hiding you. As of right now, the world believes you to be dead."

"That's how I got my injury? They did this to me?" Again, I reached to the back of my head, fingers running over my skull.

"I wish I knew all the details. I do know that someone has been trying to assassinate you ever since your mother's death. This time, they very nearly succeeded. We found you on the edge of death. Luckily our alchemists could heal the wounds, but nobody could help your brain. You were in a coma for a few weeks before you woke up; even still, your memories of the last year may be permanently erased."

I shook my head. "That's not a good thing."

Something in his face twitched. Did he agree? Finally, he nodded and cleared his throat. "Which brings me to my next point."

"Jessa?" I needed to know more about this mystery woman who had infiltrated my thoughts.

He nodded. "We need to talk about your wife. It's time you learned the truth about why that girl really married you."

★

My legs ached to run. I longed to feel the endorphins rush through my body, longed to hear my heartbeat instead of the million questions that rolled in my head. But everything else in my body told me to take it easy; I wasn't fully healed yet. Sure, on the outside I looked as healthy as ever, but the headaches still plagued me, a constant reminder of my lost memories.

I groaned and continued on my walk around the orphanage grounds. The snow had melted, leaving pools of mud. It caked my shoes, but I wasn't bothered. At least I was outside, where the air was crisp and refreshing, where I could breathe, where the sun could warm my face and I could try to piece my life back together without Richard standing over my shoulder.

He hadn't left my side in three days, constantly quizzing me on my past. This behavior was exactly why he and I were usually at odds. He was just so demanding, his presence so consuming that it took away from everyone else. If anything was going to help my headaches, it was getting away from him.

Lucas? The voice shot through my mind.

Her voice.

Lucas, are you there? It's me.

I stopped midstride and put my hands on my waist, huffing into the blue sky above. My breath spread before me, like smoke billowing into the cold air. If only I could see this girl too, then maybe I could decide for myself what she really meant to me.

Jessa, I replied. *Yeah, I'm here.* It was strange, that I didn't have to audibly talk and yet we could have a whole conversation. But then again, maybe it shouldn't have been strange, considering who she was.

You're using magic to do this, right? I continued. *My father told me you're an alchemist, which explains how you're able to get into my head. But he never mentioned that you had this particular talent.*

Did you tell him about this? Lucas, he can't know! Her voice came through the connection, sharp and fearful.

I paused, considering the implications. *You're afraid of him, aren't you?*

As I should be! she rushed, her words all jumbling together. *He hasn't followed through on his threat to take me to the frontline, but I know it's only a matter of time.*

That's probably because he's here checking up on me.

Where's here? Lucas, where are you?

I'm somewhere where I hopefully won't be assassinated. You ask a lot of questions.

And you aren't really answering any of them. She quieted for a while, long enough that I wondered if she'd severed the connection. Finally, her voice came through as a soft surrender. *Do you remember me yet?*

I squinted into the horizon, studying the empty landscape but for a few trees.

I sighed. *That is a question I can answer. No, I don't remember you. Not even a little bit.*

There was a long silence before a simple, *Oh*, filtered through my head.

Sorry. I squeezed my hands into fists, exasperated. *I don't know what happened to me, how I got this head injury, but I think maybe you can enlighten me.*

What is that supposed to mean? she bit back.

The pain was returning to the back of my head, but I pressed on.

You were the last one to see me before whatever happened to me. Richard thinks it's possible that you were the one who did this to me. That you tried to kill me.

I would never! I love you.

I scoffed. *Really? If that's true, then why are you with the Resistance?*

Yes, Richard had told me all about this Resistance group trying to undermine everything he was doing, making it harder for us to win this war against West America. It was bad enough to have one major enemy, but to have another one working within our very borders? They needed to be stopped. Even I knew that!

Your dad is trying to turn you against me. Don't let him, she begged.

Are you denying it?

Another long pause. Finally, she let out a sharp, *No.*

I huffed. *So why would a Resistance spy marry the prince to the kingdom she's trying to take down? Sounds a whole lot like treason if you ask me.* I laughed again. *And I'm supposed to believe you love me? Pick a story.*

If you could remember the last year, you'd know I'm telling the truth.

It's all very convenient for you, Jessa. And tell me again where you were when I hit my head?

You got me out of the palace before that ever happened! You sent me away to protect me!

I couldn't believe this woman. Her story was so twisted, and Richard's was a clear, logical line. Who did she expect me to believe? He was my father, and yes, he was intense and incredibly persistent when he wanted to get his way. He wasn't the best dad or husband, and at times he drove me mad with frustration. He could be cold-hearted, and he could be oblivious to people who weren't on his radar. But was he evil? Was he the tyrant Jessa thought he was? I didn't think so.

I'm almost healed, I continued. *And when I can convince my father to let me out of hiding, I'm going to come with him to interrogate you. You're part of the Resistance, you've already admitted it. You were with me the night I hit my head. They found me in the Guardian wing, Jessa! You're an alchemist! What do you expect me to think? If anyone knows what happened to me, it's probably you.*

You're making a huge mistake!

And I intend to find out whatever dirty little secrets you've been keeping from my family, I finished with an angry sneer.

Maybe you should look in the mirror! You were Resistance before I ever was.

I froze, caught off guard, but only for a moment. *I highly doubt that.*

It's true, she snapped. *You were the one who convinced me to keep my red alchemy a secret from your father for as long as I could. You were the one who wanted us to get married in the first place. You made a bargain with your father, so he would allow it. And in the end, it was you who snuck me out of the palace after our wedding. You knew your father was about to figure everything out and wanted to protect me.*

Why would I be Resistance? I'm the prince!

Because you found out the truth about your father. He's a bad man, Lucas. He's done terrible things and you didn't want anything to do with his legacy.

Bad how? What aren't you telling me?

You say you can't trust me, but how can I know if I can trust you? Apparently, you're right back in his pocket.

I took a deep breath and let it out with an angry growl. *You can't trust me*, I finally said. It was the truth. I didn't know anything about this girl, had no memory of ever meeting her, let alone wanting to marry her or doing the things she'd claimed.

Perfect. Her tone was angry now. *I get captured coming back to try and help you and now I have nobody I can trust. Not even you.*

Something deep inside tugged at me but I refused to let her manipulations sway my opinion. I also wouldn't let my father do the same. I needed to figure out the truth all on my own.

Maybe you should stop talking to me like this.

Fine by me. And by the way, maybe you should check yourself before you blab all your secrets to your father. You might not be able to remember it, but there are good reasons why you hate him.

I'd never been best friends with my dad or anything like that, but hate? That was a big word.

I'll figure it out on my own.

Good. I also hope you figure out if you love me or not while you're at it. It'd be nice to know if I still have a husband.

I didn't reply. What was there left to say? I pushed the connection away. Screw it! I ran. The pain in my head exploded with the effort but I ignored it, instead clinging to the exhilarating feel of movement in my body. This was freedom.

Jessa and I were married. So what? I didn't remember making any vows. She was Resistance, a traitor, and had no place in my life, at least not while I figured things out. If it came down to it, if I learned the truth and it didn't include real love, I would find a way to end our marriage. My father had already suggested the idea; he said we could play it either way, though his preference was a quick annulment. I wasn't convinced either way.

First, I needed to persuade him to let me go back into society. Right now, the world thought I was a dead man. Maybe it was better that way. I didn't know. But I figured if I was going to get answers, we probably needed to start with the truth.

No more hiding.

SIX
SASHA

"Come back with me," Christopher said for what was probably the fifth time in the last few days.

"You know I can't do that."

Dad frowned, tugging awkwardly on the sleeves of his smudged white shirt, but nodding. He did know. In fact, he understood better than most. I actually thought, given the opportunity, he would've chosen to stay and fight, too. But Lacey and Mom were safe on the other side of the country and he needed to be with them. They'd been separated for too long.

"Promise me, if given the chance, you'll help Jessa?" His expression was torn with regret. This had to be an impossible choice for him, having his family spread out and one of his daughters missing.

"You don't even have to ask," I said. "If the girl wasn't so stubborn she'd be the one you'd want going back with you, not me."

His face fell, the shadows under his eyes appearing darker. "Don't say that."

"I know," I replied. But did I?

I'd forgiven my parents for abandoning me all those years ago. The truth was, they didn't know what they were agreeing to when they gave me up. They didn't realize they'd never see me again. At least, that was what my father told me. He'd said he knew I would be raised with the alchemists, but not that the officers who'd taken me would completely cut my family from my life.

I sighed. No matter what happened, or what my parents had believed, it was in the past. It was over and done and there wasn't anything anyone could do about it anymore. And truthfully, it wasn't their fault. It was King Richard who was to blame—it was the result of a failed system.

He leveled his head with mine. "I mean it, don't say that. Your mother and I love you just as much as your sisters."

"Okay." I smiled, the feel of it on my cheeks was tight and forced.

He meant what he said, but that didn't mean I wasn't still hurt. His kind words didn't take away the feelings of abandonment that lingered within me. Maybe only time would heal that, or maybe it would never heal.

"How's your friend doing?" He dropped his gaze, digging a line along the dirt with his boot. "The one you came back with who was hurt?"

I smiled wide, thinking of Tristan. "He's fine. I healed him as soon as I could."

"He's lucky to have you." Christopher winked. He put an arm on my shoulder, squeezing once. "And you're lucky to have him. Take care of each other out there."

I nodded, biting my lip, fighting the urge to hug him. It was stupid. I should just hug him.

"Are you sure you can't come with me?" he asked one more time.

We stood together outside the barracks where I'd spent the last three days anxiously awaiting orders for another mission. People rushed around us; it seemed everyone had a job to do but me. They paid us little attention. Dad watched me, and as if sensing what I needed, he pulled me into a hug.

I breathed him in, gazing out at the distance, trying to focus on something other than the torn emotions inside. The sun was rapidly setting over the horizon, the orange semi-circle dipping low and sending out shards of golden light in its wake. With it, a biting chill had settled into my bones.

"I'm sure," I replied. Something came bursting from me in that moment. Love, maybe? I hugged him back as hard as I could, letting myself sink into him like I had when I was a child. It was unexpected. From his quick intake of breath, I gathered he hadn't been expecting it either. This was new for both of us.

"Take care of yourself," he mumbled into my hair. "When all of this is over, we will be a family again." Then he released me and, giving me one final nod, walked away.

I hoped he was right.

But at the end of the day, my mission wasn't to my family; it wasn't even to West America. It was to take care of the alchemists. When this was over, someone needed to make sure alchemy wasn't treated like a weapon anymore. Magic wasn't something to be feared, but rather, something to be celebrated and used for good.

I chuckled at the madness of the idea. When had I become such an idealist? As long as those in charge had control over alchemy, our freedom wasn't a likely scenario. It was too tempting of a power, and too ... different.

But I had to try.

I walked around the base camp for over an hour, ignoring

the biting air, trying to survive the torrent of emotions that burned me. Night fell, and still, I continued, arms tight around myself, coat doing little to keep out the cold, boots clomping on the crisp earth. Under the icy air was the faint smell of gasoline and gunpowder. The camp was a mix of metal buildings and thick canvas tents, with clear roads between the buildings. It was sparse but had everything we needed.

Everything I needed was here.

What if I really do want to be part of my family? Should I have left with Dad? I shook the fool-hearted thought away. This was my place. I needed to fight, and I couldn't do it from anywhere else. Still, why did I feel so broken inside? I'd just given up the opportunity to get out of this mess and let someone else deal with it. Why did I have to be so determined and passionate about protecting the alchemists, when it was my own heart that needed tending?

I groaned and dug my boot into the dirt, leaning forlornly against the nearest building. The cold metal bit into my back, not that I cared. A hot tear fell down my cheek, and I hurried to wipe it away.

"Ugh, get a grip," I said, slapping my cheeks. I'd turn into Jessa by morning at this rate! I hated acknowledging my emotions. And I especially hated to cry. It was too ... exposing. And weak.

"Are you okay?" Mastin's voice split through the darkness like a bullet.

I closed my eyes for a second, shame burning, before turning to meet his worried gaze.

"You've been avoiding me," I stated.

He nodded once and then moved to rest against the building next to me.

"Why?" I asked, though I was pretty sure I already knew.

He was angry with me for nearly getting us killed back in New Colony. It didn't take a genius to know that. Truth was, I didn't blame him.

"You confuse me," he finally said.

I glowered at his profile, the darkness broken only by the security lights and the sounds of distant soldiers. "What about me is so confusing?"

"It's not you, exactly. It's not even what you do because your actions are rather predictable." He seemed to be weighed down by his statement.

"Wow, thanks," I grumbled.

"It's how I am when I'm with you that confuses me." The light caught the planes of his face, eyes piercing.

I let out a breath. "So actually, it's you who confuses you. Not me."

He laughed, an addictive sound I wasn't used to hearing from him. It unnerved me, setting me off my axis, as if everything I saw in him was magnified by that one single laugh.

"What is Tristan to you?"

I stilled. His question threw me off guard. "He's my best friend."

"Is he more?"

"No." But even as I said it, I wondered if that was the truth. Lately, even I didn't know what Tristan was to me.

"He's a good man," Mastin stated.

I nodded. "He's a good friend." I emphasized the word friend.

"Nothing more?"

I stared at the ground, dragging my foot along the dirt in a line. "There was a time when I thought maybe Tristan and I would become more." My voice caught in my throat. "But no, we're friends and that's all. That's what is best for both of us."

"I don't think he agrees." His voice was low and questioning.

I laughed, the feel of it bitter in my lying mouth. If he'd overheard the conversation Tristan and I had back at the farm, the conversation where Tristan had told me to date Mastin, I don't think he'd be so argumentative. "Trust me," I said.

He leaned in closer, shifting so we were only inches apart. I studied his green eyes, now shadowed in the darkness. His boyish scent washed over me, making me almost hungry. I fought the urge to roll my eyes at the thought. "Still, I don't think I can compete with that." He said as he held me in his intense eyes and then they flicked to my lips. A sense of urgency welled up inside me, the hunger begging for a taste.

"Who says it's a competition?" I whispered.

His eyes shot back to mine. "Isn't it?"

Never breaking eye-contact, I slowly shook my head.

Then I closed the distance between us, pressing my lips to his. He stilled for a moment, holding me at arm's length, but then pulled me against him. My mind emptied as he deepened the kiss. For once in our relationship, I was happy to let him take the lead. He was relief and danger all in one, safety and risk. He was everything I wanted. As my lips muffled his inner groan, I wondered if maybe I was everything he wanted, too.

★

My legs burned. My breath raced in and out as my heart rate climbed. I pushed on, one foot in front of the next, careening forward. It did little to quiet the thoughts tumbling in my head. Normally running was my escape, the best way to work through my problems—or better yet, to forget them entirely.

Today was not that day.

I careened to a stop, panting for breath, shoulders heaving up and down, waiting for my body to adjust. The morning sun pressed down, the unseasonably warm day reaching into my core. A smile swelled on my salty lips. A bead of sweat trickled down my temple, and I wiped it away with the back of my forearm. The nerves anchored like a rock in my stomach, I stood, taking in my surroundings.

People bustled between the rudimentary steel buildings. The smells of ozone, packed dirt, and rain on its way circled me like a shiny-eyed crow, reminding me of where I was, of what I was, and what I needed to do.

Today I had to tell Tristan about Mastin.

It wasn't as if Tristan hadn't seen this coming—he clearly had. Tristan knew me better than anybody. And he and I were just friends, had always been just friends, so it wouldn't be a big deal that I was dating someone. He would probably be happy for me and that would be the end of it.

Still, I hated how much I was bothered by the thought of telling him.

I walked down the gravel path that led to the main gym. Although Tristan liked to run, the man had always been into boxing, and that's where I'd likely find him. I pushed the nerves down, opened the heavy door, and strolled inside.

The first thing that hit me was the heat, so stuffy and thick, it was like walking into a wall of air. That could be blamed on the multiple bodies lifting weights and boxing in a small building without air conditioning. But it was the smell that hit me next, an odor truly assaulting, like an onion that had been left to rot in the sun all day. I wrinkled my nose, held my breath, ignored the grunts of testosterone-infused men, and scanned the room.

It didn't take long to find him. My heart dropped.

His dark hair shined with sweat, his expression set in determination. He landed a punch on his opponent with so much force the other guy fell onto his butt. Unfortunately, the other guy was Mastin.

"What the hell?" I ran forward. "Are you two fighting?"

Mastin sprang back up, barely fazed by the blow. But I could tell he was frazzled, not only by the line of his mouth but by the swiftness of his rebound. Frazzled *and* angry. The pair didn't glance my way, instead matching each other blow for blow and kick for kick. Relief washed through me to see they had gloves covering their fists, considering their punches seemed to be fueled by more than the need for exercise. Tristan's eyes blazed as he took a punch. Mastin jumped out of the way, a goading smirk curving his hardened mouth.

"Seriously!" I yelled at them. "This is not normal."

Another round of punches flew, blood and spit spraying from both men's bruising faces. The gloves were making little difference. Couple of idiots! They needed to be focused on the common enemy, not each other.

"We're just sparring," Tristan growled. "Nothing to worry about. Isn't that right, Mastin?"

"Right," Mastin grunted, and then he dove for Tristan, who used the sharp jut of his knee in retaliation.

Most of the other soldiers had stopped to gawk at the show. I sent the group a pleading look, knowing they could stop this. But they only cheered the fighters on further with their hollers and bets. I rolled my eyes, annoyed, but also angry. This spectacle was ridiculous and embarrassing. I put my hands on my head as Mastin took a right hook to the chin, spittle and blood arcing from his face. I grimaced, sharing the pain. I should walk away, let them get this immaturity out of their systems. But my feet were rooted to the floor of packed dirt. My fingers itched to use my magic and intervene, but that might make things worse.

Mastin rounded a kick right into Tristan's kneecap, and he fell with a pained yelp. Mastin used the momentum to attack, jumping on Tristan's back.

Oh, screw it!

Luckily, my necklace was refreshed with new stones, and I connected with the yellow. It spun out in little strings before settling into me. I jumped between the guys and used my strength to separate them. It was easy, as if they were children and not grown men practically twice my size.

"Sasha, don't!" Mastin growled.

"I got this," Tristan snapped, pushing back at me. I didn't budge.

"If you two aren't going to act like civilized adults then I'll have to do it for you," I said.

I stood my ground, keeping them apart with outstretched arms. For a moment, they pressed against my palms, each flailing to get at the other. Mastin stood back first, arms crossed over his chest as he huffed the air from his lungs. He studied Tristan, then me, pained calculation lighting his jade eyes as they flicked back and forward between us.

I turned back and switched to the green magic, letting it pour into Tristan, who was now unfocused and giving in to the pain. He was bleeding in a few places, and I was certain his knee was broken after that kick. His face scrunched in agony as he held his leg slightly off the ground, finally sinking to the earth, a low groan emitting between gritted teeth. The green magic wormed its way into all the broken parts, healing him in a matter of moments and clearing the pain from his face.

But only momentarily.

He jumped up, brushing himself off and leveling me with a steady gaze. "We were fine."

"That's right," Mastin added, voice deadpan. "We were sparring, a little fun between friends."

Tristan scoffed. "Yeah."

"You two are so full of it." I threw my hands in the air. "But fine, if you want to beat the crap out of each other, so be it." I pointed east and glared. "Forget that our actual enemies are out there, right now, planning ways to kill us all. Sorry if I think your time would be better served doing other things than injuring yourselves!"

"You're right," Tristan said, backing away. "Forget it."

He stormed from the gym, anger rolling in his wake. I ran after him, catching him just outside the gym.

"What's wrong with you?"

He spun to face me, squinting against the sun. "Shouldn't you be back there helping your boyfriend?" All the venom had left his voice now, only defeat remained. Any anger I'd been harboring was lost in an instant.

I stopped, lost for words. Was Mastin my *boyfriend*? Part of me bristled at the word. Such a needy little word it was. But another part of me lurched forward. We hadn't technically defined it as such, we were busy with the war, after all. But we were definitely something. And we had agreed to see where that something went, at least when we weren't busy kicking enemy butts and saving the world from evil dictators.

Last night had been amazing. But it had also been private.

"How do you know?" I asked. And here was the real question. "Why do you care? We're friends, you and I. You were the one who told me I should date Mastin in the first place."

He looked up to the sky and closed his eyes, jaw clenched

tight.

"Are you counting backwards from ten right now?" I challenged.

It was one of his ways to cope when he was angry. Tristan hated to be angry, said it made him feel like his father. I'd never met the man, but Tristan had confided in me long ago that his father had been abusive toward him and his mother. He still felt guilt for getting out because he'd had to leave her behind in the process. That had been years ago, but the pain of it still lived on.

He snapped his eyes open, raking his hands through his hair. "Yes, I know about it. The guy told me."

"I was supposed to be the one to tell you. I'm sorry." Embarrassment washed over me and I shifted squeamishly on my feet.

He shrugged, his face softening. "It's okay. Really, I just want you to be happy." He paused, holding my gaze. "If he's who you want then that's okay with me. I won't fight him again or anything."

"I thought you said it wasn't fighting, just good-natured sparring?" I rolled my eyes.

He laughed. "It started off that way, if that's any consolation."

I nodded, though I wasn't sure it was.

"Anyway, I've got to go." Tristan backed away. "I'll see you around." He turned and jogged away.

I stormed back to the gym in search of Mastin. He was lifting dumbbells and smiled broadly when he saw me, the earlier pain in his expression now vanished. And that was fine by me. I didn't want to deal with jealousy; I had already picked him!

It appeared he'd already wiped away the blood by the look of his dirtied shirt. His biceps pulsed as he lifted, eyes squinting through the bruising that was purpling his cheeks. I placed my hand over my necklace with the intention to take care of him, but he brushed me away with the shake of his head.

"I'm fine."

I wasn't sure if it was on principle or because so many of his friends were watching, soldiers who were still uneasy about my magic. Now they'd seen it in action again, they were staring at me like I was contagious. A few were standing with arms folded over their chests, eyes glaring in attempts at intimidation. And still, others seemed to pay me no attention at all, going about their business.

But they all had one thing in common. They all kept their distance.

"All right," I replied to Mastin. "Let's get out of here."

Mastin's smile curved and he dropped the dumbbells to the earth with a thud and a small cloud of dust. We strode out together, a few whistles in our wake.

The moment we left the gym and had a moment of privacy, he ran his hand down my arm and laced our fingers together. We walked down the path between the buildings. Quiet for a while.

"Why did you tell Tristan?" I asked. "We agreed I was going to do that."

"He asked." Mastin shrugged. "I wasn't going to lie to him. And besides, you don't need that guy."

I tugged on his arm. "Don't say that. You know he's my best friend."

He pulled me close, wrapping his arms around me, a knowing smile lifting his lips. "Yeah, I know. But he doesn't get to do this." He widened his stance, dropping closer to my level, eyes flicking to my lips.

He softly kissed the side of my face, trailing the tip of his nose down my jaw until his mouth found mine. I sunk into him, losing myself in the feel of it. We stayed like that for a few minutes, caught up in each other, when someone cleared their throat loudly, breaking us apart.

Mortified, I jumped back, wiping my lips and staring a hole into the gravel.

"Hello father," Mastin said calmly over my shoulder.

Blood rushed to my cheeks, and I turned to face General Nathan Scott. As usual, he was flanked by men dressed in tan army fatigues. They watched us carefully, like we'd committed a crime and had been caught in the act.

Or something like that ...

After a long, tense minute, Nathan laughed. It bellowed out of him freely.

"I wondered when you two were going to get together." He eyed us, face growing serious again. "This better not get in the way of our mission here, neither of you need the distraction."

"It won't," Mastin said and I nodded. But was that even possible? At that moment, I was most definitely distracted by Mastin.

"All right then." Nathan nodded. "Sasha, I'd like you to spend the day with me. We have a new prisoner, an alchemist. And I'd like your help with this one."

"I'm coming, too." Mastin inched forward.

"Very well." Nathan strode away purposefully, motioning over his back for us to follow.

Mastin slipped his hand into mine again, and despite my better judgment, I warmed at the attention. I ought to be annoyed with myself. This thing with Mastin, whatever this was, needed to stay second to what mattered most: protecting the alchemists.

As our group neared the area of the prison, the very one I'd helped to set up, a sense of foreboding fell over me, and also, a trickling of guilt. How many more alchemists was West America going to catch? And how many more times would I be forced to watch my own kind be beaten and tortured, treated like animals and punished for their magic?

I gathered determination within me like the magic that pulsed through my veins and followed the group inside.

SEVEN
LUCAS

"Are you really going to try to conduct your business from here?" I said, leaning against the doorframe of my father's, apparently new, office. He'd set up shop in one of the guest rooms of the orphanage. Hunched over a small desk in the middle of the makeshift office, he looked completely out of place and utterly uncomfortable.

"Until I decide what steps to take next, this is my new office." He sighed and reclined back in his chair, folding his arms over his broad chest, shirt stretching with the movement. He wore casual clothing. Well, about as casual as he got, anyway. The first two buttons on his starched white shirt were undone.

"Lucas, I don't know what to do with you. That's the truth."

"What do you mean?" I stepped into the room and slumped into a red velvet armchair, body relaxing like butter left to melt in the sun. The back of my head pounded, the persistent throb ebbing with wave after wave of dizziness. At least it wasn't the sharp knife it had been yesterday. At least the churning nausea had subsided.

Richard leveled me with a sparkling gaze. "I announced to the entire kingdom that you were dead."

I raised an eyebrow and smirked. "Why?"

"What else was I supposed to do? Once again, someone made an attempt on your life, and this time they very nearly succeeded. You were in a coma for over a week and even our best alchemists couldn't pull you out of it."

"And that's how I ended up here," I moaned. It wasn't that I disliked the orphanage. I loved the people here. But I had nothing to do here, and I still hadn't been given a new slatebook. The doctor said if I got misinformed it was possible I wouldn't regain my memories. I wasn't sure I bought it.

"Yes," Richard continued. "I decided to move you to an unknown location and wait until you woke up to take further action. It was easier to tell the world that you were dead—still is." He rested his elbows on the collage of papers and open journals on the desktop, linking long uncalloused fingers. "This way, whatever assassin West America sent, Jessa or someone else, will back off. Once we have more answers, we can tell the truth about what really happened."

I still hadn't told anyone about mine and Jessa's telepathic connection. It seemed nobody knew to ask, and from her reaction, I had to guess it was a secret. Now that I knew what it was, that I wasn't crazy, I should've said something. But I didn't. I had too many suspicions to let go of my secrets just yet.

"It makes sense." I nodded, rubbing my stubbly chin with my palm. "But you also have to consider the fact that I did wake up and I'm fine now. Am I just supposed to stay hidden until the war is over?"

"That's not a bad idea."

The very idea of being stuck here sent dread sweeping

through my body. Growing up, I'd often thought of the palace in the same way. Always trapped within its stone walls usually left me itching to get out, but at least that had been my home. At least that had space to breathe and answers instead of secrets.

I bristled. "But I want to help, *and* I want my memories back. I'm not going to remember anything stuck here. Besides, don't you want me to remember who killed me?" I pointed to my head. "The answer could be unlocked if I was taken to the scene of the crime."

"You're not going to the palace," Richard snapped. "It's too dangerous. We already discussed this. That wife of yours is the number one suspect; we just need to confirm it and find out who her contacts are."

I watched him carefully, noticing the way he broke eye-contact, and for a moment, I wasn't so sure he was being honest about Jessa. The way she talked to me wasn't the way a person talked to someone they'd just tried to murder. No, she'd seemed completely horrified at the accusation. But as I studied my father, I knew he was set in his assessment of the situation. Which meant I wasn't going back home. Not yet.

"Okay, fine. Why don't we work from here, together? I want to avenge Mother's death just as much as you do. How can I help?"

He stared at me for a long moment something in his gaze shifted. "Okay, Lucas, that's something I can agree to."

"Great, where do we start?"

"One of my most trusted advisors is en route as we speak. I'd planned to keep you hidden while he and I discussed the latest reports. You can join in on our meeting."

I nodded, a little surprised with myself. I wasn't normally the type to care about politics. But then again, I *did* have a head injury. I chuckled to myself, the little bit of comic relief going a long way to ease my inner turmoil.

Richard stood and sidestepped around the desk, placing a heavy hand on my shoulder. "You're missing a lot of information, but I will do my best to fill you in. You are going to be the king one day and you're right, I should let you help."

I peered up, meeting his steely gaze. His eyes softened with pride.

"I have to admit, I like this new Lucas."

I cocked my head at the comment.

New Lucas? What was that supposed to mean? Had I really changed so much in the last year? A warning bell rang inside my head, and I held my tongue, tucking the questions away for a later day. It wasn't like I didn't already have secrets from my father, secrets I'd kept hidden for years.

My curse of alchemy being the number one culprit.

But I didn't use it much, not since I'd found a way to keep it locked away. What else had I locked away over the last year? From the way he was looking at me, the relief in his eyes, it almost seemed like we'd hated each other. Jessa made it sound like that. But had it really come to that?

While we had always had a rift between us, I'd never hated him.

"Anything else?" he asked, a question in his eyes. "Is there something you would like to tell me?"

I shook my head.

I'd learned at a young age that he believed magic was a blasphemy to be controlled. He already had enough hold on me. I didn't want to add another.

"Are you sure?" he pressed. "Son, you can trust me. If we're going to get through this, we have to be honest with each other."

I smiled, guilt tugging deep inside. "I know." I stood and

walked to the door, running my hands down my jeans. I'd be expected to dress up for dinner. "I'll see you tonight."

The weight of his stare bored holes in my already aching head, but I refused to turn back.

Jessa claimed that I'd worked for the Resistance, too. If that was true, it meant I'd wanted to see my own father dethroned. But that couldn't be. The idea of it twisted and caused my headache to return with a vengeance. Still, the question remained: who was telling the truth and who was the liar?

Maybe they were both being dishonest. Maybe I was simply a pawn on their shared chessboard and not the one playing the game.

★

I placed a stack of gravy-stained plates on the counter. They clanked together as one of the kitchen staff patted my arm and took them to the sink. The scent of dish soap and hot steam filled the room. The playful sounds of giggling and pattering footsteps on the floor above made me smile. It felt good to be up and moving. I went back to the dining room and leaned against the doorframe, watching as the staff expertly reset the table.

When the orphans had finished their meal, helping with the clean-up had made me feel useful, even if I hadn't dined with them tonight. Instead, I would be eating dinner with my father and his guest. The table was quickly finished and ready for us. Crystal wine flutes, silver cutlery, and white porcelain plates all gleamed under the low lights. The staff scampered off, and still, I waited beside the oak door, eager for whatever came next. It wasn't like me to care so much about this kind of thing, but with my memory—and my life—on the line, things had changed.

On the other side of the space was another door and my eyes flicked to it the second I heard them. Voices, murmuring conversation, the low rustle of my father's voice, filtered through the door. He talked fast, urgent, and without thinking of the consequences, I rushed forward, pressing my ear to the door, straining to eavesdrop.

A woman's velvety soft voice joined the men.

"I hope you don't mind that we came along," she purred. "I simply had to apologize for my husband in person."

A male voice interjected. "Yes, truly, Your Highness, I'm so sorry. I deeply regret my insensitive and unwarranted actions toward you."

"It bordered on treason," Richard replied in an unreadable tone.

"You're absolutely right. I let my role as a father get in the way of what was best for this kingdom."

"And he had too much alcohol," the woman added. "It was foolish."

There was a long pause. Finally, Richard replied with a relaxed tone. "It's forgiven. And forgotten…for now. I am known for my strength, but I am not without mercy."

The last part didn't ring true, and I wondered if the people on the other side of the door agreed.

Another pause, and then the woman spoke. "Thank you, your Royal Highness. You are too gracious."

"Yes, thank you," the man added, voice as washed with relief as a summer rainstorm.

"And I think you're right," Richard continued. "I do think we all had a little bit too much to drink that night."

The group laughed together. The woman's high cackle and the man's low guffaw sounded a touch too forced. Something intense had certainly happened between this couple and my father, and I wanted to know what it was.

Add it to the list of questions.

"Speaking of family, mine is here as well," Richard said smoothly. "Or, what little there is left of it, I should say."

"What?" The woman's question came out sharp.

"Lucas!" Richard's voice boomed through the door I skulked behind. "Please come in now, Son."

Finally! I flung open the door and strolled into the dining room. Not two, but three new faces gaped back at me. They were vaguely familiar, but I couldn't quite place the family. I assumed they were part of the royal court and I'd dined with them before, but not recently. Well, not in recent *memory*. They stared at me as if I was stark naked or brandishing a butcher knife or something equally unsettling.

"Um, hi." I cleared my throat. "Thanks for letting me join you. I've been getting bored up here, hidden away like this. It will be nice to have a change in pace for the evening."

"You're alive?" a new voice breathed in a soft cry. I frowned at the girl who was so striking in resemblance to the couple, that I knew she had to be their daughter. She brought her dainty hand to her painted lips as she gawked at me like I was the stuff made of nightmares and redemption. Her auburn hair fell in soft waves around her shoulders and her pale cheeks filled with color.

"Uh, yeah." I shrugged.

Richard's laugh boomed good-naturedly, as if to break the tension. It didn't work. Nobody took their eyes off me.

"There was another assassination attempt on my son the night of his wedding," Richard said. "You already know Jessa disappeared, that much was true. But Faulk and I made the call to twist the truth on my son's behalf."

I raised my hand sheepishly. "Not dead."

"He's been in hiding. I'm still trying to decide what to do

about him."

The family was still ogling me like I had risen from the dead. The man's eyes were wild and slowly, so slowly, he inched himself back toward the door.

"Unfortunately, Lucas has suffered quite a bit of memory loss," my father continued. "He hasn't been able to identify his attacker yet, but I'm confident, given time, it will all come back to him."

Richard was still convinced Jessa had been the one to harm me. He'd gone into great detail about how she'd tried to get to him first, and how she wasn't to be trusted because of her red alchemy. I had taken everything on face value, but the more I mulled it over, the more I questioned it. And now this man, with his face so clearly terrified to see me alive? What part of the story was I missing? And what did it have to do with him?

"You really don't remember anything?" The older woman glided forward with complete assuredness and ran inquisitive milky-blue eyes up and down me, inspecting.

I shrugged. "I know who I am. I remember plenty. But the brain injury made it so that I've forgotten the last year."

Her eyes widened. "Remarkable."

"More like annoying."

"You don't remember Jessa?" the quiet member of the family asked. When I caught her eyes she quickly looked down at the floor, as if ashamed, pink burning the edges of her cheekbones. But then a small smile formed on her rouge lips and I wasn't so sure. "And you probably don't remember me?" Her head popped back up, eyes sparkling under long, dark lashes.

"No." The back of my head was starting to throb again. "I think that my memory-impaired status has been sufficiently established. There's nothing more to say about it, really." I cleared my throat, sheepishly. I hoped I didn't sound rude. "We're here for dinner and a debriefing, correct?"

"That's correct," Richard motioned to the table and swept his hand toward his guests. "Lucas, this is Mark, Sabine, and Celia Addington."

An air of civility fell upon the group as they shook my hand before we all approached the fine white tablecloth and the array of place settings on top. The rich smell of expertly prepared food wafted through the air, warm and welcoming. I pulled out a chair for Celia, the legs scraping the polished oak floor. Her eyebrows drew in as she sat, puzzlement returned to her face as she peered up at me. There wasn't anything I could do to unveil her reasoning, so I found my own chair, resolved to pay attention to every word, said and unsaid.

Richard pulled off the gleaming silver dome covering his plate, leaned over his roasted chicken and vegetables, and inhaled. "Let's eat."

The early tension dissipated over dinner, replaced with a new sense of urgency as we discussed the status of the war and the recent battle. New Colony wasn't faring as well as we'd like. We had taken more ground, only to be pushed back again. The battles were a mix of weaponry, magic, and even hand-to-hand combat. Our losses were nearing two hundred casualties, but West America's were far higher, reaching into the thousands.

Sometime during the discussion, I stopped eating and pushed vegetables from one side of my plate to the other. I dropped my head into one palm, fighting the growing throb, gritting my teeth against the distraction.

Occasionally, I would meet Celia's gaze, simply because she was constantly watching me. I could feel those eyes on me like a shadow. She never said a word, just stared as if she knew all my secrets, as if she were the greatest one of all.

We wrapped up by indulging in a rich chocolate cake. I took a couple of bites and instantly regretted it, the dessert sitting in a pained lump low in my stomach. The conversation continued on around me as the party said their goodnights. I could hardly hear a word over being so focused on the ice in my head and the heat in my stomach.

I did catch one thing. They would be sleeping in the guest rooms before heading out in the morning to return to their post. With the new status of things, my father was itching to leave, as well. He wanted to be in the action—not that I blamed him. If only I could convince him to let me come along, maybe we'd both get what we wanted.

★

Warm air tickled my ear, an exhalation of breath that woke me moments before a soft voice whispered into the darkness.

"You really don't remember?"

I blinked the sleep away and rolled to face Celia.

"What are you doing in here?" I hissed, sitting up, shoulders knocking into her thin frame. The night fell heavy through the gap in the curtains, only the light of the moon to see by. "What time is it?"

She pulled her legs under her and crawled up onto the bed, knees tucked under exposed thighs, sleep dress riding up. Heat burned through me and I forced myself to look up.

"It's just after 2AM." She blinked through thick lashes, the moonlight lighting her features just enough for me to see the gentle sweep of her neck, the soft angles of her face, and the parting of two full lips.

I cleared my throat and looked away, trying to take in the darkened room, but really a little bit uncomfortable with the situation. A warning bell was alarming in my head, coupling with the persistent ache.

"It was a two-part question," I continued. "What are you doing here?"

She reached out and gently ran her palm down my arm, ending at my hand. Her fingers were cool and held onto mine for a moment before she tugged, as if to pull me closer. "Isn't it obvious?"

I eyed her smile and the way her earlier sweet expression had turned far from innocent. She was right. She was being obvious.

"Besides, we used to date. This isn't anything new."

I stilled, and for a moment I was tempted by the proposition. It would be so easy. She would make me feel better, if even for a few minutes. Didn't I deserve that?

But I couldn't, not with all the questions circling me like hungry ravens.

I pulled away, inwardly groaning.

I hate myself right now. Because really, what did I have to lose? She was gorgeous and willing. Heaven knew I needed the distraction. But the simple fact that I couldn't remember having dated her was enough to give me pause; that and the fact I was still a married man, something that *had* been confirmed to me, even if I didn't remember that either.

In the end, my mother had raised me to be respectful, to view marriage as sacred. I couldn't dishonor her, not when I didn't even get to say goodbye.

"I'm sorry." Confusion laced my tone and I bristled. It made me sound too vulnerable—and I didn't like that. I added more firmly, "I don't remember you."

I expected some kind of retaliation, hurt or shock or something. She only smiled again, dropping my hand to run hers through her long, loose hair.

"Lucas, I already knew that when I came here." Her lips quirked into a demure smile. "But doesn't that make it more exciting? We can erase the past and start afresh." She crawled closer to me as she talked, sitting in my lap. The scent of citrus and sugar surrounded me. Her breath was hot, minty, and ran along my lips. I gulped, trying to ignore my own mixed feelings, most of which leaned toward giving in to this beautiful creature. My breath sped, and I pressed myself back against my headboard, trying to find space in my brain to tell her no.

Because she was a beautiful, all right. But sometimes the most beautiful things were the deadliest.

I didn't know for sure if I could trust her. Just like I didn't know if Jessa could be trusted. Or really, anyone…

I needed to remember!

If only I could get my memories back, then I would know what to do with this girl and this whole thing would be so much easier to say no to—or yes to.

"You should go," I said, my voice more solid than my decision.

Her lips parted in a silent protest, but she scrambled off the bed.

"Seriously, Lucas? I don't know what has gotten into you. You and I used to be close, and now we're not even friends. What we had was unique and special. You don't even care."

I held up my hands in protest. "I do care, but I just don't know if what you're saying is true."

She folded her arms over her chest, dejected. "Are you calling me a liar?"

I rubbed my temples. "I can't act on a past I can't remember. I'm sorry."

"Tell me one thing." She glowered at me. "If it were Jessa, would you have acted any differently?"

I shrugged. "Probably not. I don't know. I don't remember her, either."

But according to this girl, I was cheating on my wife. As much as I enjoyed spending time with beautiful women, that kind of behavior didn't sound like me. But how was I to know? Maybe it was true. I dropped my head into my hands and ran them through my messy hair as I considered the possibility.

The bed dipped, and I looked up to find Celia kneeling beside it, her wide eyes once again innocent and careful. "I'm sorry this happened to you, Lucas. It's not fair," she whispered, a long curl cascading around her exposed neck. "I'm being insensitive. Of course, I can't expect you to act the way things used to be." She paused and closed her eyes, as if considering something. "I want to show you something."

She reached to the nightstand, to a slatebook, and after a moment of fiddling with the screen, turned it around to reveal a photograph. My mind flashed to the last time this happened, when Callie had shown me my wedding photograph with Jessa. This time, however, it wasn't a wedding photo. It was a picture of this red-headed girl and me, arms wrapped around each other and kissing.

She powered down the device and smiled sadly. "We were engaged, Lucas. Our wedding was only a few weeks away when your father decided it would be a better fit if you married an alchemist. He flung Jessa on you, didn't even give us a choice. And then he showed her off all over the kingdom in the weeks leading up to the wedding, boasting about how it was time to celebrate alchemy publicly, and wasn't it so great that the royal family was marrying into magic."

"How was I supposed to compete with that?"

Without thinking, I cupped her cheek in my palm, hoping to comfort her, but finding it was wet with tears. Guilt rolled through me, sharp and disarming.

Something clicked within and I froze, uncovering a small piece of the puzzle.

"Is that why I overheard our parents apologizing to each other. Was it over our broken engagement?"

She nodded and then stood, backing up toward the center of the room. "My father and your father got into a bit of a scrimmage at your wedding. It got out of hand. It was childish, really," her voice trailed off.

I didn't know what to say to that. This whole thing was getting more and more complicated, unraveling like a ball of string, only to run into new tangles every time I thought I'd figured it out. If her father really had accosted mine, there was no way King Richard would be so forgiving unless he knew he was in the wrong. Jessa was technically my wife. That much was confirmed. But could it be Celia who truly had my heart?

As she stood there, curling her bare toes against the rug, body deflating like a wilted flower, an overwhelming desire to discover the truth pulsed through me. There was one way to find out ...

I flung back the bedcovers and strode to her in two long steps. Taking her into my arms, I pulled her to me and pressed my lips to hers. Soft and eager to please, she responded with fevered movements and a deep moan from the back of her throat. I pressed my eyes tight, focusing on our kiss, listening to my heart, to my body. It felt good, pleasant. But not perfect. Sparks didn't fly, and my mind was easily distracted.

We didn't have chemistry. It was just a kiss.

Maybe because I couldn't remember her. Or maybe because she wasn't mine after all. Could this whole spectacle tonight be a ruse?

I explored our connection for another minute, just to be sure. More of the same. Mind relieved, body disappointed, I released our embrace and stepped back. She smiled, lipstick smudged and teeth gleaming in the darkness. When she leaned in for more, I shook my head. Her face fell, eyes sparking and a soft gasp escaping from her swollen lips.

"I'm sorry," I said. "I'm not the one for you. I can't be who you want me to be."

Hand flying to her mouth, she spun and fled the room.

My feet edged forward across the plush rug. I shouldn't have been so mean, so abrupt. She clearly cared for me, but I wavered… What if that only made things worse? I didn't want to give the woman false hope. Not to mention how coming into my room like she had wasn't allowed. I wasn't at fault here; she shouldn't have done it in the first place.

That seemed off to me, too.

How had she been allowed in? That had never happened before. Sure, I wasn't at home surrounded by my normal guard, but when I'd been whisked off to this place, Richard had still brought a security team along. It was a small one, only a few of our most trusted men, but they knew better than to allow someone into my room while I was sleeping.

Deciding to investigate, I found one of the team members in the hallway. The lights were low, and the long row of doors were closed, tucking away whoever was inside for the night. He stood directly across from my door, hand resting on the gun at his hip.

He bowed, the shadow lengthening on his stony face. "Your Grace, how can I help you?"

"Why did you let Celia enter my room?" I questioned.

He paled, eyes shifting. "I thought you would have wanted her. I'm sorry if I misunderstood the situation."

I cocked my head, noticing the way his voice sped as he

explained. Was he lying or just embarrassed at his mistake?

"Did she pay you off or something?" I pressed. "You can tell me the truth, I won't turn you in for it."

"Of course not," he replied. He bowed again. "I'm so sorry. Truly. It won't happen again."

I looked at the back of his lowered head, annoyed. Had he bowed simply to avoid eye contact, or was it because he was truly apologetic?

"It's the middle of the night. I was sleeping and completely unaware and vulnerable, and you let her into my room unannounced," I stated. "I don't care what your reasons are, don't do it again."

"No, Sir." I turned back and closed the door, making sure to lock it this time.

It was possible Celia had paid him off or blackmailed him. If not Celia, maybe her parents. Perhaps she wasn't the one to keep an eye on. The Duke and Duchess had seemed rather alarmed when I'd first walked into that dining room tonight.

Why weren't they more excited to see me alive and well?

I blew out a shaky breath and approached my bed. A glossy surface caught my eye, shining in the darkness like a beacon. Celia had left her slatebook on my nightstand. I smiled, relief soaring through me. It might be the middle of the night, but I wasn't going to stay in the dark for long.

EIGHT

JESSA

The door opened, sending my heart into a flutter. Was it Richard? Or Faulk? Would I be taken away? I pressed myself against the far wall, standing tall, trying to appear strong, fear rippling under the surface.

A maid scudded inside, dropping off my evening meal. Eyes downcast, she placed the silver tray on the dresser right next to the door and rushed away, the lock clicking into place behind her. I let out a deep sigh, allowing my muscles to relax. Never in my life had I been so grateful to be kept waiting. The longer I had to wait, the better it was for not only myself, but countless others. So, despite the boredom and the worry, I didn't ask for anything and I kept quiet.

The day Richard had informed me he'd be taking me to see Reed the next morning, I'd spent the night in utter turmoil. Since then, I'd imagined countless scenarios where something happened that changed the course of my fate. Maybe there was an attack and I wasn't the priority. Maybe Lucas remembered me and had stepped in to help. Or perhaps there was something I said or done during our meeting that made the King drop his plans, after all.

Never had I considered he wouldn't show up.

Eventually, I wouldn't be able to avoid the interrogation. I was here, prisoner, and it would happen sooner or later. People were counting on me to keep their secrets and their identities hidden. Lily and Jose, Madame Silver, the others who'd helped me to flee New Colony. What would happen to them if Reed got me to tell the truth?

They would probably be executed.

I skipped over to the food, drinking a sip from the tall glass of creamy milk as I surveyed the items: soft white bread with a swath of butter, thin slices of flaxen cheese, white crackers stacked atop each other, a handful of pale nuts, and my favorite, a diced pear. As expected, there wasn't any usable color.

I crunched on a cracker, relishing the way the salt melted over my tongue, and then popped a cube of pear in as well.

Maybe I was worrying for nothing. It was yet another day that Richard hadn't come for me. I'd spent the last week holed up in this room, twiddling my thumbs with nothing to do and nobody to talk to. It was better than the alternative. Twice a day, one of the palace maids dropped off a meal. They were quick, and they never spoke to me. No, I was stuck in here, and I was on my own.

I returned to the plate of food, feeding not only hunger and boredom, but depression, too.

The first thing I'd done in this place was search for color, but of course, I'd come up short. And with guards stationed outside of my door at all times, I wasn't going anywhere. All I'd ever wanted was to be free, to follow my heart and my passions, and yet, I'd ended up here.

The worst part of it all was Lucas. He wasn't here with me, wasn't mine anymore. Not only that, but Lucas wasn't even the same man anymore. He'd forgotten me, forgotten us, something I couldn't wrap my mind around. It dug at me, made me desperate with heartache.

There was nothing I could do.

I stood at the window, staring into the bitter landscape behind the fog of my breath on the glass. There were several problems with it being early February. The first was that it was freezing out. The second was that the grass was brown from winter, hibernating until the sun returned and the earth thawed, and it could return to full glory once again. Even if I could break the window and jump out like I had months before, I didn't have the summer grass to help me heal any resulting breaks. It was at least a twenty-foot drop, and I couldn't get away while hobbling on a broken leg. No, jumping wasn't the solution.

The only other thing I could think of was the telepathy, but that was also turning out to be a dead end. I had tried to use what little I had left of the purple material hidden in my bra to reach out to Lily. She was one ally here that might be able to do something. And since we already had a telepathic connection, it should have worked, I should have been able to talk to her.

But I got nothing. And that probably meant she wasn't at the palace or anywhere near it.

Lucas was close enough that I could talk to him. Maybe he was hiding somewhere in the city, or possibly on the outskirts of town. But he wasn't going to be the solution. It seemed he wanted nothing to do with me, that his father had turned him against me. Our love was one-sided at the moment, at least until he got his memories back.

What if he never gets his memories back?

I shook the thought away. I needed to think of something else—and quick.

I returned to the bed and clutched the white bedding in my fists. I willed the magic to work for me, to ignite in my veins and do what it did for Lucas. Invisibility would be the perfect escape. I was desperate, and I needed it. If only sheer willpower alone could make it work. I sat there for what felt like ages, desperate, pleading, but nothing happened. Nothing at all. Exasperated, I gave up.

Angry tears rolled down my cheeks. I was seriously going to go crazy in this room. I needed out!

I leapt back up and returned to the window. Maybe it would be fine, maybe I wouldn't break anything if I jumped. It wasn't *that* high. And the glass? That was nothing. Even without my yellow magic I was sure I could break it. I would have to be quick to jump before the guards heard the glass and came to investigate.

A flash of movement caught my eye and I froze, icy foreboding dripping down my spine. My window faced the main drive and a line of sleek black town cars were pulling up. I gripped the window frame, fingers digging against the wood, and stared down at the scene below.

Faulk strode from the palace, quick on her heels, surrounded by her officers in gleaming uniforms, as white as sharpened teeth. They fussed over the people exiting cars. I immediately recognized Celia's parents, and then Celia herself. I released a stilted breath. Maybe it was only the Addington family.

Another door opened, revealing a new pair of legs sliding from the car.

King Richard.

I stilled, the fear threatening to rip me apart. He was here for me. I knew it. Deep in my gut, in the marrow of my bones, in every cell that was me, I knew…

He glanced up toward my window, squinting against the

sun. Something dark flashed across his expression. I dove from the window and ran for the door.

I need to get out of here. I may not have my magic at the moment, but I still know how to fight!

I flung open the door and attacked the first guard I saw, determined to make this quick, shock and adrenaline powering through me. He barely knew what was happening, barely had a chance to respond, as I ripped my fingernails across his face, drawing blood. It only took a second, but the liquid pooled under my fingers, slick with salvation. Red alchemy spun into the air and then settled into the man, his face going slack.

"Give me your gun," I roared, my growling voice not sounding like my own.

He immediately reached into his holster and handed over his gun. It was heavy in my hand, anchoring me into the moment.

"Stand back," I commanded. He did, but he wasn't the only guard I needed to deal with. Two more had their guns trained on me, fingers hovering over the triggers. They watched me, equal parts caution and rage in their careful movements and wild eyes.

"Drop the gun." One of them scrunched up his nose and motioned to me with large well-trained hands.

"No," I said, lifting it to point right back at him. "You're not going to shoot me." Because if that was allowed, no doubt they would've already done it.

I had limited training with guns. It wasn't exactly the GC's number one skill. But I knew how to point the thing and I certainly knew how to pull the trigger. "Just let me go and nobody will get hurt."

"I can't let you do that." Richard's deep voice boomed from behind me and a prickle of fear overran my senses, my grip weakened. The thud of approaching boots, the black guns cocking in aim, and then at last, the man himself, filled my vision.

"Put the gun down. Right now, Jessa." Richard strode forward, his eyes angry slits.

Defeat fell over me like a shadow. There was no way I could fight off this many people by myself. I was outnumbered and didn't have enough color close by.

I dropped the gun. It scattered across the floor and a guard scooped it up before I had a chance to reconsider.

Faulk snaked through the crowd, shoving people twice her size out of her way. Her white uniform gleamed pristine. Venom poisoned her eyes, pure and unfiltered hatred, as she moved toward me. "That's enough out of you, Miss Loxely."

Defiance roared up inside like an untamed lion. The lion and the snake. Who would win? I had little power in this situation, but at least I had my wit, at least I had my voice. "Actually, it's Mrs. Heart now, remember?"

She shoved me to the ground, my face slamming against the smooth marble. Pain ripped across my jaw, blood filling my mouth. I spat it across the floor in an arc of spilled rubies. If only I could use my own blood on someone else, then I could get out of this situation in seconds; but unfortunately, it didn't work that way.

"We are taking you to see Reed now."

She wrenched my hands behind my back, and once again, I felt the cold sharp grip of metal handcuffs snapping around my wrists. "It's about time you answered for your sins."

★

I shivered on my cot and pressed my back against the wall. Three days of interrogation and my resolve was breaking to pieces. Weak, tired, and hungry, my emotions fought my determination. A lone bulb shone light from the middle of the room, illuminating the concrete floor, lighting the gray box. Even smaller than the palace prison cells, the place was beginning to eat away at me. No windows and one door. No way out. I pressed the heels of my palms into my eyes, wishing I could relieve the anxiety long enough to sleep. At least sleep was a temporary out.

So far, only Reed had used his magic on me. His influence was strong, stronger than I remembered. But it wasn't foolproof, and my willpower was even stronger. I'd revealed most of my incriminating past, but I had yet to give up any actual names. Maybe I could make it out of this place.

Maybe no one else had to die because of me.

The door opened and Faulk stomped in. She looked down on me with disdain as she curled her lip and glared.

"Back so soon?" Antagonizing her wasn't going to do me any favors, but I couldn't resist.

"It's my job to get answers out of you, and now that I know you're Resistance, I will not stop until I do. You have names. One way or another, you will give them to me."

She spoke with absolute certainty, but we'd been at this for days, and as far as I could tell, she wasn't getting anywhere. Blue meant influence, it meant suggestion and persuasion, but it wasn't control. It wasn't red.

"I don't know what else you expect." I shrugged. "You already brought me all the way down here and that didn't change anything."

Her eyes narrowed in challenge.

The suite in the palace had been a much cushier jail cell than this. Now that I was on the frontline where the bulk of the alchemists and real officers were, things had gotten more serious. They'd thrown me into this dark and slightly humid room as if suffocating me would get me to talk. Reed had been so smug at first, but as the interrogations continued and he failed to extract any names from me, he'd become frustrated—right along with Faulk.

Proof that there was a silver lining to everything—even this.

"Where's Reed?" I tilted my head.

"He won't be coming today," Faulk replied.

I chuckled. "Oh, scared him off, did I?"

She smiled. "I thought it was time we changed tactics."

I'd expected this, but still a shiver of dread mocked me.

"Come to beat it out of me, have you?" I stood from the cot, yanking my gray oversized t-shirt over my squared shoulders. "Try your best."

Since my handcuffs had been removed shortly after my arrival, I could fight back. Color or not, I did remember what Branson had taught me. I should attack her. That might make me feel a little better, might change my fate. I would scratch at her, use my fingernails to shred her skin and blood, use it to fuel my power, use it to end her.

But that was only a fantasy. It wouldn't matter; there was a barrage of people outside waiting to step in if needed. But it would throw her off and that alone would make my day. I glanced up at the camera blinking down on us from the ceiling. Indicating that somewhere, behind the safety of another wall, the King was watching. He'd attended a few of the interrogations in person but then this thing had replaced him, with its blinking, watchful red eye.

The urge for action ticked through me like a countdown clock.

If Faulk sensed it, she wasn't fazed. She studied me, looked me up and down with a sneer, and then ushered in three Guardians of Color. They strode forward with complete confidence, each one of them glowering. They hated me. In their opinion, I was the worst kind of human. Maybe they didn't even see me as human at all, but an animal, a traitor, a beast deserving death at the hands of its master.

"Hey guys." I raised a defiant eyebrow.

I knew them, not personally, but enough to hate them doubly for participating in my interrogation. They had been some of the most difficult students in the class I'd taught on red alchemy. All three men were close in age to my seventeen. They were also the same guys who had competed at the first exhibition, expert fighters. I caught the eye of the one I liked the very least, Dax. He and I had bad blood. As he stalked in front of his friends, he glowered down at me, excitement flaring in his dangerous eyes.

Oh, great.

"Dax is one of our expert telepathics," Faulk said. "We have a handful of them in our organization. It really is quite a useful skill. Would you like to try it?"

My face burned. Did they know? As the boy strode toward me with clenched fists and a determined swagger, I questioned everything.

Purple alchemy twirled from his palm before shooting at me, connecting.

Well, hello Jessa. Just so you know, I won't be calling you Your Highness or anything like that, so don't pull that rank crap on me again.

I rolled me eyes, trying to fend off the worry building. I didn't want to connect back. I didn't want to talk to him. But it happened as if by accident, my magic leaping out to join his.

Can you hear my thoughts?

Fire lit his eyes, and he nodded to Faulk.

Close enough. His voice cut sharply through my mind.

I crossed my arms over my chest and glared. *Get out!* I slammed back on the magic. It didn't waver. He was too strong.

I will, once you tell me who you've been working with.

"You think it's going to be this easy?" I cut the question back toward Faulk. "Your alchemists are full of tricks, Faulk. They're all show and no substance."

She leaned back against the wall and flicked her wrist. The other two alchemists dove at me so fast I didn't have time to react and pummeled me with large, bony fists. Pain broke out across my jaw, my ribs, my sides, everywhere. I screamed. The agony rose, spilling over.

I'll ask my question again, Dax said. *Who are you working with? Names! Now!*

No, I won't.

"Hit her harder," he called out.

A heavy boot slammed into my stomach, and I went down hard, landing directly on my right elbow. Bone cracked, and agony soared through me. It was rawer, more direct, than anything I'd ever experienced. It burned up and down my arm, like liquid fire. I cried out, losing sense of time and space. My vision began to blur, and I was sure I'd pass out.

Tell us. Give us names and we'll heal you. If you don't, this will continue, and it will only get worse. Don't be so stubborn!

"Get out of my head!" I screamed.

There was no use. He kept asking his questions over and over while his friends beat me. All they needed was a slip up and they'd win. My blood spattered across the floor like spilled berries, filling my mouth to the point of gagging.

Faulk's voice filtered through the room, saying something I couldn't even begin to make out. The alchemists stilled, and Faulk walked over, leaning in with a jovial, sickening grin.

"Are you ready to cooperate?"

She had me.

And yet…

I shook my head, coughing up blood. The attack resumed, and I screamed, losing myself kick by kick, feeling my body break.

Tell me! Tell me now! Jessa, give me a name! Dax screamed into my mind. *Who else have you worked with in the Resistance? Who else is a traitor? Tell me. Start with one name. One name! Who is it?*

I didn't mean for it to happen.

It was the worst possible thing I could have done, but I did it. In the midst of all the pain, the barrage of questions and the suffocating fear that I was about to lose everything, my thoughts drifted to my love. To Lucas.

And somehow, I replied with his name.

The alchemist stopped and held up a hand. He stepped back with an odd expression. The pain still raked through me as I watched, horror ripping me up.

"I can't believe it." He shook his head slowly, but realization lit his face, drawing out a sly smile.

"Who?" Faulk yelled. "Did she give you a name? What did she say?"

"When I asked her who she's worked with, I wasn't expecting her to say his name."

"Out with it!" Faulk snapped.

He turned, glancing up at the camera then over to Faulk, almost apologetically. And the name dropped from his mouth.

"Prince Lucas."

★

As the prison cell door swung open, I braced myself for another interrogation. They'd healed me after the last one, so at least I'd had a break. But the mere thought of more pain sent me reeling. I scrambled back on my cot. I couldn't take any more! My heart kicked into overdrive and my breathing sped.

But it wasn't Faulk or Reed or any alchemist who walked inside. The fear deflated, and I relaxed. It was the people I'd least expected. But I couldn't help but smile at the royal hair and makeup team: Lars and Lainey. The way the pair looked at me, faces scrunched, huddled in the corner of the room, mouths agape, was nothing short of pathetic.

"I don't need your pity," I grumbled, peeling myself off the cot.

"Come along." Lainey tossed the command over her shoulder. She didn't need to tell me twice! The very thought of getting out of the cell had me practically giddy, my heart leaping for the first time in ages. Along with the guards, they escorted me down the nondescript hallway, into a sparse but clean bedroom with a large white-tiled bathroom attached. After giving me space for a quick shower, the two got to work.

"Am I going on camera?" I asked Lars, eyeing him through the mirror, noticing how his amber eyes didn't have the same spark they'd had on my wedding day. The lines in his tanned face deepened as he tugged at my wet hair with his hairbrush. I winced.

"Shh!" he warned me. "We're not allowed to talk to you this time."

"That's dumb." I watched them suspiciously until they spun me away from the mirror. Biting my lower lip, I looked around for a chair. Sitting down would be amazing, but I wasn't that lucky. Not that it mattered.

I could always try to use my red magic on them, get them

to talk, but I decided against it. They were innocent in all this, two people doing their jobs, trying to stay alive like the rest of us.

After an hour or so of primping and prodding, they turned me back to face the mirror.

"And they call me magical." I sighed, taking in my transformed reflection. I'd gone from a dirty, bloody, sweat-covered mess, back to a princess, perfectly styled to adorn Lucas's arm. My hair was curled gently around my shoulders, my lips painted a soft coral and my eyes bright.

"Put this on and someone will be here to escort you to see the King," Lars said, passing me a white cocktail dress and matching high heels. From the way Lainey glowered at him, I guessed Lars wasn't supposed to add the last part about King Richard.

"Thank you," I croaked, fighting back the anxiety that was bubbling in my chest.

"Sorry about this," Lars continued, pulling out handcuffs. "We've been ordered."

Lainey stepped back, steeling herself. But I wasn't going to fight them on this.

"I understand." I held out my wrists, looking away as he slipped the cool metal into place.

"Remember who you are. You're a fighter," Lars whispered under his breath.

My eyes popped back to meet his, and he nodded, eyes alight with brilliant fire.

Sure enough, a couple of minutes later, I found myself following a barrage of silent, watchful guards, and entering a cozy dining room. So far, I hadn't gotten too many glimpses of the operation here. It was some kind of military stronghold, and nothing like the lavish accommodations of the palace. Still, the room King Richard was to dine in had been artfully decorated, as if we were still in the palace.

The moment I sat down, he entered the room. He was dressed, not in the royal regalia, but in a crisp business suit and tie. His presence filled the room, thick as smoke and just as toxic.

"I'm going to get right to the point," he said, sliding into the chair across from me. "I need to be able to trust my son, and as such, I need you to tell me everything."

His magnitude was enough to intimidate anyone, myself included. Everything about him made me want to crawl out of my skin. It wasn't that he was outwardly evil. It was his incredible skill for manipulation, his way of twisting every little thing to his advantage—that bothered me most.

"I don't know what you mean," I said carefully.

"Don't lie." He held my gaze. I was struck by how similar his eyes were to Lucas's, the gray so penetrating, it drew me in. "I know what happened in your interrogation this morning. You claimed the prince was Resistance, and given the nature of said interrogation, I'm inclined to believe it."

Oh, no. That was not what I was hoping for. It would have been better for Lucas if they'd thought I was raving mad!

I sank into my white padded chair, having no clue how to fix this. Lucas had been Resistance, but he wasn't anymore. What good would it be to turn his father against him? It would only put the man I loved in more danger, something I'd vowed not to do ever again. Lucas had enough on his plate, the last thing he needed was to be thrown in a prison cell and put through the same kind of interrogations I'd endured. If that happened, it wouldn't be long until he accidently revealed his biggest secret.

His alchemy.

"You're a smart girl," Richard continued, leaning over the polished oak table. "I never gave you enough credit; I see my error now. You really do know how to play politics with the best of them. Maybe you deserve the crown, after all. Too bad after everything you've done, you'll never get another chance to ruin my family. Even if I let you live, you will learn to get in line, I can promise you that."

His perfectly preened eyebrows pulled together and lowered over unblinking eyes as he delivered his monologue.

"I'm going to give you two options, so listen carefully. Option one, you tell me everything, you surrender yourself to my will, and I'll graciously let you live. With that comes the agreement to adhere to my story, my way, and always, my version of the truth."

My stomach hardened to stone. His version of the truth. My hands turned to fists, pulling at the cuffs in my lap. His version was whatever version gave him the most power, and with the war in full swing, what would happen if he managed to win?

"My son has no memory of the last year, and as much as I'm eager to learn who tried to kill him…" He paused midsentence, looking me over with knowing eyes. "I'm more eager to make sure he never realigns himself with this traitorous Resistance group ever again. So that means you will feed him whatever information I tell you. You will help me help him. Because can't we both agree that it is in Lucas's best interest to support his father, to uphold the tenants of his role of crowned prince?"

It wasn't a question. He kept going, caught in his own delusion.

"It is either that or option two. Do I need to continue? I assume by now you know what option two is. It is rather obvious."

I lifted my chin. "Enlighten me."

"You take the fall for everything."

I flinched.

He smiled. "And that means you'll be publicly shamed and executed."

I sucked in a breath, letting everything settle over me. The world stilled. I didn't want to die, but I also couldn't tell Richard everything he wanted, and I certainly couldn't help him turn Lucas into his prodigy. If I revealed the names of the other Resistance members, I would be trading their lives for mine. How could I possibly value my life above theirs? Especially when they'd trusted me?

"Hurry and make your choice," he said, nonchalantly. "I really must be getting to my dinner soon."

I stood and pushed back my chair, placing my palms flat on the table, despite the pull of the metal cuffs.

"Thank you for the offer; it's an easy choice."

He grinned, triumphant. "I knew it would be."

"I choose option number two."

NINE

SASHA

"I so don't want to do this." I sighed, leaning into Mastin's warm shoulder. He didn't respond, but did reach down to squeeze my hand. Maybe he understood.

Since the second alchemist prisoner had arrived a little over a week ago, I'd been called back in four times to work with the new arrivals. That's what they called them. Really, they were prisoners of war. I understood the magnitude of winning this thing and how important it was to the future of not only both countries, but the world at large. Still, I absolutely *hated* doing it like this.

"Are you ready?" Mastin asked, nodding toward the door. On the other side was another prisoner about to get the "Sasha Welcome Party." That's what I'd termed the pathetic attempts I made to bring these people to my way of thinking. So far, I was zero and four.

There had been small battles nearly every day, and with that meant casualties and prisoners. I'd been forced to stay back after our botched mission to save Jessa, the General's way of making me pay my dues and prove myself.

Again.

At least he saw the value in allowing me to tend to the wounded. That was one area where my alchemy was making a huge difference. But if only I could be in the middle of the battle, I could save more lives. I'd tried to argue the fact, and even added the idea of letting me join the fight so I could lend others my yellow alchemy.

Nathan Scott had shot that down immediately.

He said it was too untested and should only be used as a last resort. He also made me promise not to tell any others about the ability. His failure to see the advantage was totally foolish, but I could argue with him all day and he wouldn't see my point. I wasn't desperate enough to use magical means of persuasion.

"Sasha." Mastin nudged me. "Are you ready?"

I groaned. "As ready as I'll ever be," I replied with a huff, blowing a wayward strand of hair out of my face. I ran my hands down my black clothing, stretchy jeans and cotton top with a zip-up. My necklace of stones rested underneath it all, steady against my skin. It was nothing compared to the combat gear the Guardians wore, but considering West America didn't have black uniforms, I was happy to make my own.

Making my own way in life was kind of my thing, anyway.

Mastin turned the deadbolt, opened the steel door, and ushered me inside. My eyes lingered on an older gentleman, pegging him to be in his mid-fifties. Of course he had been stripped of his alchemy gear, now wearing the light gray prison suit. He looked up at me with challenging hazel eyes, the overhead light reflecting off his bald scalp.

I hate this part.

The business of interrogation made me wonder if I was

any better than King Richard, Faulk, and all the minions who'd tortured me. The roles were reversed now, but did that make it okay?

Probably not. I knew how this went. I would try my best; he wouldn't budge, his loyalty steadfast in the King. So, I'd go and the American interrogators would get to work, a work much more effective than mine. And also, much more brutish.

"I'm here to help you." I smiled softly at the man as I strode into the room, taking position a few feet away from him. Mastin stood with crossed arms and a lethal expression at the door, my protector should I need him.

The man's focus returned to the floor, mouth twisted in something like defeat. He stayed hunched in the corner of the room, on top of the threadbare mattress on the floor. His elbows rested on his knees, not seeming to care one bit that I was attempting to start a conversation.

If only I could use magic and somehow make him talk. But no, that would be a huge mistake. Nobody here needed to know about that ability. Once they found out about red, they would turn from tolerating me to locking me up.

I held up my hands and slowly inched into the room. "I don't know if you recognize me—"

"I recognize you." His face shot up, eyebrows drawn in. "I know exactly who you are, should have known it when you came back but you'd changed so much."

"What are you talking about?" I narrowed my eyes, trying to place him.

"I remember you as a child, had you in my class back then."

I raked my memory, searching through all the teachers I'd had back then, but came up short. Trying to sort through the past was like trying to sort through the rubble of a burned down building. There wasn't much left, and what was there, was tainted.

"Sorry," I said, trying to sound as friendly and kind as possible. "It was a tough time for me, I actually blocked a lot of those memories, I think."

"And I know what you can do," he continued, grumbly voice growing sharp with every accusatory word. "So I know there's no use in fighting you."

Anxiety rolled through me. If this man had been one of my teachers, that meant he knew about the red alchemy. Magic I'd suppressed when I was still a kid, leaving it far in my past, underneath all that burned rubble. I hadn't dug it up, and I wasn't planning to now.

But if this man told interrogators about my secret, what would they do with that information? What would happen to me?

"Go ahead, just get it over with," the man said sharply.

I retreated, pressing my back against the cool wall, blinking rapidly, and pushing down my memories. But it was no use. They flooded me, drowned me with what I'd done.

I was so young then, and the King was testing the boundaries of magic—namely, my boundaries. I'd been used to interrogate people, to control people, and ultimately, to kill them.

I shook my head. "No," I muttered, clearing my throat. "No," I said louder. "That's not why I'm here. I come in peace, as a friend."

The man's eyes bulged with contempt as he slowly stood to full height. He towered over me, yellow teeth bared, and cracked his knuckles. "You're no friend of mine."

Mastin came to stand behind me, anger rolling off him, but I held up my hand to stop him from intervening any more than he had to. This was my fight, and if I could pull it off, there wouldn't be a fight whatsoever.

"Really," I said, turning back to the captured alchemist. "This is your chance to cooperate. You should. If you don't, they're going to use whatever means possible to get what information they can from you. This way, you won't have to suffer."

His eyes narrowed, the lines of his face lifting and stretching with the move. "And help them?" He spat on the floor, right at my feet. "Never."

"But don't you see? King Richard will stop at nothing until he has ultimate power. He doesn't care who he hurts in the process, he's—"

"Foolish, traitorous child!" he yelled. "King Richard is a visionary. He is taking back what is rightfully ours, restoring alchemy to full power across the world. I will never betray him."

And then he lunged, knocking me to the floor. I landed on my back, the wind rushing from my lungs. I pushed back, a frenzied scramble to get him off. Thin, tight hands gripped at my throat, and at first I thought he was trying to choke me, but then I realized he was looking for my stones. I beat him to it, connecting with the yellow. It pulsed through me and I threw the man off, slamming him against the far wall.

Mastin was there in an instant, throwing him onto his stomach and wrestling him so that his arms were wrenched behind his back. Then Mastin cocked his gun and aimed it at the man's sweat-shined head.

"She was just trying to help you," Mastin growled. "Move an inch and I'll kill you myself."

The man lay frozen, eyes facing me, burning as they glowered at me like I was the lowest form of filth he'd ever seen.

Mastin looked up at me, running panicked eyes up and

down my body. "Are you alright? Did he hurt you?"

"I'm fine," I replied as I stood.

I wasn't upset about being attacked so much as I was upset that these alchemists coming in were so blinded by their adoration of Richard and New Colony. How could they not see what was plainly before them?

"When I get back," Mastin spat toward the man, "you will pay for daring to *touch* her."

Then he tucked me under his arm and led me from the room.

★

"Didn't go so well, did it?" The general strode down the hallway, eyeing the room we'd just exited with the raise of a thick eyebrow. "Sasha, why don't you go back to your bunk and take a rest? You've been through a lot with these people over the last week. I'm sure you're exhausted."

His "these people" comment bothered me, but I bit my tongue and let it slide. "I'd like to stay and help. Maybe I can try again after the interrogators see him." What I didn't add was that I also wanted to make sure this man didn't tell the others about my red alchemy. The very idea of diving back into that sordid magic made my skin crawl.

Nathan Scott frowned, studying me for a long minute. "You really do need to take a break. I'm sorry, but this isn't a suggestion, it's an order."

He was used to giving orders. And he was used to people following them. But I, on the other hand, wasn't.

I opened my mouth to challenge him, no longer caring about holding back, but Mastin stepped in between us, resting his hand on my shoulder.

"I'll come find you soon as I can and debrief you on

everything. Will that work?" He held my elbow and stared earnestly into my eyes, pleading with me to back down.

"Fine," I grumbled, spinning on my heel. As I did, the exhaustion overpowered me, making my eyes burn. Maybe they saw something in me before I did, and Nathan Scott really was just looking out for me. Maybe I was reading too much into things because of the lack of sleep and I shouldn't be so annoyed.

The prison was in its own building, separate from the others. It was small, with a series of rooms on either side of a long hallway that turned at a 90-degree angle down the middle. At the far end was the exit, where I was headed. I turned the corner, out of sight from the men, and a tingling of suspicion caused me to slow. Before long, that tingling grew, forcing me to stop.

Don't be foolish. Why would they be so eager to send you away? You've been tired plenty of times and they didn't say a word. Maybe there really is something going on here, something they don't want you to know about.

I bristled, hating the idea that Mastin was keeping something from me. But despite my desire to trust him, I had to know. There wasn't time to stand around and debate it. I had to take action.

I drew the blue alchemy around me, knowing it would quiet any sound I made. Nobody would hear my breathing or footsteps. I wasn't as lucky as Lucas to have white alchemy to become invisible, but this was the next best thing, and I needed to take it. I needed to be smart, to be brave, and stop being so naïve.

The blue magic swirled around my body, then settled over me like a glove.

I relaxed and listened to a conversation happening just around the corner.

"What happened in there?" Nathan Scott asked his son.

"The man isn't willing to cooperate with us. Big surprise." Mastin's reply dripped in sarcasm.

"How dangerous do you think he is? Did he tell her anything?"

"No, he didn't. But aren't they all dangerous?"

Nathan let out a sharp laugh. "That's true."

I ground my teeth, trying not to be bothered by the flash of annoyance. Because really, they were right. We were dangerous. Case in point, I was listening in on their private conversation, and they had no idea I was there. *Thank you, alchemy!*

I pressed myself harder against the wall, not that it would really help anything if someone saw me, but it made me feel a little bit better than standing right in the open.

"How many more rooms do we have?" Mastin asked. "These alchemists that are filling up our prison are not exactly easy to keep under lock and key."

"We have enough for now. And if we need to make more, then we will. But keeping them in does worry me. Because what happens if they break out?"

It was a question I'd been afraid to ask myself.

"Are we going to bring in Weapon X?" Mastin lowered his voice.

The conversation paused, silence filling the hall for a long moment. "I think we are going to have to, and probably soon. I already got permission from Madam President."

"Sasha won't like it."

My body prickled at the sound of my name, senses kicking in.

"What did we talk about, son?" Nathan Scott was gentle in his scolding. But nonetheless, even I knew the sound of a scolding father when I heard it. "You cannot let this girl, no matter your feelings for her, get in the way of what we're doing here."

"I'm not. I won't."

"You are a soldier first."

"I know," he replied boldly. "I'm saying that we're going to have to find a way to tell her about it, at least prep her for the blow."

The blow? What the hell was Weapon X?

Nathan's voice came out firm and commanding, "Under no circumstances are you to tell her anything about it. It's a State secret, and something above your rank, need I remind you?"

There was another long pause. I waited for Mastin to argue, but I also questioned if he would. He wasn't the type to argue with his father, not only because he was his parent, but because he was his ranking General. And this wasn't about fathers and sons anymore, not to a man like Mastin.

General Scott was right. Mastin Scott was first and foremost, and would always be, a loyal soldier.

"Yes, Sir," Mastin replied in a steady voice.

"Maybe you need to take a break too." General Scott sighed. "This has been a lot for you, too."

Another "Yes, Sir" quickly followed.

Mastin's boots clapping on the concrete floor echoed through the hall, heading right toward the corner where I was hiding. Any second, he would round it and see me standing here like a lunatic.

That wasn't going to happen.

The yellow magic zapped through me like electricity, the blue still there, an undercurrent of silence. I ran from the building at lightning speed, bursting out the door before Mastin even turned the corner. Immediately, I released the magic and slowed to a steady pace toward the barracks where my bunk waited for me; where those men had sent me away!

Clenching and unclenching my fists, I fumed at this new revelation. They were hiding secrets from me! Secrets that had to do with alchemy, I was sure of that. And I was also sure Mastin wasn't going to clue me in. As close as we'd become, and as much as we cared for each other, those secrets between us weren't going anywhere.

It's not as if you don't have your own secrets. You have your red alchemy!

Yes, and he had knowledge of this mystery weapon.

As I continued down the path, dodging the soldiers in my way, glaring at the shanty buildings of the base, ignoring the cold biting at my cheeks, I found myself not heading back to my room, but to Tristan's quarters. I missed him.

He was allowed to participate in the battles, and because of that he'd quickly become one with the military men. He was trained, he was smart, and he was able-bodied. Not to mention loyal to a fault. Of course, they loved him. I hated that I wasn't able to go along, but I checked up on him after each and every battle. He was always okay.

But I wanted more than okay. Tristan was still my friend, he always would be. But he was colder toward me now that he knew Mastin and I were an item, less likely to joke around or even smile in my direction, but I realized I couldn't expect to have it both ways, and at least he still talked to me, still let me care about him.

I stood outside the building where he was likely hanging out and took a steadying breath. I was bunked with the women across the way, and every time I went into the men's area, I had to be on my guard. There were still plenty of soldiers who didn't like me, some who even wished me dead. I saw the way they watched me with their calculating eyes, felt their whispers behind my back. They put up with me because of Nathan Scott's strict orders, but for most of them, that was the only reason.

The men's barracks were practically overflowing the last time I was here, but as I walked in this time, there were fewer occupied bunks.

That wasn't a good sign during wartime.

I found him on his lower bunk; one in a long row of rudimentary metal and plywood structures, complete with thin mattresses and canvas sleeping bags. His nose was deep into a novel and he didn't seem to notice me standing over him.

I smiled and spoke low, "Tristan, I need to talk to you in private."

He dropped the novel to his chest and gave me an exasperated look, mouth downturned and eyes twinkling, but the second he caught the seriousness in my expression, he threw the book aside and nodded once.

"Let's go on a walk." He stood and led the way from the room.

A military base in wartime wasn't exactly open for anyone to walk anywhere they pleased, but despite that obstacle, we'd figured out where we were and weren't allowed to roam. As we maneuvered through the metal buildings and the gravel and dirt pathways, we walked close together, shoulders brushing, and kept quiet. There was so much unsaid between us, and the air was thick with untold confessions.

"Have you ever heard of Weapon X?" I asked, peering up at him.

He shook his head.

"I hadn't either, until today. I overheard Mastin and his father talking about it in regards to the alchemists imprisoned here."

Tristan laughed, a low rumble that made me feel nostalgic. "You overheard them or you eavesdropped?"

"Shut up!" I shoved my elbow into his ribcage.

He smirked. "That's what I thought." He didn't say more, and for that I was grateful. It would've been the perfect opportunity to question my relationship with Mastin. Girlfriends were supposed to trust their boyfriends, not spy on them.

"What do you think it is?" he asked. Our boots crunched against the gravel as we dodged passersby. One particularly ugly guy gave us a deadly glare, his lip curled in disgust, hand perched on the gun in his belt, before continuing on his way up the path. I glared at his retreating form.

"I don't know but I don't like the sound of it," I whispered, turning back to Tristan. "Mastin seemed to think that it would not make me happy. He wanted me to know about it and his father told him that I was not to be told anything."

Tristan folded his arms and nodded. "Poor guy."

"What is that supposed to mean?"

"He is stuck between you and everything else he cares about." He shrugged, looking away. "That can't be easy."

I hadn't thought of it that way and I certainly hadn't expected Tristan to defend my new boyfriend. Well, maybe he was my boyfriend. It was stupid to define it when we all had better things to worry about. Despite that, I found myself fighting a mix of annoyed frustration and clawing jealousy, and then mentally kicking myself for being such an idiotic girl when who I dated should be the least of my worries.

"Whatever," I grumbled as we turned a new corner and kept walking up the path wedged between two silver buildings. "We need to figure out what the weapon is and why they're bringing it here. That's the other thing. General Scott said something about the president giving him permission to move the weapon here."

We mulled it over, neither one of us all too happy about it.

An idea popped into my brain, painfully obvious. "Do you think Hank knows anything?"

"I actually talked to him yesterday. He's doing really good. Loves his new job training the baby alchemists." He winked at me. "But he didn't mention anything about a weapon. If it's some big secret, I doubt he would know."

"I need to call him," I said, hand absently resting against the mostly unused slatebook currently resting in my pants pocket.

"You need to call him *and* call your family. Why do you always do this?"

I bristled. "Do what?"

"You push away the people who love you the most."

Like I pushed you away for Mastin? I didn't voice my thought. Didn't want to go there. We kept walking as I burned with frustration at his accusation. Was Tristan right? Did I push people away?

"You have to give me some credit." I kicked a pebble, watching it clatter ahead. "Lately, I've been trying to connect with people. I went back for Jessa, didn't I? Even though it was totally stupid." I gulped, pushing the fear at being vulnerable deep into my chest. "And I did what you said, I am seeing if I can make things work with Mastin."

We stopped, gazing at each other. I couldn't read the expression in his eyes as they peered back at me. "Relationships aren't always easy for me," I whispered, letting out a long-held breath.

"You're right." He smiled softly and pulled me into a tight hug, our tense bodies relaxing together in their familiar way. "I'm sorry. You're doing great, kid. I'm just upset about something else," his voice trailed off.

There were so many more questions left to be asked, so much I longed to know. I could feel those same questions rising and falling in him with the rise and fall of his chest against mine.

But in the end, I didn't ask. And neither did he.

Sasha, a voice shot through my mind like an arrow. *Can you hear me?*

I stilled, frozen.

"What's wrong?" Tristan asked, pulling back.

"Hold on," I whispered. "Something's happening."

I closed my eyes and concentrated.

Jessa, I thought the words back at her, aware the telepathic connection was weak. But the fact it was there at all meant she had to be close. *Where are you? I've been worried sick about you. Are you okay? Can I help you?*

They caught me, she replied and my heart dropped.

Okay, where are you?

I'm in holding somewhere along the frontlines—or something, a military stronghold. I think. I don't really know. I'm scared. Lucas doesn't even remember me!

Wait, Lucas is alive? That was good news, at least.

Yes.

Are you okay? Have they hurt you? My mind flashed to my own interrogations, and my stomach flipped. Jessa wasn't strong enough to handle that kind of thing. If she broke, there'd be many people caught in the crossfire.

I need help. Her voice was laced with panic. *I don't have much purple left. I had a little hidden that they still haven't found.*

Okay, calm down. Tell me what you know.

I don't know anything. They had me in the palace for a while and then they moved me south, but I don't know where to exactly. I've been in a cell without windows.

It's okay. I think I might have an idea of your proximity. We'll get you out. It wasn't going to be easy, might even be impossible. I wanted to promise it to her, but I couldn't. *If you see Branson, you can trust him. I think he's there, too. I saw him not long ago.*

I haven't seen him. But either way, I need you to hurry.

I'll see what I can do. I shook, and Tristan reached out and grasped my hand, steadying me.

There's more. Jessa's voice broke through the darkness, shrill as it faded, the connection wavering. *King Richard just informed me that I'm to be executed.*

Our connection severed. My knees gave out and I crumpled to the ground.

TEN
LUCAS

I pressed my hand to the back of my head for no reason other than habit. The pain had subsided, but the day the doctor, nurse, and the alchemist left the orphanage was the day I knew I was in more trouble than I'd first realized. The memories hadn't returned. Those people had done all they could, but ultimately they'd given up, and I was more confused than ever.

Now it was just me, the guards, the orphans, and the staff left to occupy the estate. They were busy with classes and projects, and I was completely bored out of my mind. I moseyed about the different rooms, reading books, people-watching, and when things got particularly bad, staring holes into walls. At the moment, I was doing just that. My thoughts rolled around in my head like an unwanted companion.

I still didn't have a slatebook. Unfortunately, Celia had come back for hers the next morning after our…little conversation. I'd given it to her without question, and she'd agreed not to tell anyone I'd used it if I kept her secret. She didn't want anyone to know she'd entered my room like that. Shaking on the agreement had felt like making a deal with a viper. By then, I'd seen the footage of her attacking Jessa.

Didn't matter. I had more important things to worry about. Namely, getting my memories back, or at the very least, getting my life back, but I'd barely had a chance to talk to my father. He hadn't stuck it out in this new office for more than a couple days; no surprises there. He'd said there were only so many things he could oversee remotely, but he would come to visit as soon as he could.

I wasn't counting on it.

And he still kept my slatebook from me, kept *all* technology from me. It was all based on some medical advice from the doctor about not putting too much information into my head while I was still suffering from the memory loss. Considering I'd already secretly read everything I could that night using Celia's slatebook, I wasn't holding my breath. Even with all that, all the news stories about Mom, all the twists and turns with my two engagements, the public alchemy exhibitions, I still had amnesia. And I was still without answers.

"How are you doing?" One of my favorite workers, Martha, smiled pityingly at me as she approached me in the main family area. Since the kids were in classes, I was alone. My hips ached from sitting here like a lump. I rolled my eyes congenially at her and patted the armrest of the seat beside mine.

"You already know I'm going crazy with boredom," I said as she sat in the plump velvet chair. "How do you do it out here? I mean, don't get me wrong. I have always loved a short visit. But to stay? The isolation is awful."

We leaned back in our chairs, strategically placed next to the large window. The room was cozy, with wood-paneled walls and floors, plush rugs, and chairs throughout. A few wooden block toys had been left outside of a toy chest tucked away in the corner. My gaze flashed to the outside world, one blank as a canvas. We'd had another snow storm last night, and everything was once again covered in the stuff. A shiver ran over my arms, despite the fire crackling in the fireplace nearby.

The older woman laughed, her plump body bouncing jovially. "It's not so bad. I'm used to it. It's lovely in the summer. And besides, some people prefer the country to the city." She smiled, mossy eyes lighting in amusement, gray bun pulling at her ruddy cheeks.

I guess I could understand that. There were times in my life where I would have agreed with her, but then again, I wasn't much of a country boy, especially in the middle of winter.

"You really won't let me use your slatebook?" I asked, already knowing her answer. It was the same she'd given me day in and day out since my arrival. Still, I kept asking; I might eventually wear her down.

She shook her head, eyes crinkling. Her round cheeks balled as she smiled at me, clearly finding my persistence amusing. That wasn't going to get me very far.

I needed to find a way to convince my father to reintroduce me to society again. Whoever tried to kill me could face my guards, if needed; I wasn't going to live my life in hiding, especially over an incident I couldn't even remember. The war had started a few months ago and, for all anyone knew, it could last for years. I wasn't about to spend years hidden away in this place, no matter how much I loved the people.

"What about this." I flashed Martha my best smile, turning on the charm. "I won't go onto any of the feeds or check the news or anything like that. I only want to use the slatebook to call my father."

She eyed me warily. "Lucas, I don't know."

"Just one call, that's all I'm asking for. Let me talk to him one time. Let me lay out my case. Whatever he says, I'll take it. And I'll stop pestering you about the no tech rule."

"I really shouldn't—" Her voice faltered—I had her.

I leaned in, wrapping her round shoulders in a side hug and looked down on her with big, sad eyes. "Please, Martha. I really need this."

She sighed, resigned. "Fine." Weathered hands shaking, she pulled her device from the pocket of her floral housedress. The slatebook wasn't nearly as advanced as mine, but it would do just fine. "You better mean it, Lucas. One call. And you're doing it right here. I can't afford to have you run off with this. Your guards were in the hallway when I came in here."

My guards could shove it.

Okay, truth was, I didn't really want anyone to hear this conversation, Martha included, but I wasn't about to argue with her logic. The slatebook was in my hands now, I couldn't waste this.

It only took two minutes to get what I needed.

Two minutes. One phone call.

And just like that, I'd conjured up the exact words to convince my father that he absolutely had to have me with him.

I shut the device down and smiled gleefully at Martha, who stared back at me with worried eyes. The poor woman probably wasn't expecting to hear that. Oh, well. I was leaving this place—that's what mattered.

And I wasn't going home. The palace would have to wait.

No. I'd be joining King Richard on the frontline. That was fine by me; I wanted to be a part of the action. Who better to question Jessa before her execution than the man she supposedly claimed to love? I stood, patted Martha on the shoulder, and strode from the room. I had to get ready to leave since I'd be on the road within the hour.

I had a few pressing questions for my wife.

★

Gravel rumbled underneath gargantuan tires as we pulled up to the military stronghold. Rain pelted the metal siding, drowning out any sound from the outside world. The black armored vehicle had tinted windows, presumably so that the soldiers here couldn't get a peek at me inside. From my vantage though, I could see everything. The setup was much more established than I'd been expecting. The brick and metal buildings weren't hastily done or makeshift. How long ago had Richard built this place? With freezing rain pelting down in a torrential downpour, there wasn't much else to see. Aside from the stationed guards and patrols, nobody was out here.

What would they make of it if they could see me here? According to Richard, he'd already had a small, closed casket funeral for me. He wasn't ready to let all that hard work go to waste and reveal me to unsuspecting soldiers.

If only he knew about my white alchemy, this could make things so much easier. I could just go about my business, here, at the palace, wherever, and nobody would be any the wiser. But no, I had to keep that to myself. And maybe I could use a little bit to get around this base while I was here. I just hoped that in the last year, I'd still managed to keep my secrets my own.

I leaned back in my heated leather seat, rubbing the side of my stubbly cheek.

The driver was a bulky, quiet man, known for being

discreet—one of our regulars. He carefully maneuvered the vehicle into a large storage shed. Soldiers slid large metal doors closed behind us, and he cut the engine. He slid from his seat, pacing the space of the small garage. Burly shoulders relaxing in satisfaction, he trotted to my door and swung it open.

"Your Highness, you're requested to enter through there." He pointed to a heavy steel door on the far end of the garage, a lone guard stationed in front. "Your father has accommodations below ground for his safety."

"Makes sense." I slid from the car, feet dropping to the concrete floor, and shook the driver's cold hand. Then I steeled myself and strode to the door.

The guard in front stood tall, eyes forward, as if ordered not to acknowledge me. I shrugged and reached for the door, swinging it open with ease. A wide set of concrete stairs led to another door several stories underground. The long staircase was lit by low-hanging light bulbs, reminding me of our unused bunker back at the palace. I'd never liked that place.

"Here goes nothing," I mumbled to myself, and took the first step.

As I descended, the already-cold air grew colder, goose bumps rose like pinpricks on my skin, and a gnawing sense of importance gripped me like a fist.

I couldn't screw this up.

The door at the bottom waited. I tried the handle, but it didn't budge. Locked. It appeared to be as thick as a bank vault door, metal and cold as ice. I pounded on it, not sure what else to do. A slight jab of pain ignited in my wrist, but I ignored it, pounding harder.

A crack echoed through the hallway, the lock unhinging. The door pulled open, my father standing on the other side, lips lifted in a bemused smile.

I sighed and stepped inside, warming instantly as heat blasted, vision adjusting to the change in light.

"Well, it's not the palace, but it will have to do," I said jokingly, taking in the vast room sprawled out in front of me.

Truthfully, it was more impressive than I'd been expecting, and much bigger than the bunker below the palace. The two of us stood side by side, studying the family room and kitchen suite. Gleaming stone countertops, dark wood accents, leather sofas and patterned rugs, complete with framed oil-painted landscapes hung artfully on the off-white walls. Along the main wall was a series of oak doors, leading to what I assumed had to be equally elegant bedrooms and bathrooms.

The place looked like Mom could have decorated it, and my heart pinged painfully at the mere thought. She should be here with us.

"Welcome to your new home." Richard smiled, narrowing his eyes. "Since you couldn't sit still at the last place, you'll just have to make do here."

I stifled a breath, already feeling enclosed by the four walls.

"I brought her to you." Richard motioned to one of the closed doors with the quick flick of his wrist, and I froze.

"You brought her to me?" The question sounded strained and confused as it left my mouth.

"Jessa. Yes, she's here. Locked in one of the bedrooms, all the color removed ahead of time. I can't have you walking around the prison quite yet, that's where she has been staying up until now."

He looked up at the ceiling, eyes growing thoughtful. "I haven't decided how I'm going to reintroduce you to the world…or when."

"Great," I mumbled, spinning in a slow circle, my gaze

traveling high and low as I picked up on smaller details of the space. There weren't any windows. I sighed; at least at the orphanage, I'd had windows.

"Aren't you going a little overboard?" I questioned.

Richard glowered at me from across the room, arms folded over his broad chest. "No. You've almost died multiple times. You're my only heir, Lucas. We have to be more careful."

"If you say so," I grumbled. I eyed the door to Jessa's newest prison cell as I toed my way toward it. "I guess now is as good a time as any."

"I'll wait out here. At least, for your *first* meeting together." He grinned, eyes far-off, as if remembering something funny. "But be quick, and don't let her manipulate you."

"What do you mean?" I stopped to study him, something about his tone causing me to falter.

"Remember what I told you, Lucas. It's the truth." He nodded toward the door. "That girl is Resistance. You can't trust her. You should only try to get names out of her."

"Obviously." I smiled. I already knew all that, he'd explained it to me when I'd first asked about my supposed wife.

"Don't get smart with me," he snapped back, but there was a playful glint to his eyes. "And don't make me regret letting you go in there alone."

I shrugged. "It's probably better if you're not there. I assume you and her don't have the best relationship?"

He barked a laugh. "You could say that. But I mean it, Lucas. You can't trust everything she says."

"I don't have to trust her. She just has to trust me."

I pulled open the door without a second glance in his direction.

The light was on, but she was asleep, her lanky body curled up in the corner of the bed, arms tucked against her chest. A wad of white sheets gathered between her legs, her body wrapped up in them, leaning on them for support. Her unruly, dark hair spread out around her like a halo, a stark contrast against the white pillow.

I stepped closer, searching her face. A purple bruise had blossomed across her chin, creeping up toward her eye. I sucked in a breath. Why hadn't they healed her? She'd obviously endured some beatings. I shouldn't have been surprised, or even upset, she was an enemy of New Colony. She'd gotten less than she'd deserved. But still, seeing someone so young and innocent, sporting bruising like that, made my protective instincts flare. The urge to punch a wall, to scream, to do something, *anything*, rocked through me. It caught me so off-guard, the visceral reaction so stunningly intense, that I had to catch my breath.

I kneeled next to the bed to get a better look, careful not to jostle her. The girl laying before me had tender, full lips softly parted as she slept. Her eyelids had a soft purple hue, framed by dark lashes. They fluttered as if she were dreaming. She smelled of soap and something floral. Lilac? Her smooth and pale skin had a slight pink flush just on her cheeks. Oh yeah, she was beautiful.

And a longing deep within me tugged hard at my heart.

So why didn't I recognize her? And why weren't the memories of us rushing back to me?

Beyond the photographs, I'd hoped seeing her in person would spark something in the hidden parts of my brain, but so far, there wasn't anything new. Suddenly, she began to turn in her sleep, a frightened moan escaping her lips. I sat back on my heels.

"Stop," she breathed, panic ringing in her high voice. "Please." Long strands of her unruly hair wrapped around her face, and a faint sheen of sweat along her brow glistened. My heart pounded, the heat rising within, as my body reacted to her.

I didn't think, didn't question my instincts. I just reached out and gently shook her. "Wake up, Jessa. You're dreaming."

She blinked rapidly, eyes only inches from mine and delirious with sleep.

"Lucas?" The pain on her face was replaced with relief. She flung her arms around me, pulling me toward her and closing the distance between us. Shock burned within me as her lips melded perfectly to mine. Shock, and then something else, something much more primal.

My eyes slammed shut and I deepened the kiss. She smelled of lilac and soap and warm summer nights. She felt like coming home and the inertia of free fall. And although my mind may have forgotten her, my body remembered. The way her face fit perfectly in my palm, the angle at which her jaw jutted upward to me, the gentle tilt of her cheek, the soft flutter of eyelashes against my skin. It all poured over me like salve to a wound.

Of one thing, she hadn't been lying.

I rocketed back to standing, ashamed. I didn't remember her! I couldn't be kissing her, not like that. Her eyes opened wide, following me as they blinked away the previous moment. Embarrassment crept across her cheeks in deep red strokes as she sat up, stretching her body out like a kitten. The hem of her shirt rose above the hemline of her gray cotton pants, briefly exposing a line of pale stomach.

I imagined roots extending from my feet and into the floor, grounding me in place. It was either that, or pick up where we left off. But I couldn't let myself, not with so many unanswered questions. Not with how dangerous she could be.

I glanced down at my clothing, relaxing at the all-black ensemble.

"I'm sorry," her voice chirped. "I wasn't fully awake. I was just so happy to see you. I didn't think." Her bright ocean eyes shone with such intensity, and I couldn't turn away.

I cleared my throat. "It's okay. Let's just forget about it."

She shook her head. "If only you knew how long it took you to get me to forgive you…" Her voice trailed off.

"What do you mean?"

She glanced around the room. Even though we were underground, no expense had been spared. The bedding had been stripped save for the white sheets, and there wasn't a rug, but there was a black couch along one wall, a black dresser and furniture set, smooth white walls adorned by black and white landscape photography, and a small crystal chandelier hanging above the bed.

I noticed her eyes lingering on the oak door, painted black on this side. It matched the black trim lining the room.

"It's okay," I said. "Those things are thick. Nobody can hear us."

I wasn't sure if that was actually true, not if my father had a certain kind of alchemist with him.

She looked skeptical but nodded anyway. "Are you okay?" she said. "I assume you still don't remember anything?"

"I don't."

"But, they haven't punished you? Have you talked to Richard yet? What did he do to you?" Concern knit her brow, eyes pleading. One hand was fisting the sheet anxiously. What on earth was she talking about?

I shrugged, relaxing onto the couch. "I'm fine. My father is fine. I just talked to him."

Her eyes flashed skeptical. "He didn't say *anything*?"

I cocked my head at her, trying to figure her out. "About what?"

She took a deep breath. "Lucas, they've been torturing

me."

I sunk into the couch, guilt pulling me down. "I know."

"No, I mean, they want names. I didn't mean to give them yours."

"*My* name?" That didn't make sense.

"Yes, Lucas. They know you were with the Resistance. Or well, they don't know any of the details, but that you've been involved somehow."

I shrugged and shook my head. "I don't remember. Guess it doesn't matter. Everything is fine." Even as I said it, I didn't believe it. I needed answers, but I also needed her to be on my side—to trust me.

She frowned, jumping from the bed and coming to join me on the couch. Her gray cotton outfit was rumpled from sleep. She looked at me so earnestly, I almost felt sorry for her. This was too easy. She slid in close, leg pressed to mine, heat intermingling, and I stilled. Discomfort and longing warred within me, each fueling off the other.

"Don't you want to know what happened?" she asked.

"I do. It's hard to know who's telling me the truth and who isn't. Richard thinks you tried to kill me."

I gave her a knowing look, knitting my eyebrows together. Then I chuckled when she sat back, eyes wide and appalled.

"I would never hurt you, Lucas!" she challenged. "Someone needs to tell you everything that happened." She chewed her lower lip, nodding once to herself. "I'm the only one who knows everything. It needs to be me."

"It's against my doctor's wishes." I sighed. "He wants me to remember on my own without anyone else putting their versions inside my head."

Too bad it was already too late for that! The image of Celia's slatebook popped into my mind.

"But aren't I allowed to defend myself?"

I smiled. "You're right. Tell me your version of events."

Over the next hour, she did.

By the end, I sat motionless, bile rolling in my stomach. Jessa's hand was in mine, caressing my palm as she cried silent tears, as I was held captive by her rendition of events. Was it true? It was all so detailed, and hard not to believe it. But if she was telling the truth, it meant I was on her side. And she on mine. It meant my father had secrets beyond what I'd ever imagined, secrets so dark, there was no way to shine light on them without revealing the man he really was.

That he was manipulative beyond anything I already knew.

It also meant I needed to convince him to keep her around a little while longer. Last thing I wanted was to wake up one day with all my memories and emotions returned, only to realize my wife had been executed for protecting my sins.

I had to verify her story, and if it checked out, to keep her from being killed for it. I just didn't know how that was ever going to be possible. Because there was one place her story and my father's coincided.

Jessa was a traitor to the royal family and her actions were punishable by death. When it came to that, Richard was in the right. What could I do to convince him otherwise?

And I also wondered just how much of this conversation was really between Jessa and I. Richard had sent me in here on the pretense that I get names, that one-on-one time with her would soften my wife up to helping me, but what if all of that had been another game?

Fear unsettled me as I considered why I was in here alone with her. It was very possible that my father had found a way to hear every last word of Jessa's confession to me. If that was the case, she had dug herself in even further than before. And I'd helped her do it.

ELEVEN
JESSA

"I've struck a deal with my father on your behalf," Lucas said with triumph as he slipped into the room. He'd spent a lot of time in my new prison cell over the last couple of days, mostly to ask me questions. Each time he came through that door, I was reminded of how much I loved him, but also, of how worried I was for him. And for us.

I eyed him wearily. Any deal with Richard wasn't a good one—not for me.

"He agreed to put the Resistance names behind him for now, if you'll help him win the war. Then, when this whole thing is over, we can go back to normal."

I stared at him, not really believing the insane words escaping his mouth. "Are you serious?" I sputtered, catapulting from where I'd been lounging on the couch. "You really think things can ever go back to normal? Haven't you listened to anything I've been saying? And forget the fact that you still don't remember me!"

He frowned, running a hand through his hair and closing

his eyes briefly. "I can't help that," he said, voice low and gravelly. "It's called compromise, Jessa. If you don't want it, if you'd rather die, then so be it."

I stilled, returning his challenge with a glare of my own. Did he really mean that? His eyes were set, his mouth a flat line, as our gazes battled. Frustration tightened, pulling me to him like a string.

"So we're helping your father now? That's the plan." I stalked the length of the room until we were inches apart, the space between us charged with electricity. "I won't do it."

He glowered down at me, any semblance of sincerity in his expression now lost. "You will do it," he barked between gritted teeth. "You will help us. You will do as my father asks. You will do whatever is needed to stay alive, Jessa. *You will.*"

Silence stretched between us. I jutted my chin. "No, Lucas, I won't."

He growled, lips pinching, eyes darkening. Folding his arms over his chest, his biceps bulged against the black fabric of his t-shirt. "Are you trying to get yourself killed? Do you want to die? You're being unreasonable."

"I can't," I said low. "You don't know what you're asking of me."

"And I don't think you know what's going to happen to you!"

His voice reverberated off the walls, hardening the thick tension that was now suffocating the room. I knew what I was doing. I'd rather die than see Richard take over West America. I wasn't going to step in line. There was no going back for me. Either way, I figured I was dead. If that's how I was going, I was going out with dignity.

Lucas and I stood toe-to-toe as I held my ground.

An alarm erupted through the room, shrill and persistent. We flew apart, looking around wildly for the source of the noise.

Woop! Woop! Woop! It assaulted my ears, bringing me to my knees. I pressed my hands into my ears, scrunching up my face and squeezing my eyes shut. A wave of sheer panic overtook me.

"What does that mean?" I yelled, looking up to Lucas.

"Enemy on base!" He replied, his voice barely audible over the screaming siren. Panic transformed into hope and my heart slammed into overdrive. I needed to get out there!

A red light popped out of the ceiling, flashing in blinding intervals. A second, deeper alarm echoed along with the first.

"And that?" I pointed to the light, squinting hard.

"I don't know. I think it's best if we stay put."

Yeah, that wasn't going to happen. I sprinted for the door. Adrenaline propelled me forward, my legs aching at the sudden movement.

"Don't!" Lucas called, but it was too late. I tore out into the main room of the underground bunker, looking for threats. Except for one lone guard, standing by the door and fiddling with his slatebook, everyone else had left, probably to aid the fight above.

The guard was distracted, not looking at me when I jumped him. My training with Branson all those weeks ago kicked in, returning in an instant. I disarmed him in one kick to the stomach, sending him sprawling. Then I took off for the stairs, Lucas right behind me.

"You can't go up there! *I* can't go up there!" Lucas shouted, but it didn't matter what he said now. His influence over me had vanished minutes earlier. He wasn't on my side; he was on Richard's now.

Through all the changes, nobody had thought to check inside my bra. Thank God! I connected with the only color I had—the purple—and reached out.

Sasha, I screamed through the connection. *Is that you? Are you guys here to get me out?*

Jessa! Where are you? This isn't going well, we're going to have to retreat soon.

I don't know! Some warehouse. A bunker is below it, they've put me with Richard and Lucas.

Richard is with you?

My legs pumped up the stairs, and I sprinted into the empty space above. It wasn't more than a fifteen by fifteen foot room with a garage door on one end, next to that, a closed steel door.

He's not. It's just me, Lucas, and one guard right now for all I can tell.

Gunfire pummeled outside, bullets hitting the garage door, bending it. I dropped to my knees, crawling to the door, needing to escape.

Lucas grabbed my ankle, but I kicked at him as I strained for the door handle. Thankfully, I gripped the metal and turned, swinging it open.

I caught the flash of a blonde ponytail, recognizing Sasha at the other end of the alleyway. Hope blossomed and tears sprang to my eyes.

"I'm here!" I called out, desperate and relieved all at once.

Lucas's hard body jumped on my back and flattened me to the floor with a crack. Pain burst through my ribcage and I gagged, the breath knocked out of me.

I don't see you, Sasha's voice shot through my mind.

I peeked up, spotting her as she sped closer, her eyes zeroed in right where I was lying with Lucas. One hand pressed over my mouth, the other pinning me to the floor, his body covered mine.

I'm here! I pushed back. The magic began to fade. I needed more purple. *I'm almost out of purple. I'm right in front of you. I'm with Lucas. He's covering my mouth!*

I bit at his hand, but he only gripped harder. He stayed silent as I writhed under him.

I don't see you. She turned and sprinted further away.

"Hey!" The guard from downstairs was in the garage now, Lucas rolled us out of the way just before the man stepped into our path. He looked around for a moment, then took off out the opened door, gun raised.

My magic faded, and I knew the strip of color hidden inside my bra had too.

I wriggled, trying to break free of Lucas. But there was nothing I could do; he had total control over me, his dominance overpowering. I craned my neck around to shoot him a nasty look, realizing he'd made us invisible. There was nothing to see here, no sign of our struggle, nothing but an empty room.

No wonder Sasha hadn't seen me.

I continued to fight, but he held strong, keeping me detained in that god-forsaken building, watching a small slice of the action unfold outside, completely unable to take part.

From our vantage point, it appeared that the fight was moving out as West American soldiers retreated. New Colony soldiers and alchemists charged after them, war cries, weapons brandished, and strands of brilliant color weaving and darting from the hands of alchemists that followed.

All at once, the area fell into silence.

"Come on," Lucas said, letting go of my mouth.

"Get off me!" I screamed, hot tears streaming down my face. "Sasha! Sasha, I'm here!"

It was no use. We both knew that. We were alone. I crawled to my knees, overwhelmed by the heavy disappointment that buried me.

He stood, leaned over, and he had the audacity to pick me up.

"Get your hands off me! You don't know what you're doing."

"I know exactly what I'm doing," he said, charging toward the staircase. His hands gripped me under my legs and around my shoulders, holding me tight against his chest. His heart pounded so loudly, I could feel it against my side. "I'm saving your life! You think people know you're here? Very few do and even less know about me. We have to be careful, Jessa."

"I was getting out of here! What did you think? That West America was going to kill me? They came for me!"

His body tensed, step faltering. "Either way," he supplied, "it's too risky."

"Oh, and staying here and getting executed is a better plan?" I shoved at him as we moved down the stairs, wriggling and jolting with each step. "I mean it, Lucas, put me down!"

"You're not going to get executed because, like I said, I already worked out a deal with my father on your behalf. A deal that you're going to graciously accept."

"We already had this conversation. I said no."

"And now any hope you have of getting out of here is gone," he snapped. "You're going to do it, Jessa. I need you alive."

He carried me into the main room then back to my prison cell, dropping me on the bed with a huff.

I bounced, then hurried to standing, hands fisted at my sides. "Why do you care if I'm alive?"

"Because," he replied, exasperated. "I don't know if I believe everything you've told me, but I do believe one thing."

"And what's that?" I asked sarcastically.

"I believe we were in love." He glared, pain burdened behind his gray eyes. "I believe I wouldn't want you executed, nor would I want you running off to West America."

What a joke! He was the one who snuck me out of the palace in the first place.

"What makes you think that? You're crazy. You're selfish and so—"

He didn't let me finish. His hungry lips crashed into mine, devouring me, possessive. I shoved him away. Hard. At first he didn't budge, but on the second shove, he stumbled back, hands flying into the air. He let out a groan and stormed from the room, slamming the door behind him so forcefully that a picture frame fell from the wall.

I picked up the broken shards, smoothing out the black and white image of a beach scene. There wasn't any glass. Nothing to get at someone's blood.

★

He left me there for hours, locked in that room without a clue to what was happening above. The alarms had long since stopped and I was left to stew. I slept on and off, despite attempts to stay awake. I'd decided that the moment the door opened, I'd be ready to pounce, to make my case, to fight, anything would be better than sitting here. But when the door finally did open, it wasn't Lucas on the other side.

King Richard's tall frame took up most of the doorway, his long shadow falling into the darkness of the bedroom.

"Let's go," he said gruffly. "I have something to show you." He stalked away.

Despite an undercurrent of trepidation, I rolled from the bed and took off after him. Any chance I had to get out of this room was one I was going to take.

Flanked by a half a dozen guards, we ascended the staircase. Save for the sound of their boots clomping up the stairs, everyone was silent. Barefoot, I ignored the cold that gripped my vulnerable feet. There was no time to delay. Whatever Richard had in mind to show me, I was going to go along with it, and maybe if I was lucky, formulate a plan.

I glanced around for Lucas, but he was nowhere to be found. I breathed a small sigh of relief. The feeling was one I'd never expected to have when it came to that boy, but after today, I didn't know how we'd ever get back to the way things used to be. The Lucas I knew never would have done that to me.

We left the warehouse, out onto the tarmac, the cold air ten times worse. Sunrise peeked over the horizon. I told myself that it was refreshing and breathed in a deep breath of the cool air. A thin sheen of moisture covered the ground, which immediately soaked into the hems of my gray cotton pants as we marched down the street. Small pebbles stuck to the bottom of my feet. The base was orderly, brick buildings in neat little lines, soldiers and the occasional guardian crisscrossing the path, the faint smell of gunpowder and smoke, the low hum of vehicles in the distance.

Turning a corner, a large military helicopter waited in the distance.

I skidded to a halt and turned to Richard. "Where are we going?" The chopper was not a welcomed sight. Just thinking about the last time I'd been in one, when I'd nearly crashed to my death, sent me reeling.

Richard didn't reply as we approached the machine, its black surface shiny and gleaming. He climbed inside, reaching his hand out to help me. I eyed it suspiciously, refusing to touch him, and hoisted myself inside without help. Being unencumbered by handcuffs certainly made things easier, but I wondered how long that would last. His guards climbed in after me, passing massive black semi-automatic rifles between them and facing toward the two exits.

"Sit by me." Richard patted the seat next to him. I hesitated, but did as he said.

As we lifted into the air, a thundering roar surrounded us. Three jets zoomed out into the sky ahead. I gripped the sides of my small seat, stomach dropping with the inertia.

"They're added protection," Richard yelled, smiling gleefully as his eyes followed the fighter jets.

"Where are we going?" I called back, pushing down the sense of foreboding. Why was he talking to me like this? Like he and I were on the same side now that Lucas had convinced him not to execute me? I would never be sided with this man. Never.

His answer was filled with triumph, like a little kid who'd won a playground game. "We had a lot of success last night. We're setting up the occupation of Nashville."

Success? What did that mean? Success at killing innocent people, most likely. I watched the scenery fly by outside the window, green and brown landscapes mixing into a blur of color.

"What's Nashville?"

Richard smiled. "One of their largest cities near the border. More than a million West American citizens live there. Only a small amount evacuated before we set up occupation."

"Okay…" My voice trailed off. I didn't get what this had to do with me.

"Alchemy is treated like a crime in West America. Did you know that?"

I eyed him, biting my lip. "I've heard that."

But I also knew my sister was there, my family, and so far they seemed okay about their situation. At least, I thought so. I hadn't exactly been able to talk to them whenever I'd wanted.

"At least with me, you stand a chance," he said.

I laughed low. "Oh, really? Is that why I'm scheduled for execution? By the way, when is that? Because I'm assuming it's still on. Even if Lucas did cut a deal for me, I don't expect you to honor your end of the bargain."

He turned a dark look on me, eyes pointed, shining like razor blades. "Don't test me," he snapped. "I'm giving you one more chance to come to our side and abandon this Resistance nonsense, and I'm only doing that for my son's sake."

"It has nothing to do with my red alchemy?"

This time, he laughed. "Of course that's an added benefit, but not if it means having a traitor living in my own home."

I rolled my eyes, lost for words.

"Before you give me your final decision, I need to show you what costs are involved."

I grit my teeth and nodded. I already knew the costs involved.

As we flew further away from our base and toward the warzone, I noticed several fields of stark gray against the otherwise normal land. I knew about the Shadow Lands up north, but not about these. The desolate earth sprawled out for miles, everything dead.

I turned on Richard. "Are you crazy? Why would you do that?"

He smirked at me like I was a complete idiot. "It was a show of strength," he replied with a reptilian smile that made my skin crawl. "It wasn't the first spot we did this, and it won't be the last."

I shook my head.

"You need to realize that West America is going to lose and the Resistance will go down with it."

I held my tongue.

We continued until we flew over the city itself, a city that appeared to be recovering from a devastating fight. Thick smoke billowed from several buildings, and a few small fires were still burning bright as sunrise. But from this height, I couldn't make out any people. My heart ached for them.

How many were dead?

"Soldiers are rounding up anything that could be used against us," he said. "Most of the people are taking this better than we'd expected. Then again, we're not holding back anything. I've ordered an excessive show of force. No mercy."

"You're sick," I whispered low.

"What was that?" He shot me a dangerous look, a challenge in his eyes that sent a shiver of fear down my spine.

Once again, I held my tongue. I needed to be smart if I was going to make it out of this alive. A possibility that seemed further and further from reach.

"I wanted to show you this so you would understand how important it is that you use your red alchemy to help us."

I held up a hand, not quite understanding his meaning, but also not wanting to fully understand this man. "I'll stop you right there. If your son can't convince me, what makes you think you can?"

He smiled softly, turning back to the window. We hovered over the city, and up ahead, I could make out the jets flying low. Beyond that, something in the distance burned. I squinted, trying to make it out, but all I could see was flames and smoke.

The jets approached the area, and a black speck fell from one, landing with an explosion. It billowed out in an all-consuming flame, the noise penetrating the entire landscape with a screaming boom.

My mouth fell open, tears springing to my eyes. "What are they bombing?"

Richard sent a conspiratorial grin at me. "That's the West America military base." A dark laugh fell from his lips as he leaned forward to get a better look. "Or at least, what's left of it."

Terror overtook me, pressing on my chest, confusing all my thoughts. My sister was there. Her friends! Maybe Dad? So many others. This couldn't be happening.

"Why are you showing this to me?" I gasped, the fear cutting me like a razor.

"I already told you, Jessa. I am going to win this war. And you're going to help me do it. This isn't the first bombing; some have been on the city."

"On all those innocent people?" As I stared wide-eyed at this monster, blood drained from my face, heartbeat thudding in my ears.

"If you don't have the decency to make this easier for me, *for everyone*, then I will use whatever means necessary."

"You can't blame me for a bombing!"

He tilted his head, eyes two pinpoints of rage. "Can't I? You have undermined me at every turn and I will no longer allow it. Lucky for you, my son convinced me that we do need to keep you. Your execution is postponed until further notice."

"This doesn't change anything!"

He motioned toward the pilot and we spun around. Even though everyone was strapped in, our bodies veered with the movement. I slammed up against him and the need to vomit rose up, clawing at my throat. I began gasping for air, unable to get enough.

The chopper righted itself and flew closer to the city.

"See that?" He pointed toward the wreckage of a building. "That was a hospital."

Tears burned my eyes and I choked out a sob.

"And see that?" His finger moved toward an intact building. It stood tall and regal, like it was important to the city. "It's currently filled with dissenters. You can either help me control these people, or you can watch them die."

"No," I said with the quick shake of my head. "You're bluffing."

"Am I?" He slid a slatebook from his pocket and pressed a number. A moment later he held it to his ear. "Do it," he said to whoever was on the other end. "I'm making the order."

I faintly made out the reply of a woman's voice. Faulk?

A jet flew over the capitol building. As the small speck fell, screaming filled my ears. My screams. "No!"

But it was too late.

The bomb exploded, sending chunks of the building flying, practically shaking the entire thing off its foundation. A ball of fire plumed up from its center, black smoke at the edges.

"It's no big loss, really," Richard shrugged with nonchalance. "Casualties are expected and those fools were asking for death. Plus, we'll be destroying any state buildings once we take over anyway."

My heart thudded. My breath caught.

He turned his evil eyes on me, talking slow, making sure I heard each and every word, "You could have prevented that. If you had agreed to help me with those people, I wouldn't have killed them."

I shuddered.

"There are more. There are others."

Dark understanding crawled over me. My vision dimmed.

My mouth opened and closed repeatedly as I realized the truth. I was stuck. I had no choice but to help him, to become another weapon in his arsenal. If I didn't, he would end up killing even more people.

I nodded. "Fine." A hot tear fell down my cheek. "You win."

TWELVE

SASHA

The early morning sun glared down on us, the sunrise washing the carnage and destruction in a strange yellow light. Overnight, the world turned to chaos. What was supposed to be a quick extraction mission had quickly transformed into an all-out battle to the death. Not that anyone should've been surprised—least of all me.

"Go!" Mastin yelled over the deafening roar of gunfire.

He pointed toward the armory on base. My necklace was running low on everything. I needed to get over there to replenish it with what Nathan Scott had supplied for me. And my gun's ammunition had long since been depleted—making it to the armory was the next best move.

"You're coming with me." I pulled on his arm.

"I can't," he replied, scanning the battle ahead, the battle that had unfortunately followed us back to the base. "You go. I'll catch up."

I closed my eyes briefly, the ratcheting sounds of combat caving in on me. The smell, equally jarring with its mix of smoke and blood, sweat and metal, gunpowder and rain.

I didn't want to leave Mastin. Something told me that if I left him now, we'd be separated for good. Perhaps it was foolish or short-sighted, but my heart just couldn't do it. We needed to stick together.

The New Colony forces had moved in quickly. Swift as an axe, they'd unleashed their fury. We'd poked at them one too many times, and now had woken the beast. The moment we'd retreated from their base after things had taken a sour turn last night, they'd used the opportunity to attack. They'd started with several bombs that had thrown everyone to the ground, left us scrambling, and then their alchemists had moved in, crossing into our territory in droves.

The Guardians of Color were the worst.

Lethal, they moved like panthers, quick and cunning. They all had yellow and green power at their disposal, though some were better than others. Some were better than none—which was our biggest problem. Using the strength alchemy to their advantage, they cut down our soldiers like weeds. Whenever one of their own or a nearby New Colonian soldier was injured, they were quick to administer healing magic. But it wasn't just the green and yellow that was the problem. Other magics were at play, too.

"What's he doing?" Mastin questioned, terror rising in his voice. It was a new sound for him, something so foreign, I stepped back, his wave of panic sweeping over me, too.

I peered over his shoulder at a group of our soldiers. They had their guns trained on a male alchemist, but one by one, they dropped their weapons. Our men were surrendering!

When the alchemist turned, and I caught a glimpse of Reed, I froze.

"It's blue alchemy," I whispered in Mastin's ear. "He's using it to persuade them to stand down."

"We have to stop him."

"It's not that simple."

The moment the last of the soldiers had dropped their weapons, Reed lifted a handgun and began firing. Arcs of blood shot out of the defenseless soldiers' bodies as they crumpled in on themselves, dropping to the mud with sickening thuds.

Mastin tensed, a growl escaping his throat, hand lifting his gun, and clearly ready to run from our hiding spot and intervene. I surged yellow magic through my veins, holding Mastin back with my strength, rooting us in place.

"You can't," I gasped. "He's too powerful. He'll kill you."

"I'd like to see him try," Mastin snarled, yanking at his arm, trying to free himself. "Let me go."

"Please, come back with me," I begged, running my hand up his arm, willing him to look at me, to listen to reason. But he wouldn't. He craned his neck back to get a better look, craned it away from me, fire still burning through him, fire that I needed to extinguish if I was going to keep him from running in there and getting himself killed.

By this point, several more Guardians had joined Reed. They moved up the alleyway in a determined line, taking out anyone in their way. Swirls of color magic swung around them, mostly yellow, with a mix of Reed's deadly blue. The men in their way didn't stand a chance. They fell, landing on their knees, bloodied, faces scrunched up in confusion, before flopping to the earth. Before dying.

"We need to move," I whispered. "They're going to see us."

"I have to stop him," Mastin challenged again.

"You can't if you're dead!"

Why couldn't he see reason? His bloodlust had taken a firm hold, the desire for revenge overpowering all sense of reason. If he didn't snap out of it, I'd lose him.

A thin trail of blood ran down his forearm where some shrapnel had launched itself into his bicep earlier in the night.

I could use red alchemy... The thought pulsed, taking root in my mind. *It's been years, but what if it still works?* It would be so easy to make him come back with me.

But no, that would reveal my secret. And he would hate it. *But if it saves his life, wouldn't it be worth it?*

"I was wondering when I'd find you again!" Reed's cackle echoed down the alleyway, making my decision for me. His gaze zeroed in on us as he ran. I might've been able to resist him, but I couldn't risk Mastin. Reed had made the mistake of going easy on us once and we'd gotten away. From the shine of excitement lighting his eyes, from the way he and his gang stalked toward us across the gravel, that wouldn't be the case a second time.

He was far away still, but he was the predator and we were the prey. And he loved it.

I glanced around, desperate for escape. There was only one way I saw this going. I didn't let myself debate for another second. I grabbed Mastin's bloody bicep and thought only of red. The magic came back in an instant, as if it had never left, just waiting for me to accept its presence. The electric power surged through me. Red strings of shining magic danced through the air, and I immediately pushed them into Mastin. Eyes still on Reed, he never looked my way, never saw the alchemy.

"Come on, we have to save ourselves. Follow me," I said, pushing what little I had of the yellow in with the red. It was our only shot at outrunning Reed. "We have to get to the armory. Now!"

Mastin didn't argue. I knew that he wouldn't, that he couldn't, not with my power reigning over him. I caught a glimpse of his eyes, glazed over with a singular focus on my command, and refused to feel guilt. I'd have time to beat myself up later. Boots kicking gravel behind us, we sprinted around the corner and toward a heavily fortified steel building. The wall of soldiers lining the front, guns trained, let us through without a flinch of hesitation. They barely looked our way as they shouted to each other, taking shots at the incoming enemy. The thick burn of smoke still hung in the air, paired with low moans and arresting shrieks of the injured.

We stumbled into the room, packed with bodies. Apparently, we weren't the only ones who needed more ammunition.

"Load up!" the deep voice of General Scott echoed through the large room, basically a small scantily-built warehouse with shelves upon shelves of weapons along the sides. "We're retreating. We've lost too much ground here. We're going west. Head for the airfield. Now!"

Men and women gathered supplies at lightning speed, carrying boxes of ammunition and slinging guns over their shoulders. Some worked together to carry large crates. They streamed for the exits in crushed lines. Mastin followed me, ever the faithful servant with the red magic running through him.

I crossed my arms over my stomach, trying not to be sick. This was why I hated red alchemy so much. I never wanted this kind of power. It was too much, too much for one person to have this kind of control.

"Snap out of it." I turned on him. "Do whatever you want."

He blinked, confusion running over his face, as he looked around wildly. "What just happened?" His eyes narrowed on me. "Did you do that?"

"I'll explain later," I rushed the excuse out, breaking his

intense eye contact just as I'd broken his trust. Now was not the time for this conversation—would there ever be a time for it?

"There you are!" Tristan's frenzied voice jerked me out of my thoughts. "I've been looking everywhere for you." A trace of anger rung heavy in his tone as he pushed his way around the crowd of retreating soldiers. "You disappeared! We were supposed to stick together."

"We took cover." I shrugged, biting my lip as more guilt ripped through me. "It's fine, we're here now."

He held my eyes, mouth in a thin line. "You heard the General, we need to get out of here. Get what you need. We're leaving." He hooked his weapon over his shoulder, drawing his eyebrows together.

I nodded, and the three of us sped off to replenish our supplies. Luckily, all of us had been trained to understand the layout. My stones were in a box in the corner of the room, resting high on the farthest shelf. I sprinted toward it, relieved to find the box waiting for me. Just the sight made it easier to breathe.

But when I heaved it down from the shelf, it jostled into my hands like nothing, as light as if it were empty.

I flung it open, furious. Empty.

I cussed and threw the box against the floor, splintering it along one edge.

"What's wrong?" Tristan jogged over, an added gun slung over his shoulder.

"Someone took my stones! And I'm pretty much out of everything useful."

Pulling it from under the hem of my black shirt, I studied my necklace in my fingers. The stones hung in a line along the leather strap. There was hardly a trace of yellow left and the green was completely gone, the stone a sickly shadow of itself.

"It's okay." Tristan tugged me after him. "We'll worry about it later."

He was right. As much as I wanted to scream and punch something, there wasn't time. We took off, finding Mastin who was busy loading ammunition into his current handgun and slinging another, much larger one, onto his back.

"You ready?" I asked him.

He nodded once, looking me over with a trace of suspicion in his green eyes. His jaw clenched for a moment and then he spoke, "Yeah, let's go."

We hauled it for the building's one exit, Mastin taking point as usual as we moved from the relative safety of the place. Gunfire rained down on us the moment we slipped out the door and sprinted for the airfield. We dodged the bullets as they ripped at the ground around us, sending dirt and gravel flying. The airfield stretched out next to the armory, so we didn't have to run far, but with death all around us, it felt like miles extended between us and the nearest machine.

Soldiers were climbing into the opened doors of jets and choppers. The second one filled, the doors slammed shut and the machine rose into the air. I eyed the nasty New Colony jets circling the base, white demons that roared through the sky, hungry for more death.

So far, they hadn't dropped any more bombs.

Probably because so many of the New Colonians were on the base now. Richard wouldn't care about his civilian soldiers, but he wouldn't want his alchemists to be blown up. No, those Guardians were the difference between winning and losing.

Our feet slammed against the pavement, puddles of rainwater splashing in our wake. At last, we made it to one of the mammoth helicopters just as it was getting ready to lift off. Mastin jumped in first, reaching out to pull me in after him. As I was hoisted inside by his steady arm, I landed on my butt. A prickle of relief ran down my entire being, settling in. I closed my eyes, catching my breath, running hands down my legs to wash off the mud. I spun around to make sure Tristan had plenty room as well.

He was gone.

I blinked, disbelieving. "Tristan!" I jumped up and screamed out the door. "Where are you?" My voice was a mere squeak compared to the onslaught of battle raging outside. I frantically scanned ahead, taking in the last of the soldiers, watching as the enemy approached, but Tristan wasn't anywhere to be seen. Had he gone to another chopper? No, he wouldn't have left me. Not on purpose.

Someone pulled the door shut with a sharp clang. The chopper lifted and climbed, and my panic climbed with it. No, I couldn't leave him!

I wrenched the door open, calling on the last bit of yellow magic I had, and dived down to the pavement ten feet below. I tucked and rolled on my landing, ignoring the pain as I popped up to full standing.

"Sasha! What are you doing?" Mastin screamed down but it was too late. He was too high to jump down after me.

I held up a hand. "Don't worry!"

Looking around the airfield, there were still several choppers that hadn't taken off. There was still time. All the jets had left, but all I needed was one chopper. Just one. I would have to be quick. Find Tristan, then get back before it's too late.

You can do this. Everything will be all right. I repeated the words over and over again as I took off running.

Gunfire blew bits of the dirt right next to me, and I dove for the ground in the opposite direction. I crawled to my knees and searched for cover.

That's when I saw him.

Leaning against the metal siding of the backside of the armory, Tristan hunched over, clutching at his stomach. His face shone with anguish, his mouth pinched.

I ran for him at breakneck speed, dodging bullets and crying out in both terror and relief. I was well aware that there wasn't green near me, so if I got shot, I wouldn't be able to heal myself. But more than myself, it was Tristan who I worried for. He needed my healing alchemy. I had nothing to offer. The entire area was a tangle of metal and pavement, dirt and gravel, shrapnel and wreckage, but no greenery in sight.

I skidded to a stop in front of him. "Are you okay?"

He blinked up at me, a mix of relief and fear drowning his features. "What are you doing here?" He coughed, thick globs of blood spilling out of his mouth.

"I came back for you. What else?"

He didn't seem to hear me, head shaking, his eyes rolled into the back of their sockets. The remaining color drained from his face, black hair flopping across his sweat-covered forehead.

I had a little bit of yellow left, the barest amount. I prayed it would be enough to get us to safety. Quickly, I called on what was left of the amber stone that lay, mostly gray, against the hollow of my neck. The second the surge of strength ran through me, I reached around Tristan and picked him up. His arms fell on either side, his head rolled against my collarbone as I stood.

"Hang in there!" I demanded. "You are not allowed to die!"

Magic bursting through my legs, I took off for the chopper. It was the last remaining one but the propellers were already spinning. A man with a smoke-smeared face leaned out to slam the door shut.

"Wait!" I screamed, my voice shriller than I'd ever heard it before. The man caught my eye, looking to me and then to whoever was advancing behind us. I didn't look back. It was now or never.

Mercifully, the man waited with the door opened, someone at his side leaning out and firing at whoever was chasing us.

My heart pounded, catching up to the chopper just as it was lifting off. I threw Tristan in first and jumped inside. As I turned to close the door, a sharpness tore through my upper arm. The pain was so searing that it was almost unbelievable. I cried out, panic surging alongside the agony.

"You've been shot!" A gruff voice called as I stumbled further into the chopper.

"I'll be okay." I winced, holding my arm. The pain crawled into my bone, deep and reaching. "Any chance one of you has some green on you?"

Nobody answered. I turned, absorbing the looks of a dozen astonished and weary expressions. Honestly, they didn't look much better than I did. Their uniforms were filthy with matted soot and blood, faces bruising. But at least they didn't have gunshot wounds!

"I didn't think so," I muttered, straining on the words.

I looked down to the blood pouring out of my arm. It was bad, but it was nothing compared to what Tristan was enduring. His entire shirt was soaked crimson, and he was still passed out, body slumped awkwardly beside me. If we didn't get him help right away, he would die.

The chopper flew over the blurred landscape, gaining speed.

"Land!" I yelled, lumbering to the front of the chopper.

The pilot didn't seem to notice me. Or if he did, he didn't

care enough to glance back in my direction.

"We need to get to land," I said again, gritting my teeth against the pain. "Somewhere green." My breath caught. "Please."

No response. I could overtake him. I could fly this thing. But that wouldn't happen with all these soldiers here; they'd stop me.

"We need land!" I chocked back a sob. "Please, just really quick so I can save my friend and anyone else on here who needs help." I pointed to a field of sprawling green grass in the distance. "There. Land there!"

"Are you trying to get us all killed? Get out of here!" the pilot replied. "I have orders."

I turned back to the men behind me, eyeing three more injured bodies crumpled in on themselves.

"I can save people if you land this thing. I can heal them. Please!"

Should I use red alchemy on him? I don't know if I can with so many witnesses, but Tristan needs me. I'll do anything to save him. No question, I'm desperate.

Resolved, I reached toward the man.

"Fine!" The pilot relented, just before I touched him. "But you'd better make it quick."

"I will. I promise!" Pure relief cascaded through my breath as I exhaled.

We descended quickly, landing in the middle of the glorious green.

Using my good arm, I swung the door open. Landing on both feet, I reached down and tore at the grass, fistfuls of it.

"Come on!" someone called out to me. "We need to go!"

In the distance, several jets circled the base, much lower than they were earlier. A black speck fell from one of them. I stilled as I watched it, knowing what it meant. A bomb. It landed on the armory, the structure exploding and erupting into flame.

I sprinted back to the chopper, scrambling to get to Tristan as quickly as possible. The other injured would have to wait, myself included. Tristan came first.

We jolted into the air, flying low over the ground. I worked the green magic, the color twisting into the air. Saving my very best friend, my favorite person, wasn't what I'd planned for today, but I was certainly grateful for the chance.

After a few minutes, he woke, blinking up at me.

"Thank God," I breathed.

He smiled, eyes dark as storm clouds, searching mine. "Yes. Thank God for you, Frankie."

Who was I? Was I the Frankie from years ago, in love with my unavailable best friend? Or was I Sasha, the warrior destined to start a new life? So many things had changed, starting with the introduction of my family. I didn't feel like the same girl from all those years ago, but sometimes, I wondered if maybe I still wanted to be her. Maybe it was possible to meet in the middle, to be both.

I looked away, sitting back on my heels, and tended to the wound in my arm.

"I owe you. This is at least the second time you've saved my butt, you know?" Tristan teased, brushing the sweat from his brow.

Shaking my head, I laughed. "It probably won't be the last, either."

✭

"I can't believe we lost Nashville." I ground out the words as I sat down next to Mastin. The dirt and rocks mixed uncomfortably with sparse grass, but I paid them no attention. I would endure much worse to spend time with this man. "And Jessa, I don't know what's going to happen to her." I sighed, defeated, an emotion I didn't know how to handle.

Mastin sat on the crest of the hill that overlooked the endless horizon when I found him, his knees bent, elbows resting on top, and his hands cradling his face. Tense, he didn't say anything in response. Frustration rolled off of him and I bristled. Was this all my fault? I'd convinced his father of the importance of rescuing Jessa, and when we'd failed the mission, everything had gone to hell. So there was that. There was also the fact that for the first time in years, I'd used red alchemy, and it just so happened to be on him.

I stared out into the sunset, blinking back the tears. I was not going to cry! I was not that girl.

I craned back to get another look at our newest home. We'd taken up occupation in a tiny town a few hundred miles west of Nashville. The residents had already evacuated, so we were able to start reorganizing ourselves in the homes and businesses. The place was quaint, a jewel in a field of vast grasslands.

My head ached, a throb that pulsed in my forehead. The entire day had been terrible as we'd realized just how many people we'd lost back in Nashville.

Guilt ripped through me. How was it that the sky could be so beautiful, a wash of bright pink and royal purple, and yet I could feel so hollow inside?

"Are you in love with him?" I froze, Mastin's question catching me off guard. He leaned back on his palms, staring off into the distance.

I took in the firm set of his profile, turning the question over in my mind. I could pretend I didn't know who he was talking about, but of course I did. "I love Tristan. I've loved him for years. But I don't know if I'm in love with him."

He winced, eyebrows drawn. "You don't know? How can you not know?"

I shrugged. "But I do know how I feel about you."

"And what's that?"

Was it love? I hadn't gotten to there yet, but I was close. "I feel like you and I are the same, like we get each other. I feel like we're supposed to see where this goes." I reached out and placed my palm on top of his, intertwining our fingers. This level of vulnerability was hard for me. I wanted to jump up and run away, but I forced myself to stay.

My heart, usually so guarded, was opening for him, and quite honestly, it hurt. But wasn't love supposed to hurt?

He sighed, closing his eyes and breathing in deeply. "How are we going to do that if you're more concerned about your friendship with Tristan than you are with your relationship with me?"

I started pulling away from him. "That's not fair."

"Isn't it?"

"Is this because I went back for him? I couldn't leave him there to die. You can't get mad about that."

He twisted his lip, nodding slowly. "It's not that you went back for him. I understand that and I would have done the same. Even though it bothered me, I know that's a selfish reaction and I don't want to be that guy."

I laughed coolly. "What? The jealous boyfriend? It's kind of too late for that, don't you think?"

It was a mean thing to say. But I was too stubborn to take it back. And actually, he wasn't my boyfriend, was he? We'd never defined it that way.

"I'm serious." He looked me up and down with his piercing green eyes. They traveled slow, landing on my lips. I tensed in anticipation. "And it's not because you went back for him that we're having this conversation." He paused, twisting the words around in his mouth before speaking, "It's the way you look at him. It's the way you *are* around him. I didn't want to see it at first; it was easy when you were staying at my house out west and he wasn't there, but I can't help it now we're all on this base. He's always around."

"No he's not. He's been avoiding me ever since you and I got together." I sat back, folding my arms over my chest. Why was I being so defensive? I could just tell Mastin that I had zero feelings for Tristan and this conversation would be over.

"And the fact that he's been avoiding you hurts you. I can tell."

"Because he's my best friend."

"Nothing more?"

I bit my lip. We'd circled back to the burning question. The truth was, even if somewhere deep inside I still wanted Tristan, he didn't want me. He'd told me to date Mastin. And that was fine. Mastin and I were the same, we belonged. I'd chosen him and wanted to keep choosing him, if he'd let me.

"Nothing more," I said.

He watched me carefully, guardedly.

"Please, don't do this," I said, letting out a stilted breath. "I can't choose between my best friend and you. I want you both in my life. I need you both."

He sighed, anger leaving his expression only to be replaced with sadness.

"Fine," he relented. "I guess it's better than the alternative."

I stilled. What did he see as the alternative?

"If it's not you and me," he continued, "it's going to be you and him. And I'm selfish, I guess, but I want it to be you and me. I–I really care about you, Sasha."

I leaned in, scooting closer. "I feel the same way about

you."

Tentatively, our lips met. The argument was quickly lost to the passion that overtook us. As he held my face in his rough palms, I knew I'd meant what I'd said. I did care about him. I wanted this moment to go on forever, to live in this place where we could save each other.

THIRTEEN
LUCAS

"Start with the inner circle." I leaned against the wall, looking down at my father. We'd been arguing his reasons as to why I wasn't allowed out of the bunker. They all made sense, but that didn't make it any easier for me. My hope in coming here had been to get Richard to let me go back to the way things were. If I'd known that helping him with Jessa would result in being confined underground, I wasn't sure if I'd have done it.

Of course you would have. You wanted to meet Jessa.

"You said you got Jessa to agree to help with red alchemy." I crossed to join him on the chestnut leather couch. "So let's start with the inner circle. Let's find out who's been trying to kill me and then we can remove them and I can get out of here."

"What makes you think it's someone in my inner circle?" His jaw clenched, disbelief in his eyes.

I scoffed. "Come on, it's the only thing that makes sense."

"Plenty of people were in the palace that night."

"Yes, but what about the plane explosion, or the fire, or even the funeral?" I pressed. It was obvious to me.

He let out a breath. "You've been doing some research. You weren't supposed to look into your past until your memories returned. We talked about this—the doctor agreed."

I couldn't meet his gaze, ashamed at lying, and also, in getting caught. *Yeah, so what? Anyone in my position would have done the same.*

"Where did you get a slatebook?"

"I stole one," I deadpanned. "Did you really think I wouldn't look into my past? If it were you in my position, you'd have done the same."

He hummed, thumb running along his jaw. "True enough. I'm wondering how you can learn all of that and you *still* don't have your memories back."

I shook my head. "I don't know if I ever will."

He smiled. Why the smile? If he wanted me to remember who'd tried to kill me, I needed those memories. But at the same time, I wasn't even sure I *wanted* the memories anymore. What if Jessa was telling the truth about everything? What if I was Resistance and had turned on my own family?

"Answers," I pressed. "I need answers, as do you. Let's start with using Jessa's red alchemy."

Richard's smile spread even wider. "I never thought I'd see the day that you'd put our family's interests before Jessa."

I bristled. What was that supposed to mean?

"Luckily for you, I have to agree," he continued. "We'll do as you suggested. Let's start with our inner circle and work out from there."

"Let's start with Faulk." I'd hardly seen the woman lately. She was busier than ever, doing my father's dirty work, no doubt.

The silence between us stretched as we studied each other.

Faulk and I had never seen eye to eye, Richard knew that as well as anyone. It made sense; she hated me. She could be the one behind the attempts on my life. Why not the woman who'd felt the need to point out my weaknesses all throughout my childhood?

"She has no reason to betray us." Richard's voice was smooth as ice.

"That you know of."

He grumbled. "She won't like it."

"Only if she has something to hide."

He leaned back into the couch, looking up at the ceiling, considering. I waited, anticipation creeping up me. As far as I was concerned, Faulk was the perfect candidate to start interrogations on. And we had to start somewhere, right?

"We'll get started right away," he relented, looking back to me with a pained nod.

"Do it here," I said. "Faulk already knows about me. I want to see this." Was it wrong that I wanted to see her squirm? Maybe. I didn't care.

"I'm proud of you, son. You've become more cunning than ever since your accident. You're turning into the prodigy I'd always hoped for. I'm just sorry your mother isn't here to see it." He stood, patted my shoulder, and then strode from the room.

Pride swelled like a balloon within the deepest part of me, but there was something dark there, too, something that twisted my insides and pricked my skin. I realized with a start that the feeling was shame. It was guilt and disgust and a mix of so many things and it left me reeling. What did I have to be ashamed of? My mind flitted back to all the claims Jessa had made about the last year, about my father. Even though my mind disbelieved, maybe the rest of me was trying to tell me something, trying to prove once and for all that Jessa was right.

★

She came willingly. Maybe it was like I had said; maybe Faulk didn't have anything to hide. As she walked into our bunker, I eyed her up and down, taking in her pressed white uniform, gleaming silver buttons and flashing adornments.

"Nice to see you're doing well." She said it in a way that felt much the opposite. I raised a mocking eyebrow.

"Let's get this over with." She sneered and marched across the room, arms folded defensively over her chest. She crossed to Jessa's door, unlatched the lock, and threw it open with a clang.

"Get out here, traitor," she taunted. "You should be thanking God for that red alchemy trick. You should know you'd be dead otherwise."

My fingers itched to wring her neck. She shouldn't be talking to Jessa that way. Her hate was so all-consuming, it turned her from agitating to downright obnoxious, but I kept my mouth shut and pushed down the white-hot anger that had flared within.

Richard leaned against the wall of the bunker's family room. He watched the whole exchange with unrestrained amusement playing at his lips. Guards stood at attention in the four corners of the space, hands resting on their holsters, eyes assessing for threats.

Jessa gingerly shuffled from her doorway, reluctance etched into every line of her body. Her complexion had paled but she held herself solid, shoulders back, chin up, a look of sheer defiance lighting her eyes. Her unruly hair was gathered in a knot on top of her head, one small piece loose and bouncing against her long neck. I grew jealous of that lock of hair, longing to run my fingers along that tender spot of milky skin. As if sensing my lascivious thoughts, she turned a savage glare in my direction; I couldn't help myself, I stared back.

She was gorgeous, reminding me of a wild animal, a mare that needed to be broken, but the very idea of breaking her untamed spirit left me reeling.

"What's this about?" she demanded, peeking about the room. We'd already cleared out any color that could be detrimental to us, but I could tell she was checking. Just in case. Smart girl.

I didn't blame her.

"You work for me—you already agreed. Don't look so put-off," Richard said, peeling himself off the wall and stalking toward her. In his fine suit, with his tall frame and broad shoulders, she looked positively weak, but I knew better than to underestimate her. "We're going to start with a few interrogations. You'll be using your red to get answers from our leaders, and so on down the pipeline."

Her eyes popped. "W-what?"

"Let's just get on with this." Faulk stepped forward. "I don't have anything to hide." She slid a bony hand into her pocket, pulling out a shiny pocket-knife. Flipping open the small blade, she cut a thin line into the flesh of her forearm. Blood surfaced, little crimson beads that she held out to Jessa.

The mood shifted. Jessa visibly relaxed, as if accepting the inevitable, and then reached out to Faulk. The small bubble of blood that dripped from Faulk's arm changed color as Jessa touched it. It pulsed through the air, a red swirl, before running back into the woman.

"You will answer anything we ask with 100% accuracy," Jessa said, and Faulk nodded, her normal spark of personality now extinguished.

"Do you know who's been trying to kill me?" I asked, moving to stand next to the pair. Jessa looked up at me from under her dark lashes, eyes fixed with animosity. She was still angry at me for stopping her escape; probably always would be. Didn't matter, I needed her here.

"I don't know, yet," Faulk said, voice as even as slate. "Jessa is the best explanation for the night of your wedding but not the other attempts. We're still working on it."

Jessa glared, mouth pinched.

"Don't you have any leads?" I continued.

"No living ones."

Richard strolled over, power shining in his hungry eyes as he leaned down to stare directly into Faulk's placid eyes. "Are you loyal to me and my family?"

"Yes."

"Have you always been loyal?"

"Yes."

He nodded, straightening. "Is there anything you've been hiding from me? Anything at all that I should know?"

"I wasn't upset to see Natasha die. I should have been; it was my job to protect her."

Hot pinpricks clouded my vision. Next to me, Richard's temper snapped like a whip. He struck out and backhanded Faulk without a second's pause.

She flew back with the force of it, thudding against the wall and sliding down onto her butt, knees bent awkwardly. She sat there like a lump of clay; nothing in her eyes. Nothing but focus on her task, waiting for the next question that she could answer, a puppet on a string.

"Why?" I asked. Queen Natasha had been loved throughout the kingdom, and especially by anyone she worked with. She'd been kind and beautiful, smart and strong. She was the perfect queen, and even when her headaches had stolen her daily life, she'd still fought to be the best queen she could be.

"Natasha wasn't good enough for you," she said, voice even as she glanced up at Richard. "She never did anything to help you expand your reach, never really saw your vision. She held you back. Look how far you've come since her death."

His chest rose and fell haughtily as he took it all in.

"Did you know she was going to die?" His question bellowed through the small space, causing everyone to jump in alarm. Everyone but Faulk who'd lost all emotion the moment she'd offered her blood.

"No," the woman replied evenly. "But I suspected the alchemy, as you know, we talked about that on more than one occasion."

"Thomas," Richard growled. "He got what he deserved."

"Yes." Faulk's voice rang in affirmation.

The two watched each other over the long, drawn-out, pause. I wrinkled my nose, unable to stomach what was likely to come next. If we kept at it, Faulk would probably confess some unrequited love for my father. It made me ill just thinking about those words coming out of that snake.

I turned on him. "Can we be done here? I think we got all we needed from her. Let's move on to the next person."

Richard nodded once, and after eyeing Faulk one last time, stormed from the room. Faulk hadn't exactly done anything wrong, but since she was his number one advisor, the fact she didn't mourn the Queen's death was big news. I glowered down at the woman. "Get up!"

She didn't move.

"Get up," Jessa repeated, and Faulk stood. "This is over. Go back to your normal self. If you could try not to be such a cold-hearted witch, the rest of us would really appreciate it." A small smirk lifted the corner of Jessa's lips and the desire to feel those lips again crashed through me. As if sensing my thoughts, her eyes shot to mine in warning.

"Not happening." Jessa pointed at me, jaw clenching tight. Then she spun on her heel and charged toward her room, slamming the door behind her.

Faulk took several heavy breaths as her cognition returned to her. Her mouth pinched as if she'd just tasted something sour. Her gaze drifted toward Jessa's closed door and she sneered. Then she, too, escaped from the room.

I dropped to the couch, relaxing into the cool leather and rubbing my hands along the sides of my nose, warding off a headache. That had been an interesting reveal. So, it turned out that Faulk really did have something to hide. She idolized Richard for more than just her boss and king. Maybe I shouldn't have been surprised. Maybe deep in our cores, in the places we thought were hidden from the rest of the world, we were all harboring a secret or two.

★

I paced the length of the room, the book in my hand bouncing uselessly against my leg. If I didn't get out of here soon, I swore I was going to lose my mind. Over the last couple of days, Jessa's red alchemy interviews had continued. Unfortunately for me, they rarely happened in our bunker, since only those who knew about me were permitted down here. Of course, I had argued incessantly to go upstairs but still couldn't make any headway with Richard on the issue. He thought I was being unreasonable, but what was so crazy about wanting to get out of this god-forsaken dungeon? Deep in my bones, I ached to get out, almost as much as I ached for the whole truth of my past.

Footsteps clattered down the hallway and the bunker's door swung open. Jessa and Richard entered the room, glowering at each other and barely glancing in my direction. The tension between them was thicker than anything I'd witnessed previously. Something had shifted.

Richard threw his coat on the kitchen table and strode for the refrigerator, rooting around through the drawers. Jessa, she didn't move. She was a changed woman. I saw it the second I met her stormy eyes, looking for the familiar charge between us. But it was gone. It was all gone. She was no longer the wild mare I'd likened to her energy. She'd been broken. My hands clenched into fists, the desire to punch something strong.

"What happened?" I demanded, striding around the couch to where Jessa stood aimlessly by the door.

She shook her head. "You wouldn't care." Slowly, she peeled off her white jacket, revealing the usual gray cottons underneath. Carefully, she hung it on the rack and padded to her room, the door closing silently behind her.

One of my father's guards locked her inside before returning to his post, a silent statute in the corner of the room.

My gaze shot to Richard. "What was that about?"

He bit into a yellow pear, juices running down his chin as he beamed. "Just that things are going well for me. Nothing for you to worry about, son."

I narrowed my eyes and he shrugged, wiping the back of his face with his arm and moseying off to his bedroom. Anger and desperation surged through me at having been left in the dark once again. Letting out a breath, I knocked on Jessa's door, wanting nothing more than to talk to her about whatever the hell was going on. She didn't say a word and I didn't let myself in. Too many lines had been crossed already.

Something huge has happened and you missed it! I chastised myself. *You can't let this continue, not if you're serious about figuring everything out.*

I threw myself back on the couch, staring dully at my surroundings. The white walls, the oak trim and doors, the plush rugs in dark reds and blues. The kitchen had more of a modern look, the bare glass dining table gleaming in the middle of it all.

I squinted, the idea rushing to me. Not just an idea, a solution.

Jumping up, I pounded on my father's door this time.

"What is it?" he called through the metal, voice muffled. Then he swung it open. His face was tired, worn down, but also, happier than I'd seen him in ages. It made my stomach churn to know Jessa felt the opposite.

I cleared my throat. "You know Mom's favorite flowers are, or were, white roses?"

His eyes flashed indignantly. "So?"

"We always had several vases back in the palace. I was thinking maybe we could get some for down here. To liven up the place and to remember Mom."

The request sounded utterly stupid now that I said it out loud, but I held my ground, trying to look as earnest as possible. I sighed. "I'm just, missing her, is all."

And that was the truth.

Richard's expression softened. "That's a great idea."

Relief overtook me, and I nodded, a wide smile taking over my face.

"I'll make a call right away. Is that all? I'm exhausted, Lucas. We've had a lot of success in Nashville and in our interrogations as of late, but it's been a lot of work."

I wanted to know more. But I couldn't let him forget about the roses. "That's all. Get some sleep. Do you want me to make the call?"

I raised a playful eyebrow.

He laughed. "Nice try," he said, and then reached into his pocket, pulling out his slatebook and flashing it at me as he closed the door.

I stepped back, smiling for an entirely different reason, and reveling in the knowledge that, as far as I knew, I still had my secret. Before long, I'd have access to the white roses. It was the kind of organic material I needed. I had used a sheet when I'd worked alchemy on Jessa upstairs, but this was different. It was best to use something natural, regardless of the length of time. The white roses had always been perfect. They would be again. I had tried doing things Richard's way, and it hadn't gotten me any closer to the truth. It was time I stopped complaining about my situation and did something to change it.

★

The guards weren't in the bunker with us very often; they were usually outside the door and upstairs. That helped. My father was still asleep in his room, which also helped. And Jessa was locked away. It meant I didn't have anyone checking up on me, which was perfectly okay with me.

I woke the next morning before the bedside alarm, hastily dressed myself and padded into the main living space. Confirming that there weren't any guards, I smiled. The place was empty and my plan was working.

Case in point, in the center of the glass tabletop stood a tall crystal vase overflowing with white roses.

I snagged one, ripping the stem off an inch below the rose. I tossed the stem into the trash, and taking one last look to make sure I was in the clear, I used the white rose to make myself invisible. As far as I knew, it had been a while since

I'd done it, and I was a little worried it would exhaust me quickly, or worse, not even work at all. But true to form, the white magic did its job. My body and anything touching me faded into nothingness, like sand lost to the wind.

I waited. It didn't take long.

Richard, dressed for the day, exited his bedroom and moved toward the exit, swinging the door open wide to let in a stream of guards. Then he stomped across the living room to pound on Jessa's door. She didn't fight it. She opened up almost immediately, body slumping from the room with a detached, stony expression lining her pale, forlorn face.

"We'll continue where we left off yesterday," he said.

She nodded and followed him from the bunker. I peeled myself off the wall and crept as close as I could without bumping into one of them and giving myself away. Painfully aware of the insane risk I was taking, the rush of adrenaline and magic surged through me, pushing me forward. Once I knew what Richard was doing with my wife, it would be worth all this trouble.

My wife. Why did I keep calling her that?

It was a different me that had married her. A different time. Now, she obviously hated me, barely looking at me and recoiled from my touch. She probably didn't see me as her husband. I was the enemy. I was the predator and she was the prey, the bird in the cage.

I didn't even know if we were on the same side.

Just because I'd convinced my father not to execute her didn't mean it wouldn't happen eventually. But then again, Richard had invested so much time and money into getting the public to accept her during the alchemy trials. As far as they knew, she was still missing. She was still the beloved princess, stolen from her bedroom the night her husband was murdered.

When all of this was over, would he reintroduce us together? I tried to imagine what that would mean, but came up short. Would we become partners again? Doubtful. I shook the questions away as we stepped out onto the military base. The fresh morning air blasted my skin, smelling of ozone and smoke and rain, but I didn't care. I breathed it in, filling my lungs to the brim, relishing in it.

As a group, we navigated along the brick buildings until we approached a massive helicopter. It was the kind that could hold a bunch of soldiers all at once. Everyone climbed inside and I quickly scrambled in after them before someone slid the door shut. I assessed the space, worry pinning me in place. How was I going to pull this off? They were strapping themselves into seats, not something I could do in my current state. What if I sat down and someone else sat on me? The chopper was being boarded by a stream of soldiers. I jumped out of their way and eventually settled into the farthest corner, sitting with my back against the wall, fingers gripping at the smooth metal wall. I'd have to hold on for dear life if this chopper did anything out of the ordinary. This had better be worth it.

My heartbeat pumped wildly in my ears as I waited, eyes lingering on Jessa, on her sadness. A minute later the chopper purred to life and we took off, cutting through the brilliant red sunrise. The machine's vibrations soothed me and I relaxed. *No, don't let your guard down.* I gripped the rose in my hand, the petals soft against my clammy fingers. What if this was a huge mistake? As far as I knew, I couldn't go long as invisible before the magic would become too much and I'd succumb to sleep. If that happened, I would become visible and my secret would be revealed.

But ... I should have been feeling the effects of that by now, and I wasn't, not even a little bit. How much had I practiced with white alchemy over the last year? The question burned me up, bringing more curiosities to my mind.

I studied Jessa's profile, wondering if maybe she really was telling the truth about everything that had happened to us. Had I turned against my father?

Before long, we landed in a sprawling parking lot. I heaved a sigh of relief to have made it this far and jumped out after the rest of the group. Long cracks had split fissures into the gray pavement, tall weeds growing between the divides. For early February, it was surprisingly warm out, the sun now higher in the sky and pressing down. Or maybe it was just my adrenaline kicking in that made heat rise in my cheeks. I longed to remove my jacket, knowing that was a terrible idea. I had to keep my hands as free as possible. I ignored the sweat gathering along my spine, left hand gripping the rose in my pocket harder than necessary, and trudged after Richard and Jessa.

They entered a one-story red-brick building, so old it looked like it should have been demolished decades ago. Leyland Elementary School was written in boxy script across the entrance, the Y crooked and hanging awkwardly by a single bolt. The brick had crumbled in several places and the railing that lined the steps was so rusted entire parts were missing. What was someone as regal as my father doing in a place like this?

"How many today?" Jessa's question echoed down the steps as they disappeared behind a pair of double doors. The doors swung shut before I could follow.

I inwardly cursed and scrambled up the steps, waiting for someone new to open the door again so I could follow. I didn't have to wait long. Faulk ascended the steps with no less than ten alchemists in her wake. I was so used to seeing her with Royal Officers that the sight of Guardians sent a shockwave through me. They were dressed in their specialized military uniforms, not just the black outfits I remembered from the palace. They had a rainbow of glittering stones embedded into their gear and helmets with shiny visors. Some had their visors pulled down, covering their faces. They looked nothing short of extraordinary and terrifying.

I followed, figuring that where Jessa and Richard had gone, Faulk would soon be joining them. I was right. We entered a large room with scuffed white tile and children's drawings perched on the walls. From the looks of it, it had probably been the school's cafeteria. Sitting along the edges were people grouped together. Families. West American citizens, I had no doubt. Had they taken refuge here during the attack? They huddled together, wide-eyed and afraid.

My ears buzzed as I took it all in. Richard's voice boomed, finishing up some kind of speech that I'd hardly paid attention to. Boots echoed as Faulk marched into the room.

Jessa got to work.

I stood off to the side, both fascinated and horrified as I watched Richard's plan unfold in front of me.

"Hold out your hand," a guard barked, nodding toward a man in threadbare clothing. Taking heavy breaths, the man did as he was told. Knife gleaming, Faulk cut a thin line into the man's palm. Jessa touched the blood with the tip of her finger. The red twirled into the space between them, and the man's eyes bulged. A few nearby observers gasped as Jessa sent the red alchemy back into the man.

"Repeat after me," she said, voice cracking. "I hereby swear my total allegiance and devotion to New Colony and His Royal Highness, King Richard."

The man repeated the words and Jessa moved on to the next person. One by one, Jessa secured loyalty to my father. With her power, these prisoners of war did exactly as she asked. The second they repeated after her, they physically changed. They transformed from reluctant, afraid, or defiant, to malleable and agreeable; the kind of citizens a king could only dream of. They gazed at my father like he was their savior.

Some of the adults waiting their turn held on tight to their crying children.

Others resisted.

The guardians used their brute strength to force those people forward. Jessa worked quickly, Richard at her side the entire time. As she moved from family to family, I could make out the anguish in her eyes. It killed her to control them like this. Someone who was part of the Resistance would hate to comply with such a task. The Resistance…if Richard was willing to do this to West Americans, eventually he'd be doing the same thing to his own citizens. What better way to cut the Resistance down than right where they grew?

It was genius.

I doubled over, clutching my knees and fighting the rush of blood prickling in my brain. It was too much. These people were no longer free, and they didn't even have a choice. Was it worth it to be in power if it meant controlling people's choices like this? How could my father think this was okay? This wasn't the kind of king I wanted to be.

And yet this will be your legacy.

I twisted the angry thought around in my mind, unsure of what to do with it. I couldn't just forget it, couldn't push it away. Did I file it under "necessary evil" or just plain "evil"? A bead of sweat trickled down my spine.

"Don't touch us!" A woman screamed shrilly, clutching a toddler to her chest. She stood against the wall. Her son, wrapped around her waist, erupted into tears. She ran a trembling hand down his matted hair, shushing him gently.

Jessa, only feet away from the pair, held out a dejected hand. "If you don't fight it, it will make it easier for him."

"You're sick!" The woman stumbled to the side, shaking her head, her eyes round circles of fear. They flicked toward the exit, right near where I was standing. She didn't see me, looked right past me, but something inside reached out to her, longing to be able to help, and I took a step forward.

"You don't want to do that," Jessa begged. "Please, don't run. You know what will happen if you do."

"How can you do this to people?" the woman replied. "I won't let you touch my son. He's innocent. You'll hurt him; you'll scramble his brain. You scrambled my husband's brain yesterday! You saw what it did to him; not everyone can handle your sick blood magic."

"I'm so sorry," Jessa said low, shoulders caving in. "More than you know."

But the woman didn't respond. She took off for the door, feet slapping the tiles, her son still clutched to her middle.

"Don't!" Jessa yelled after her, but it was too late.

A single bullet ripped through the cafeteria, shattering the silence and sending the inhabitants into frightened hysterics. The woman fell, her body crumpling to the ground. Her son flew from her arms, bawling hysterically.

Blood pooled around her as she held her stomach.

Faulk stood just beyond, her gun raised and a sick smile on her lips.

"Let me heal her." Jessa pushed past Faulk but she didn't get far. Richard ripped her back toward him, holding her in place with a grim expression.

"No," he said, voice booming. "She made her choice."

Jessa let out a sob as the entire room watched the woman on the floor. She bled out in less than a minute. The child that had fallen from her arms continued to wail as he climbed back onto his mother's body, her blood soaking him. He couldn't have been older than two. His face was a red ball of tears and snot, his blonde hair disheveled, the blood turning it pink. His chubby fingers clutched her vacant face, body shaking.

I stepped closer, the urge to comfort him overwhelming. Someone needed to do something! One of the alchemists, a tall man with the visor covering his face, pried the child off his mother without an ounce of sympathy, dumping the boy onto a nearby family.

"Shut him up before I have to do it for you," the man barked.

The family scrambled to calm the traumatized boy, but it was no use; the boy only grew louder, reaching toward the body. "Mamma!"

"Let me calm him," Jessa begged, tears streaking down her face.

"He's of little importance," Richard replied, not even bothering to look at the boy. He pointed to the next family in the row. "We have work to do."

And so they continued on, turning person after person into loyal fans of New Colony and the royal family. Anyone who resisted, anyone who tried to run, was murdered by Faulk without a second thought or a shred of mercy. If she had any remorse over taking innocent lives with such brutally, she certainly didn't show it, but seemed to revel in it, victorious.

Her glee-filled eyes mirrored her King's.

Exhaustion wore me down, starting as a trickle, but soon becoming a downpour. It tugged at my eyes and fell heavy through my limbs. I squeezed the velvety rose in my pocket, knowing I couldn't take any more. I couldn't do this. I slipped from the room, rushing for the nearest empty classroom.

Crawling into a dusty closet and closing the door, I dropped the invisibility and fell into a mind-numbing sleep.

✱

Thud, thud, thud, the whirling sound of rudders woke me with a start. I scrambled for the white rose, grateful it wasn't all gray, yet. In the dim light of the closet, I could barely make out the white stands of magic as they swirled out of the flower. The magic seeped into my skin and the invisibility washed over me, covering me like a blanket. I jumped from my spot, ignoring the pulsing ache in my body, and sprinted from the room, sped through the dank hallway, and outside onto the pavement. The blinding sun was setting over the horizon, a wash of citrus hues painting the sky. Squinting, I could make out the huge chopper my father used had already lifted into the sky. Terror ripped through me like razor blades and I sunk to my knees, gritting my teeth.

What would happen when they got back to base and I was missing? Better yet, how was I supposed to survive out here, defenseless and hungry? It was a warzone, after all, and no way everyone here had been turned.

Boots clomped in the distance, but I couldn't see anyone. Figuring they were on the other side of the building, I took off. Relief poured over me when I spotted Faulk and her people climbing into a second chopper. I sped forward, barely making it inside in time. I barely dodged the soldier who was in charge of closing the door, and then not seeing a better place to hide, I pressed myself against the door and prayed it would be an easy flight.

The occupants seemed tired, all buckled-in and closed-lipped. Holding my breath, I slid down to sit on the metal floor. I just needed to get my breath under control, my heart to stop beating in rapid-fire succession. After a few minutes, we lifted and I let out a long slow breath, studying the men and women surrounding me.

Were they traumatized by what they were doing? Did they agree with it? Or had they been changed by Jessa already and didn't care either way?

Their faces were unreadable, some even still covered by black, shiny visors. Maybe it didn't matter, maybe they were as loyal as anyone in this army.

My muscles ached and I longed to stretch my legs as I counted down the minutes. Finally, mercifully, we landed back at base camp without any problems. The red brick buildings, lined in neat little rows, both beckoned me and frightened me.

I slipped out of the helicopter. The second soldier opened the door and moved out of the way as the people in the chopper streamed from it, boots clomping in succession as they headed in different directions. I needed to get back to the bunker before my father realized I was gone. And even that seemed like a feat. Sucking in a breath of chilled air and helicopter exhaust, I sprinted toward the garage with our bunker beneath.

Just as I was about to enter, something in the corner of my eye caught my attention. Two familiar people were arguing, their voices rising above each other. They stood only twenty feet from the garage, their body language tight and angry.

Curiosity got the better of me and I made the detour, creeping forward on the balls of my feet, hand still gripping the rose in my pocket. I needed to be quick.

"I saw you go into his room." Callie's normally sugary voice had turned sour, arms folded over her chest as she stared at her companion. "I saw you do it that night at the orphanage, so don't even try to lie to me." Her Guardian armor gleamed with crystals in the setting sun, giving her an even fiercer appearance.

My body prickled, realizing they were arguing about me.

Celia glared down at the girl, nose turned up in disgust. She wore a white fur-lined coat, her red hair styled in loose curls around her face. Her tongue clicked as she thought of what to say. "It doesn't matter what you saw, whatever your name is. Nobody cares. It's really none of your business."

"The hell it isn't!" Callie stepped forward, pointing a finger at Celia and pressing into Celia's coat. "Jessa is my friend and she's *married* to Lucas, not you."

"So what?" Celia laughed, turning away as if bored by the accusation. "He doesn't remember her."

"When they find her, you'd better believe they're going to get back together. They love each other. Stop trying to get between them."

Celia smiled, eyes gleaming in victory. "You really are out of the loop, aren't you?"

"What are you talking about?" Callie glared.

"I take it you aren't one of the alchemists going over the border this week?"

"I haven't yet," Callie replied suspiciously.

"Maybe you should ask your friends who's been helping them over there." Celia rolled her eyes and turned around, hair whipping in the wind like a raging fire as she stormed away.

"Everyone knows you're a dirty gold digger!" Callie yelled after her, voice furious. She huffed, dropped the visor on her helmet, and ran in the opposite direction.

My body still tingled with what I'd heard. Making sense of everything hadn't been easy, but that argument had certainly helped. Callie was Jessa's friend, but she could also vouch for her, too. That had to count for something.

Richard and Jessa appeared from around the corner, tired gazes set on the bunker. I balked and ran full force to beat them to the door. Rushing inside, I dodged the guard, waiting with the door opened, and hurried down the staircase. The door at the bottom was closed, so I had to wait. Nervous energy pulsed through me, my hand tight on the rose as Richard and Jessa descended the stairs. The guard opened the door for them, and I slipped in right after they did. Then, I went straight to my room, where I'd mercifully had the foresight to leave my door open this morning. I didn't give myself time to think it through or to debate it. I just jumped into the bathroom, closed the door, and turned on the shower.

Nobody came knocking.

I breathed in deep shuddering breaths, letting the stress wash off of me as I undressed and ducked into the respite of hot water. I washed away the adrenaline of the day, sorting though everything I'd witnessed, muscles relaxing, breath slowing to a steady cadence. But even as I relaxed, I knew, no matter how hot the water was or how long I stayed under the pelting stream, I'd never be able to clean the images from my mind.

The crying toddler, his plump body frantic for his mother.

Her bloodied, broken body.

And all the people with their glossy-eyed allegiance.

These were the images that clawed at me, that poured through me like the water poured over me. Now, more than ever, I believed Jessa's outrageous story of our past together. Memories of it or not, there was something rotten about this war, and as much as I hated to admit it, it was my father who lay at the center of the decay.

FOURTEEN
JESSA

The interrogations, the manipulations, the forcing people to bow down to Richard against their will, it all continued. *I let it continue.*

It was either that, or they'd kill more innocent people.

I'd become the thing I'd always feared. I was the puppet, the weapon, and the right hand doing the bidding of an evil family. And yes, I had decided to start thinking of Lucas as evil, as well. After he'd held me down, silencing and hiding me from my sister, forcing me to stay in New Colony, I couldn't think of him as anything but evil. He'd ruined my chance to break free.

The Lucas I knew, the one I loved, the one I'd been through so much with, would have never done that.

I finally accepted that Lucas was gone.

I was living with a different Lucas now, one who was in league with his father. One who may not be as bad as Richard now, but that was only because he was in hiding. I feared the inevitable. One day, he would not only catch up to Richard, but he would surpass him in the amount of destruction he would cause. The Heart Family wouldn't stop at West America. This was only the beginning.

I shivered, my heart breaking deeper than I'd ever thought possible. How had the sweet man I'd fallen for turned into this? I closed my eyes, pushing back the tears.

"Focus!" Faulk snapped, ripping me from my downward spiral.

I blinked up at her. "Can't we be done?" I begged. "We've been at this all day. I can hardly keep my eyes open."

She smirked, folding her arms over her chest and rocking back on her heels. "I thought you'd have enjoyed this respite from our mission in Nashville."

I looked up at the plain white ceiling and sighed. "Fine. One more and then I need to get some food and sleep."

She clucked her tongue and motioned toward the steel door to our right. We waited in Richard's specially-appointed interrogation room, the same gray box I'd spent time in before being transferred to the bunker. I still didn't fully understand that move, but knew it had something to do with Lucas, with his memory, and with my loyalties. Didn't matter.

I focused on the task at hand. Between these walls, it was my job to sort through the minds of the New Colony operatives. One by one, with Faulk at my side, we searched for a spy. Each time some unsuspecting victim entered that door, I held my breath, praying it wasn't a fellow Resistance member, or even someone who could be misinterpreted to be Resistance. Because as much as I wanted to know who'd hurt Lucas, I was more worried about hurting *my people*, or harming more innocents.

The door opened, and Branson walked in, eyes focused and clear as they settled on me. He nodded once, confirming he knew what was about to happen. For all the unsuspecting people who'd walked through that door, he wasn't one of them.

No. My mind reeled and my body tensed. There had to be another way.

"Take a seat," Faulk said, nodding at the metal folding chair across from where I sat, waiting to ruin his life. He followed the directions, relaxed. He was dressed casually in black cottons and scuffed boots. His broad shoulders pulled at his shirt as he rolled out his shoulders, breathing deep.

"No problem," he said, smiling conspiratorially up at the woman. "I understand this is a formality and everyone will get their turn. Now is as good as any time."

Did he have a plan? A way to get out of this? A gnawing pain rolled through my stomach, and I imagined asking Faulk for a break, but it would be no use. I eyed the three guards standing by the wall behind Branson, eyes narrowed, backs straight, hands resting on the guns in their holsters.

How long will it take before they fire those guns?

Sasha had said I could trust Branson, that he was on our side. Branson's ties to the Resistance had been my suspicion since the first moment I'd met him. He was a good man, through and through. Good men wouldn't condone the crimes we were committing on West American citizens. Good men would stand up and fight. Was that what he was about to do here?

I gulped. Faulk split an inch of his tanned skin with a small blade. Branson didn't even flinch. Our eyes met in solidarity as I reached out to his wounded arm and tapped a drop of his warm blood with the tip of my finger. The red danced between us and with a single thought, I sent it back into him. His eyes grew hazy, arms settling at his sides, blood falling in long drops, splashing on the concrete floor.

I knew how this worked. I'd done it enough times. I would have about ten minutes before the numbing magic would wear off, that assuming I wasn't forced to alter his mind permanently with some kind of blood oath like what I was doing to the people of Nashville. But no, these were interrogations, through and through. I would ask questions, get answers, and that would be all.

And we wouldn't even need five minutes to get the job done. Heck, in this case, we may not even need one.

"You will happily answer all of Faulk's questions with 100% accuracy and truth," I said, my voice foreign in my ears. Then I sat back, fists clenched and heart quickening, as Faulk began her questions.

"Are you loyal to King Richard and his mission?"

Branson didn't hesitate. "No." The word hung in the air, final.

Faulk sucked in a breath, anger rocketing through her. She slapped him across the face. "How dare you!"

He was calm as he looked back to her, expression pleasant, simply waiting for more questions.

She kneeled in front of him, arms folding behind her back, teeth bared in disgust. "Are you Resistance?"

"Yes."

She stiffened, and then slowly, she smiled, her face smoothing, her eyes sparkling with delight. Goosebumps prickled up my arms and I stepped back against the wall, trying to catch my breath. *Click*, the guards readied their weapons.

"And who else is Resistance?"

He pointed to me. "Jessa."

"I know. And who else?"

"Jasmine was. I don't know any other names."

Her scream pierced the room and she leaned into his face.

"How is that possible?"

"We kept everything separate, all of us in the palace answering to Jasmine."

"But there were others in the palace who were Resistance? How many?"

"There are, but I don't know who or how many."

"Guess," she spat, the reflection of the florescent light above shining off her immaculate blonde bun, lighting her head like a halo.

"If I had to guess, I would say anywhere from five to ten."

She stood, cracking her neck and knuckles, mouth grim, the anger rolling off of her in waves. "The traitors," she whispered. "I will find them and I will kill them all."

She continued on for a while, asking question after incessant question, the need to needle out every small piece of information from his mind driving her. I stood back motionless, silent tears running down my face. She would kill him. And even though he didn't know much, he would somehow reveal too much. She would find a way to root more information from him. More people would die. And if she didn't get to them today, eventually, I would. Eventually, they'd walk through that door, just as Branson had.

His eyes flickered over to me for the briefest of moments, a flutter so quick, I barely caught it. Heart racing, palms growing sweaty, I realized with sudden and absolute clarity that Branson's red alchemy had just worn off. The timeline made sense. Faulk had so many questions. Ten minutes had slipped by unnoticed.

She froze, tilting her head, eyes squinting. "Jessa." She turned to me. "Get him again. I'm not finished here."

"Too late." The words fell from my mouth, barely audible, lost in the sudden crash. Branson was out of his metal folding chair in an instant, picking it up and throwing it at Faulk. It hit her with a crack and fell to the floor with a clatter. She staggered, falling to her knees. He was quick to move on to the guards. He attacked them faster than lightening and with the force of a bulldozer, his years of skill and practice kicking in.

"Catch!" he called to me, tossing a gun into my outstretched hands. It was heavy and detached, but I steadied it.

"Shoot him!" Faulk yelled at me. I looked at her with a sneer. Why didn't *she* shoot him? And then it dawned on me that in the middle of all the commotion, he'd managed to disarm her, as well. The sight of her gun missing from its belt sent a wave of triumph over me. Maybe I should shoot her instead?

I hesitated. Branson didn't.

He grabbed me, pulling me close and aiming a gun at Faulk and her guards, all now lying injured on the floor.

"I'm sorry about this," he whispered low in my ear. "Just go along with it. I'm getting us out of here."

He then wrenched me against him, turning his gun on me.

"Come closer and I'll kill her," he said. "You wouldn't want to lose your precious red alchemist now that you know how powerful she is."

Faulk's face drained of color—he was right.

Days ago I'd been facing the execution block, but now everything had changed. Richard had gotten a taste of what he could do with me, and he wouldn't be very happy to kill me and lose his greatest weapon yet.

"You wouldn't dare!"

"Oh yes, I most certainly would." He cocked the gun and even though I knew what he was doing, my body automatically reacted, trying to fight him off. It was no use; he was way too strong, pinning me to his massive body with ease.

"Hide your gun," he whispered as we moved for the exit. "You might need it soon."

He shoved us out the door and into the hallway.

Chaos swept through the area in a cacophony of angry shouts as he shuffled us down the narrow space. The entire time, the cool barrel of his gun pressed against my temple. My heart beat so loudly, I heard the blood whooshing through me, a reminder that I might not make it out of this. I held my breath and forced myself to stay calm.

I could use the red alchemy. His wound wasn't healed. It would be easy.

No.

I had always liked Branson. He was one of the only good ones left. Besides, I hadn't seen Lily or Jose since arriving here, not once. Branson might be my only chance. I had to trust that he knew what he was doing.

Faulk and her people circled us with guns raised as Branson led us to the exit, using his hip to push it open. Pelting rain assaulted the earth, some of it splashing my face, spreading cold everywhere. Night had fallen, and freezing air filtered into the hallway fog.

"Let her go!" Faulk barked. "She doesn't belong to you."

He laughed. "She doesn't belong to *anyone*."

"Actually, she's the property of New Colony." Faulk's eyes were bright, her mouth set in a thin line. She stepped closer. "You're going to get her killed."

"She'd rather that than be your slave."

He said the words as if he knew it were true, as if he knew me better than I knew myself. And I realized, he might be right. The thought of losing my life settled over me, and a strange sense of peace rose inside. I didn't want to die, but faced with it now, I'd rather die than continue on the path of harming others.

Branson shoved me out into the rain behind him, still using me as a human shield. Rain slid down my face and arms in rivulets of ice, making the world seem muffled. I sucked in several sharp breaths, blinking away the water.

"It's going to be okay. They won't kill you," he said against my hair.

More and more soldiers from all over the base stomped in, weapons trained on us, as Branson and I trudged through the mud and toward the airfield. Faulk followed closer than anyone else, drenched by the rain, gaze fixed and determined.

"What do you think you're going to do?" she cackled.

"Yeah, what's your plan here," I said low, meeting Branson's eyes. He squinted against the water that ran down his face, breathing deep.

"Just trust me," he replied.

"You're going to give us a pilot and a way off this base," Branson yelled back, his voice sure as anything.

"I don't think so," she replied coolly.

He pushed the gun harder against my face, and I yelped.

"I *do* think so!" he screamed.

We shuffled through the puddles and mud, inching closer to our destination. Worry found its way to my core with each step. But also, a flickering hope rose inside me; what if he pulled this off? What if he got us out of here?

Maybe, I didn't have to die. Maybe, I was minutes away from freedom. The idea was so sweet I could taste it.

A chopper came into view and my heart leapt. This was it.

"Stop right there!" King Richard's voice bellowed through the stormy night, slicing through me like a knife. The crowd of armed soldiers parted as the King ran forward, water sloshing out around his black shoes. He was dressed in nothing but a white button-up shirt, and slacks. The clothing stuck to his body like a second skin.

"We're leaving," Branson said. "If you don't let us out of here, I'll shoot her."

Richard shook his head. "What makes you think I'll agree to this?" He laughed, his teeth flashing white in the darkness. "You should know me better than that, Branson."

"I know she's nothing to you if she's dead."

"That's true," he replied. Rain dripped down his chiseled face, but he hardly seemed to notice or care. He stared at us with a strange intensity. "But I would rather she die than work for my enemy."

The air knocked out of me so fast that my knees became weak.

Of course, it was true. Richard didn't care about me as a human; he cared about me as a red alchemist, as a weapon. He would never allow his most powerful weapon to end up in the wrong hands. Never.

Branson cursed and his body instantly tensed against mine, perhaps realizing the gravity of his mistake.

"It's okay," I said to him. We could figure this out.

"Stay strong," he growled into my ear as he raised his gun.

Then he shoved me down into the gravel. I landed on my hands and knees, mud and rocks and water flying. Guns shots blared, and Branson fell to the earth next to me, already dead. His blood splattered against the splotches of mud, mixing with the earth. I screamed, crawling back, my cries garbled in the sound of rain and shouting.

"Help the King first!" a voice pounded through the chaos, and an alchemist kneeled down next to Richard.

My mind tried to make sense of what I was seeing. The King had fallen? When? Everything seemed to be in slow motion and happening all at once.

Richard clutched his arm, crimson blood blooming against his white shirt. An alchemist was quick to use healing magic, the green ribbons twirling around Richard's injury. His face relaxed, and I knew he would be just fine. Branson wouldn't be so lucky. I looked away, hot tears burning my cheeks. They were quickly lost to the rain, like so much else on this awful night.

My eyes scanned the ground, noticing a few more bodies that had been caught in the crossfire. Blonde hair stained red shone from one of them, an arm awkwardly bent beneath. My entire body stilled, burning with a prickly sense of understanding.

Faulk.

I tilted my head, so overcome by the surreal sensation of seeing her dead body right in front of me. It wasn't the Faulk I knew, the determined woman with the flawless appearance and cruel center. It was a shell of her, only a shell, entirely broken in the end. A small red dot was centered on her forehead, a trickling of blood falling into unblinking eyes. They glowed like two full moons. Blood moons.

I squeezed my eyes shut and rolled to the side, fingers clutching at clumps of cold mud, and violently lost the contents of my stomach.

★

I thought sleep would never come, but somehow it did. It wasn't a blessing but another curse, accompanied by tormented dreams, darkness so thick and heavy it threatened to destroy everything, to stifle the breath in my lungs. It left me sweaty and panicked, gripping at thin white sheets.

"Shush," a deep voice whispered against my neck. "It's okay. You're okay."

My body stiffened as awareness surfaced. Two arms wrapped around my body, a hard chest pressed against my back, and hot breath tangled in my hair.

"Lucas?" I croaked. My voice burned, and I swallowed hard. The tears came again, salty and thick. I couldn't hold back the sobs, and wondered if they'd ever stop. The wound was too deep. They wet my face, reminding me of being outside in that rain, of the blood, and the death, and just how much death would still come because of my *life*.

"It's okay. I've got you," he said. "Go back to sleep."

I wanted to fight him, shove him off, tell him to get away, but my body betrayed me and the comfort was far too good to pass up. I relaxed, eyes shutting as if my eyelids were weighted down. I sighed, breath steadying, and before I could process any more thoughts, I fell back into the darkness.

Later, I woke with a start, reaching around the bed.

I was alone.

Had I dreamed him? Had Lucas really come in here and held me in the middle of the night? My brain filtered through the thoughts, sleep giving way to lucidity, and I knew that he had. It wasn't a dream. But, why? He wasn't supposed to do things like that. He was supposed to be the enemy. No. He wouldn't have come in—it must have been a dream. That was the logical answer.

I rolled over on my pillow and breathed in, the scent of sandalwood and grass and something else, something so entirely Lucas, filled me up, soothing and heart-breaking. I held it there for several long minutes despite my better judgment. He *had* been here. Maybe he'd changed…

Enough.

I jumped from the warm sheets, tossing them to the floor. I couldn't be weak. I needed to be stronger than this. Stepping into the scalding hot shower, I allowed the water to wash away any lingering scent of Lucas as quickly as possible.

✦

"Let me guess," I said, sliding into the chair of the ghastly interrogation room. I looked up at a man I hardly knew, but his was a face I would recognize anywhere. He had the same features as his daughter, Celia. "You're the new Faulk?"

He raised an eyebrow. "I'm taking over where she left off."

"Because she's dead," I supplied. "Don't need to tip-toe around it. I was there."

"Yes." His expression turned sour, two red eyebrows arching over amber eyes. "She's dead." He straightened in his black suit and tie, oozing confidence.

"How very convenient for you." I cocked my head, satisfied when his cheeks grew red.

"Let's just focus on the task at hand," he replied. "We have orders to go through all the alchemists and continue from there."

I barked out a quick laugh. "And what about the thousands more in Nashville that haven't been brainwashed yet? There's only one of me, you know."

"We'll get to them in time. The King thinks it's more important to make sure we don't have any more situations like Branson's. We're spending a few more days here, conducting more interviews."

My stomach fell. There would be more. The second Lily or Jose walked in that door, I would be facing my worst horror all over again.

"Interviews. That's one way to put it."

I eyed him, up and down, thrilled to be taking my anger out on him.

"What's your name?" I pressed, the question coming out like an accusation.

"I'm a Duke," he replied shortly. "Mark Addington. And I

don't answer to the likes of you. I'm in charge here. No more attitude."

I grinned slyly. "Okay, Duke, why don't we start this interrogation with you and your precious little family? Your daughter did attack me, in case you've already forgotten. I think that's reason enough to question her, don't you think?"

He blanched, thrown off. Something murderous flashed in his eyes. I held his gaze for a long moment before turning to smile nonchalantly at the three Royal Officers standing watch. Not one made eye contact.

"You have something to hide," I said, leaning back in my chair and smirking. "It's painfully obvious. I'm surprised you showed your weakness so quickly. Faulk always knew better than that."

"I don't know what you're talking about," he snapped. "You'd be smart to watch your mouth. Faulk was a lot of things, but I won't be as kind to you as Faulk was."

"You call that kind?" I raised an eyebrow. "I'm not afraid of you."

"You should be."

"Why? In case you couldn't tell, I no longer have anything to lose."

He stood, pointing a finger in my face. "I'll be bringing in our first appointment shortly. Behave!" Then he stormed from the room, slamming the metal door with a clang. I crossed my arms and tapped my black boot against the smooth floor, replaying the scene.

Curious.

What was Mark Addington hiding?

FIFTEEN

SASHA

Enough was enough. I still couldn't find my array of stones, the color so precious to me it was like water to a fish or air to a bird. They'd never shown up after the evacuation, which didn't make sense. Someone had gotten them before I'd had a chance, so where did they go? I'd been patient, had listened when Nathan Scott advised me to hold off jumping to conclusions, but I couldn't hold my tongue any longer. Most of the soldiers tolerated me, some even liked me, but enough sent me hateful looks and muttered obscenities whenever I was near, that I couldn't go on pretending.

Someone had tried to sabotage me.

I stalked across the mess hall, hands fisted at my sides, eyes zeroed on a group of soldiers who'd glowered at me and whispered among themselves the second I'd walked in the door. They were also the idiots who'd cornered me that day while jogging, threatening me because of their prejudice against my magic. I refused to put up with their intolerance any longer.

I slammed my palms down on their table, rattling their bowls of stew. All three of them stood, glaring down at me. The youngest of the group, an ordinary-looking guy with buzzed hair and muddy brown eyes, also happened to be the mouthiest. He stepped into my space, sneering.

"What makes you think you can come over here, huh?"

I scowled at him. "Was it you?"

Realization dawned in his eyes and he smirked, stepping back and nodding to his friends. "Was what me?" His voice came out innocent, and his friends laughed.

"Which one of you fools tried to sabotage me? Who took my crystals?"

The oldest of the group closed in on me, breath reeking of alcohol. I didn't know where he got it and why he was drinking it in the middle of the day, but it sent a shiver down my spine. He flexed, tanned and tattooed muscles popping.

"You missing your little rocks, ya? Is that what this is about?" He cackled. "I also notice you're missing your two body guards. Not very smart of you, Sasha, to come over here all alone."

I tensed my jaw, ready to fight if it came to that. It was true, Mastin was meeting me any minute for lunch and I didn't know where Tristan was at the moment. Actually, I didn't know what he was up to most of the time, these days. But there were men and women all over this dining hall who could step in, and more importantly, the stew had a colorful array of vegetables. I'd be fine.

"I want my crystals." I sent each of the men my most menacing look. "Return them to me, or pay the price."

This sent them into a fit of laughter and hoots. The younger of the group put a sweaty hand on my bicep and I froze, itching to rip his filthy hand off of me.

"All I can say is you're not going to see those crystals again."

"Is that a confession?" I challenged.

He tilted his head, leaning in to whisper in my ear. "I'm pretty sure I saw someone throw them into the fire, but damn it, I can't remember who it was."

He patted me once and turned back to his meal. The other two men smirked, the older one chewing on his lip and traveling his eyes up and down my body in a way that made me want to either punch him or hurl, probably both.

"Sasha!" Mastin called out, striding through the mess hall. "There you are. Are you ready to get something to eat?" He stopped short when he saw the men, now returned to their table, but who were still peering up at me with distain in their eyes. The energy between the four of us was charged with such animosity, it didn't take a genius to pick up on it.

"You okay?" Mastin gently touched my elbow.

I exhaled, trying to relax. So, these men had destroyed my crystals? I wouldn't let that stop me. And I wouldn't let them get to me any longer. Nathan Scott said more crystals were coming. Next time, I'd keep them with me instead of in the armory.

I sent the group one final glare and then plastered a sickly sweet smile on my face, turning to Mastin.

"I'm great. Let's eat."

★

I stared down at the sidewalk, watching my shadow move beneath me, as my thoughts spun. I was upset about what had happened at lunch, sure, but it was thoughts of Tristan that were really bothering me.

I was losing my best friend.

He'd distanced himself from me, whether he acknowledged it or not. I felt the ache in my gut, like something was missing. I would turn to smirk at him over one thing or another, but lately, he wasn't smirking back. He barely even looked in my direction anymore. The truth of our crumbling foundation lingered in the subtle movements of his body, in the way his expression closed down whenever Mastin was around. I told myself that this was only natural, friends grew apart all the time. And anyway, we had already been apart for ages after I'd left to be an undercover operative, so it wasn't like I should be so upset. I should be used to the distance. Maybe Tristan didn't really see me as his friend anymore, maybe he hadn't for a long time and I'd stupidly assumed we could get back to the way we used to be.

I ran my hand through my hair, huffing in annoyance.

"What's going on in that brain of yours?" Mastin asked, squeezing my hand gently.

It felt like there was a rock in my stomach, the stew I'd just scarfed down curdling. Our boots slapped the cracked sidewalk as we walked back from what had become our new mess hall. The mess hall that was basically an old abandoned grocery store, cleared of the shelves. Tables had been set up in neat rows down the middle and the building had quickly become the gathering place for the crew out here. A crew that still shot me withering glances every so often.

"What do you mean?" I returned lamely.

"There's something going on with you." Mastin shrugged. "I keep trying to figure you out, but just when I think I do, you change."

I winked. "Doesn't that just mean I'm mysterious? Don't guys like that?" I was avoiding the question, and quite brilliantly. Maybe.

"Mysterious is definitely a good word to describe you." He sighed, unrelenting. "But I also want to make sure you're okay."

"I'm okay."

He frowned. "It's just that ever since you and I started dating, and believe me, it's been great on my end…"

"What?"

"Well, ever since we started dating, you've seemed, I dunno, distant? Sad? Something just isn't right."

I held my breath for a moment, trying to think of the right thing to say. "I'm fine." The words fell flat. "I'm just really worried about my family. Jessa's stuck over there." I pointed east. "And this war is crazy. I guess it's a lot to take in."

Liar. It's not just about family unless Tristan is also the family you're referring to.

The thunderous sound of a military aircraft pierced the sky, and tension at its arrival ran through the camp like a tidal wave. I reached up, instinctively running my fingers along the stone necklace, even though most were sickly gray. I would be able to replenish everything as soon as the next arrival came and I couldn't wait.

I vowed to never be without my tools again.

Mastin automatically rested his hand on the gun in his holster. And as the aircraft flew closer, he relaxed. It was only an airplane, not an enemy jet.

"It's one of ours," he yelled, voice booming over the area. "Stand down!"

I smiled, knowing more of my stones might be on board!

He ordered the men around him, many much older than his twenty years, with complete ease. His voice rang out with confidence, naturally drawing attention. It was one of the most attractive things about him. Appreciation purred through me as I watched the man take action. The more I got to see him in his element, the more I understood why he was one of the youngest ranking officers. He had been bred for this life. Literally.

He marched off, and not wanting to be left out, I caught up to him quickly. "What are they doing here?" I asked, pointing to the airplane.

"No," he muttered under his breath. "They weren't supposed to get here until tonight. I wanted more time..."

My eyes narrowed on his sheepish expression, on the way his hands were fisted at his sides and his gaze didn't meet my own. "Who are you talking about?"

His face hardened, looking over at me. "Please don't shoot the messenger."

I glowered. I wasn't shooting anyone, but it didn't mean I wasn't about to open up the full force on my magic if he didn't open his stupidly handsome mouth and start talking! "What? What aren't you telling me?"

"I wanted to tell you, but I was ordered to keep it to myself."

The realization sunk deep. "This is about Weapon X, isn't it?"

His eyes flashed, mouth dropping open. "How do you know about that?"

Yeah, I wasn't going to answer that one. I didn't want him to know I'd been eavesdropping on his private conversation. But then again, it involved me, didn't it? We were supposed to be a team.

I shifted my weight onto one leg, defiance rolling through me. "What *is* it? And why are you keeping it from me?"

"I have my orders." He ground his teeth.

This was where we disagreed. "Screw your orders."

He reached out and grasped my hand. "Come on then." He sighed. "I can't say anything, but that doesn't mean you can't figure it out. You're going to want to see this."

We jogged for the highway. It stretched out into the flat horizon like a never-ending runway. And that's essentially what it had become to us. It was used as a makeshift tarmac for any planes that needed to land in the area.

As we approached the airplane, its exterior gleaming black, a sense of foreboding washed over me.

"Like I said, please don't shoot the messenger. I wasn't supposed to tell you that they were coming, but now that they're here, you're going to find out soon…" His voice trailed off.

"Just out with it, Mastin!" I challenged.

"See for yourself." He pointed to the mammoth airplane.

The bottom opened, a set of stairs rolling down to the pavement. I watched, horrified, as one by one, alchemists descended from the belly of the beast. They had to be alchemists. I knew immediately, from the gray clothing they were wearing, but also, from the man who was leading the group.

Hank.

My beloved Hank, with his grizzly appearance, quick mind, and ruddy smile. As much as I loved to see him, I didn't want it to be like this!

"What are they doing here?" I growled.

Mastin rocked back on his heels. "It's been decided that they are needed. And so…here they are."

"Weapon X." I spat the name like it was a dirty word.

He narrowed his eyes slightly and shook his head.

Okay?

Then, dropping my hand, he ran ahead to greet our guests.

Anger stirred within as I slowly walked forward to join the newcomers. My eyes landed on Hank, who was talking privately with Tristan. They stood off to one side, talking in low voices, probably as upset by this as I was. Just as I was about to join their twosome, my eyes caught a flash of familiar hair.

Smooth, blonde, and glossy in the afternoon sun.

Lacey.

I balked, feeling as if my entire body was sinking into the pavement. No! This couldn't be!

But it was. And my parents were at her side. Bile rose, so nauseating I doubled over. She was a child! She had no place in a war zone!

I sprinted over to Hank. "What are you doing here? And why are *children* here?"

He held up a hand, the lines around his eyes deep as he grimaced. "We got orders. There wasn't a negotiation."

I poked my finger into his chest, needing someone to blame. "You should've refused. You're better than this!"

"Like I said, we got orders," he replied, dejected. "What was I supposed to do? They were coming either way, so I had to come too."

I shook my head, feeling like my body was sinking into the group, swallowing me up before I could get a grip on things. This couldn't be happening!

Tristan stepped in, resting his steady hand on my lower back. "It seems that the American leadership is getting nervous about this war and decided they needed to fight fire with fire."

I gulped.

"Or in this case," Hank added, "alchemy with alchemy."

I ground my foot into the pavement. How could anyone think this was a good idea? I couldn't picture the president I had met agreeing to such a thing. But then, there'd been that man, the general so convinced on doing this very thing. Maybe he had been the one behind it. Either way, it was wrong.

I spun back to study the newcomers. Most were young, some children, and I doubted any of them had much training beyond what Hank had provided. His couple of months with them wasn't enough. Bringing them here was foolish. No, not just foolish—selfish. Someone had essentially sent these innocent people to the slaughter!

This was not okay.

My mind returned to the incident in the mess hall, to the protestors outside the airport, to all the nasty comments and opinions about alchemy. Maybe someone had known they were sending innocents to die, and that's exactly why they'd done it. Anger pulsed through me once again, red hot and ready to burst.

I searched the crowd until I found General Nathan Scott. When he caught me staring, I glared. If looks could kill, he'd be so dead right now! He pinched his lips and shrugged, as if to say, what else did you expect? Then he walked away, vanishing amongst his soldiers. The coward!

Mastin, who was also in the crowd, kept sending me chastised and sorrowful looks whenever he had the chance. I put my hands on my hips and raised my eyebrows.

We'll be having a discussion about this later, buddy.

"There she is!" My mother's voice carried across the tarmac like a kite on the end of a string. My three family members beamed at me, and I tried to find a smile, I really did. But it just wouldn't come.

They ran forward, pulling me into tight hugs. Tears burned my eyes, and I breathed them in. It felt so good to be with them again, but I was breaking inside for the circumstances. I couldn't stop looking at Lacey's young face, the sweetness that was still bright in her eyes, and imagining those eyes cold and dead. "What happened?" I said as we broke apart. "What are you doing here?"

Dad looked around before speaking low, his voice gravelly with worry, "We didn't have a choice. All the alchemists were suddenly ordered to come here. Even the kids."

"This is dangerous," I replied, stating the utterly obvious.

"We know," Mom replied. "Thank God they let us come with Lacey."

I shook my head. "None of you should be here. This is a war zone."

They shared a knowing look. Christopher tucked Lacey against his leg but she resisted, side-stepping to get into the middle of our little circle. She placed her hands on her hips and cocked her chin up, looking so much older in that moment. Too much. Too soon.

I squatted, placing both of my hands on her shoulders.

"Are you doing okay?" I asked.

Her eyes were smaller mirrors of my own, a blue that shone back at me, no longer innocent and sweet from moments before. They sparked with the same kind of defiance I saw in not only myself, but in Jessa.

Oh, she was a Loxely, all right.

"I'm great," Lacey replied. "I've been practicing my magic every day. I'm really good now. I can't wait to show you."

I smiled weakly. "I would like that."

And in any other place and time, I would have.

★

I smiled despite myself. Nearly all my loves were seated around one table, and I couldn't help the happiness warming me. This was what I'd wanted for so long, if only we'd come together under different circumstances. I'd learned to push the "if onlys" of life away a long time ago, and yet here I was, foolishly wrapping myself up in one of the most dangerous ones of all: family.

I didn't run from it.

Because I'd also learned over the last year that the more courageous thing was to let them in.

We'd found each other in the dining hall—Lacey and my parents, Tristan and Hank, and of course, Mastin. All of us had never talked about sharing a meal together, it just happened. As we began to settle into our spots on the long benches and dug into the array of fresh-cooked food, an unspoken rule had fallen over the group. Nobody talked about the war. For that, I was incredibly grateful.

"Can you pass the butter, dear?" my mother asked me shyly.

Things with Dad and me were going okay, probably because we'd shared so much during our time in the New Colony prison. Mom and I, on the other hand, hadn't had a lot of time to talk, and the energy between us was still strained. I couldn't avoid her. We'd have to air everything out eventually, but as I'd watched her from the corner of my eye, saw the way she'd doted on Lacey, it stirred old resentment inside my chest — and I knew I wasn't ready.

Another time.

I passed her the butter with a guarded smile and turned back to Mastin, who was busy shoveling food into his mouth at my side. The man could *eat*. I'd learned that living with his family. The Scott men worked hard and practically worshipped their mealtimes. Not that I blamed Mastin; the food spread out in front of us was better than anything we'd had since leaving the west coast. The plane that had brought the alchemists had also brought provisions, and General Scott had decided to treat everyone to a feast of steak and potatoes, fresh dinner rolls, green salad, and rich creamed corn.

"Here, try it like this." Mastin lifted a chunk of potato he'd stabbed with a fork. He'd slathered it in creamy salad dressing, so much it was dripping. I wrinkled my nose.

"I like to keep all my food separated," I teased.

"What? It all ends up in the same place."

"But it tastes better if it doesn't start out in the same place." I leaned into his side, his familiar warmth surrounding me.

"Don't be a baby." He chuckled, and I elbowed him in the ribs. Not willing to let him get the upper hand, I dove in and bit the potato off his fork. The hot food mixed in my mouth, savory and sweet, and I swallowed, licking my lips.

"Okay, fine, you win."

His bright green eyes stared intently at my lips and I became immediately and unbearably aware of how we weren't alone. I sighed and looked away.

Across the table, Tristan joked with my father, his voice ringing out like a church bell. Dad doubled over in laughter, nearly choking on his food. Tristan always did have a way of making people laugh until they cried. I'd lost count of how many times he'd done it to me. A small part of me was jealous of my father; I'd love to be the one on the receiving end of one of Tristan's jokes. It had been a while since he'd treated me that way.

"Look what I found." Lacey's sweet voice tickled my ear and I smiled down at my sister.

She held up a jug of some kind of frothy orange punch or juice, her eyes twinkling in delight. The citrus scent wafted through the air and my mouth watered. I glanced around, noticing that over the chatter of the room, the other alchemists, all dressed in simple gray uniforms, were enjoying the meal. Before they'd seemed nervous, but now that had melted away. Good food could do that to just about anyone.

"Can I pour you some?" she asked, nodding at the jug of juice.

"Of course. Do you need any help with that?" I reached out to steady the jug that looked a tad too heavy for her small arms.

Determination filled her normally timid expression and she shook her head. "No, I don't need help. I got it."

I sat back, impressed, as she filled my cup to the brim. She was growing up so fast, and just thinking that made me feel like an old maid. I laughed to myself.

She continued around the table, charming each and every person along the way.

"She's cute," Mastin whispered in my ear. We watched her, both of us clearly enamored. I let out a laugh and elbowed him in the ribs.

"She *is* cute," I agreed, joy rising up. Tears gathered in my eyes—I was so happy.

Wait a minute…

I caught Lacey's eye and raised my eyebrows. She nodded once, giggling, before moving on to the next person.

Holy crap! She'd become incredibly adept at orange alchemy! We'd had some lessons on it back at the Resistance basecamp, but I had no idea she'd come this far.

Everyone at the table fell under her spell. They were alive with happiness. She'd made a connection with each person, giving them this gift. And quite honestly, with everything going on, it was an amazing gift to be had. I tried to get my mind to focus on something else, but I couldn't. I was simply *happy*. The orange had taken what I was feeling and enhanced it, and it would continue to enhance whatever I felt until it wore off. I eyed the orange bubbly drink in front of me and smiled from ear to ear.

Talented little stinker!

"I've been wondering where you went." A female voice cut through the chatter, voice flirty. I looked over to find the source, noticing a woman had come to chat up Tristan. "You still owe me a rematch."

Tristan turned to converse with one of the soldiers... one of the *female* soldiers. Envy riled up in me. She was beautiful—exotic, sweeping dark hair and hooded eyes, gorgeous caramel complexion, curvy in all the right places. What the hell was she doing talking to Tristan?

She slid in next to him, straddling the bench, facing him, body leaning in with a knowing smile, laughing in a low, throaty voice.

Rage burned through me, closing in on my clenched fists and my tense jaw.

"Are you okay?" Mastin's question lingered on the outside of the haze, yet not strong enough to penetrate it. I ignored him, glaring darkly at the woman. The intruder!

Why was she so openly flirting with Tristan? He wasn't interested, couldn't she see the way he was treating her like anyone else? She needed to back off!

But then he reached out and tucked a strand of hair behind her ear, smiling intently, and I lost it.

I sprung from the table, my plate clattering.

"Sasha!" Mastin jumped up with me. "What's going on?"

A handful of nearby faces swiveled, chatter growing silent, as the joyous mood flipped to something much more curious and invasive.

I sucked in a breath, realizing what had just happened.

Damn that orange alchemy, always getting me into trouble.

"You've got to be kidding me," I spat, annoyed with myself. The magic flitted away into nothingness, and my emotions settled back to normal.

I'd gotten jealous, insanely jealous, of Tristan flirting with that girl. It was so stupid! Where had that even come from?

It had to be because I cared about Tristan. *As a friend, my best friend.* And surely, if it had been Mastin the girl had touched and flirted with, I'd have gotten even more angry. I probably would have punched her.

Right.

Okay.

Breathe in. Breathe out. Everything is fine.

"I'm good." I laughed awkwardly, belly flopping, and grinned at the people who were still staring at me like I'd just picked my nose or something. I couldn't meet Tristan's eyes—nor Mastin's. "I'm fine. It's nothing."

I sat back down, gripping the seat. My cheeks burned. That was so weird. And so embarrassing. And everyone was still gaping at me! Oh, heavens, I needed to get out of here. I needed to go for a run *alone* to clear my head.

"Thank you all for your service." Nathan Scott's deep baritone voice rang out over the mess hall. Five hundred voices quieted as every pair of eyes turned to watch their leader at the front of the room.

"We have *three thousand* more forces moving into the area at this moment," he continued. "They'll arrive shortly, ready to fight."

The room grew even quieter. Mastin shifted next to me, stiffening and transitioning into his usual soldier-self.

"I hope you all enjoyed your meal. You deserve that much." General Scott cleared his throat, steadying his gaze and sweeping it across the crowd. "Please prepare yourselves tonight. Tomorrow is a new day, a day to stride forward in our valiant efforts. Tomorrow we join our comrades in battle. We leave at first light."

SIXTEEN
JESSA

Nashville was a fallen city. As we landed in its center, my heart sank. Fewer buildings were on fire, the rubble was beginning to get cleaned up, and many more people were out on the streets. It was starting to resemble a normal city, and all that meant that Richard was gaining control faster than anyone had anticipated.

After another long day of conducting interrogations on his own people, Richard had announced it was time to head back into Nashville. I didn't know how many lived here, or how long it would take, but I knew that eventually, I would get to everyone. Richard would make certain of that.

First, he'd secured the borders, trapping everyone inside. Then, he had alchemists enforcing the rule of law, rounding people up in hordes. And finally, he had his secret weapon to finish the job.

Me.

And so we continued, taking over the city like a swarm of deadly wasps. Our job was to go from shelter to shelter where the soldiers had rounded up innocent people and forced them inside while they awaited my arrival. We would tell the West Americans what to expect and what would happen to them if they didn't do as we asked. Then, I got to work. It was usually over quick, people didn't have anything to fight with and most were trying to keep their families together, but it was still exhausting and emotionally draining work.

Mark Addington and his wife Sabine had taken over so Richard could do whatever kings did during wartime. It didn't take long to confirm why I disliked the couple for reasons that had nothing to do with Celia and the broken engagement. They were pushy, self-important, and constantly leered at me. I was beginning to think they either saw me as their enemy or as their salvation, I couldn't tell which. And I didn't know which I'd prefer.

Our boots clomped across the pavement, the soldiers leading us into yet another school turned into an internment camp. It was our first of the day and already my body ached for rest. I hadn't been getting much sleep; I was too haunted by the faces of those who'd died, not to mention the countless people who'd been turned because of my interference. It felt like a spindly pit was twisting in my stomach and I groaned, squinting as the morning sun shone off the reflective surface of the glass building. This one was bigger than any of the others and a pool of dread welled within me.

"Chop, chop!" Sabine Addington barked, her arm motioning for me to hurry through the door she'd propped open. She was a classic beauty with delicate features, a slender face that had aged well, and vibrant ruby hair perfectly coifed in a twist at her neck. I'd learned that sometimes the most beautiful people on the outside were the most ugly on the inside. The Addington family was proof.

"Can't we go easier on them today?" I said, eyeing the

door wearily.

Mark laughed, smoothing a wrinkle in his pressed dress shirt. "Whatever do you mean?" He matched his wife in style, almost like they'd grown to resemble each other over the years. He motioned to some of the guards and alchemists at his disposal, urging them to take position.

"I've been thinking about it and I have a question," I continued, trying to sound as persuasive as I could. "Why do we immediately kill them if they won't willingly participate with this? I mean, if we can restrain them, then I can use alchemy on them and bring them to our side either way. This way, we don't have to kill so many people."

They both glowered at me like I was a total and complete idiot, their expressions dripping in utter disdain.

"You really don't understand social pressure, do you?" Sabine finally replied coolly, looking down her nose.

I shrugged, because actually, I didn't know what she was even talking about. Social pressure?

"Those who are killed are used as an example," Mark supplied with exasperation. "They keep everyone else from rising up. If we show leniency then we also show weakness."

I glared, stepping back. "You call it weakness. I call it mercy."

They shared a knowing look, smirking in unison.

"We give them a crystal clear understanding of what will happen if they fight us. They know what they are doing and they know there are no second chances. Period." Sabine explained it simply, as if she were rattling off a recipe. She spun around and strolled through the door with her husband in tow. I followed closely, drilling holes through their backs with my eyes. Inside this building were innocent people whose entire way of life was about to be changed, all with little force and a lot of manipulation.

I could relate to these poor people more than they knew.

I had lost count long ago of how many of them had been shot and killed in front of me. If the King had no qualms about murdering people right in front of me, then how many more had been killed when I wasn't there to witness it? I had no idea what the death count was, but I couldn't imagine it was anything short of staggering.

It wasn't totally my fault, but still, I was ravaged by guilt. Truth was, at the forefront of everything happening here was *my* red alchemy. I was working for the King now, plain and simple. Now that his threats to kill more people if I didn't help him had become plainly evident, I didn't see what other choice I had. So, I worked.

I did exactly what was asked of me, taking away people's freedom to the point that they didn't even realize it. Deep inside, I kept hoping my magic would wear off and the people would return to normal, but so far, nobody had changed. Even if the magic was gone, their minds had been twisted by my power. They now saw Richard as their savior come to deliver them from their terrible democracy, rather than the other way around. Apparently, many of them had even enlisted in our army. He'd boasted last night about how they'd willingly joined up. It seemed I'd swayed these people to Richard's plans because they accepted my words as absolute truth. It was brainwashing at its finest.

And I hated myself for it.

"Don't you look chipper this morning," a sly voice echoed down the long glass hallway. I looked up to find not only one unwelcomed man leering at me, but two. Reed stood next to Dax, the intense broody kid with purple telepathy who made my skin crawl. Dax sneered darkly, and Reed ran his eyes up and down me, exuding sheer creepiness.

"Come on, boys," Mark called to the pair. "Remember

what we talked about."

I folded my arms over my chest and glared right back at them. If I ever had the chance to get at either of their blood, I would take it. I would make them pay for the way they so clearly enjoyed their roles in this war. They had probably become murderers ten times over at this point, and not a lick of remorse showed in either of their cold expressions.

Hello Jessa, Dax's scratchy voice pilfered through my mind, like nails on a chalkboard. *Nice to see you again, Princess.*

I refused to reply through the telepathic link that he'd opened between us. The very idea this psychopath could talk to me anytime he wanted, assuming I was in close enough proximity, made me sick with anger.

I know you can hear me, he pressed.

I didn't say anything. Didn't react in any way. If I was lucky, I'd make him paranoid I couldn't hear him. If I could make him sweat, that would at least be a silver lining to this awful morning.

Reed and I have made a little bargain with Mark, in case you're wondering why we're here. In fact, if things go as planned, you'll probably be seeing a lot more of us over the coming months. I can't say I'm happy with your presence here. I've never liked you and I never will. You're an entitled little bitch. But oh well, he cooed. *Once this is all over, it will be so worth it.*

My eyes flickered to him, giving me away.

His grin was slow and wide. *As they say, the ends justify the means.*

I continued to refuse a reaction or a reply, but curiosity was getting the better of me. I held my breath, the questions bubbling over. These two had made a deal with Mark and Sabine? What kind of deal? For what reason? And what did I have to do with it?

Frustrated, I kept my mouth shut, my eyes forward, and followed the couple into the gymnasium. Reed and Dax peeled off the wall as we entered, the pair bounding in after us like excitable puppies with a new chew toy. I could feel Reed staring at me from behind. I clenched my fists so tight my fingernails razored into my palms. I wanted nothing more than to turn and punch him square on the nose.

How had I ever been friends with him? My first impression of the guy had been so good. He'd come across as funny and charming, a friend. I knew now that it was his blue alchemy at work. He had charisma in spades because of it, but that didn't make him a good person. Reed had shown his true colors, and those colors were ugly as sin.

There wasn't a minute off-script about our time in the gymnasium. One by one, I used my magic on at least a hundred people's blood, turning horrified faces into ones eager to please their new King. Two fought back. They were shot. Even though it wasn't unexpected, wasn't a surprise, I was still a shaky mess. Tears burned my eyes and blurred my vision through the whole thing.

Was this my life now? We'd go from city to city, rounding up everyone we could get our hands on, turning them into Richard's puppets. He wouldn't stop, not until every last citizen bowed down to his rule. And then what? Would we move north to Canada? South? Would this continue, on and on, until the Heart family ruled the entire planet? I couldn't do it all in my lifetime, there was no way, but somehow I wondered if Richard expected me to try.

We finished with the gym in record time. Our group exited the building with haste, soldiers swarming around us in a wall of protection, and we marched back to an armored vehicle that waited to take us to the next location. The grass was brown and squishy under our boots as we crossed the sweeping lawn to the parking lot. The muggy smell of distant rain wafted through my nose, the humid air filling up lungs. I stared up into the gray sky, wishing my power away. I'd give anything to not have this burden anymore. If that was taken out of the equation, then none of this would be so easy for them. Or just take me out. If I wasn't here…

Thwomp thwomp thwomp.

Helicopters pilfered the sky. Jet engines intermixed, loud as blow horns. I peered up at them, little black specks growing larger by the second.

"Red alert!" Mark shouted, holding up his shiny black slatebook. "We're under attack."

A swell of hope rose inside me like a brilliant sunrise. This could be my chance. I didn't stop to think about it. I took off running, my feet powering me forward. Without access to yellow, there was nothing that could save me from the other alchemists. But I had to try.

A body slammed into me, pounding me to the ground. Dax.

"Not so fast, pretty princess," he growled, twisting his hand into my ponytail and yanking me to standing. I gasped, straining against him. He tugged again and I stilled; it was the only way to get him to stop. Our eyes met and his flared with desire.

I like you in this position, he purred through my mind. *You should learn to be submissive to men all the time. It makes you even prettier.*

I wrenched my body around to face him, kneeing him directly in the groin, hoping for a direct hit. Success! He fell like a log. I didn't stop and gloat. I exploded into a run, legs pumping me forward. My eyes roamed the horizon, neck twisting side to side as I frantically searched for help. I had to get away from these people, take cover, and find usable color. With purple alchemy I would be able to tell Sasha where I was. She'd be able to get me out of here. Maybe.

It was all I had.

Angry shouts exploded behind me, my pursuers gaining ground. Scratch that. I needed to get yellow first so I could fight, but more than that, so I could stay ahead. I'd have to worry about purple later.

"Get back here!" Reed shouted, voice way too close for comfort.

My eyes continued to scan the area, looking for anything. Anything! It was February, and had been raining like crazy, but there had to be color somewhere. I'd even settle for nonorganic material—it was better than nothing!

And yet, I saw nothing.

The buildings in this area were all glass and steel. The grass was dead for the season. The trees and bushes were mostly barren, and any green they did have wouldn't be helpful. Not now. I didn't need healing!

Come on! Yellow. Anything yellow.

Reed caught up to me, only a footstep behind. His panting breath warmed the back of my neck. "Don't make me shoot you," he warned. The sounds of more footsteps in his tracks echoed through the air.

"You wouldn't dare!" I shot back. We neared the corner of a block, and I prayed I'd find what I needed once we rounded it. "I'm too valuable."

How many pursuers did I have now? I mentally tried to count the guards from today but my mind was too unfocused.

"Not if you're playing for the other side," he growled. "Remember?"

I careened around the corner, skidding so fast that I began to fall forward. Panic ripped through me as the ground rose up.

Reed took care of the problem for both of us.

He tackled me, and we rolled several feet before landing in a decaying flowerbed, arms and legs flying. Weeds scratched at my exposed skin, and I screamed. Not for the pain, but for the fact I'd been caught. Tears prickled my eyes.

I blinked them away furiously. I needed to think, to keep moving, not to start crying, and definitely not to feel sorry for myself.

Gunshots exploded on the other side of the street. People yelled, some cried out in agony. The battle had begun. If I was going to get any help, I'd have to create it myself. I had to use the battle's distraction to my advantage, and fast!

I focused on what was right in front of me. Underneath the brush, a small sprinkling of purple flowers grew. Salvation!

Reed ground my face into them as he straddled me, wrestling my hands into cuffs. I let him, not fighting. Instead, I focused on the purple smashed against my cheek, connecting with the magic instantly.

Sasha, I called out. *Are you there?*

Jessa! she returned instantly, her tone frantic. *Where are you?*

A wave of comfort crashed over me, tears springing to my eyes. Her take-charge voice was exactly what I needed.

I'm with Reed and some others. They've got me detained over by Imperial High School.

Okay, hold on, we're coming!

We're not in the high school, though. Don't go in there! There's a ton of people loyal to Richard in there. I don't know what they'd do to you if they saw you. The words rushed our connection, horrified to think what the West American soldiers were about to face. We hadn't made it through the entire city, yet. Not even close. But still, there were many who would most likely fight their own countrymen.

What do you mean? Sasha's question pulsed through me, the guilt inside raising its ugly head again.

I had to use my red. Richard made me. Don't trust anyone and I'll explain the rest later. Just please, come get me out of here!

Reed wrenched me up from the ground, pushing me forward, oblivious to the purple magic I'd deployed. I smiled faintly, quickly replacing it with a frown, glaring savagely at Reed.

I don't know how long this purple will last, I continued. *I don't have the flower on me anymore. But I'll describe my location as long as I'm able to reach out to you.*

Okay. Just do your best. I'm in the middle of something here, but I'll come get you as soon as I can. We're coming to save you, Jessa. My sister's determined voice warmed me from the inside out. If anyone could get me out of this mess, it was Sasha. I'd never met anyone quite like her.

In fact, she continued confidently, *we're coming to take back Nashville!*

★

Reed kicked in the door and we swept into the little house. Dax ran ahead to check the rooms. "All clear," he called down after a moment and the four of us shuffled inside.

"This battle won't last long," Mark said, steering me into the living room. He peered out the window before drawing the burgundy curtains. The hems sat heavy against the scratched wooden floor, blocking the bulk of the mid-morning light.

Dax ambled into the room, running a slow finger over the stones in his uniform as he leered at me.

"Sit," he pointed to a brown, threadbare recliner.

I dropped into the chair with a huff. "You should be out there fighting," I challenged, glaring at the group of four people who'd basically taken me hostage. They'd sent the rest of the guards out to fight. "You're all cowards."

"Shut up!" Dax hissed at me, fire in his eyes.

A guy like that? Oh, I was sure he wanted nothing more than to be out there fighting. It probably killed him to be locked up, hidden away from all the action. Reed only laughed, leaning against the far wall.

"We can't afford to lose Jessa," Sabine purred, manicured fingers dancing against her chin, eyes thoughtful, as she walked the perimeter of the small room. "She's far too valuable. So, we will wait this out and make our move once it's over."

The family wasn't here, luckily. I could only imagine how Dax would have treated them if he'd discovered someone on his search. Whoever the people that lived here were, they were probably in the gymnasium, waiting for further instructions, or maybe they were out fighting their own people, brainwashed by my alchemy. Considering their home was across the street from the school, it made sense. It was either those explanations, or they were already dead.

The home had a cozy, well-loved energy that made me think of my home, the place where I'd lived a beautiful childhood, but could never return to. My heart squeezed, the truth clearer to me than ever. I studied the home, seeing the similarities. Even though the wooden floors were heavily scratched, the homeowners had centered beautiful rugs throughout. Pictures lined the walls with clean glass frames. Some held images of family, smiling faces shining back at the camera, and others were of beautiful landscapes. A fireplace with a massive wood mantle centered the room, leftover charred wood giving the room a faint smoky scent.

I'll never get to go home, but maybe I'll get to see my family again. That was most important, a thought I needed to hold onto, no matter what.

Sabine and Mark stood in the farthest corner from everyone else, whispering quietly between each other.

"I don't think that's a good idea," Reed interjected from across the room, a twinkle of blue light moving between two fingers. "She will have to agree to it *willingly* for it to work." His eyes flashed to me. "She's strong. She needs to come by things in her own time. It's either that, or you'll need really good blackmail. Might I suggest the prince as collateral? She still loves the guy, and yes, I know he's alive." He laughed. "People always underestimate my gift."

The couple glared back at Reed, Sabine's eyes were sharp ice and Mark's were incredulous. Yeah, so he invaded their privacy. What did they expect? I stifled a laugh. *Serves them right!*

But considering they were talking about a plan that included my consent, it was about time they stopped all their whispering.

"What the hell is going on? What aren't you telling me?" I asked with a sneer.

You had better agree to this, Dax's snarky voice infiltrated my mind. *If you don't, I will get you alone and I will strangle you with my bare hands. Don't think I haven't been daydreaming of it since the moment I laid my eyes on you. You're a spoiled brat and you need to be taught a lesson.*

Panic rose in the back of my throat and fear prickled up my spine. I pushed away the clear mental image he'd conjured in my mind. All these people were messed up, but Dax was truly sick. One look was all I needed to know I never, ever wanted to be alone with the kid.

Not willing to back down, I shot a heated glare in his

direction. "Say that out loud so everyone here can listen to your disgusting thoughts," I snapped.

He looked away, greasy black hair flopping, heat creeping to his cheeks.

"I didn't think so." I leaned back in the chair, annoyed at the cuffs still pinching my wrists, restraining my arms behind me.

"Whatever," he growled, charging toward the door in a few short stomps. "I'm going to go find something to eat. If you need me, I'll be in the kitchen."

"Get me something, too!" Reed yelled.

"I'm not your maid. Get your own damn food," Dax called back.

Reed laughed, throwing his head back as if it were the funniest thing ever. Like it was really hard to focus on something other than food at a time like this? Breakfast wasn't that long ago. They were both idiots.

I returned my attention to Mark and Sabine, who were both looking disdainfully in the direction of the boys. They didn't find it funny either.

"You might as well tell me your big secret," I said. "I already know there's something strange about you two. You're hiding something."

"I'm not sure." Mark leaned against his wife.

"You can tell me now, or you can tell me eventually in the interrogation room." Because sooner or later, it would be *their* turn.

"She's right! We're running out of time," Sabine replied, reaching down to grip her husband's hand and losing a bit of her usual cool. "We can't have the whole country aligned with Richard, let alone all of Nashville. Not if this is going to work."

Wait a second...

I sputtered, my entire body growing sickly warm.

"You're not loyal!" I perked up in my chair, a bead of hope growing in my chest. "Are you Resistance?"

Mark spat. "We're not part of that damned Resistance!"

Sabine held up a hand, poised once again. "Please, dear. It should hardly come as a surprise that we're not loyal to the Hearts. Richard, foolish man that he is, has many enemies. We are only one of them."

"But you work for him!" I challenged. "You seem so besotted. How am I to believe you're telling me the truth?"

She smiled. "Yes. It's all very convenient, don't you think? I certainly do. Thank you for getting rid of Faulk for us, by the way. That woman was getting on my last nerve. Things will be so much easier now that she's dead."

A million questions pummeled my brain, but the biggest came out first. "Is it you? Are you the ones who hurt Lucas?"

They shared a guarded look, something dark flashing between them.

"No," Sabine said. "That wasn't us."

Mark eyed her as he nodded fervently.

"Though the boy probably deserved it, after what he did to Celia," she continued. "It's not really him we're concerned with at the moment. Lucas has always been harmless. The boy has no spine. No. It's Richard that needs to be removed."

They were lying to me. I couldn't know for sure, but I felt it in my gut.

If I could get at their blood, I could find out the truth. I foolishly yanked on my cuffs, which they'd neatly rearranged through the slats in the chair where I currently sat. I groaned. For now, I wasn't moving.

"And what does this have to do with me?" I asked.

It was a stupid question. Of course I knew. But I had to buy time. Sasha was on her way…

Sabine cackled. "Don't be daft. We want you to help us. Align with us. Use your red to end Richard. You can stay married to your little love. We'll help Lucas run things. He needs our guidance. Our families will unite."

I glared. "Am I really supposed to believe you won't somehow end up on the throne yourselves? You'll probably annul my marriage and have your daughter married to him within the week."

Her eyes widened—I had her. It didn't matter what she said next, I saw it written all over her face. I'd thought their family was after the crown when their daughter had been engaged to Lucas, but this confirmed something far worse. It wasn't just their daughter they wanted to see in power, it was themselves. It was Sabine and Mark Addington behind the whole thing.

"But why? Why not be loyal and reap the rewards of your high position?"

Sabine sneered, "Our family has been through hell for the Hearts, especially our daughter. We've been so close, for generations, really. And that's how we're repaid? A broken engagement? A never-ending war? No, it simply won't do." She strolled closer as she spoke, eyes boring into me as if it all made perfect sense. "Besides, we'll do a better job at ruling. You do see Richard's foolishness, don't you? He thinks he can take over the world by ripping it to shreds. We will create diplomacy and peace, give our society better advantages, and use alchemy to create abundance for those most deserving."

Off to the side, Reed stood with his arms crossed, nodding along to the whole thing. No doubt he would get some sort of leg-up for helping them.

"And *you* will help us," Mark pressed. "I know you hate Richard as much as we do. This is the right thing to do."

I scoffed. "Never."

"Like I said," Reed sighed, "you'll need to blackmail her."

Boots scuffled, someone groaned, and two forms appeared from around the doorframe. Dax's teeth were bared, eyes wild, as he held a steady gun pressed to the back of a woman's head. She turned, blonde ponytail swooshing, and grimaced at me. Sasha.

I jumped up trying fruitless to bring the chair with me. Reed strode across the room, pushing me back down. Mouth opening and closing, unable to speak a word, I held Sasha's eye contact. She squirmed against Dax, mouth pinched, regret and anger burning in her gaze. Nothing needed to be said, we both knew we were on the losing end of the situation.

"Look who I found," Dax sneered. "It's your precious sister. What should I do with her, huh? Should I kill her?"

"Careful with that one," Reed interjected. "Cuff her. She's a tease just like Jessa here. Not to mention more dangerous than you."

Dax scowled at Reed and then tossed Sasha to the floor, the force of his magic ripping through his sinewy muscles. Her stone necklace dangled in his free hand. He shoved it in a pocket and then set to work cuffing her arms behind her back.

Reed flicked a wrist toward Sasha, "There's your blackmail."

Mark smiled, crouching down to stare into my eyes. "And what about now? Now will you help us?"

I opened my mouth but was unable to answer. What was I supposed to say? Reed was right. Sasha was the perfect blackmail. She was the key, the bait, someone I would do anything to protect.

I was out of choices.

SEVENTEEN
LUCAS

"You have to take me with you." I followed my father up the stairs, taking two at a time, trying to catch up. We'd just received news that a battle was waging in Nashville. From the initial report he'd gotten downstairs, West America was on the losing end. Again. Of course, my father's pride had reared its head and the man had wanted to see it for himself.

"Absolutely not," he barked over his shoulder. "You're still supposed to be dead, remember? Besides, it's too dangerous for you out there."

The lights in the stairway sent his long shadow pressing down on me. "That's pretty hypocritical coming from you, don't you think? Seeing as you're going out there."

"I will have an entire team to protect me. At the first sign of trouble, I'll be back. But for now, I need to steer the ship."

He was serious with that analogy which only made me chuckle in disbelief at the size of his ego. Steer the ship? Really?

"So? Your team can protect me, too."

He turned on me then, face cast in shadow. I could only make out his silhouette, but I knew from his heavy breaths that he was done with this conversation. Didn't stop me. "Very few members of my team know you're even here, Lucas. Need we have this conversation again? My answer is no."

He whipped back around and slammed his wide shoulders through the door. I sped up but the door closed in my face, the sound of a lock clicking in place. I bristled and stepped back, my jaw dropping.

Since when had he installed a lock on the *outside* of the door? There was a huge lever on the inside of this door and the one below, which made sense, considering it was a bunker. But to purposely make a way to lock me in? All my bugging him about being down here must have finally gotten the best of him.

Either that, or he's suspicious.

I sighed and rested my head against the cool metal, momentarily lost for a solution. Jessa was over there. She was stuck in the middle, and I needed to make sure she was okay. As much as she hated me, I couldn't pretend there wasn't something there between us. I'd felt it from the moment I'd met her. I needed to see that something through and that wasn't going to happen if she was dead. Besides, I wanted to join in the battle if it came to that and help where I could. After I witnessed what she was being forced into and how broken she'd become, I wanted to offer help.

I slammed my fist against the door, cussing. *Stubborn man!* I tested the handle, just in case. It was still locked.

Running back down the stairs, I jumped over the last four in one swoop, and flew through the door at the bottom. I needed yellow. If I could just get my hands on some yellow, I could break that lock myself. But it had to be organic yellow like a stone or a plant or something.

Why hadn't I stocked up?

I tore through all the bedrooms, rummaging through cabinets and drawers. I even lifted up the couch cushions.

But there was nothing.

I plopped back onto the misshapen couch, tossing the book laying next to me across the room. It hit the wall and clattered to the floor, pages flying open. Breathing fast, I ran my shaky hands through my hair and stared up at the stark white ceiling. White was in abundance down here, even the flowers on the kitchen table were fresh. But what good would invisibility do if I couldn't get through the door?

At that thought, I heard the click of the door handle.

"Hey you," a silky voice chimed behind me. "Are you doing okay? I heard you were stuck down here."

I stood and spun around—Celia Addington. She sauntered into the room, casually removing black gloves and unraveling a long cream scarf. She unwrapped the soft fabric from her neck several times, eyeing me with interest. She tossed the items onto the table like she owned the place and sashayed toward me.

"How did you get in here?" I asked. And more importantly, was the door upstairs still open?

"Leo let me in."

I stared at her. "Leo?"

She giggled, the sound forced. "Your guard, silly."

Okay, why was she acting so weird? If she thought this was flirting, she was trying way too hard to pull it off. She was attractive, but this was not. And why were my guards so easily paid off? It didn't make sense. What did Celia have on them?

"Umm, okay," I replied, clearing my throat and focusing

all of my attention on her. "And what are you doing here?"

"I came to keep you company." She smiled seductively, walking her fingers across the back of the couch as she worked her way around it, finally standing right in front of me. She tugged on the collar of my shirt, biting her bottom lip and looking up at me through a set of dark lashes. "I bet you have a lot on your mind, hmm?"

"Uh, yeah," I sputtered. "You could say that."

A lot of *Jessa* on my mind. Or maybe the problem was that I didn't have *enough* on my mind, namely my memories that still hadn't come back, and the full truth. Even though, I was beginning to piece that together on my own.

"I can help you take your mind off those troubles for a while." She ran her hands down my chest. "Nobody has to know," she whispered.

I narrowed my eyes and stepped back. Hadn't we already had this conversation?

"I'm not interested."

She pouted. "Don't pretend you haven't been thinking about our kiss."

"I haven't."

She put her hands on her hips, attitude flaring. "I don't believe you."

I shook my head, annoyed. "Believe it. I haven't thought about it once since that night."

Hurt flashed across her face, breaking her smooth exterior. "Why are you fighting this, Lucas?" She stomped her foot like a spoiled child. "You know, I've never had a guy turn me away before you. I'm sick of your prudishness. And by the way? Things will be a lot easier for you in the future if you don't fight this."

Umm, okay?

She turned, her hair flipping as she stormed toward the

door.

"Wait!" I called out. I didn't want her here, but I also didn't want her to leave and lock me up again. Her arrival had marked the only opportunity I had to get out. If that door upstairs was still unlocked…

She spun back around, raising her eyebrows. "What, Lucas?"

"I'm sorry." I cleared my throat and looked down. "I didn't mean to be rude. You can stay. We can hang out for a bit… as friends."

She laughed, her cold anger thawing quickly. "Sure." She winked. "*As friends.*"

"Sit," I said, motioning to the couch. "I still don't have a slatebook. But, uh, we could read or something? That's pretty much all I've been doing lately."

That, and sneaking out a few times under the guise of white alchemy.

That, and obsessing about Jessa and what she really meant to me.

Jessa, who spent her nights sleeping on the other side of my wall.

"You're an interesting character." Celia relaxed into the couch. "We could talk, ya know? We don't have to *read*."

"Yeah," I returned. I jogged over to the roses, sliding two out from the massive arrangement. I strode back and dropped one into her lap.

"Uh, thanks?" She giggled.

"One for you and one for me," I said, feeling and sounding like a total idiot. It was a necessary evil. I needed to play this whole thing off as nice, as funny, as anything other than what it really was.

"You're sweet." She buried her nose in the rose.

My eyes caught on a flash of metal sticking out of her

pocket. I frowned. "Is that a knife?"

Her eyes popped to mine, red brightening her cheeks. Slowly, she nodded, pulling the long, thin blade from her pocket. She twisted it around in her hand, a smirk playing on her lips.

"A girl can never be too safe," she purred.

It didn't ring true. Something about this whole situation was off. A small alarm bell went off in my head, a warning to play it cool.

"Don't worry, Lucas," she grinned at me, pressing the tip of her finger to the knife. A tiny bead of blood swelled on the end. She placed in her mouth, sucking it for a moment. "When all is said and done, you and I are going to have a great life together. And if you can't see that, well, I think you know what that means."

The threat prickled over me, pins and needles covering my skin.

I narrowed my eyes. "Are you saying if I don't agree to a relationship with you, you'll what? Slit my throat?"

A smile played on her lips as she feigned innocence. "I never said that. Of course I would never hurt someone I care about so deeply, especially because I know how strongly you feel about me. Besides, it's best for Jessa this way, too. She's too busy with alchemy to be a good wife to you."

I nodded once and she slipped the knife back into her pocket. The message was clear. She was threatening me. And not just me, Jessa! I didn't think I'd ever have the urge to punch a woman, but I did right then.

"I told them you'd come around," she leaned into me, cuddling into my side.

"Who?" I stilled.

"My parents, silly. They wanted this match from the beginning. They're with Jessa right now, did you know? She's their little puppet." She laughed lightly, sighing, a craze to her eyes that I'd never noticed before. This woman was truly delusional if she thought I was in love with her, that I would dump someone as sweet as Jessa to be with her.

Taking a long breath, I ran a hand down her arm. My other still held the white rose and with a quick squeeze, I remembered my plan.

"I'll be right back," I peeled her off of me and strolled to my bedroom. "Stay right there, I have a present for you."

She bounced in her seat, beaming.

The second I rounded the corner, sure I was out of her eye-line I worked the white magic into my veins. I popped off the head of the rose and squeezed it between my fingers, the silky texture releasing a sweet scent into the air. As the white seeped from the rose, my form also seeped from view.

Entirely invisible, I carefully walked out of the room, past where Celia sat primping on the couch, and through the open door into the stairwell. Then I hurried up, my legs burning.

"Lucas? Are you okay? I'm ready for my present now!" I heard her voice call from below as I slipped through the door above. I thanked God it was unlocked.

The guard, Leo, leaned lazily against the wall, completely unsuspecting. It wasn't the same guy from the first time Celia had snuck in. She must have bribed a second guard to get to me yet again. *Gee, some guards you got there, Dad.*

To throw the guard off his game, I slammed the door shut with a loud clang. He jumped up, eyes wide and hand reaching to his rifle. The second he rushed forward to inspect, I took off in the opposite direction. It wouldn't be long until I'd be on board some helicopter, speeding away from the base. But I did wonder how long it would take to actually find Jessa. It didn't matter to me if New Colony was winning the battle at the moment. The soldiers of West America would kill Jessa on sight if they knew what she was doing to the people of Nashville.

If there was anyone I wanted to be stuck in a bunker with, it was definitely that mysterious wife of mine. In order to do that, I had to find her and get us both out of Nashville alive. And then maybe I could work on figuring out how to get my father to stop hurting so many innocent people. Because one thing was starting to become clear, one thing Jessa had revealed that I couldn't believe at first. Richard had lost his mind, and it was up to me to stop him.

✱

I dove from the chopper, rolling across the pavement. Gunshots rang out, pilfering the city street. I trailed behind the line of soldiers as they jumped from the machine and took their positions. Ducking into an empty alleyway, squeezing the white rose in my left hand, my breath came out fast. Shaking racked through my body, taking in the sounds of battle. I needed to calm down, to make a plan. My ambition, my need to be part of the action, had gotten the better of me, and that realization stared me straight in the face now.

I'd overlooked getting a gun.

How could I have been so stupid as to not bring a weapon? To make matters worse, I didn't have any other colors on me besides the white rose. And I still had no idea where Jessa was. This was a huge city, and she could be anywhere.

Searching eyes darted in every direction as I thought through my options. Weapons. Those needed to come first. I slowed my breathing as I scanned the area. No luck.

I ran to the opposite end of the alley, peeking out. The street was in ruins—an all-out battle waged in front of me.

My belly churned as men and woman destroyed each other, blood and bullets flying. Our alchemists wore their gear, the advantage obvious: a rainbow of stones embedded into their uniforms. The shiny black helmets made it impossible to tell who was who, creating a menacing uniformity. They fought alongside our soldiers, and to my astonishment, what appeared to be West American civilians also putting up a fight.

Most of the civilians were on our side. It didn't surprise me, but it didn't feel right. I doubled over as I watched one kill his own countryman.

On the other side of the battle, some fighting in hand-to-hand combat, others using guns and even hand grenades, were the West Americans. They moved lithely in their khaki uniforms, skills just as impressive as any of our soldiers. They had a trained synchronicity to their attacks, a lethalness not to be underestimated.

I squinted, making out the occasional West American alchemist, head to toe in black with a ropy gemstone necklace wrapped around each of their necks. The news of West American alchemists left me staring, hands fisting and aching to help. Many of them were young. Too young. They were novices, quick to succumb to the battle. What was going on in West America that they'd send untrained alchemists into battle?

A young teen West American alchemist fell into the mud, gasping out a curdled scream, blood gushing from his right side. A West American soldier sprinted forward to help. Hunching, he hitched his gun over his shoulder and stretched out his arms. A masked Guardian jumped in between the two, shooting the soldier down, his body landing inches from the boy. Then the Guardian quickly tended to the wounds of the fallen alchemist with streams of green magic, all the while restraining the kid with a zip tie. He hauled the lanky boy into his arms and ran. I squinted, eyes following them, questions burning.

"Remember, orders are to keep as many alchemists alive as possible," someone shouted from down the street. Their barking orders barely carried over the roar of battle. The Guardian carrying the kid ducked around the fighters, disappearing into the distance.

Keep the alchemists alive? It had to mean one thing: Richard didn't want to waste magic. He saw no problem with everyday soldiers and civilians losing their lives, but the alchemists were too valuable. He would keep them, like pets.

The carnage continued and revulsion boiled up inside. Bodies littered the streets, streams of alchemy shot alongside the bullets. It tore me up, seeing something that could be used for such good, twisted in this horrific way. How much longer could this continue?

A West American alchemist stumbled into the alleyway. I threw myself against the brick building before the woman careened into me. Was she hurt? I held my rose to my chest, blood rushing through my ears, as I looked her up and down. I didn't see any wounds. Dressed in black, her wrinkled hands ran along her gleaming necklace as she gasped in short breaths. She dropped her hands to her sides and a second necklace appeared, one full of black stones. They were stacked in neat rows, shiny orbs that blended with her clothing. My breath caught, confusion bubbling inside.

Was she a black alchemist? What did black magic even do?

I forced myself to remain against the wall as I studied her. She was older, maybe in her sixties, and something about her was incredibly familiar. She had silvery blonde bobbed hair and light knowing eyes. Sweat soaked her skin in the sunlight, as if she'd exerted herself more than usual. She was powerful beyond imagination, dressed like that in a place like this.

A slatebook pinged at her belt. She fumbled, pulling it close to her mouth, talking low. "I'm here," she said. "I made it this far. Now what?"

"You're only five blocks east from Imperial High School," an authoritative male voice replied, booming from the speakers. She must have turned the sound all the way up because of the noisy battle. "That's where we have reason to believe King Richard just landed and many of his troops are there to guard him. Get there and use your weapon."

She nodded, a little reluctantly, squinting up into the sun. She slid her slatebook back into place and squared her shoulders. "Here we go," she muttered. And then she took off, jogging as fast as her body would take her.

Imperial High School?

Use your weapon?

Confusion interlaced with sinking dread filled me, making my feet feel like anchors, pinning me to the concrete. If my father was near that area, then I had to assume Jessa was near as well. I took a resolute breath and ran back down to the other side of the alley, deciding it would be better to travel in the areas that weren't currently a bloody battleground. My boots pounded against the pavement, dodging rubble and the occasional fallen body.

I tried not to look too closely at the dead, tried not to picture the way their lives should have gone, with family and friends, with happiness and living into old age. But I couldn't help it. The guilt flashed the images through my mind anyway.

Before long, I rounded the final corner of the fifth block, the school's patchy green and brown lawn sprawling out in front of me, a field of death. The entire area swarmed with soldiers, their magic and bodies and guns clashing in a cacophony of cries and smoke and blood. The sun arched high, making the air as hot as the battle.

Or maybe it was nerves that made me feel like I was boiling from the inside out.

I lunged forward. The gratitude for my invisibility pulsed through my veins as my boots tore through the field, escaping notice. After a minute that felt like an hour, I approached the high school, fully unscathed. Taking the front steps two at a time, I rushed through the doors and skidded to a stop in the large lobby.

I eyed the glass partition, looking into what appeared to be a large office on the other side. Inside stood my father, his advisor Mark and Mark's wife, Sabine, a few alchemists and soldiers, a blonde girl dressed in black who was apparently under arrest, sulking in the corner with guns trained on her, and in the center of it all, Jessa. My heart burned when I saw her, saw the way she was standing, saw the pain etched in her every line and curve. She had her arms crossed over her chest, lips turned down in a frown, and eyes so full of fear I thought they might spill over.

I crept across the lobby and waited for someone to open the door. A couple of soldiers with determined gazes careened into the lobby, going right for the door and giving me the very opportunity I needed. I followed easily, pressing myself against the far wall the moment I entered the office.

"Your Royal Highness," one of the soldiers said, dipping low in a quick bow. "Something is happening outside. They have some kind of…unknown weapon. I think you need to see this."

Richard's mouth fell into a flat line, and he trudged past me and out the door. "I'll be right back," he called after him, the door swinging shut as he went.

Perhaps I should have followed, but something held me rooted in place, my back against the wall.

"You should have done it then," Sabine turned on Jessa, her eyes two angry slits. "You were standing right next to him!"

"You don't understand," Jessa sputtered. "I tried to do this once before and I failed. It's not that simple. He'll kill me if I mess up again."

"Don't be so afraid to do your duty."

"It's *not* my duty."

The woman slapped Jessa across the face, the sound a sharp crack. Jessa stumbled back. Hate shot through every cell in my body. Who was this woman that she thought she could touch Jessa?

Mark held up a hand, eyes drawn in understanding. "Sabine, none of that. She'll do it; she just needs the perfect opportunity. She knows her sister will die if she doesn't."

My breath caught. In the corner, the blonde girl in black laughed, blue eyes shining. The same eyes as Jessa. "You think you're going to be able to use me as leverage forever?"

Her sister. It clicked into place. Jessa had told me about all of this. Why hadn't I believed her when I still had the chance to help?

"Shut up," one of the alchemist guardians ground out the insult, hitting her with the butt of his rifle so hard she slumped down against the wall, head awkwardly tilting to one side.

"Don't you touch her!" Jessa yelled, angrily charging the guy. "What did you do?"

He spun, pointing his gun at her. "Careful, Princess."

"Don't you dare point that at her!" Mark shot out, and the boy dropped his gun, a sheepish expression rising on his lips.

"Jessa, you need to relax," Sabine said, touching her auburn hair gently as if a strand were out of place. "Sasha has only been knocked out. She'll be fine."

Untapped rage built as I watched these people treat Jessa like some kind of prisoner, like a tool to use however they saw fit. What did they have on her? Was my father part of this? I considered Sasha, a girl Jessa would do anything to protect. A sister.

"You will order the King to kill himself," Sabine said, finger pointing at Jessa. "Next time he's near, you will do it. It will be easy. You will scratch him and use your red or I swear we'll kill your sister. The world would be free of one less alchemist pest, but I have a feeling she'd rather live."

Jessa nodded, face ashen, fat tears breaking loose and streaming down her face. I ground my teeth.

"And then, as we discussed, you will get to Lucas. We'll have to talk to Celia again, see if Lucas still deserves a place in this," Mark continued. "But for now, let's head outside and see what this West American weapon is all about."

The group moved toward the exit, one Guardian gripping Jessa's upper arm, shoving her forward. The other standing watch over Sasha, kicking at her boot. He let out a huff and reached down to haul her over his shoulder. Her arms and head flopped against his back as he strode forward.

I was still pressed against the wall. The rage that had been building came to an all-out eruption.

They were going to blackmail her to kill my father and then me? They were using my wife to take control of New Colony for themselves? Or maybe they were West American spies.

I didn't think so.

I dove forward, tackling Mark around his middle and slamming him to the ground.

Someone screamed, but I didn't pay that any attention as I pummeled the traitor's face. Blood sprayed in all directions. His eyes shone full of terror, probably because I was still invisible!

Realization dawned and he fought back. He kicked out at me, arms flying. He connected with my nose and blood pooled in my mouth as his meaty fist crashed against my teeth.

The sick bastard. I would kill him.

At some point, it was not only his arms that I could see flying, but mine as well.

I had dropped the rose.

His gaze leveled with mine, first widening in surprise before transforming into mocking enjoyment.

"Oh, Lucas, have you been hiding a dirty little secret?" He cackled.

Over his shoulder, I caught the sight of the others fighting as well. The girl who'd supposedly passed out was alive and well, kicking the ever-loving crap out of the two alchemist dudes who'd been guarding her. Jessa was attacking Sabine, quick to overtake the polished woman who didn't have magic or a gun.

"I should have done a better job the first time I tried to kill you," Mark ground out. My gaze returned to the man pinned beneath me, confusion peaking. I reached out my fist again, ready to strike, when he slammed me back, shifting the balance of power. I fell to the ground, landing hard on my back, elbows scraping against the rough carpet. He jumped up, kicking me with his steel-toed boots. Pain overpowered the thoughts in my brain, sweeping over my body.

"Does this look familiar?" he continued.

Outside, muffled screams and bullets and chaos echoed faintly. If anyone saw what was happening in this office, they didn't come. They couldn't. They were too busy with whatever New Colony's new weapon was to come inside here. I had to get myself out of this mess, but I could barely push past the agony as Mark pummeled me again and again.

I blinked up at the man, seeing red. Something flashed through my mind, taking in his words. *Does this look familiar?* It did. Was it a memory? Déjà vu?

I had been in this position before.

My brain sent flashes of images, electric pulses of memory. The night he'd tried to kill me overtook my vision. I saw it all. The look on Jessa's face when I'd told her we had to get her out of the palace. The same look when I'd said goodbye to her at the safe house and when she'd dropped my mother's ring back into my shaking hand. My deep sadness as I'd wandered around the palace that night. Mark hiding out in that darkened nursery. His rage when he realized it was me who found him, me who'd shamed his family, his name. And the way he'd ruthlessly attacked me, had so clearly tried to kill me.

"It was you," I coughed, copper filling my mouth. My arms and legs didn't seem to know how to fight back anymore. They lay useless at my sides, paralyzed by pain. I was succumbing to the agony. It covered me like a thick blanket.

"It was, and it has been," Mark continued. "We've been trying to get rid of your nasty family for months now."

Another boot connected with my face.

"Your mother's funeral."

A crack broke my rib.

"The jet explosion."

Something crushed against my skull.

Fight back.

I willed every ounce of strength I had, wanting to live. I couldn't give up now. I couldn't let him win.

"You should have married my Celia," he continued.

He jumped on top of me, blood dripping as he leered close to my face. My eyes were so swollen that he blurred above me.

"This time I'm going to finish the job."

And I believed him.

More memories flashed through my mind. Meeting Jessa, the way she'd hated me at first, the way she'd used alchemy on me by accident with the fire. Sharing a meal with her out on the grass, a picnic under the stars. How much I had wanted to kiss her, despite my better judgment. And the moment I *had* finally kissed her, how amazing she had felt wrapped up in my arms. And then that helicopter had come, spinning the wind around us, pulling us apart.

And Sasha. Her sister.

The Resistance and everything that had happened with them.

I squinted up, trying to focus on something else. Jessa's sister, Sasha, was finishing off her fight with the blonde guy. He collapsed and she turned, staring down at me with wide eyes.

"Sasha!" I called, my voice sounding gargled and far away. "Help Jessa."

She darted forward, gripping at Mark's shoulders with a shrill war-cry.

Jessa appeared, on the other side of Mark, also screaming.

"No," I tried to tell her, but the word was swallowed by blood. I didn't want her in this fight, he was crazy. And she, she was everything...

Out of everything I remembered, what came through with absolute clarity was how many times I'd failed Jessa. I'd hurt her, the one I loved most. I couldn't do it again. I would die if it meant she could be free of the destruction I always seemed to bring down on her world.

Mark's rage burned down on me as he hit me one last time.

The two sisters wrenched him back and connected with the blood that coated Mark. He screamed in retaliation. But he had no chance.

The blood between us faded to gray.

Hope surged.

And then my consciousness fell, lost to the gray, faded to black, before I could even catch my breath.

EIGHTEEN

JESSA

Fury poured through me, white hot and cutting. My vision blurred and narrowed in on Mark Addington's body. I pulled and pulled at his blood, draining the color, leaching it until it was nothing but a mess of lifeless gray liquid. Too angry to direct the red magic to go anywhere or do anything productive, it swirled around Sasha and myself in a tornado of unused energy. She didn't care. Her hands also pushed against Mark. Her anger was just as thick.

I blinked at her, realizing the truth. My sister had my same power. She was doing this, too. We smiled at each other. We couldn't stop, wouldn't stop. The masses of gray blood were our salvation. We knew what it meant. Death. The power of it thundered through us, strengthening our bond, and building the magic of the moment into a frenzied, lustful, never-ending storm.

"No!" Sabine screamed. I turned the magic on her, reaching out a second hand to snatch her bloodied arm.

"Go!" I commanded. "Don't tell anyone we're here. Get

away from us!"

She ran.

I turned back to the horrible man at my feet. He deserved it. More than anyone, it was Mark I wanted to hurt. And I was almost there. If I went on longer, he would die and that would be justice. His body would become nothing but a dead mass lying on top of Lucas.

Lucas...

I stopped. I didn't want to be a murderer, no matter how much Mark deserved to die. That wasn't who I was. That wasn't why I was doing this. And Lucas was the one who needed attention right now, not Mark.

I lifted my hands and sat back. My eyes connected with my sister as she did the same. "I didn't know you could do that, too," I said lamely.

"I never wanted you to know." She shook her head, sadness seeping over her deflated body. "I never want anyone to know. I put that kind of magic behind me a long time ago."

I nodded. "I get it. If I could wish it away, I would."

We were alone in the office with all of these injured men, two powerful girls who wanted nothing more than normalcy. Sasha crawled over to the two passed-out Guardians. She touched their bloodied forms, whispering for them to sleep, to sleep until tomorrow, to dream of nothing but darkness.

Outside, the battle continued.

I frowned down at Lucas, mind finally cleared enough to help him. He was passed out, but once I healed him, I was sure he'd be fine. He had to be fine. My heart couldn't bear it otherwise. Wrenching Mark's huge body out of the way, I kneeled before my prince, ready to assess the wounds. My breath caught.

Wait–No...

Lucas was white as a sheet, unblinking eyes lifeless. He

didn't move. Not even his chest rose or fell. Panic swept through me as I ran my hands over his body. The once vibrant blood that had covered his face was now completely gray, dripping off him in streams of iron.

I shook him, gently at first. "Lucas?"

He didn't respond.

I shook him harder, tears springing to my eyes. "Lucas, are you okay? Wake up!"

"Lucas, please!" My voice came out cracked and hoarse. I found Sasha's gaze. She would know what to do. But she sputtered, horror struck.

"We took too much," she whispered, a lone tear rolling down her cheek.

"No." I frowned. "No. We were using it on Mark, not Lucas."

Sasha's eyes mirrored back at me, brimming with pity. "It was an accident," she said, voice even. "You have to remember that this was an accident, Jessa. We would have never done this on purpose."

"What are you even talking about?" I growled. I looked away and leaned over Lucas, shaking him once again. But he was gone.

No...

What happened? We'd gone after Mark. It was never supposed to be Lucas. I looked around horrified, everything sinking in as I realized that both of their blood had been all over each other. When we'd stepped in to stop Mark, we must have somehow also pulled alchemy from Lucas.

Lucas, who had already lost so much blood.

Lucas, who'd been on the edge of death.

No!

"He's dead," my sister confirmed. "They both are. I'm so sorry."

I screamed, a high-pitched eruption that transformed into a guttural moan.

"Go find some green," I begged. "Please."

She didn't question me, didn't tell me it was too late. She sprinted to the desk behind us, fumbling with the mess sprawled across it, papers falling to the floor.

"Here!" She tossed a small bamboo shoot growing out of a little yellow pot. I caught it, staring down dumbly at the sparkly trinket wrapped around the green shoot: a tiny golden elephant.

Refocusing, I grappled at the green, shooting the magic through Lucas.

Nothing

This couldn't be happening!

Sasha stood above me, her body trembling. "This is why I never wanted to do it again," her voice croaked. "This was why I ran in the first place. I never should've done it again. I knew better." Her head dropped into her hands. "I am so sorry."

I couldn't deal with her. I couldn't do this. I couldn't believe it.

I pulled Lucas's head to me and tenderly laid it into my lap, brushing the strands of dark hair out of his face. We'd been through so much together. Had it really come to this? Had I just murdered my own husband?

I'd been so afraid he was turning into his father but it was me who'd been overcome with power. I was the one who'd used my magic to kill, the one who'd relished in the feel of it. If anyone was like King Richard, it was me. I was nothing but a destructive force of nature.

My mouth fell open in a silent scream and hot tears rolled down my cheeks, the salt sinking into the corners around my mouth. I gasped, my heart ripping out of my chest, this day sinking in deep.

I'd been so worried about Lucas, and yet, I'd turned away from him. I'd been so frustrated with his memory loss, so annoyed, when none of that was even his fault. He didn't choose that. Mark had done it to him!

And in the middle of what had happened over the last few weeks, I'd forgotten just how much I loved him.

But I did. I loved him.

I knew it the moment we'd first kissed. I knew it again when that farmer told me Lucas's death had been announced. But here I was, with him lying before me, really dead this time, and the pain was more unbearable than anything I'd ever experienced before. It was too much.

And it wasn't enough.

"We have to get out of here," Sasha said. "There's something going on outside. I think West America's gaining ground right now. We need to take this chance while we can."

I was numb. I couldn't move, could barely hear Sasha.

"Come on, Jessa," Sasha pressed. "We need to go."

"No," I snapped. I wasn't giving up on Lucas; there had to be a way. This couldn't be over. This couldn't be the end. I couldn't accept that.

"You need to come." She reached out, tugging on my arm.

I slapped her away, my voice turning dark. "I said no. Leave me alone."

More gunshots ricocheted outside. An even louder bang shook the floor. Or maybe that was just my body shaking?

She groaned. "I'll be back." Then she ran for the door. I didn't watch to see where she went after that. I didn't care.

I took in the room, blinking.

Dazed.

Mystified.

Mark was dead. Sabine was long gone. The two alchemists

were still asleep. But it was Lucas who needed me. I couldn't leave him.

I brushed his swollen face with the back of my hand, my tears still falling in droves. One dropped and landed on his forehead, splashing and then rolling off the side. Another fell and hit his eyelid. If I squinted, I could almost believe it was his tear.

No, there has to be another way. I can't give up. I just need more color.

Even as the thoughts came into my head, I knew they were foolish. I didn't care about that, either.

Carefully placing his head on the floor, I pried myself off the floor and looked around the office. Anything, any color would have to do. I would try it all, push everything into him and maybe something would work.

I grabbed a flag first from where it was tacked to the wall: red, white and blue. I pulled over a chair, an ugly burnt orange color. I grabbed a blue book off of the desk, tugged at the purple sweater left on the back of the desk's rolling chair.

I gathered the items around me and unleashed the colors. The magic came from synthetic materials so they were mostly weak, but I no longer cared. I had to try. It was all I had left.

And I was determined, more determined than I'd ever been in my life.

The color swirled, a weaving, dancing, pulsing messy rainbow. What color would possibly help him now? I had no idea, but I pushed them, one by one, at Lucas.

Nothing took.

Frustration left me gasping, the tears falling again. But I was not ready to give up. I kept going. And kept failing.

I doubled over, gathering the scratchy purple sweater into my hands and burying my face in it, sobbing.

"Please don't leave me, Lucas," I begged. I inched my hand away from the sweater and grabbed at him, shook him. "Please don't leave me here alone. I can't do this by myself. I need you."

The color from the purple sweater swirled in the air, a physical representation of the passion currently roiling inside me. I knew what I wanted in this life and it was him. As much as I'd always loved to dance, as much as I'd always loved my family, as much as I had loved anything, *I loved Lucas.*

I loved him more.

More than anything.

He was my reason. He was my reason for living and I couldn't go on without him. I couldn't imagine my life without him in it.

"Please," I whispered again, pulling my face from the sweater.

The purple alchemy swirling around the office separated, the color changing to red and blue. I had done this before. This wasn't new. On several occasions, I separated a color down into its two primary sources. But all it had ever done was exhaust me. It was useless! I hadn't ever been able figure out what these primary colors could do. What was different today?

At first, I was annoyed. Angry. This was the last thing I needed. It would only exhaust me and I didn't want to fall asleep in this moment. I wanted to be here with Lucas, to keep trying.

A startling thought popped into my mind.

Why not? Why not try this new magic on Lucas?

"Come back to me," I whispered to him, one last time, a new kind of power taking hold, running through me like wildfire.

Instinct as my guide, I pushed the color, the blue and the red, down into Lucas's body. The blue bounced away, became frenetic, almost electric, and bounded through the room.

The red, however, was quick to take. It swirled into him like a loving caress.

I gasped, a jolt of adrenaline shooting through me. Hope swelled, my eyes hardly believing what I saw. The colorless gray blood that covered him from head to toe was changing.

Slowly, it transformed back into its original red.

The shine of steel gray blood disappeared, vibrant red taking its place.

I shrieked, pushing green alchemy at Lucas once again. His pale face began to brighten, blood flowing.

The tears in my eyes streamed down my face as I stared, mystified, at everything. At Lucas, and at the colors still whirling through the room. The purple I had separated had created a rare kind of red magic, not the kind that destroyed, but rather the kind that *restored*. It had started that night of the ballet, and for months and months I had been wondering what this separation magic meant. Now I knew. Once separated, a color could return what had been lost. My mind raced to the Shadow Lands, to all this could do for our world. But that only lasted for a moment as I stared at Lucas, he was all I could see. I collapsed on top of him, sobbing with relief and awe.

"You okay?" Lucas asked in a scratchy voice. "Why are you crying? Are you hurt?"

I hugged him tighter. "I'm fine," I mumbled between the sobs. He winced against the pressure of my body. I reached out behind me until I found the bamboo shoot and pushed what little green I could into him, healing the last of his wounds. Then I sat back and looked at him, running a gentle palm down the side of his face, staring into his sparkling gray eyes, my breath catching, my heart filled.

"Seriously, Jessa, are you okay?" he asked again.

"Am I okay?" I shifted off of him, giving him space and studying his eyes. "Lucas, you died."

He sat up slowly, rubbing his head, looking me up and down like a man returned after years away from home. He smiled. "Well, whatever happened, I'm not dead now."

I crawled over, sitting on his lap and gripping his face between my fingers, kissing him as hard as I could. He met me with equal passion, and my tears once again broke free. To be here, in this moment with him, it meant everything. I never wanted it to end. I'd lost him once, maybe more than once. I couldn't lose him again. After a moment, he gently pried me off him, eyes gleaming with mischief and passion.

"What was that for?" he asked.

"I love you," I said. "I love you so much."

He smiled as his eyes darkened. "I love you, too. And Jessa?"

"Yes," I breathed.

"I remember everything." He wrapped his warm arms around me and kissed me all over again. He tasted of everything I'd ever longed for, his lips the comfort I'd been longing to find.

Another blast of sound followed by a violent shake of the earth pulled us apart. "We'd better get out there," I said.

He held me back. "I'm not supposed to be alive, remember?"

I frowned at him.

"What I mean is, my father has been hiding me. I had to use invisibility to get out here in the first place. I'm supposed to be back in the bunker right now. I can't just walk out there like this." He motioned to himself.

I scrunched my nose as I looked around the mess of

objects and the splattering of blood. Under a pile of fallen papers, I located the edge of the rose. I pulled it out with a smile and held it out to Lucas. "There's still some white left," I said. "We can't stay here."

He took it in his hands and I wondered if he had enough strength after dying and all, but that question was answered as he instantly turned himself invisible. He grasped my hand in his free one and changed me, too.

"Come on," he said. "Let's see what's going on outside and take it from there."

I sucked in a breath, knowing I had to ask the question. "Umm, Lucas? Whose side are we on?" Now that he had his memories back, how did he feel about this war? He had to know Richard was evil. If I told him about what his father had been making me do with my red alchemy, he'd be livid, but I felt so much shame in admitting the truth.

"Not my father's," he answered quickly. "But also, I don't know how I feel about the other side, either. Mostly I just want things to go back to the way they were. I want to step up and do a better job with what we have, to make the best of it instead of trying to change everything."

I laughed. "I don't think that's going to happen."

I felt his gaze looking fruitlessly for mine. "Don't say that. We can still try."

I nodded, even though I knew he couldn't see me. Together we stood, hand in hand, and left the office. The double doors to the outside world loomed ahead. This was the beginning, or maybe it was the end, but at least this time we had each other.

"What will we find out there?" I whispered.

"I honestly don't know," he replied, his voice catching in defeat.

I squeezed his hand in reassurance. If he could be strong

for me, I could be strong for him. "Don't worry. Whatever is next, we'll figure it out together."

We burst through the doors, confronted with chaos. On the front lawn and out into the streets, soldiers and citizens fought in a clash of hand-to-hand combat. Occasional bullets streaked through the air. A small bomb detonated, crumbling the side of a building. A window broke, the sound crashing through the moment of stillness.

And the alchemists? They were retreating. All of them.

I froze, not quite sure what I was seeing. Most of those left were New Colony's super-soldiers, proud Guardians, suits embedded with stones making them nearly impossible to fight. From the yellow that made them strong and fast, to the green that allowed them to heal instantly, to the more unique situations, like the persuasive blue, or the telepathic purple, or even the emotional driving force that was orange. All of that should've meant The Guardians of Color ought to be running into the fight, not away from it.

"Come on." Lucas hauled me forward, talking low into my ear, "Nobody can see us. I have the rose, remember? We need to figure out what is really going on here and make a plan."

I nodded, realizing too late that he couldn't see me. Not that it mattered. We ran down the steps together, solid in our agreement.

I caught sight of Sasha sprinting across the lawn toward us and faltered.

"Sasha!" I screamed, not even thinking.

She must have heard because she stopped, looking around with confusion and panic lighting up her glacial blue eyes. Lucas and I ran over and I spoke normally when we were a couple feet away from her.

"I'm with Lucas. He's alive. What's happening?"

She blinked. "Jessa?"

"Yes, we're here. White alchemy. Remember?"

Her confusion cleared and she spoke, words rushing out, "We have to get out of here. Our powers, they're not working. If she gets close enough to you."

"What are you talking about?"

Sasha didn't answer me. Her head swung side to side, taking in the sight of more retreating alchemists.

"There!" Lucas called out, tugging me back against his warm body. He very well could have been pointing to something off in the distance but I couldn't see it. It didn't matter. I saw exactly what he was concerned about. Fear welled up inside of me, fear, and the realization that nothing would ever be the same.

An older woman dressed in the black garb of alchemy strode up the lawn. Around her, West American soldiers held out their guns, as if protecting her. In the center of the mass of soldiers, was a familiar face. I knew him! I knew that closely cropped white-blonde hair and those intense brooding green eyes. I knew that confident swagger, the way he looked at the world as if he were in charge of keeping it. He was Sasha's friend! One of the two guys who'd come to get me out of the cellar the night I'd run away. He looked different in full daylight, younger somehow, but just as intense as before. Actually, way more intense than before. He looked deadly.

"What are they doing? Who is she?" I turned to Sasha.

Sasha growled. "She is the American President! And Apparently *she* is Weapon X!"

"Weapon X?"

"I'll explain later…" Sasha's voice trailed off.

She didn't have to explain because I saw it. A dark cloud of black billowed at Weapon X's feet, like a supernatural mist. The president was an alchemist? The news was both shocking and completely reasonable. No wonder she'd been rumored to be such an advocate for alchemy.

"See that? It's black alchemy," Lucas said.

"I didn't know such a thing even existed. What does it do?" I asked.

As if in answer, a string of the black snaked out from the woman, swirling around one of the fleeing alchemists. The speed at which the man had been running slowed to almost nothing. He stumbled and fell, and the West American soldiers swarmed him, placing him under arrest.

"It's rather obvious, don't you think?" Sasha replied, but not in a mean way, but a defeated one. "It makes it so we can't use our powers. We need to go. One lick of that black over here and you two will be visible again."

The president jogged up the lawn, her eyes darting around as she looked for her next victim. Suddenly, she closed her eyes, intense focus lining her features. The cloud of black multiplied, billowing out across the lawn, moving in all directions.

"What the hell are you still doing here?" A guy ran out in front of us, arms waving at Sasha. He turned back toward the group of West Americas, yelling over the chaos at the woman. "Stop! She's one of us! Remember?"

She froze, black magic pausing.

I also recognized the guy as another of Sasha's friends. Wasn't his name Tristan? I'd met him the first time I'd dropped my parents off at the Resistance camp, and then again later. He was the other soldier who'd accompanied Sasha to the farm to get me.

"Don't go after her!" Tristan yelled, standing in front of Sasha. "She's one of us."

"Stand down," the blonde soldier called out. "Our orders

are to collect all of the alchemists, on either side."

"So that's why you brought all those untrained alchemists out here!" Sasha yelled angrily. "Most haven't even fought, you know. They all ran and hid the second we landed, my sister included."

"We have your sister," the guy replied, voice carrying over the lawn. "She's fine. I made sure of it myself."

Sasha shook her head and crossed her arms over her chest, eyes roaming the field as if she were trying to decide whether to give in to the order, or to make a run for it. The soldiers surrounding the president were much closer now, moving in succession and ready to strike. Lucas and I crept back but my sister seemed to be totally transfixed on the men in front of her.

"Sasha, come on!" I called out as loud as I dared.

She didn't budge.

"What does that stuff do to them long-term?" Tristan yelled at the group, staying put in front of Sasha. His black hair gleamed in the sunlight, so sweaty it stuck to his face and neck. His arms were folded, a rifle slung over his back. "Does it wear off?"

Nobody replied. The black magic had snapped out again, catching another alchemist, and the soldiers were at work detaining the screaming woman. Again and again, it went on. A piece would reach out from the small billowing cloud, travel across the ground like a snake, and wrap itself around an alchemist from as far as a hundred feet away.

Sasha, Lucas, and I? We were much closer than a hundred feet away. All it took was that woman deciding she was going to send her magic at us and that would be it. We'd be caught.

"Sasha, let's go," I ground out again. "We're going to leave your butt here if you don't get moving."

"They won't stop," Sasha replied angrily. "This was never

part of the deal. I can't believe she kept this secret for so long! Well, the military must have known…"

She gasped and pointed. I caught sight of someone I knew. Someone I loved!

"Callie!"

She fell to her knees, helmet popping off her head and glasses flying. In an instant, West American soldiers surrounded her.

"Please!" she screamed. "I didn't want to help Richard, I never wanted this."

I held back a scream, remembering the time she'd questioned me out on the terrace about the Resistance. She hadn't been one of Faulk's spies. She'd been honest, wanting to help, to join up, and I'd lied to her. Guilt swept low in my belly and I turned away. I couldn't help her, not without magic.

"Mastin!" Sasha called. "What is this? Why didn't you tell me ahead of time about this?"

The crowd parted and he stared from across the lawn. His face faltered as he met Sasha's angry expression. He broke from his group and ran forward.

"I'm sorry," he replied, coming to stop in front of her. Tristan stood to the side, glaring. Both men were dirty and bloody, both looking at Sasha like she meant the world. "We'll sort it all out later. Right now, we need to finish this thing. Where's Richard? He was just here."

She shook her head, hands clenching into fists. "I can't believe you would do this to me, after everything. I really want to punch you right now, Mastin."

His head dropped and he stepped back.

"Whatever, I'm out of here," she grumbled, and took off running. Lucas and I followed, footsteps light on the grass, heartbeat loud in my ears. Tristan caught up quickly, bringing in the rear.

"It's the only way!" The president called out, apologetic. "Please forgive me."

The black magic shot out across the grass, lightning fast. It swirled around us like a tidal wave. A dull aching pain burned through me, creeping up my bones, coupled with overwhelming exhaustion. I stumbled, losing Lucas's hand.

It didn't matter. The magic wrapped around him, too.

Visible now, we fell to our knees.

Just ahead Sasha laid on her side, face pinched in frustration. Tristan tried to lift her into his arms, but he was too slow. Soldiers swarmed. My mind was too tired to notice much of what else was happening. I pushed through the fog anyway, trying to find coherent thought or a way out.

Zip-ties cinched my arms behind my back. I was under arrest. Lucas, too.

"Don't you dare touch him!" Richard's voice bellowed over the landscape. I blinked up against the grass, the black mercifully gone, to see the King's beet-red face.

My exhaustion was beginning to weigh on me, and now it was stronger than ever. But it was my magic that concerned me. My magic, a faint humming sensation, a flowing presence in my body that I didn't even know existed before, was gone.

The King ran, guards and officers flanking him. A group of three shuffling just behind them. Immediately, I recognized Jose and Lily. I had wondered where they'd been, but had been grateful not to see them until now. Had I interviewed them like I had Branson, they'd be dead, too. They were Resistance, but as I saw them now, a tug of confusion pulled at me. Jose had a gun pressed to a man's head. A man dressed in the kind of West American regalia that meant he was important.

"Dad!" Someone called out in a horrified tone. It was blonde soldier from before that Sasha had called Mastin. My heart dropped for him. I knew what felt like to see your own father in that kind of situation.

Richard cackled, eyes angry. "It really is a family affair."

Jose, sparkling in his white Royal Officer uniform, pressed the gun closer to the man's head. "Don't come any closer or he's dead," he snapped, nodding at Mastin and the others.

"Everybody put your hands up," Richard spat. He glared at the group of enemy soldiers. "Do it, or watch your General die." The group froze, nobody wanting to relent.

Richard walked forward, "Who's the highest ranking here?"

"Me," Mastin replied coolly with the jut of his chin.

I craned my neck, looking for the president. She was the highest ranking! But in all the chaos, she'd disappeared.

Very convenient.

"Give me my son and I'll give you your father," Richard replied. He was splattered with blood and dirt, soot smeared across his cheek. But even with all of that, he was the same commanding man he'd always been.

Silence filled the area as if everyone had forgotten to breathe, and maybe they had. I forced the air from my lungs, taking it all in. The West American soldiers on one side, weapons drawn. Richard on the other, his loyalist people surrounding him. Lucas, Sasha and I, kneeling in the dirt. Jose, Lily, and the General, the gun pressed to his head.

It was too charged, too intense. My heart pounded, my palms grew sweaty, my heart racing ahead of my thoughts. Before this was over, someone was going to die.

Finally, Mastin nodded.

Jose pushed the general forward, spinning his gun on Richard.

I gasped, hope spreading. Richard balked, stepping back, confusion flashing across his face, followed by a wave of pure fury.

"You!" he growled. "You will die for this, you traitor."

"Shut up," Jose replied, shoving the gun closer. "I'd like nothing more in this moment than to kill you."

"You'll die too," Richard snapped. He nodded toward his people who'd also raised their guns. "They'll kill you the second you pull that trigger."

"It would be my pleasure to die if it meant taking you with me," Jose growled. "Unfortunately, we made a deal to turn you over to West America alive."

Richard glared. "A deal?"

"That's right. As soon as the battle started we reached out to General Scott."

He pointed toward Sasha, who had now walked over to join the group. "Sasha was able to set everything up for us and make the proper introductions. It was her idea, you know. You always did underestimate the young ones."

"You're under arrest," Scott snapped at Richard as he stood. He brushed himself off and glared triumphantly at the crowd. Sasha sidled up next to him, her arms crossed, as she sneered at Richard.

"That's right, old man. The Resistance and West America joined forces. Bet you didn't see that one coming, did you?"

Richard barked a laugh. "You're pathetic."

Sasha cocked her head. "And you're the one under arrest."

There were still plenty of guns pointed in all directions, but it was clear West America now had the upper hand. And they also had Richard right where they needed him. I met Lucas's gaze and saw a flash of peace there.

"You okay?" I whispered.

"It needed to happen," he whispered back.

"Please, if you don't surrender this very minute," Lily stepped forward, her voice as sweet as chimes blowing in the wind, "you will die. I've seen it myself."

Lily was the King's personal oracle, and he was used to taking her word as gold. His eyes flitted up to her, resignation filling them. He still didn't know she was Resistance too, though he probably had his suspicions now.

"You saw it?"

She nodded, her ethereal voice high as she continued to speak, "If you don't surrender, you won't make it off this field alive. Please, Your Highness."

He fumed, but ever so slowly, he sank to his knees, raising his hands in surrender.

"Give me those," Sasha said to one of the Royal Officers. The man handed her a pair of gleaming silver handcuffs.

Satisfied, she slapped them over the King's wrists, squeezing them as tight as possible.

NINETEEN
SASHA

During my early teenage years, whenever I'd gotten extra grumpy, Hank had always told me to count my blessings. I'd found that notion ridiculously annoying and immature. But now, I didn't think so. Here I was, rattling off blessings one by one, trying desperately to feel better. Because tonight? Oh, tonight I was extra grumpy and surrounded with blessings.

Blessing number one: my family was reunited again. Or at least, we would be soon. I was assured Jessa would be released within the hour. Lacey had been returned the moment we'd come back to our base, because what did they have to question a six-year-old for, anyway?

Blessing number two: after Mastin had found out I'd been keeping Branson's email address from the General, he'd made me turn it in. I hadn't thought much about it until the morning we'd left for battle. I had gone straight to General Scott and told him my plan. I didn't know every member of the Resistance but he was able to fill in the gaps. And it was how he'd been able to join forces with Lily and Jose, pulling off the incredible stunt that had led to Richard's capture. I found Lily's role in it particularly amusing.

Which led me to blessing number three: the capture itself. That was enough to keep me happy for the rest of my life. Richard would be behind bars for war crimes and I would never have to deal with his level of evil again. It's what all of this had been for in the first place.

So why did I still feel so angry?

I trudged across the hill overlooking the little town that had become our base, my favorite spot so far out of all the places I'd stayed since joining the West American cause. The town was quaint and secluded, the sweeping views calming. But I didn't find myself calm today. Not in the slightest.

I'd been pacing back and forth along the top of the hill for nearly an hour, thinking of all the things I was going to say to Mastin. Like, how dare he keep Weapon X from me like that. And where did he get off allowing her to use that blasted black magic on me? It wasn't what friends did to each other, let alone what you did to someone you cared about on a deeper level.

The betrayal burned deeper than I cared to admit.

"I thought I might find you up here," his voice called out gruffly. He stalked up the hill, boots smacking against the dewy grass. He had his tough-guy attitude on but his face said it all; the man knew he was in big trouble.

The second our eyes met, my anger drained away.

And was replaced by hurt.

And sadness so much bigger than I'd expected. How could he?

I dropped my head, tears prickling. Maybe I didn't want to talk to him, after all. I wasn't ready for this.

"Look," he said, sighing, stopping in front of me. "I'm

really sorry about what happened. I was ordered not to say a word to you."

I turned on him, studying him, looking for a crack in his story. He was as beautiful as ever, with his flaxen hair and striking green eyes, with his high cheekbones and perfect bow lips. None of those things pulled me in as they usually did. They were a lie, an elaborate set-up to break my heart and win his war.

"Let me ask you this," I said. "Did you fight your father on those orders?"

His face fell. "No."

Because he probably agreed with it. The betrayal multiplied, but I held it in. "And if you hadn't gotten those orders, if you'd been allowed to tell me the truth ahead of time, would you have told me about her?"

Her. The wonderful, thoughtful, spit-fire president who'd gained my trust only to turn it against me. Her. The weapon who'd come between us.

He glanced away, face grim as he took in the sunset. "Probably not," he finally relented. "You wouldn't have understood. We had to do it; it needed to be perfect. This has been a military secret for so long, we couldn't just tell anyone."

"Why the kids though?" I challenged. "That doesn't make sense to me."

"That part I was never okay with," he said. "But we never actually expected them to fight and we knew Richard's people would try to keep them for him. So that's why they were ordered as soon as we landed. The idea was that Madame President needed to subdue as much alchemy as possible. She needed to get everyone in one swoop before the surprise was lost. It was the best advantage we could think of to win this war in the long run."

I huffed, disbelieving the level of their secrecy and awed at the brilliance of their plan. Had I not stayed in their home? Shared their meals? Is this what they thought of me? I was just a flame in need of snuffing out.

"How long does it last?" I asked.

"Not forever," he said. "But…a while."

"How long?"

His eyes shot back toward mine. "Sometimes a few days, sometimes a few months. Or…years."

My jaw dropped, and for once I was speechless.

"Look, if we were going to win this war, we needed to take alchemy out of the equation."

That was so backwards from everything I believed! I'd been fighting for alchemist rights from day one and he knew it. "And what else can you tell me about black alchemy?"

"That's classified," he said, visibly shutting down, mouth flattening to a thin line and eyes growing vague.

I struck out, shoving him in the chest and pushing him to the ground. He didn't fight me. "Just tell me!" I shouted. I had wanted to punch him before, and now that feeling was back ten-fold!

"We've had her for a while, okay? Why do you think we didn't really need alchemist prisons before we got out here? There was no need for all that gray nonsense when we had *her*."

I stomped my foot and stalked across the hill for a minute, catching my breath and glaring out at the happy fuchsia sky. Then I hiked back, plopping down on the ground beside him. So many emotions spun within that I was dizzy with them. I couldn't keep up. My fingers dug into the grass.

"I still can't believe you did that to me," I said, defeated.

"I'm sorry," he whispered. "It was the only way. I did it for your own good. I did it because I care about you and I want you to be safe."

He didn't get it, but there was nothing I could do. What was done was done.

"We have to break up," he said, tormented. I glowered back. "I mean, if we're even together, if that's what you think we are, we can't be *that* anymore."

"After everything you did behind my back, you have the nerve to break up with me? Oh, no, buddy." I laughed, my own voice bitter in my mouth. "It's the other way around. I'm breaking up with you. And also, we weren't ever officially anything. So whatever."

He winced. "I'm not breaking up with you because of what happened out there. I'm breaking up with you because you're in love with Tristan."

I stilled, blood rushing to my cheeks.

He sighed and laid back on his elbows, gazing up into the darkening sky. "I always knew it, but I thought maybe you could get over him once we were together. Clearly, that never happened."

I chewed my lip, wanting to disagree. I couldn't. I'd said it to myself a thousand times, hadn't I? Tristan was home. What was love, if not that?

He sat up. "Truth time. You need to stop lying to yourself about Tristan. What you and I have, or had, it was special too. Don't get me wrong. But I think it was physical attraction more than anything else. And with the war, we never really could get it off the ground. You and Tristan however…" He trailed off. "Are you really going to make me do this?"

I frowned at him. The words wouldn't come to my lips, they were caught in my throat with all the emotions. I dropped my head into my hands, breathing in the smell of grass and sunset and life-changing realizations.

"There's love between you two," he relented, "Real love. I

don't know what all of it means or if it's physical, or attraction, or really just an incredible friendship. But it's more than we ever had and there's no use in competing with it anymore."

"You're chatty all of a sudden," I sighed. "I don't think I've ever heard so many words come out of you before tonight."

He was right. I knew it. But I wasn't ready to do anything about it.

I stood, brushing off my pants. "Good luck with your life, Mastin," I said, the anger lost from my voice. "I mean it."

I did want him to have a good life, even if I was no longer willing to be a part of it. I turned away and walked down the hill.

Mastin was a soldier, through and through. His first love, his only love, it wasn't me. It never had been. It had always been war, the strategy, the thrill of the fight and impressing his General of a father. And he'd gotten his dream, after all.

But Tristan? What did he love?

Me.

And it went both ways. He was my comfort. I loved him, too, more than I could ever put into words. But did that mean Tristan and I were suddenly supposed to fall into each other's arms and ride off into that stupid pink sunset?

I wasn't ready for that.

I needed to lick my wounds.

Because the truth was, Mastin had hurt me. Deeply. What he'd done had stung more than I cared to admit. I wasn't sure how long it would take to heal that. And what if, in the end, Tristan did the same thing?

I couldn't take that kind of pain. Not when it came to him.

Besides, Tristan deserved better than to heal my wounds, the way he always did. He deserved better than to be a rebound or second choice. Maybe one day it would be him and I together, but for now, we needed to stay friends.

Best friends.

So why did that thought make me cry?

I wiped away the tears, growling at myself. I would focus on lobbying for alchemists' rights. With Richard and Lucas in custody, there was about to be a lot of change for everyone, and I wanted nothing but positive change for my people. That was more important than a boyfriend. My heart could wait.

I strode toward the small town hall building, more determined than I'd ever been. Inside, General Scott was meeting with his advisors and the president. After the stunt these people had pulled today, after what they'd done to alchemists—my alchemists—security had better let me in. West America had better be prepared to give in to my demands.

I wasn't in the mood to negotiate.

★

I strode into the building with all the confidence I could muster, every step echoing determination. Holding tight to the knowledge that if I wasn't going to stand up for alchemists, maybe nobody was, kept me moving forward.

I never expected to be let right in, but I was.

I glanced around, hungrily seeking out someone important to yell at, or I don't know, something…

"They're just through here," one of the stoic soliders said, pointing to a set of closed doors. "They're expecting you."

"Oh-kay," I said, drawing it out.

I straightened my rumpled black outfit and ran my fingers through my limp hair, then took a deep breath and opened the door. The room fell into silence, everyone turning in my direction.

"There she is," the president's calm voice sparked through the space. "I've been wanting to talk to you, specifically, Sasha."

I raised an eyebrow, because if that were the case, why wait until now? Taking a deep breath, I considered the room. We were in some kind of city office building, with thick maroon carpet, wood trim, and cream walls. This room had a large round table in the middle, with leather chairs and couches strategically placed throughout. Everyone sat around the table, the seating giving the appearance of equal footing. But given who was here, equality probably wasn't first on their minds.

Next to the president sat General Scott, and next to him another man, the one from my time on the base out West. The guy who'd wanted to make the children go to war. I glared at him. The sicko had gotten his way, after all.

Beside him were a few faces I didn't recognize. I scanned the group, coming around the other side of the table until I found Hank and Tristan, and next to him was that Royal Officer, Jose. A woman smiled up at him, the purple alchemist teacher, Lily. And then my eyes landed on Jessa.

And Prince Lucas.

And a very perturbed-looking King Richard!

I doubled back.

"What in the blazes is *he* doing here?" The question fell from my mouth. "He should be locked up!"

"Have a seat." The president motioned to the empty chair in front of me.

Okay, this was beyond weird. But I kept my mouth shut and sat down in the closest chair, which happened to be on the other side of my sister. There wasn't a mess of papers littering the table, maps on the walls, or anything about this meeting that resembled the many I'd attended over the last couple of months. The war was over. Richard surrendered. West America should be making their demands, and maybe that's what this was about.

"I always thought if we could all just sit down and have a conversation together, we could talk this whole mess out and nobody would have to die," the president said, eyes running across the group and landing firmly on Richard. "Of course, that is assuming we are all reasonable people. After everything I've seen over the last few months, I know now that's not the case."

Richard glared. "After what your people did to my alchemists, I would hardly call you reasonable, either."

The president paused, her expression soft. "In any event, blood has been spilled, and we need to talk about what's next."

As Richard leaned forward, I noticed that his arms and legs were restrained in his chair. The sight of him this way sent a thrill down my body. Everything I'd been through had been worth it to get to see this.

"Death is a necessary evil of war," he spat.

General Scott's face turned red and he glowered. "A war that you started for no good reason!"

Richard growled. "You sent someone to kill my wife."

"Father, you know that isn't true," Lucas interjected.

Richard rounded on his son. "How dare you interrupt me!"

The president cleared her throat. "That's enough of that. It's time we talk about what's next."

Richard's laugh was crazed, the result of the world's most egotistical man not getting his way. Or maybe it was something more delusional. "Like you aren't going to execute my family the second this farce is over? I'd rather not play games with the likes of you."

She raised her eyebrows and the white bob framing her diplomatic face twitched with a hint of annoyance. "If it comes to that, have no doubt, we will execute you. The way I see it, Richard Heart, you now have two choices. You can die by lethal injection, or you can live in one of our maximum security prisons, that is assuming you'll even cooperate with me, which would be a requirement to your survival."

"I'd rather die," he spat out.

"Can't say I didn't try." She peered at Lucas. "And what of you? Are you going to join your father?"

"Lucas had nothing to do with this!" Richard ground out. "He is innocent."

"It's true," Jessa's small voice squeaked. Steeling her shoulders, she looked at each person in the room, courage growing. "He's only ever tried to do the right thing. He's a good man."

"He's an alchemist," the other General interrupted.

"What?" Richard sputtered, "That's a lie!"

"It's true," Lucas relented, sinking down into his chair. "I hardly use magic and have kept it a secret for years."

Richard turned on his son with a look like he was seeing him for the first time. Perhaps he was.

"But why?" Richard asked, voice cracking in a way I'd never heard out of him. The two stared at each other for a long moment, the weight of truth and lies too much for their already tumultuous relationship.

Lucas took a deep breath and explained, "I grew up hearing the way you talked about alchemists when they weren't around, how you and Mom thought it was unnatural. So I learned how to hide what I was from a young age and always kept it that way."

"I didn't know." Richard's voice was low, tormented. "If I had known, it would have changed everything."

Lucas sighed. "No, I don't think it would have."

Richard's nostrils flared, anger sparking in his cold eyes. I thought back to everything he'd done, knowing deep in my gut that Lucas was right.

"While this little confession session is fun and all," I piped in, "I can also attest to Lucas's true loyalties. He saved me on more than one occasion. He helped the Resistance when he believed we were doing good, but he didn't when he thought we weren't acting in his kingdom's best interest. I can truly say, having known him since he first aligned with the Resistance, he shouldn't be punished for his father's crimes. He is nothing like Richard. He's a *good* man."

As I spoke, Richard's silver eyes became dark holes, glaring openly at his son. But he didn't say another word.

"Well then," Madame President said, leaning back in her chair, "where do we go from here? What's next?"

"Once the magic is returned to the alchemists, we can heal as much as possible and reestablish the borders," Lucas supplied, breaking his father's eye-contact and letting his shoulders relax.

Nathan Scott laughed. "And just pretend this never happened? I say we take over New Colony and ensure this never happens again."

"I agree!" the other general added sharply.

The president shook her head, calm as ever. "Let's not get too greedy. We don't want to become like our enemy, do we?"

Richard sneered.

"I believe I can heal the land," Jessa's voice rang out, excitement growing in her tone as she leaned forward in her seat. Her curly, dark hair glowed under the florescent light. "And I even think I can help your people who had their minds turned in support of New Colony."

I whirled on her. This must have something to do with Lucas being alive. I still hadn't gotten to ask Jessa about it, but one thing I did know: Lucas had been dead. Something miraculous happened in that room, and I had to know what it was.

"Explain," Madame President instructed, curiosity burning in her intelligent eyes.

Jessa gulped. "Well, it turns out I have this *other* power, this ability to separate colors. I discovered that it's restoration magic," she said. "I can turn back the effects of other magic with it. And umm...I saved Lucas's life with it."

My eyes grew huge. "It's true," I attested, everything clicking into place. "He was dead. I was there. And then the next time I saw him, he was alive and well."

Well was relatively speaking, of course. Technically, the next time I saw him we were all attacked by the President's black alchemy, but something told me to bring those questions up later.

Jessa beamed, shooting a look of pure adoration at Lucas. "I figured it out just in time!"

Madame President nodded. "There will still be retributions to be paid to our country, but I think for now, Lucas and his bride should return to the throne in exchange for your help restoring our land and people, paying for all damages rendered, and signing a border agreement so this doesn't happen again."

Jessa nodded eagerly.

A cacophony of voices rang out, some angry, some pleased, and everyone deciding now was time to state their differing opinion. Tristan caught my eye from across the table and winked. I smiled back, warming at his gaze. Maybe everything was going to be okay after all.

"What about the alchemists?" Tristan's steady voice rose

over the arguments and everyone quieted, listening.

"What about them?" the other general in the room snapped back.

"I think they should have rights, too," he said confidently, his voice smooth and commanding. "They've also been victims in this, maybe more than anyone."

The silence stretched between the group.

"And from both sides," he added.

"What do you propose?" the president asked.

"Don't ask me." He shrugged. "Isn't that why she's here?" He pointed to me.

I sat up taller in my chair. "Yes, ever since alchemists were discovered, we've been treated as heathens and criminals, or we've been used to serve other people's interests, and not always the good people."

My eyes darted to Richard and narrowed.

"I propose all alchemists be properly trained, given a code of ethics to live by, and given the freedom to choose their own paths in life. If some of them would like to serve the royal family or their country, then so be it. But they shouldn't be forced into servitude, nor should they be unfairly imprisoned."

A few people shifted uncomfortably.

"It should be illegal to harm them without cause." My fingers stabbed at the tabletop, adrenaline kicking in. "And if they break the laws, they should be treated just like anyone else and given a fair trial. At the end of the day, alchemists are as human as anybody else, and so they should be treated as such. With dignity and respect, with rights and equality, and as assets to our society."

The president beamed. "I whole-heartedly agree."

Pride swelled, and I smiled so wide that I could feel it in my entire face.

"And since my election, I've found most of my people agree, as well. Change is in the air, for all of us. It may take lifetimes to end the bigotry. As long as we have differences, there will be people who twist those differences into justifications for hate and greed. But that doesn't mean we'll ever give up on fostering what really matters." She paused. "And that's love."

A huge weight lifted off me and for the first time in my life, a sense of hope bloomed square in my chest that maybe I would actually get to taste true freedom. Maybe with someone like her in world leadership and Richard behind bars, I would get to live life on my terms. I could find myself instead of always looking out for everybody else.

"That's preposterous," Richard spat. "What a waste of resources. Alchemy has its place in serving King and country."

Everyone glared at him but he held himself strong.

"Why else would God create magic, if not to use it to strengthen those in power?"

"You will be quiet," General Scott snapped. "You've had your say. Don't forget, your time in power is over."

We discussed everything for a little while longer until it became clear that Richard wasn't going to stop interrupting. He hated everything, literally everything, proposed. Of course he did. He was a narcissist who hadn't gotten his way.

Finally, the president had had enough.

"All right, get him out of here," she called to the soldiers standing on the back wall.

Four of them ambled forward, carefully unlatching him from where he was restrained in the chair, though he still had shackles and was cuffed. He began to move from the room, chains clinking, hatred rolling off him.

Then he dove.

Not toward the president.

Not toward his son or anybody else.

But toward Jessa.

"This is your fault!" he yelled, voice dripping in venom. "You turned my son against me. Did you use red to do it?" He was quick, wrapping the cuffs around her neck and yanking hard. Her eyes welled, blood pooling.

A brief pause was followed by an explosion of action.

"Don't touch her!" Lucas jumped on his father, clawing at the man's arms. Others charged, grabbing. I went for Jessa, trying to pry her loose. But the man had just the right angle and just the right madness to keep his hold on Jessa. Her eyes rolled back into her head, her body slumping. He sneered, pulling even tighter, resilient to our attempts to rip him away.

"You're going to kill her!" I screamed, my voice joining everybody else's, lost in the panic of the moment. Fear and anger doubled with the knowledge that I was weak without my magic.

"You're pathetic!" Richard screamed. "All of you." But his eyes were zeroed in on Lucas. He spat in his son's face.

"Drop her now, or you will die," General Scott said, gun clicking into place and trained on the back of Richard's head.

"As long as she dies with me," Richard replied, yanking infinitely harder on the cuffs choking Jessa.

She wasn't going to make it. Lucas jumped up, pushing away from his father and yelling at Scott, "Do it!"

Scott hesitated as he looked at Lucas. The two men shared a quick look of understanding.

"If you don't do it," Lucas continued. "Give it to me and I'll do it."

Everything in his voice was smooth resolve. He meant every word.

Boom!

The bullet blasted through Richard's head, blood and tissue flying, his body slumping, cuffs relaxing instantly. Blood pooled and I choked back a mix of horror and relief, hardly believing the truth of what had just happened.

King Richard was dead.

The room fell to silence once again. Finally, General Scott spoke to Lucas, "Nobody should have to kill their own father, but you're a brave man for being willing to do what had to be done. I'm glad it was me; you don't deserve to live with this on your shoulders."

Lucas nodded once, his face devoid of color, his eyes hazy.

"Let me see her." I pried Jessa's limp body from Richard's dead grip, smoothing her hair and searching her swollen face for signs of life. I needed to heal her. I needed green. A little green was all it would take.

Realization sunk me to my knees.

I didn't have magic anymore—it hadn't returned.

None of us had it back *yet*.

"How long?" I growled at the president. "How long until the magic is back?"

She stood at the head of the table, hands pressed into the wood, staring down at us with a broken expression. "Months."

The room quieted, everyone watching as Lucas pulled Jessa from my lap into his own. He kissed her face, tears dropping from his eyes. She was still, limp as a doll, her hair awkwardly strewn across her face, Richard's blood splattered across one cheek.

"Please," he whispered. "Now it's your turn to come back."

Time slowed. Ever so slightly, her chest rose, her lips parted, and then suddenly, she inhaled a gasping breath.

Her eyes fluttered open, arms flailing toward her neck, and she coughed, choking for a long minute.

"Am I alive?" she asked between coughs, blood-red eyes blinking in rapid succession as she looked up at her husband.

Lucas laughed once. "Yes." He kissed her on the forehead. "Yes, we're both alive. Everything is going to be okay."

EPILOGUE
EIGHTEEN MONTHS LATER - LUCAS

I love watching her dance. Quite honestly, it's one of my favorite pastimes. The way she moves, it makes me forget myself and remember at the same time. Of all her magics, this one is my favorite.

"I wish I had passion like that," I say, pushing myself off the wall of the private dressing room and wrapping her in a tight hug. I bury my face in her warm neck and inhale her floral scent.

"Ew! I'm all sweaty." She laughs, but lets me hold her anyway. "It's the nerves. I don't know why I'm so worried."

"You look perfect," I say, because it's the truth, but also because I don't want her to be afraid. In her white flowery costume, she reminds me of how she looked on our wedding day, and that is a look I'll never forget again. "You're going to be amazing out there."

"Thanks." She smiles, excitement flashing in her eyes.

She's been preparing for this performance for months, adding extra practice time on top of the rehearsals at the theatre. Her private studio back at the palace has quickly become her favorite place, of which I take full advantage—always popping in to say hi, maybe sneaking in a kiss if I'm lucky, but mostly I watch her in her element.

"Actually, on second thought," I muse, "I do think I have your kind of passion about one thing."

She peers up at me from under long, fake lashes, nodding. They make her blue eyes stand out more than usual and I lose my breath. "Rebuilding the kingdom," she says.

I shake my head. "Well, that too, I guess. But I'm talking about you."

And I mean it. I thought losing my parents would break me, and while I was still sad about everything that happened to them, I found solace in my marriage. Jessa had helped to make me a better man and a better leader. I was starting to believe I was growing into the kind of king I always wanted to be. A king who put his people first, no matter their station, and no matter their utility.

One of the first things I did was create a parliament system where the people could vote in representatives, and those representatives help me run things. I saw too much of my father in myself that year when everything went down. I hurt innocent people. It wasn't something I could risk again. Our royal family had ruled New Colony for generations, but what had once been an idealistic leadership had turned into a greedy dictatorship. I feared if I was the sole person in charge, I might one day turn into that, too.

Never again.

Jessa trembles under my touch. Her mind is racing.

"What are you thinking about? Are you still feeling nervous?"

"Yeah, a little."

I kiss the top of her head. "Don't be. I have a surprise for you after the performance. So don't be nervous. Be excited. You're going to look back on this night with only fondness."

Little does she know I've flown her older sister in for the performance. They haven't seen each other in over six months.

And okay, the fondness line is cheesy, but it instantly calms her.

She gives me a quick kiss and then breaks free of my arms, moving back to double check her makeup in the mirror. "If it's a surprise from you, then I'm sure I will love it."

A knock sounds on the door. "Sir, it's time to take your seat."

I wish Jessa good luck one last time and then find my place in the crowd. I won't be sitting up in a box like my family had done all those years. No, I'm in a plush velvet seat, front row center. A jolt of my own nerves rips through me. Not because I think anything might go wrong, but because I know how much this means to Jessa.

She'd given up dance for most of the last eighteen months. We had to focus on rebuilding, and dance had taken the backseat. We started with the government. West America followed through with their promise to change laws and enough states voted to add a constitutional amendment ensuring alchemists' rights. There is still a heavy prejudice against magic that runs deep, but for now, things are improving, people are beginning to accept it as part of the world.

Unwinding what happened in the Shadow Lands and freeing the minds of those harmed in Nashville was a painstakingly long and brutal process, but we finally finished the job two months ago. It didn't help that the effects of black alchemy took most alchemists months to wear off. Jessa hadn't gotten her magic back for seven months. Mine had taken a full year.

"There he is!" Christopher, Jessa's dad, walks down the space between the row and the orchestra pit, arms outstretched in greeting. "How are you doing, son?"

I jump up to offer him, Lara, and Lacey tight hugs. Christopher has taken to calling me son, and I can't say I mind. They all look great, smiles beaming from ear to ear. Both of her parents look much younger than I've ever seen them before, the lines around their eyes less pronounced, their skin warmer, eyes brighter. But it's the peace that has settled over them that makes the biggest difference. The family is dressed in their best outfits, matching in bright blue dress clothes. The color reminds me of Jessa. Lacey skips and twirls, taking in the beautiful theatre with adoring, round eyes.

"Where's your other daughter?" I ask, looking over the crowd, trying to spot that telltale blonde hair among the sea of people.

"Thank you for flying her out." Christopher pats me on the back. "They've been traveling all day. She just called and said they're in the city. They should be here any minute."

I relax down into my padded seat, glad Jessa would get to spend time with her whole family over the next few days. Sasha, who we now call Frankie, has changed the most over the last eighteen months since the war ended. Or maybe it's not that she ever really changed, but just remembered who she was in the first place. If anyone can understand that, it's me.

About a year ago, she officially dropped her alias Sasha, happily returning to Francesca, the name her parents had chosen for her. And she hasn't come back to New Colony, except to visit family. She's chosen to spend her time working with the alchemists in America instead.

I still think of it as West America. But that was another thing that has changed. I created a campaign to right any misinformation about our kingdom's history, not to mention, the state of the world. It was never West America; it was always just called America. We need to stand by the truth, not propaganda.

"Hi, there! How's my favorite brother-in-law, doing?" Frankie plops down into the empty chair on my left, giving me a strong side-hug. Her blonde hair is pulled up into a sleek knot on top of her head and she's wearing her signature cut and color—a black form-fitting dress.

"I'm your only brother-in-law," I deadpan.

"And you're still my favorite," she teases.

"I'm doing well," I say, giving her my full attention. She has a relaxed air about her tonight, something I haven't seen in her. Ever. "And how are you?" I question with a raised eyebrow.

"I'm good. We're good." She motions to Tristan beside her. The two are inseparable, so I'm not surprised to see him here.

I say hello to him and he to me.

I have really grown to respect the man. Apparently, he and Frankie have been best friends for years. She credits him for saving her from my father the first time, when she was still a kid. Jessa keeps hoping they will get together and make it official, but they never do. As I watch them together now, I wonder if they are only putting off the inevitable, or if it simply isn't meant to be.

"How are things in America?" I ask.

She sighs, a small smile playing on her lips. "Better than ever."

"Do tell."

"Well, you know how the president is also the infamous

black alchemist? She's been able to change some of the prejudices against her by agreeing to subdue powers for any alchemist who wants it, but they have to be at least sixteen to legally make that choice. And our training has been going better than I ever thought it would. Taking away the magic from everyone during the battle meant that it slowly returned. That ended up being a blessing in disguise."

"How so?" I question, interest piqued. Maybe the American President can make the same offer to our people. I would hate to see people give up their alchemy, but I also want them to have choices.

"Well, if you think about how hard it is to train someone, imagine how much it helps not to have brand new people who were too powerful for their own good."

My mind flashes to Jessa's first few months at the palace. I laugh to myself as I think of how she'd accidentally knocked me out the first time we met. If only I had known then just how much everything was about to change, maybe I wouldn't have made so many mistakes along the way.

"It was almost as if we got to teach them from the ground up."

"And you're okay with some of them choosing out of magic?"

She nods. "Absolutely. I would never do it, and I don't advise it. I think we should accept and embrace who we are. All of us, alchemist or not. But I also believe in choice. This gives them a choice. I've learned that some people truly don't want magic. Who am I to judge that?"

"It makes perfect sense to me."

My mind settles. I'll reach out to the President first thing in the morning and find a way to get this offer available for our alchemists, even if I have to fly them out to America myself. Since I've made our own Guardians of Color optional and children are no longer being taken from their homes, there might be people who want this kind of option. As things stand right now, the GC is still housed at the palace, and people can board there if they desire. We also relocate families to the capitol and help them get new jobs so that their children can attend classes during the day at the palace, and be home in time for dinner.

It is still illegal to hide alchemy. Everyone has to train since it's far too dangerous to keep magic inside. But no one is forced into servitude anymore.

And as for those whose alliances are still unclear, those people like Reed, Jax, and the Addington family, they're on strict probation. They know that at the first sign of trouble, they'll be questioned and likely arrested. So far, they're laying low. With things working out so well for the kingdom, I expect it to stay that way, but I'm prepared for action just in case.

I lean over to Tristan and point. "Are you keeping this one in line?"

He grins, his white teeth flashing. "It's the other way around."

"Yeah, right," Frankie laughs. "You've always been the level-headed one."

She reaches out and wraps her fingers in his, bringing his hand up and pressing a quick kiss to his palm. The intimacy of the move is anything but innocent.

From several seats down, Frankie's mother pops up, eyes wide and hands clapping as she squeals. That woman doesn't miss a thing.

"Are you two finally together?" she gushes, climbing over legs and reaching out to quickly hug them both. She pulls away and watches them with anticipation. I imagine if Jessa was here right now, her reaction would be the same.

The two share a sheepish look and then Frankie nods.

"I can't keep her away from me," Tristan teases.

Frankie slaps him in the arm. "Oh, shut up. You know you love me."

"I really do." He meets her eyes and the air between them grows as thick as the magnitude of that four-letter word.

The rest of us share looks of *I told you so* and *it's about time*. Lacey bursts out laughing, a rosy blush spreading across her round face as she stares at her oldest sister. As Lacey grows older, she resembles Frankie more and more.

The two lovers break their gaze, smiling at all of us.

"Well, Jessa will be happy about this development," I say. "She's been rooting for this ever since the war ended."

"We're really happy for you," Christopher adds.

"Does this mean you're going to get married, too?" Lacey comes to stand next to her mom. "Can I be the flower girl?"

Frankie's expression turns guarded.

Tristan just smirks, onyx eyes twinkling. "Absolutely."

"I mean, it probably won't be for a while, we just started dating," Frankie interjects, voice growing weak. "I'm barely twenty-two."

"But I'm an old man!" Tristan laughs, speaking directly to Lacey. "Don't worry. We're going to get married. I just have to convince her to say yes."

Frankie elbows him in the side. "Tristan!"

He laughs. "I'll wear her down eventually." He winks at Lacey. "You'll be dressing up for a wedding before you know it."

Lacey bounces back down into her seat and Frankie stares off into the distance, positively beaming.

Oh yes, these two are definitely in love.

The lights dim and everyone hurries to their velvety seats. The chatter falls away and the room surges with promise, the faint scent of perfume and floor polish wafting through the darkness.

The nervous excitement I felt before returns as the curtains lift. In the center of the stage, Jessa stands, eyes closed, arms outstretched, body elegantly tall with one foot pointed to the side. Blue light surrounds her, as do the other dancers. They are dressed in a rainbow of color and she is the white goddess in the center.

The orchestra music swells and she begins to move. The dancers are all incredible, but I only have eyes for her. Her every movement is perfect.

She spins over to a dancer dressed in deep navy blue and touches her gently, pulling the color from the costume and tossing it into the air. Then she prances to the other end of the stage and does the same with a woman in red. The colors swirl above them, a shimmering dance of light and magic.

And so, the dance continues.

I think back to the first time I ever saw Jessa. She was on this same stage but things were so different back then. She didn't know how to control her magic, was living in secrecy with her fears hidden inside. The accidental show of the purple alchemy that night started her on a path that would go on to change everything.

For the both of us.

And now she has come full circle.

Once again, here she is, dancing center stage where she belongs. And once again, she's using her innate talent and powerful alchemy to bring all of us in the audience to our knees. But this time is different. This time, as the magic grows around her, as the colors swirl and move, the radiant smile awash on her face is here to stay. I've never seen anything so beautiful.

THE END

ACKNOWLEDGMENTS

As always, I must thank my readers. Without you, none of this would be possible. Thank you for sharing in this world of color alchemy. It's surreal to have completed the series and I'm grateful you came along. I hope you'll continue to read my stories and fall in love with new characters and magics and worlds. I promise to keep writing!

Thank you to my husband, Travis. I couldn't do any of this without you. You're my anchor and you and I both know how much my Aquarius-self needs a really solid anchor to keep from drifting into oblivion. I love you.

Thank you to my Mom and writing buddy for all your support and encouragement.

Thank you to all those who worked on this book, from my talented cover designer, Molly Phipps, to my amazing developmental editor, Kate Foster, to the many proofreaders, Chelsea, Kate, Ailene, Travis, and Sarah. And to my ARC team for being willing to go on the journey first, typos and all. You people rock! I am so appreciative to each of you. THANK YOU!

And finally, thank you to anyone who's given me any kind of support, especially to the one who's behind it all, my loving Father in Heaven. The glory goes to Him.

ABOUT

NINA WALKER lives in Utah with her family, where she spends her time reading, writing, and helping women prioritize their health in online support groups. She also has a mild obsession with Instragram Stories.

Connect with Nina:

Facebook at fb.com/ninawalkerbooks
Instagram @ninabelievesinmagic

www.ninawalkerbooks.com

CPSIA information can be obtained
at www.ICGtesting.com
Printed in the USA
LVHW041221040319
609400LV00001B/62/P

9 780999 287675